Hello,
HOLLYWOOD

ALSO BY SUZANNE CORSO

Brooklyn Story

The Suite Life

Hello, HOLLYWOOD

SUZANNE CORSO

Gallery Books

New York   London   Toronto   Sydney   New Delhi

Gallery Books
An Imprint of Simon and Schuster, Inc.
1230 Avenue of the Americas
New York, NY 10020

First Gallery Books trade paperback edition May 2015

GALLERY BOOKS and colophon are registered trademarks of Simon & Schuster, Inc.

For information about special discounts for bulk purchases, please contact Simon & Schuster Special Sales at 1-866-506-1949 or business@simonandschuster.com

The Simon & Schuster Speakers Bureau can bring authors to your live event. For more information or to book an event contact the Simon & Schuster Speakers Bureau at 1-866-248-3049 or visit our website at www.simonspeakers.com.

Interior design by Meryll Rae Preposi
Cover design by Chelsea McGuckin
Cover images by Daniel Shapiro/Getty Images, Shutterstock

Manufactured in the United States of America

10 9 8 7 6 5 4 3 2 1

Library of Congress Cataloging-in-Publication Data
Corso, Suzanne.
Hello, Hollywood / Suzanne Corso. — First Gallery Books trade paperback edition
    pages ; cm
1. Single mothers--Fiction. 2. Man-woman relationships--Fiction. 3. Motion picture industry—California—Los Angeles—Fiction. I. Title.
PS3603.O7785H45 2015
813'.6—dc23
2014048836

ISBN 978-1-5011-1589-9
ISBN 978-1-5011-0606-4 (ebook)

To every girl's dream of her real-life "John Steeling"

Nothing can hinder, nothing can delay the manifestation of the Divine Plan of my life.

—FLORENCE SCOVEL SHINN

prologue

From the moment I'd told Marvin Castelli that I wanted to move out to California, he had insisted that my daughter, Isabella, would love it. But I'd had so many doubts. She had just lost her father five months earlier, and her life had been so chaotic for the last several years that I was afraid she would plunge into a blue funk. I should have known better. She was sixteen going on thirty, a beautiful young woman with her father's dark eyes, my black hair, and a personality as huge as the Pacific. She loved her new school, Our Lady of Malibu, and already had so many friends that on weekends our Malibu beach house rocked with music and laughter.

Her life had settled into a kind of normalcy that my childhood never had. My mother was a chain-smoking alcoholic, a lost soul, and my father abused her, cheated on her, and abandoned her shortly after I was born. I saw him once when I was six, a guy Mom pointed out in the Brooklyn neighborhood where we lived. I ran over to him and hugged his legs tightly. He pulled away, and I never saw him again.

I didn't have any positive male influences in my life as a kid, and that does something to you, creates this terrible inner void that begs to be filled . . . with something. For me, that inner void burned with a craving for love. True love.

That craving had caused me plenty of heartache and still did.

My husband, Alec, had been one of those people who was larger than life and, not surprisingly, had done everything in a big way. He literally swept me off my feet, and for years, our life together was about excess. We had money to burn—but it was *his* money. He controlled every facet of it and also controlled me. After Alec crashed and burned with the Wall Street debacle, after we lost everything and he ended up in a psych ward, our lives descended into darkness and chaos.

When Alec lost his money and his power, he also lost himself, his identity as a human being, as a man. His frenetic energy, once so laser-focused, scattered like dry seeds in the wind. He became someone I no longer knew.

I stayed in the marriage because I didn't know what else to do, didn't have any other recourse. I hoped I might fall in love with him again, but then I began to wonder if I had ever really loved him at all. I had thought he was my saving grace. The real knight in shining armor who came and captured my heart. After all, a modern-day Rapunzel I truly was, and all I wanted was to be loved and to give love. *What else is there?* I thought. Maybe I was seduced by the luxuries of those good years: the private jets and exotic travel, the clothes and jewelry, then to quickly adapting to socializing with the pawnbrokers to unload it all. To a girl from Brooklyn who'd spent her childhood on food stamps, Alec had represented my ticket to love and to final freedom over the Brooklyn Bridge, to the high life in Manhattan, where I would become a writer.

Well, a writer I became, all right, and moved across that bridge. But at what cost? Four years ago, I lost everything— my marriage, my home, and the millions we supposedly had in the bank. Even the million we had in our daughter's college fund evaporated. Was any of the money ever really there to begin with? Or was it all just the smoke and mirrors of derivatives? After all, money doesn't define you; it just enhances your life.

During my first trip out here eighteen months ago, my manager, Liza Corrlinks, and I were on our way to meet a producer who was interested in optioning my novel, *The Blessed Bridge*. Liza told me I would be moving to California, and when I laughed, she confessed that her friends thought she was a tad psychic. *They think it explains why I knew Stallone was perfect for Rocky, Pacino for Corleone, Michael Douglas as Gekko. Hey, it sounds like your life, Sam!*

I told her *The Blessed Bridge* sounded like my life, and that was when she explained that the producer with whom we were meeting wanted to change the title to *Brooklyn Story*, that *blessed* was too religious for them. *But they love the word* bridge, *Sam.*

Why this? Why that? Why, why, why seemed to be the litany of my life. Why had Alec, a man in his early fifties, after losing it all, managing to make some of it back, suddenly died of a heart attack thirty-five thousand feet above the Atlantic, en route to Switzerland for HGH treatments? And why had it happened right after my meeting with the producer who ultimately optioned my book? That kind of juxtaposition of events made me wonder, again and again, just who or what orchestrated our lives.

Alec's death had hurled our lives into utter bedlam— emotionally, spiritually, financially. As his widow, I was responsible for his debts, hundreds of thousands of dollars he had borrowed from his parents, friends, former Wall Street buddies. I was responsible for his funeral expenses at the Frank E. Campbell Funeral Chapel and his viewing in their chapel, his coffin surrounded by dozens of red roses and white lilies. Scattered about were wreaths of Yankee memorabilia.

Isabella and I moved in with Liza and lived with her

while I tried to figure things out. Focus groups became a way to earn easy cash and helped to improve our situation. Even when my novel was optioned, a lot of that money went toward paying off Alec's funeral expenses and our other debts. I could no longer afford the tuition at Isabella's private Catholic school. Fortunately, a dear friend stepped up and paid a year's tuition while I figured it out. What a blessing. I was grateful for the things that mattered the most and the people in my life that gave me hope to continue on my path.

Then, sixteen months ago, a man appeared at the door, and our lives spun in the opposite direction. He was an insurance agent and handed me a bunch of papers and a check for fifteen million dollars, payoff on a life insurance policy I didn't know Alec had. *Fifteen million.* Even during the darkest years, Alec somehow had been making the payments on that policy, ensuring that Isabella and I would be able to survive in the event of his untimely death. And right then I forgave Alec for everything and understood that even if we'd made a mess of our marriage, his love for his daughter had never waned. In the end, he had done the right thing, and he had done it the way he had done everything—big and grand.

Now here we were in our new lives, with new opportunities for me and a more stable environment for Isabella. I had my own production company and had convinced Marvin to move out here after he and his partner of fifteen years had split up, and now he was working for me. There was even a new man in my life, the producer, Paul Jannis, who had optioned my book. I didn't know yet if he was my other half, my true love, if he would fill that void I have carried inside me for most of my life. But I was doing what my grandmother had advised before she'd died: *You wrote yourself out of a Brooklyn story, Sam. Now write yourself into a California story, the one you really deserve.*

chapter

ONE

The blue vastness of the Pacific swept to the distant horizon and melted into the sky. Mansions perched at the edge of cliffs and beaches appeared and disappeared against all the blueness, this incomparable open *space*. I definitely wasn't in Brooklyn anymore—or in Manhattan.

"Gorgeous, just gorgeous, all of it," Marvin remarked, leaning forward from the backseat, his head popping into the space between Isabella and me. "Even after living out here for a year, I don't get tired of feasting on all this blue."

"And no winter, no snow," exclaimed Isabella, my daughter. "At night, I go to sleep to the sound of the surf. How awesome is *that*?"

"Very awesome," I agreed, and my eyes met Marvin Castelli's in the rearview mirror. *Told ya so, Sam.*

I turned off on South Winter Canyon Road. I loved the name of that road; *south winter* conjured such vivid mental images of snow-covered streets wrapped up in that strange silence that came with falling snow. And the word *canyon* was all about this area of California, a sweeping desert of canyons and valleys that humanity had sort of tamed.

Just beyond Pepperdine University on our left, I hung a right through the gate of Isabella's school. "I've got a swim meet after school, Mom, so I'll catch a ride home with Lauren."

Lauren was her closest friend in Malibu, the daughter of writers for one of the hottest TV shows this season. Even though both she and Isabella had their driver's licenses, neither of them was allowed to drive to and from school. Lauren's older brother, who attended Pepperdine, often drove them home.

"Have a good day, love, and I should be home around six. I left a veggie lasagna in the fridge that you can heat up."

She bussed me quickly on the cheek and slid out of the car, and Marvin got out of the back to join me up front. "And good luck with that English test," he called after her. "I know you'll do great."

Marvin used to teach English lit and composition in a high school in Rhode Island and had spent several hours this weekend helping her study for the test. He and his ex-partner had also written a play that I had produced off Broadway, in my other life. That was how I'd met him. That time now seemed so distant and remote that I often couldn't remember who I had been there, what had motivated me, what goals I'd had.

Isabella flashed him a thumbs-up and I stared after her, watching until my beautiful daughter vanished into the crowd of kids moving toward the main building.

"Don't worry about her, Sam," he said. "She's flourishing out here. We all are."

Yes, we were. But always, in the back of my head, there was an annoying little voice that kept warning me about becoming too complacent, too comfortable. As I knew from the past, the proverbial curveballs usually hurtled toward you out of the blue, and slammed your life into crisis mode. I'd had more than my share of crises and disasters and could do without them, thank you very much. But still, a part of me remained alert and vigilant, prepared nonetheless for what *might* occur.

"So how's our day shaping up, Marvin?"

"We've got back-to-back meetings from ten till noon, lunch with Liza after that, and then five more scripts came in over the weekend. And I haven't finished going through the email yet." He brought out his trusty iPad and went online.

Marvin was a short, handsome man with wavy blond hair and dark, compassionate eyes. There was an artistic, disheveled air about him, but he was so efficient and organized that he kept my new company on track. Despite the fact that we were new in town, we already had one TV movie in production with HBO, a thriller/love story set post-WWII, and we were actively seeking scripts for a possible TV series. *Brooklyn Story* was supposed to go into production at Gallery Studios sometime in the next several months, but we didn't have a date yet.

Liza had been immensely helpful in connecting us with the right people. Her network out here was vast and varied and ranged from actors and directors to scriptwriters and line producers. She was also steering our search for financing for a movie of my second novel, *The Suite Life*. It would have been great if Gallery had just optioned both books, but as Liza said, *Patience, love. It'll happen.*

For most of my life, I'd known people who were helpful and supportive like Liza was, but she was extraordinary. Endowed with endless energy, Liza could tackle anything, anywhere, and complete the job in half the time it would take anyone else.

Sometimes my life felt as if it was moving at the speed of light, and I just had to slow down and take some deep breaths. That was when Isabella and I would take long walks on the beach, talking and looking for shells. Or we would do girl things, like shop and get our hair cut and our nails done, stuff we rarely had done together in New York. Our relationship was much stronger and deeper here than it had been during the years when our lives were so screwed up. I hated to admit it, but with Alec gone and some money, that can happen. I guess money can do that. There was a lot of be said for financial freedom.

"Okay," Marvin said. "There's an email here from Liza. She says you're not answering your text messages and are we still on for lunch?"

"You bet. Tell her that. And tell her I just did a software update on my phone, and my texting isn't working right."

DeMarco Productions was located on Melrose Avenue, close to Paramount Studios. It was small, just four rooms on the second floor of a house that had stood on Melrose for decades. The central room was a small lobby, the walls painted a pale lemon yellow and decorated with some vintage movie posters that Paul had lent us from his collection. The other three rooms circled the lobby, like planets around the sun.

Clara Mendoza, our receptionist, was already at her desk, madly typing away at her computer; she paused to hand me a stack of phone messages. "They're all urgent," she said in her snappy, slightly accented voice. "They're always urgent."

I laughed. "Life is urgent."

She glanced away from the computer screen. An attractive brunette in her early thirties, a Peruvian who had come to L.A. looking for fame and fortune, after several years of heartbreak, she'd decided to find a real job, something in the industry, and I hired her within five minutes of meeting her. She was bilingual, a definite asset, and could fix anything from computers and broken faucets to scripts.

"Now you sound like some South American writer like . . . Marquez. Wasn't he the one who said that life is urgent? Or was it love is urgent? Well, whatever."

"I can't text after updating my phone's operating system," I said. "Any advice?"

"I'll take a look." She extended her hand, and I passed her the phone. "Paul has called a couple of times. He wants to meet you for lunch, I told him you were meeting Liza, and he'd like to join you."

"What'd you tell him?"

"*Que va, chica*. I told him you'd call him as soon as you got in. Oh, I just forwarded you and Marvin another script we received. It looks promising. I'll read it tonight."

And she was also incredibly diligent. "Great. Thanks. Can you get Paul on the phone?"

Since Paul had called the office rather than my cell, it meant he had business to discuss. I would do the same.

I hurried on into my office. Sunlight shone through the sliding-glass doors leading out to a small balcony to my right, where several gorgeous potted plants grew with a kind of wild abandon.

Sometimes at the end of a busy day, Marvin, Clara, and I sat out at the balcony table, sipping my favorite rosé wine, commiserating over possible strategies, and marveling at our good fortune. I hoped to expand the staff eventually, but I didn't intend to make the same mistakes I had made during my marriage to Alec, when money went out faster than it came in. I pondered the thought of how far I had come in my life, and finally it felt great. I was even able to exhale for a moment.

Right now it was just the three of us and a part-timer, a male intern from UCLA who had a sharp eye for what worked in stories. He worked closely with Marvin, and I suspected that some sort of romantic thing might be unfolding between the two of them. I hoped so. Marvin needed love as badly as I did.

My first ritual every morning when I came into my office was to light three candles on the little altar in the corner that held miniature statues: the first to the Blessed Mother, a second to the Archangel Michael, and a third to Buddha. In the six weeks Paul and I had been dating, he'd never commented on the altar or the items it held, but I suspected he didn't approve for "business reasons." He was too nice to say it, though. Even if he had, this was *my* office, *my* production company, and if I wanted to have an altar in here, then I would. These were my beliefs. They had taken me this far, and I was willing to go all the way with them. I hoped that the days when a man called the shots regarding what I did, who I saw, where I went, or how I spent my money were history.

As I lit the candles, I could almost hear my grandmother whispering, *Kinehora, Samelah, kinehora*, the words that always protected me. *Blessed good journey*, protecting what's to come. I asked that the week ahead would unfold peacefully. I've had enough drama in my life to last several lifetimes, and the only thing that ever came from it was more drama and heartache. I then blew the candles out and inhaled the scent of lemon that lingered in the air.

My desk faced the balcony so that I always had a view of those potted plants and the palm trees beyond them. Those palms were a constant reminder that I wasn't in New York anymore, as if I could forget that. As much as I loved being organized, *stuff* still cluttered my desk: books, scripts, notes, and pads of paper on which I jotted everything, from addresses to lines from songs that I wanted to use in the script for *The Suite Life*. So when my desk phone rang, I had to dig through the clutter even to find it. "Sam, I've got Paul on the line," Clara said, and clicked through.

"Hey," I said.

"Hey yourself, beautiful."

He had a low, husky voice, infinitely seductive, and it elicited an immediate image in my head of a younger Bruce Willis, head as bald as an egg, Mediterranean blue eyes, a salt-and-pepper goatee. Six months ago, he had asked me out for the first time. I turned him down. I didn't think it was a good idea to date the guy who had optioned my book and script. He wouldn't take no for an answer and kept finding excuses to call me. This went on for months, until he came by the office one afternoon with my favorite, a truffle pizza.

"Since you won't go out with me, I figure that if I bring lunch to you, it's not an official date. We're just two hungry people sharing the best pizza in Hollywood."

So we sat out on the balcony like a couple of old friends, exchanging stories about Hollywood's weirdness. He had more of those stories than I did—he'd been here for decades. One of my favorites was about the valet at one of the plush hotels who was eventually busted for stealing parts from Jaguars and BMWs, which he sold for a tidy profit on the black market. Then there was a woman who cleaned houses for the rich and famous and went on to write a tell-all book about the dysfunctional lifestyles of the people for whom she worked. Ordinary people, really, whose lives were corrupted by Hollywood and fame.

This sort of corruption, though, was even more prevalent among the children of Hollywood's movers and shakers, Paul had said, and told me about his son's addiction to a video game. Luke was now in rehab. Luke's friend Jake, whose father was the CEO of a major studio, had a sexual addiction that resulted in his being treated for a host of STDs that had nearly killed him. Stories like these made me appreciate just how *normal* Isabella was.

We enjoyed a couple more impromptu pizzas after that, and I really started looking forward to seeing Paul, laughing with him, just getting to know him as a person rather than as a producer. So six weeks ago, when he asked me out for the second time on a real date, I accepted. The man exuded such charm and was so much fun to be with that we started sleeping together within a few weeks.

In these past six weeks, there hadn't been a single incident with him that set off any alarms in my head. I wasn't in love with him—yet—but I suspected he was falling in love with me.

"So Clara says you'd like to join Liza and me for lunch?"

"If it's okay."

I liked that he asked. Most of the men I've known would have just barged in on the lunch as if they had every right to do so. "I don't see why not. Any particular reason?"

"News."

He was being cagey. "Good news, I hope?"

"Well, I sure as hell wouldn't bring bad news to lunch with you two."

"Give me a hint."

"Nope. You've got to wait till lunch."

"Oh, c'mon. That's not fair."

He hesitated, then said, "Principal photography on *Brooklyn Story* starts next month, on the Gallery Studios lot. I just got the heads-up a little while ago."

No one except my grandmother could possibly understand how I felt in that instant. For as long as I can remember, she was my supporter, my cheerleader, the one who encouraged me to write my way out of Brooklyn and into a better story. Gratitude nearly overwhelmed me for everything she'd given me throughout my childhood. Her support had brought me to this moment. As that Smith Corona she gave me when I was seventeen to write it.

"That's fantastic. But what happened? A month ago they didn't even have a full cast."

"What happened is that Jenean Conte has agreed to play you."

Conte had been nominated for an Oscar last year for a Spielberg film. She was only in her mid-twenties, a beautiful young woman loaded with talent. "She's perfect for the part, Paul."

"And we're going to celebrate tonight. I'm taking you out for a romantic dinner, for—"

"I can't do it tonight, not during the week, when Isabella is home. This weekend would be better. She'll be spending the night with friends."

He hesitated. Paul didn't really have any concept of

what it was like to be a single mother to a teenager. His son was twenty-four, but even if Luke were a toddler, his ex-wife would be tending to him. Maybe that was why Luke was in rehab for his addiction to Mystery Manor. Weird, but there you had it. Nothing out here—even addictions—was like anywhere else. "Okay, let's shoot for the weekend."

Maybe he felt Isabella was old enough to stay by herself—and at sixteen, she definitely was. But for me, this was about the past, about how I hadn't always been there for her when she needed me. "Great." It was tricky enough stealing time on weekends to spend the night with Paul. I didn't want to sneak around on weeknights. "I'll see you at lunch. Larchmont, twelve-thirty."

"I'll be there, beautiful."

I remembered how in the weeks and months after 9/11, Alec's relentless drive to reach the top had meant he was rarely home. And when he had been home, he'd issued orders about everything from having dinner ready to getting Isabella to and from school on time. It wore me down and left me resentful.

When I had tried to talk to him about what I felt concerning our marriage, he had blown me off at every chance he had. The few times we'd gone out socially, he hardly acknowledged me except to remark to one of his cronies about how hot I was. I constantly asked myself whether the price of staying in my marriage was greater than the cost of breaking free, or the price of being so rich that it almost made me want to be poor again.

And now, ironically, thanks to Alec's insurance policy, we were okay. No man was ever going to put me in that kind of situation again. And I would teach my daughter that very motto.

The Larchmont was one of those restaurants on Melrose that looked like someone's private home. Liza usually reserved a table in the garden, and that was where the hostess took Marvin and me.

Liza was already seated, and, as usual, she was texting or emailing someone. She had every A-list actor, director, musician, and writer on speed dial. I used to be pretty far down on the list, but that changed the day Paul optioned *Brooklyn Story*. Now Liza was like a big sister to me.

"My favorite people," she exclaimed as she spotted us, and got up to hug us both hello. "You've just got to try the scallops. They are to *die* for."

She talked fast, like the Jewish New Yorker she was, but she was pure Hollywood now. Her long black hair cascaded over the shoulders of her sleeveless Armani dress, as orange as a Popsicle; her Armani sandals matched her Armani handbag; and the diamond studs in her ears were as lovely and perfect as the rock on her finger. Her husband, an entertainment attorney, worshipped the ground she walked on, but Liza had forged her own way in Hollywood.

"Hey," Marvin said quietly, and tilted his head to the right.

I glanced in that direction. Al Pacino was having lunch with an attractive blonde. Half the fun of eating here was watching celebrities. I had no idea who the woman was. "Who's he with, Liza?"

"A TV writer. I heard that one of the cable channels is trying to interest him in a series, something epic, like *Game of Thrones*." Liza glanced at her watch. "Where's Paul, anyway?"

Right on cue, Paul Jannis made his way through the gathering crowd, pausing at one table after another to greet people hello, shake hands. He seemed to know just about everyone and was now working the restaurant. I had seen him do this countless times, working a room at a party, at a dinner, at any social event, and doing it with one intention in mind: to network. Out here, networking was how you landed jobs, made headway. Friends hired friends. He even paused at Pacino's table.

He wore California casual—khaki pants, a blue cotton shirt that matched the color of his eyes, leather sandals. He smiled broadly as he approached the table, and the moment his eyes caught mine, I could tell he was undressing me.

"Sorry I'm late," he said, joining us at the table. "Traffic's a bitch."

"Traffic's always a bitch—it's L.A.," Liza said. "But we forgive you, especially if you have good news."

"I hope Sam didn't let the cat outta the bag," he said.

Liza laughed and pointed a carefully manicured finger at him. "And which cat would that be?"

"The one called *Brooklyn Story*," Marvin remarked.

I had told Marvin the news, of course, and strangely enough, Paul seemed to resent it, like I'd robbed him of his moment in the sun or something.

"Do tell," Liza said, leaning forward, her wildly intense eyes glinting with curiosity.

So he did, spilling all the details with great relish and enthusiasm, as though *Brooklyn Story* were *his* story, as though he had lived through the dark days of my Brooklyn childhood and teen years with Tony Kroon, one of the Brooklyn mafia boys. Paul couldn't know what it was like to be treated like chattel and given impossible demands delivered over a clenched fist. That world was as far from him as Pluto was from the sun. Yet he sounded as if he had lived in Brooklyn, in my neighborhood, and had hung out with the mafia boys.

And right then I suddenly began to doubt the man I'd thought Paul was. Maybe what I hoped might unfold eventually between us was illusion, the stuff of which Hollywood was made. My doubt, coming on the heels of Paul's news about the production schedule, struck me as a grotesque irony, some sort of cosmic joke. And it brought back that age-old question: *Who's orchestrating this stuff?*

"Sam. Hey, Sam." Liza waved her hand in front of my face. "You with us?"

"Sure."

"So what do you think about Jenean Conte playing Samantha Bonti?"

"I'm totally into it. She's perfect."

"And she'd like to meet you as soon as possible," Paul said. "Just to talk and get a sense of you as a person."

"Who's going to play Tony?" asked Marvin.

"A relative newcomer," Paul said. "He's done a dozen films but isn't really well known. We figured it was best to cast a new face for this part, just like they did for the part of Peeta in *The Hunger Games*."

"Smart, very smart," Liza said. "Who's directing?"

"Carl Davidson."

Davidson had directed two blockbusters in the last five years, and in a town where you were only as good as your last movie, that boded well for *Brooklyn Story*. I'd heard he could be difficult to work with, but since I'd never met him, I would have to wait and see.

Liza nodded. "Davidson has a good track record."

"He has a great grasp of story," Paul said.

The waitress came over and we ordered. Liza was zipping through the calendar on her iPhone, and when the waitress left, she said, "Sam, now that we've got a production date, I'd like to schedule you for some publicity—*Entertainment Weekly*, *People*, that kind of thing. Not only will it create some early buzz about the movie, but it'll get DeMarco Productions out there. We could do it when you and Jenean meet to chat."

"Sounds good to me," I said.

"Me, too," Paul agreed.

"Wonderful," Liza said. "I'll get that set up this afternoon."

"Well, you'd better keep in mind that Sam isn't available on weekday evenings," Paul remarked.

Huh? Had he really said that? Was it what he'd wanted to say on the phone earlier? Liza glanced up from her phone. "What're you talking about?"

"Just that I like to be home in the evenings with Isabella," I said.

"Of course you do. And it won't be a problem. These interviews are scheduled during regular work hours."

Her eyes darted to Paul and lingered on him. I could tell she had a good idea what his remark was really about. Sometimes, Liza wasn't just a "tad psychic," as she'd once put it, but could peer down into your soul.

Later, as we left the restaurant, Paul drew me aside and spoke quietly, as though he didn't want Liza and Marvin to hear him. "I shouldn't have said that, Sam."

It was his way of apologizing. But Paul, like the other men who had been in my life, had never been able to say the actual words *I'm sorry*. "Yeah, you shouldn't have. But whatever." I turned away from him to catch up to Marvin and Liza, but he grabbed my upper arm.

"Hey, hold on."

I looked down at his fingers, digging into my skin, his nails perfectly cut and professionally manicured, then looked up at him and wrenched my arm free. "Don't *ever* do that," I snapped.

He held up his hands and sort of laughed. "Shit, Sam. What's your problem? You PMSing or what?"

"Fuck off, Paul," I spat, and spun around and hurried away from him. It seemed inconceivable that on the very day when I heard *Brooklyn Story* was actually going to become a movie, I had this weird spat with the same man who'd made that possible. I was grateful to him, but gratitude wasn't love. Then again, I hadn't reached the point where I loved Paul.

I remembered how overjoyed I was when I realized Alec, this big Wall Street guy, was interested in *me*. My self-esteem had been so low that I suddenly began to see myself in a different light, like maybe there was hope for me. Gratitude toward Alec for his interest in me quickly followed.

Patterns, so much of my life had been about inner patterns that seemed to attract these kinds of experiences with men. I needed to work on that. I needed to figure myself out in that regard.

Even though I knew I had to trust that there was an underlying order to all this, some grand plan that I couldn't see, it was difficult to do right now.

As I pulled into the driveway, Marvin pressed the remote, and the gate slowly slid open. The driveway angled steeply uphill, and to either side of it, the grounds were lushly landscaped with hedges and red and blue flowers, and the grass was so green I could almost smell the color. Palm trees rustled in an evening breeze.

I drove into my two-acre slice of paradise and stopped the Prius in front of the bungalow. Three bedrooms, two baths, a huge family room—four thousand square feet of living space and windows everywhere that overlooked the property or the Pacific. The property backed up to a canyon the color of rust, and sometimes at night, I heard coyotes howling.

The guesthouse where Marvin stayed was actually an apartment above the detached garage, and it stood off to the right, partially hidden by trees. As we got out, headlights suddenly shone through the gate at the bottom of the hill. "Is that Isabella?" Marvin asked.

"No, she's in the house. The driver's probably lost."

"I'll check it out." Marvin, my protector.

"That's okay. I'll go have a look."

"Okay, see you in the morn, Sam. It's my turn to drive."

I continued on to the bungalow, parked, gathered up my stuff. As I trotted up the steps to the front door, I noticed that the headlights were still visible at the bottom of the driveway. I felt apprehensive without quite knowing why. I doubted it was Paul. He would have texted or called me first. In fact, most of the people I knew out here would text or call before dropping by.

I unlocked the front door, set my stuff in the hallway, called for Isabella.

"In the family room, Mom. Lauren's here."

"Okay, love. I've got to check on something. Be right back."

I slipped the high heels off my aching feet and padded barefoot down the driveway to the gate. The car was a yellow cab, not something I'd seen frequently out here. A tall, thin man got out the back door.

"Samantha?" he asked, his words heavily accented. "Samantha Bonti?"

"I haven't been a Bonti for years."

He wove his way toward the gate, like he was drunk or suffering from some neurological disorder, a bulging backpack slung over his shoulder. The cabbie hopped out, ran over to the man, and shouted. "Hey, dude, you owe me twenty-five bucks. I'm not leaving until I get paid. And if you don't pay, I'm calling the cops."

The man shoved some bills at the cabbie, then came into the glare of the headlights so I saw him clearly—stubbled chin, disheveled clothes, a broken human being with eyes the color of grease.

"You gonna open the gate?" he asked.

"I don't know you," I said, backing away, suddenly terrified.

"I have no place to go. Only here."

"Excuse me, driver," I called. "There's been a mistake. I don't know this man."

"Samantha. It is me. Vito. Your father."

chapter
TWO

Vito Bonti. Shock waves tore through me.

He was the Italian Catholic immigrant and Vietnam vet who had just called himself my father, but he had contributed zero to my life except DNA. In fact, when my mother had been eight months pregnant with me, he had hurled a car jack at her belly; the resulting hemorrhage had forced her into premature labor. The doctors had told her that when I was delivered, I would either have severe brain damage from the impact of the blow or I would be stillborn. But I had survived and Vito Bonti had taken off. And now I was supposed to open the gate, throw my arms around him, and welcome him into my home?

As the cabbie backed out into the road, Vito said, "You done real good for yourself, Samantha."

"No thanks to you. What the hell are you doing here, Vito?"

"I got nowhere else to go."

"Bullshit. You've got three ex-wives and two other children."

In my head, I kept seeing my mother, her spirit beaten down by this man, who had reminded her at every opportunity that she was just a poor Jewish girl from Brooklyn. And I kept seeing my younger self running to him that day and throwing my arms around his legs, and how he pulled away from me.

"Don't know where any of 'em are."

"Not my problem." Well, that wasn't exactly true. Now that the cabbie had left, it *was* my problem. "Besides, you tracked *me* down."

"Findin' you was easy. Ran into Franco in the ol' neighborhood." Alec's brother. "He tol' me 'bout Alec's death, your book, you runnin' off to Hollywood."

"Franco is a plastic surgeon, Vito. And unless you've come way up in the world, you two sure don't travel in the same circles."

"You got that right. He was doin' pro bono work at the homeless shelter where I was stayin'. Recognized his name, DeMarco, and I asked him if he knew Samantha, said she's my kid."

I had never been his kid. I had been a major inconvenience. And the picture was getting clearer. Franco had probably told him about the fifteen-million-dollar insurance policy, too, and Vito, who was obviously broke, had decided he might be able to cash in—for old times' sake, since we were related and shared the same DNA. "Look, you can't just barge into my life after forty-five years. And you can't stay here. I'll get you a motel room for the night."

"I got no money, Samantha."

"I'll buy your plane ticket back to New York."

"But—"

"I have to get my car and keys."

"Can you open the gate so I don't have to stand out here?"

I was certain that if I opened the gate, if he walked onto this property and back into my life, he would never leave. "I frankly don't give a shit if you stand out there all night. But because I'm a good person, I'll drive you to a motel. I'll be back in a minute."

I stumbled back from the gate, horror clawing through me, then spun around and tore uphill toward the house.

Fortunately, Marvin was inside the guesthouse, probably fixing himself a bite to eat, and Isabella and her friend were still in the family room; I didn't have to explain anything to either of them. Vito Bonti wasn't going to be part of this story. It had taken me years to write myself out of Brooklyn and into the story I craved, and this man I had never known and could barely remember wasn't going to derail my dream and infect my daughter's life. I couldn't allow that to happen.

I ducked into the hallway to grab my purse and a pair of sandals and called out to Sam that I had to run to the market. I made sure I had plenty of cash and my credit cards. The closest motel was probably the Malibu Motel, just several miles up the Pacific Coast Highway.

Tomorrow, I would buy him a plane ticket back to New York, give him some money so he wouldn't land with an empty wallet, and that would be that. He was a grown man—broke and broken, yes, but he'd made it for forty-five years without help from me and could make it another forty-five without me. Vito undoubtedly had old cronies in Brooklyn who would take him in. Or he could return to the homeless shelter and maybe run into Franco again and they could share tales about what a terrible person I was. *Bitch wouldn't even take in her ol' man.*

It suddenly occurred to me, though, that maybe it was all a scam. Maybe Vito had a fourth wife and the two of them had figured he should come out here, playing a broke and broken man, and that I, bleeding heart that I was, would take pity on him and give him a couple of million. Or maybe the plan was that once I took him in, he would worm his way into our lives, then knock me off. As Isabella's closest relative, he would claim custody of her—and everything she would inherit.

All the possible scenarios flashed through my head as I drove down toward the gate. That was the problem with being a writer and a girl who used to know mafia guys. Once your imagination seized hold of even a tiny morsel of an idea, every possibility unfolded in your head.

By the time I reached the gate, I was actually afraid to let him in the car. I pressed the remote for the gate, it slid open, and I drove through it, stopped, and made sure the gate shut behind me. He tried to open the passenger door, but it was locked. I got out, locked my door, and walked over to him.

In the backwash from the headlights, he was scarecrow thin, his ragged clothes just hanging on him. His gray hair was too long and hadn't been washed in a while. He looked at me with his huge, haunted eyes. "I wanna meet my grand-daughter. I know you have a kid, Franco tol' me."

Thanks, Franco.

"Yeah, right," I laughed. "Here's the deal, Vito. I'll pay for a motel room for tonight, give you some money for food and a change of clothes. Tomorrow, I'll buy you a ticket back to New York and give you enough cash so that when you get off the plane, you won't be flat broke. But that's it. After what you did to my mother and to me, I don't owe you shit. We clear on the rules?"

Was that *me* talking?

He stole a longing glance toward the house, then looked down at his shoes, a pair of ratty old loafers with soles that were undoubtedly wearing away. I suddenly felt awful about what I had said, the way I was treating him. But then I thought of what he had done to my mother, and I didn't feel awful at all. I knew I couldn't let him touch my daughter's life. I also thought about what kind of a person I am. After all, I do light three candles religiously to my besties every morning, and they surely wouldn't treat me like this. I just couldn't help myself.

"If you don't agree with the ground rules, Vito, then start walking. It's a long way to town."

"Not givin' me no choice."

"*Choice?* What have you ever done to deserve a *choice?* You didn't give my mother or me a choice. And I'm giving you the only choice I can live with."

He nodded reluctantly. "Okay."

His acquiescence seemed too easy. I hesitated. Until I unlocked the car and he was inside, I still had the chance to drive back up the hill to my house, go inside, and shut the door—on him, on everything he represented. But that might cause an even greater problem. He might decide to camp outside the gate all night.

I pressed the remote on my key chain, and the car doors clicked open. Moments later, we headed along the highway, the air tight, tense, and filling with the stink of his body. My phone rang. I turned it off and lowered the windows. I felt like screaming. I felt like calling Marvin or Paul and asking them to deal with my father. Either of them would do it, I knew. If this were happening five years ago, I would have turned everything over to one or both of them. But those days were long gone.

"You wanna know where I've been livin', Samantha?"

"You just told me. A homeless shelter in Brooklyn. Who paid for your fare out here?"

"Franco and his mother. They felt bad for me, said you could help me out."

This struck me as a lie. "Really. Well, I'll just give Filomena a call and find out what really happened."

I pulled out my phone, turned it on, started to punch in my former mother-in-law's number. "No, don't call her," Vito said quickly. "Franco lent me the money. He said you're a greedy bitch who coulda given the family some of that insurance money. Instead, you took it all and left New York."

That sounded closer to the truth, except that Franco

made plenty as a plastic surgeon, and if he'd actually said something to Vito, he'd omitted an important detail. Alec had had a smaller insurance policy—for two million dollars—for his mother and siblings. I didn't tell that to Vito. He didn't need to know any more than he already knew. And if he'd had any idea who the hell I was, he would know I would never abandon Alec's family financially. It simply wasn't in me. I'd been through enough. As it was, I did not owe this man who stood in front of me, or anyone else, any explanation in regard to my actions.

I headed straight for the Malibu Motel, a boutique place where each of the eighteen rooms boasted a view of the ocean. He would be comfortable there for the night. He could walk to a restaurant tomorrow morning for breakfast, buy a change of clothes, then take a cab to the airport. I would buy his plane ticket this evening and use the computer in the lobby to print it out. This would work; it had to work. It was the only plan I had. I didn't want him anywhere near us.

"So Franco, he said I'm in your novel. That true?"

"You're a footnote."

"Ya owe me, Sam," he said. "If it hadn't been for me, you never woulda written it."

That much was probably true. If he hadn't abandoned my mother and me, though, I hated to think of what kind of hell we would have lived.

I ignored him and, a few minutes later, turned into the parking lot in front of the motel. "I already told you the rules, Vito. If you continue to piss me off, I'll just leave you here and you can hitch back to New York."

Vito knew he was a pathetic loser who had abandoned his wife and child forty-five years ago, had done it without a second thought, and had never looked back. He knew I meant what I said. So he pinned me with those eyes the color of grease, eyes that screamed, *Bitch, ya bitch!* Then he got out of the car, pack slung over his shoulder, and slammed the door so hard it rattled the windows.

I sat there a moment, gripping the steering wheel, struggling not to scream, cry, or—worse—run after him and throw my arms around his legs. That little kid each of us once was probably still existed somewhere inside of us, huddled in a corner, sucking his or her thumb, grinding teeth, fighting off real and illusory demons.

Again, I thought of the candles I had lit only this morning to my three protectors and couldn't understand why they would allow Vito Bonti to appear at the gates of my life. Was this some final test or challenge? Was my mettle being tested, again? Hadn't I been through enough shit already?

I watched him through the windshield, moving purposefully toward the front door of the motel, his arms swinging at his sides. Then he paused, as though he sensed my watching him, and spun around, glaring back at me, everything about his body language screaming, *Well?*

You don't control me, Vito. So I sat there a few moments longer, no longer staring after him. *I'll get out of the car when I'm ready to get out. Not a second before. I'm not following your schedule.*

I said a silent prayer, asking the Blessed Mother for strength to get through the next thirty minutes, then got out of the car. I reached the front door of the motel before he did and opened the door for him, and he walked in without looking at me.

I was relieved to see Kelly behind the desk. She was an aspiring actress who worked at the motel part-time. When she'd found out I'd written a novel that had been optioned, she'd read the book, loved it, and asked me to keep her in the loop about everything. I'd alerted her when casting started, and she'd tried out for the part of one of the Brooklyn girls and had gotten the role.

"Sam," she gushed, and hurried out from behind the desk to hug me hello. "It's great to see you. I heard . . ." She stopped, looked at Vito, frowned, glanced back at me. "Is he, uh, with you?" she asked quietly.

"Kelly, this is Vito Bonti."

Her eyes nearly bugged out of their sockets. She recognized the name. She realized that the man who had shaped the texture of my life was standing in front of her. Never mind that he looked like he was coming off a three-day drunk. Kelly was scrupulously polite.

"Nice to meet you, Vito."

She extended her hand, but he didn't reciprocate. He just stood there, immobile and pissed off. Her arm swung back to her side. She looked over at me, her eyes radiating alarm, questions, and she mouthed, *Should I call the cops?*

I shook my head. No cops. I could handle Vito as long as he didn't become violent.

"So how can I help you, Sam?" she asked.

"Vito needs a room for the night."

"Not a problem. We've got a couple of vacancies."

"Something with a view," he said.

"All our rooms have views, Vito," Kelly said. "I'm going to give you the best view we've got."

"Perfect." I pulled out my credit card, handed it to her.

Vito walked off like he couldn't care less, and paused in front of the huge window and gazed out.

Kelly mouthed, *What the hell?*

Long story, I mouthed back.

As she processed my card, she whispered, "Is it true? That Jenean Conte is playing you?"

I nodded. "That's what the producer tells me. And production starts next month."

"Fantastic. I can quit this stupid job."

"Are they paying you enough to do that?"

"More than I make here, that's for sure."

"What time do you get off tomorrow?" I asked.

"I'm pulling a double shift tonight, so I'm not outta here till noon. Why? You want me to, uh, keep an eye on him, Sam?"

"If you could just steer him to a restaurant tomorrow morning and a place to buy a change of clothes, I'd really appreciate it. Then give me a call when he has headed off to the airport."

"Not a problem. I'll get him to the right places."

I removed a couple hundred dollars from my wallet and handed it to Kelly. "That's for you. I need to buy his plane ticket back to New York."

She gestured toward the three computer stations in the lobby. "Have at it, Sam." Her eyes darted over to Vito, and she leaned forward across the counter and whispered, "Did he show up at your house?"

"Yeah."

"I'll go keep him busy." She slipped out from behind the counter and went over to him while I parked myself in front of one of the computers.

I found a direct flight from L.A. to New York at three-thirty tomorrow afternoon. I figured it would give Vito plenty of time to do whatever he had to do in the morning and get to the airport by two p.m. or so. A one-way ticket was ridiculously expensive, there were only two seats left, both middle seats, at the rear of the plane, and he would probably complain bitterly to whoever would listen. Tough shit. No way was I paying for a first-class one-way ticket. I reserved the seat, bought the ticket, printed it out. I folded the rest of my cash into the ticket, then walked over to Vito and Kelly.

"Okay, Vito, your flight leaves tomorrow afternoon at—"

He glanced up and spat, "I don't want to go back to

New York. You can't make me." Like a petulant, spoiled child.

"Then I guess Vito will be paying for his own room, Kelly."

"But I . . . I—" he stammered.

"Exactly," I said.

Kelly looked uncomfortable and was saved by the peal of the desk phone. "I have to get that."

As soon as she turned away, I handed Vito the e-ticket with the cash folded inside. "There's enough cash for you to get what you need in the morning—clothes, breakfast, a cab to the airport—and money left over for when you get to New York. Your flight leaves at three-thirty and you should be at the airport by two, Vito."

"*Dad.* I'm *dad* to you."

"No, you're not. I haven't had a father since the man my pregnant mother was married to hit her in the stomach with a car jack. I almost died in utero. I'll tell Kelly you're ready to check in."

His eyes filled with such an agonizing confluence of emotions that guilt and remorse washed through me. I didn't realize then that Vito was a master manipulator in his own way. Where Alec had wielded that manipulation through the sheer power of his personality, Vito did it through his eyes, his facial expressions, through our genetic connection.

I turned away from him, pained by his wounded-dog look, and hurried over to the desk, where Kelly had been watching the little drama between us. "He's ready to check in, Kelly."

"Wow," she said softly, shaking her head. "You're doing the right thing, Sam." She handed me the key.

I knew I was, but the Bonti in me made me doubt it.

"Second floor, first room on your right as you step off the elevator."

Vito and I rode the elevator in silence. He counted the cash I'd given him, slipped it into his pocket. The e-ticket stuck up out of his shirt pocket, already crinkled and soiled, and probably by tomorrow it would be indecipherable. I just wanted to get home to my daughter, my life, and I didn't understand why the Blessed Mother or the universe or whatever would hurl this impossible man in my direction.

Yes, I felt sorry for him . . . who wouldn't? He was a lost soul, eaten up by bitterness. But I didn't feel so sorry for him that I would back down. *You're a period at the end of a sentence, Vito, nothing more.*

As the elevator doors whispered open, he looked at me with those haunted eyes. And in a sharp, cruel voice, he said, "Nine hundred bucks? You're worth millions."

"My childhood was priceless, and you left, Vito. Be grateful you've got enough to get your ass back to New York."

"I wish that car jack had killed you 'fore you was born."

He stomped off the elevator, and I stood there, unable to wrap my head around his words, around the vitriol and hatred behind them. I hit the hold button and stuck my head out the door. "Hey, Vito, it's room twenty. Here's the key." I hurled it down the hall, and it clattered against the floor beside him.

He paused, looked down at the key, then up at me. *"Ya bitch!"* he hollered.

I stepped back into the elevator, slammed my fist against the button for the first floor, and struggled not to cry as the elevator clattered downward. He hated me, and it hurt in a visceral way, bringing back all those terrible feelings I'd had as a kid, that I was a kind of orphan, a refugee. Even though he had never been a father to me, he was the only biological family I had besides Isabella.

When I walked out into the lobby, Kelly saw that I was

upset and hurried over and put her arms around me. "Don't waste your energy, Sam. He's your past, and he'll be gone by tomorrow. You've been incredibly generous. I'll call you when I get off work and give you an update."

"Thanks, Kelly. For everything."

It was a relief to reach my car. The stink of his body still lingered, and as I drove back along the highway, I lowered all the windows and let the cool salt air wash away the odor. And I started crying. I couldn't help myself. The man who had been responsible for the terrible void that had been my constant companion since I was a kid still hated me. Would always hate me.

And I would never know why.

I would never know why about any of it—why he was my father, why my mother had married him, why she'd stayed with him through years of abuse. And why had I stayed with a gangster? Why had I stayed married to Alec when it was so obvious that the marriage was over?

Maybe it all came back to that weird adage: *Better the devil you know than the devil you don't*. Or, translated according to Sam, *Stick with what's familiar, even if it sucks. . . .*

What I did know was that even though Isabella's father was dead, he had loved her fiercely and had loved me the best he could. She would never have that inner void that had screwed me up. And Vito Bonti would never contaminate her life—I would make sure of that.

When I entered the house, the sliding-glass doors to the patio were open, and I could hear the Jacuzzi running. But I didn't hear either Isabella or Lauren. For a horrifying moment, my imagination slammed into overdrive. I was sure Vito's partner in this scam had gotten onto the property while I was driving him to the motel and had kidnapped my daughter.

I dashed out onto the patio, where the glow from the

Jacuzzi created a strange texture of light and shadows against the walls, the deck. There they were, the two of them with their earbuds in, listening to their respective music. Isabella waved, slipped the buds off her ears. "Mom, we warmed up that lasagna and already ate."

"Okay, love. I'll be inside."

I wanted to stand there for a while and watch them, absorbing this perfect scene of my daughter with her closest friend, doing regular teenage stuff. I never knew that kind of normalcy and was happy that she did. But I knew that if I stood there, watching them, it would seem weird to her, weird to her friend, like I was some kind of voyeur or over-protective parent who was checking to make sure the kids weren't drinking or smoking weed out there in the Jacuzzi. I slipped back inside the house.

I was so emotionally drained by what had happened with Vito that I could barely muster the energy to warm up some of the lasagna. When it was steaming, I carried it into the living room with a stack of scripts and my phone. Clara had fixed it, and I could now send and receive text messages without any problem.

I turned the phone back on and found a rather terse text message from Paul, telling me that Jenean Conte would like to come by the house sometime this week, at my convenience, so she and I could chat. I replied that I would meet her somewhere. After what had just occurred with Vito, I didn't want any part of *Brooklyn Story* to breach those gates at the bottom of the driveway, the gates to my new life, the story I had written myself into, as Grand-mother Ruth would say. Paul wouldn't understand that. He didn't understand the three candles I lit every morning, either.

Bottom line? Paul didn't understand jack shit about me.

I polished off the lasagna, then sat back and shut my eyes just to rest them for a few moments before I started one of the scripts. Maybe I dozed off and dreamed. Or maybe what I saw were hypnogogic images, tricksters that bubbled up from my subconscious. Whatever the source, the story these images told was clear: if I broke off my relationship with Paul, he would sabotage the filming of *Brooklyn Story*.

I bolted forward in the chair, my heart racing, my breath hitched in my chest. A warning, I thought, it was a warning.

Liza and I, over the past months, had talked a lot about prescient dreams. *We all have them, Sam. We just don't pay attention.*

Immediately, my reasoning brain interfered. Would Paul really sabotage himself just to get even with me? Absurd. I hadn't even done anything: I hadn't broken off the relationship; I hadn't made any decision yet other than acknowledging the fact that I didn't love him. Also, Paul's company stood to make an enormous amount of money from the film. And with Conte now attached to it, the overseas sales could prove to be just as, or even more, lucrative for him.

And yet, in the back of my head I could hear this small, soft voice cautioning, *Be careful, Sam. Think things through. Look at what has happened today. The signs are there.*

From my argument with Paul earlier today to Vito's unexpected arrival and the horrible things he had said to me, the signs *were* there that my dream could be derailed. Even worse, it wouldn't take much for that to happen.

My company had money coming in from our deal with HBO, and my accountant had helped me with investments and tax loopholes and all the rest of it. But the bottom line was, if the deal with Gallery Studios fell apart, I wouldn't be able to finance *Brooklyn Story* on my own.

Fifteen million was enough to set up a production company and pay salaries and buy a home for Isabella and me, but what remained could very well finance a low-budget horror film. In the end, fifteen million dollars—a sum that 99 percent of humans on the planet would never see—was just pocket change in Hollywood.

If I ended my relationship with Paul, I risked having the movie shelved. He wouldn't do it consciously; it wasn't as if he would be staying up late in the night to figure out a way to fuck me over. It would be more subtle than that, an internal thing, something born within his own childhood, the only kid of movie-industry parents, raised by nannies and hired help. It would be compounded by his son's addiction to computer games. Paul blamed himself for Luke's stint in rehab.

If I'd paid more attention to him when he was younger, if I'd been more present . . . if, if, if.

If. Our lives were predicated on that two-letter word.

Only in this city would there be a rehab center for a specific game—Mystery Manor, a hidden-objects, hunt-and-click game, now available on Facebook for the iPad. The download was free, but if you wanted to advance in the game, there were in-app purchases for diamonds, the game's currency, and for objects that enabled you to explore the various rooms. The game was endless, as infinite as the universe, and was also connected to social media, so you could ask your "friends" for stuff. And some of these "friends" became real friends. It was how Luke had met his current girlfriend. Paul had told me as much.

He'd also revealed that where Luke had gone so terribly wrong was with the in-app purchases bought with a phony credit card.

Paul's son had spent thousands on those in-app purchases and had lost his job and a three-year relationship. He'd had a breakdown not long after Paul first asked me out six months ago; once a week or so, Paul drove out to the facility in the Hollywood Hills to visit his son. Supposedly,

Luke now believed that he actually lived in Mystery Manor, *a place where something terrible had happened.*

Yeah, it was weird. Hollywood weird. But it was real. People actually went into rehab for this shit.

The point, though, was that Paul was made up of a morass of conflicting emotions, and I was afraid that if I didn't toe the line, I might find my movie—and my dream, my hopes for a better future for my daughter—tossed under the truck.

Roadkill.

I once looked up the definition of the phrase. The Merriam-Webster online dictionary provides two definitions, neither of them particularly savory:

1: the remains of an animal that has been
   killed on a road by a motor vehicle
2: one that falls victim to intense compe-
   tition

Guess which definition fits Hollywood?

It had happened innumerable times in this town. Movies with not-quite-famous actors were shot, then shelved. When and if they were released, the results were not impressive.

I couldn't risk it.

But was I willing to continue a relationship with Paul, to keep sleeping with him, so that *Brooklyn Story* would make it to the big screen?

Nope. Even I had my limits, my boundaries. Sex as a weapon, a tool, had never been my thing. My emotions simmered way too close to the surface for that kind of deviousness, for that kind of dishonesty.

I leaned back in the chair, an arm covering my eyes, and felt as trapped as I had ever felt in Brooklyn, all those years ago.

It didn't matter that I had way more money than I'd

had then. It didn't matter that at the height of his success, Alec had been worth more than a hundred million. Never mind any of that because right now, at this precise moment in time, I was a Bonti again, living on food stamps and wearing clothes from the local thrift shop.

You never escape your past.

THREE

The next morning, when I was in the middle of reading a script that both Marvin and Clara loved, I got a text message from Paul.

> *Am very sorry for what I said yesterday. Was just feeling left out. May I stop by to give you something?*

I immediately felt bad that I had told him to fuck off. I had overreacted. And wasn't this progress? Paul was learning to say *I'm sorry.*

> Sure, c'mon by. I'll fire up the Nespresso machine.

Both Paul and I liked strong cappuccinos, so I used the dark roast. When he walked into my office ten minutes later, I handed him a mug and gestured at the porch. "Let's sit out there. It's a glorious morning."

Glorious in spite of the fact that I'd slept poorly, that Vito gnawed at the back of my thoughts.

"Smells fantastic," Paul said, and sipped. "Makes my morning."

We ducked out onto the porch. A cool breeze rustled through the palms, swollen with the salt scent of the Pacific.

"I realize I've been letting Luke's situation spill over into the rest of my life, Sam, and then I take it out on the people I care about."

"How's he doing?"

He rocked his hand from side to side. "Better. They've got him stabilized with meds."

"That's good to hear."

He reached into his jacket pocket and brought out a small square box. A jeweler's box. "I want you to have these."

He popped open the lid, revealing a pair of ladybug earrings made of rubies and flecked with what looked like onyx.

"Wow, these are gorgeous, Paul. Thank you."

"Here, put them on."

He handed me the box. I hadn't put on earrings this morning, and these little beauties even complemented the red in my blouse. I slipped them into my ears. "How do they look?"

"Like they were made for you," he said. "I'm actually on my way to a meeting, but dinner when you can?"

I felt bad all over again, though, because he was trying, that much was obvious. "Sure. I'll call you."

He touched the end of my nose. "A spot of cappuccino."

We both laughed and went back inside. I walked him to the front door, and as I was on the way back into my office, Clara said, "Beautiful earrings, Sam. Ladybugs bring luck."

"Yeah? We can all use some of that."

Just then my cell rang. It was on my desk, and I hurried back into my office. It was Kelly, from the motel.

"Hey, Sam, just wanted to give you the heads-up. Vito checked out of here a little while ago and left in a cab, presumably for the airport."

Relief coursed through me. "Thanks for letting me know, Kelly. Did he give you any trouble?"

"Uh, yeah." She lowered her voice. "He called a couple of times, ordering room service. I told him we don't have room service. Then he came down to the lobby and wanted to know where he should go for takeout and to buy a disposable cell phone. He made a couple of long-distance calls from the room, and I had to charge your credit card."

"For how much?"

"That's the bad news. Both calls were to New York, and the bill came to two hundred and change."

"Shit, *two hundred*?"

"Uh, yeah. He was on for a couple of hours. I jotted down the numbers. You want them?"

"Sure."

Kelly ticked off the numbers, and I jotted them down. Both were Brooklyn area codes, and I was tempted to call them just to find out who would answer. But I was afraid if I opened that door, I wouldn't like what I found on the other side. "Great, Kelly, thanks so much. I appreciate everything you did."

"I gave my two-week notice here. I'll see you on the set!"

"You bet."

After we hung up, I sat there staring at those numbers, tapping my pen against the desk, and realized it sounded like the ticking of a clock. "Forget it." I slapped the pen down, folded the piece of paper, and slipped it into a zippered compartment in my purse. I went over to my altar and lit three new candles I'd brought from home. I liked the colors—pastel green, rose red, bold blue.

"Please," I whispered. "Keep Vito out of my life. That's all I'm asking."

The rest of the day was uneventful, a change for me. I was grateful for it and slept eight hours straight that night.

Shortly before noon the next day, I finished the script just as Clara popped her head in the door. "Liza's here."

Liza. It took me a moment to remember she was picking me up for a meeting with some Gallery Studios execs. "Okay, tell her I'll be right out. By the way, I finished the script you've been raving about. I love it."

"I knew you would."

"I think we should option this one, but need to mull it over before making a decision." I grabbed my bag, and on my way out the door, Clara handed me a leather shoulder bag that held my iPad, folders, and notes I would need.

"Go wow 'em, Sam," Clara said.

"It'll be the other way around, I'm sure."

The meeting had been Liza's idea. These two executives—Brian King and George Prince—were the ones who had greenlighted *Brooklyn Story*. Liza wanted them to connect a name with a face and a personality. Meeting a king and a prince can only be a good thing.

Paul had never suggested such a meeting, but then again, why should he? Technically, DeMarco Productions was a competitor. Realistically, though, we were hardly competitors. Paul had been in the business for more than twenty years; I was the new kid on the block. But it irritated me. Was it his way of trying to maintain control over the project and me? Of keeping me dependent on him for information or something?

Or something. All too frequently, these two words were attached to Paul's motives. Somewhere in the last six weeks, I'd overlooked the fact that he was a player.

But how could I even be thinking this way after I had agreed we would have dinner when I was free? Sometimes, my own actions bewildered me.

Liza and Marvin were chatting in the doorway to his office. As usual, Liza looked terrific, California chic and casual in classic Ralph Lauren. She had braided her hair, and it curved gracefully over her right shoulder. "You ready, hon?" she asked.

"Definitely. Where're we meeting them?"

"Blu Jam Café, breakfast twenty-four/seven."

Once we were outside, on the way to her car, Liza asked, "Did Paul ever suggest a meeting with these guys?"

"Nope."

"Interesting. In my book, Sam, that's a sin of omission."

"I was thinking the same. Of course, to be fair, I never suggested it, either."

"He's the producer, he should've suggested it. And, given your personal relationship, you shouldn't *have had* to suggest it."

"I'm really conflicted about my relationship with him, Liza." I explained how I'd felt at lunch the other day when Paul had been talking about *Brooklyn Story* as if it were *his* story. "Then yesterday he apologizes and gives me these beautiful earrings." I touched them. "Maybe I'm just being overly sensitive about all this."

"Ha. Never deny the validity of what you feel at any given time, Sam. Our emotions are our most reliable GPS."

I thought of my visceral reaction the night before last to Vito's sudden appearance and knew I'd done the right thing by not allowing him onto my property, into the life Isabella and I had carved out for ourselves here. "A part of me is afraid that if I break things off with him, he'll do something to sabotage the movie."

I blurted it out as soon as we were in her Mercedes. To my surprise, she didn't laugh, didn't offer any of the rebuttals that someone else might have about how absurd it would be for Paul to undermine himself financially. Instead, she flashed one of her winning smiles. "Which is exactly why I want you to meet these Gallery boys."

"So you think Paul is capable of doing something like that?"

"Between us, hon, yes. And in this town, you have to assume it's the standard MO."

"It's not *your* standard MO."

"Or yours. High five, sistah!" We both laughed, then Liza added, "On a personal level, I've never liked Paul very much. But he's so well connected and knows so many players in the business that I try to maintain a business relationship with him. I manage a lot of people who have worked with him."

"You never told me you disliked him, Liza."

"I didn't feel it was my place. I've heard way too many stories about how he has screwed people over—mostly actors and actresses. But he has *never* done anything to my clients. He knows I'd ruin him if he did."

"How could you ruin him?"

"A soft whisper in the ears of people who work with him. Innuendo is a career buster here."

"Remind me to stay on your good side," I remarked.

"Hon, you have been on my good side since the day we met. That'll never change. Soul sistahs to the end!"

Blu Jam had a touch of Art Deco about it in the pastel colors of its facade and the shaded sidewalk tables. Despite the fact that the lunch rush was over, the place was still crowded. Liza had made a reservation, and we were seated at a choice spot outside, surrounded by lush potted plants that gave us ample privacy. Within minutes, the two royals arrived, one tall and slender with dark hair; the other shorter, muscular, and black, his hair paling to gray at the temples. Both looked to be in their late forties.

Liza stood up and waved them over. From her descriptions, I knew the taller man was Brian King, and that his shorter companion was George Prince. Together they had green-lighted fifteen of Gallery's most lucrative films since the early 2000s. King and Prince: good names for studio royalty.

I liked that neither of them wore a suit, that they didn't look like studio executives. If anything, they looked like a couple of recent transplants from the East, both wearing khaki pants, colorful cotton shirts, and sandals. California chic, like everyone else around here.

From the moment they sat down, it was apparent that Prince was the more effusive of the two. "Just love your book, Samantha, and we're delighted that Jenean Conte is on board."

"She brings enormous talent and star power to the film," King added.

"We're going to meet later this week to chat," I said.

"Excellent." Prince nodded and helped himself to one of the warm biscuits the waiter had just brought over. "She'll have your mannerisms down in a matter of hours. She's an incredible mimic."

"You know," King said, "we've been bugging Paul for weeks to set up a meeting with you. But he was always busy and tough to pin down. So when Liza called and suggested lunch, George and I jumped at the chance."

So my suspicions were right. Paul had deliberately kept me out of *this* loop. "Do you have a date yet for principal photography?"

"Ideally, May first," Prince said. "We'll start on the Gallery studio lot, probably in early June, then move to Brooklyn for the neighborhood shots. Schedules change, though, so until we actually start shooting, nothing is written in stone. Right now, auditions are going on for the extras we'll need in some of the scenes we'll be shooting at the studio."

The waiter came over again with drinks. "Are you ready to order?"

"Three more will be joining us," King said. "They should be here shortly."

I glanced at Liza, but she looked as clueless as I was about who else was coming.

"Some changes to the original script have been made," Prince went on when the waiter left. "And since you're on

board as a consultant, I'd like you to go through them, Sam.
I'll email copies to you and Liza. We're hoping that you can
join us on the Brooklyn shoot, too."

"I'd love to."

"And on the set, if your schedule allows it," King added.
"Hey, here come two of the three."

King waved, and I glanced around and saw Paul with a
scarecrow of a man whose body seemed to vibrate with frenetic energy. He looked high strung, the kind of man who
couldn't sit still for even five minutes. Thinning dark hair,
a neatly trimmed beard, jeans and a cotton shirt, sandals,
shades. A guy who could fit in anywhere.

"Well, well. Carl Davidson," Liza said.

"We thought it was time everyone met," King said.

Paul looked good, as he always did, Mr. Cool in his
designer clothes, his affable smile. When he looked at me, I
knew he could tell I was miffed about something.

Yeah, that sin of omission.

"Sorry we're late," Paul said, and claimed the chair next
to me.

"We're not in any hurry," King said, and introduced
Liza and me to Davidson.

Davidson tilted his shades back onto the top of his head.
"Wow, the legendary Liza and the talented Samantha." He
talked fast, shoulders twitching. "The pleasure is all mine,
ladies." Then he pulled out a chair, sat down, and leaned forward, eyes impaling me. "Your script is brilliant, and this is
going to translate incredibly well to the big screen. And you,
Liza"—his eyes darted to her—"we need to have lunch soon."

"How about tomorrow?" Liza never missed an opportunity. "Noon? Twelve-thirty?"

Davidson laughed and slapped his skinny hand against
his thigh. "Love it, a woman who moves at the same speed
I do. Sure, tomorrow's perfect." He whipped out his phone,
asked for her number, texted her.

"Got it," she said.

"Now that you're on Liza's speed dial, Carl, you know you've arrived," Paul quipped.

"Shit, y'mean two blockbusters didn't do that?"

"Honey, those blockbusters are the reason you're directing this film," Liza said.

"And shame on you, Paul," said King. "Keeping Sam hidden away from us."

He looked guilty, but not for long. I suddenly realized that guilt was as foreign to a man like Paul as poverty was to any of them. "Got a lot of things on my plate, Brian. So does Sam."

"Actually, Paul, my schedule right now is relatively clear," I said. "And I'll have plenty of time to be on set." I tried to keep the frost out of my voice, smiled as I spoke, but I caught the quick, worried little frown that brought his eyes together. He apparently thought that, because he had apologized the other day and given me the beautiful earrings I was wearing, he could now speak for me. And right then, I was beyond giving a shit what Paul thought about me or what he believed was going on between us.

The waitress, a young, attractive brunette, came over to take our drink orders. "It took you long enough to wait on us," Paul said testily.

"Sorry, sir. But we're pretty busy today. What's everyone having to drink?"

"Your house red," Paul said.

"Merlot or Cab?"

"Merlot," Paul replied. By the time she'd taken everyone's order, Paul had changed his mind. "Make mine the Cab," he said. "And a glass of water. And we'll take the shrimp appetizer, too."

"I'm sorry, we're out of that one," the waitress replied.

Paul rolled his eyes. "Then you'd better get out there on the next shrimping boat, honey, because—"

"That's fine, thanks," I said. "I know what I'd like for lunch."

I gave her my order, and everyone else did the same. I could tell from the expression on Paul's face that he was pissed I had interrupted him.

"Who else is joining us?" I asked.

"One of our investors," King said. "He may have gotten held up. I'll text him."

While Prince, King, Davidson, and Liza chatted, Paul, seated on my right, leaned toward me and whispered, "What's bugging you, anyway?"

"You. Don't speak for me, Paul. You don't know shit about my schedule."

Before he could say anything, I got up and asked a waiter where the restroom was. He directed me through the café to the back and said the restroom was on the right.

I picked up my bag and headed inside the café, wanting only to put some distance between Paul and me. Before I reached the restroom, I got a text message from Liza:

You played that well.

For me, it wasn't about *playing* anything. I wasn't particularly good at head games and was even worse at hiding what I felt. Yet in those years with Tony, his rage had always been so close to the surface that I learned to hide my feelings, especially when I knew the end result would be a clenched fist.

In a way, what Paul had done—that sin of omission— was a symbolic clenched fist that could tear my dream away. That was how I had to look at it because that was what it amounted to.

I freshened up, made my way back to the sidewalk table. As I emerged into the California afternoon, I thought maybe the brightness of the light was causing me to hallucinate. The man who was standing by our table, speaking to the waiter, resembled Brad Pitt from *Legends of the Fall*, long hair worn in a ponytail, full beard. But, hey, this was Hollywood, right? Celebrities were everywhere, and big honchos were seated there, so it made perfect sense that Pitt might know them.

When the man turned and I saw him full on, I realized he didn't look like Pitt at all. He resembled Leonardo DiCaprio, but with wild, dark hair and a dark beard. His body was so well toned and honed that I immediately imagined what it would be like to put my arms around him, to feel that solidness of muscle and bone beneath my hands. It wasn't as if I thought that about every good-looking man I saw, either. But there was something about this DiCaprio clone that resonated powerfully.

The moment our eyes connected, a bolt of lightning seemed to sear through me. Sound rushed out of my world until the only thing I heard was the relentless pounding of my heart. My peripheral vision closed down. Everyone and everything else ceased to exist. It was as if he and I had been suddenly transported to some foreign place and dropped down in the same space. We stood there for what seemed a long time, unable to take our eyes off each other. Yet I was sure I had never met this man.

Gradually, sound and awareness of my surroundings returned. My vision opened up to include tables filled with other customers, employees scurrying around. I managed to look away from him and pay attention to where I was going. Good thing. I nearly barreled into a waiter holding a tray of drinks.

"Sorry," I murmured, and wove my way between the tables.

I felt his eyes searing through me as I approached the group and forced myself to look at Liza instead of him. As I took my seat, King said, "Samantha, this is John Steeling, one of our investors."

I raised my eyes. "It's a pleasure, Mr. Steeling."

"Likewise, Ms. DeMarco."

His husky voice and those penetrating blue eyes sent that bolt of lightning through me again, searing me raw inside. No man had ever affected me this way. He really did resemble DiCaprio, something about his jaw, his eyes, but he was even better looking. And he literally exuded presence. I could have been on the other side of the street and felt that presence.

"I thoroughly enjoyed your book," he said. "But I'm curious. How much of it is true?"

Hmm, was this a test . . . ? All of it. I really did have an abusive mafia boyfriend who went to prison for homicide. And when I lost my virginity, it actually did happen in a bed with a Blessed Mother painting on the wall over it. "It's fiction." I laughed. "Except that I *am* from Brooklyn."

"And there's a sequel, John," said Liza. "It's equally good. Think: the rise and fall of a Wall Street husband and the effects on his wife."

"That's been done three times already," Paul said. It was obvious he'd picked up on the electricity between John and me and didn't like it one bit. That he intended to squash it immediately, before it could become anything else. "Douglas twice, DiCaprio once."

"It hasn't been done from a female point of view, hon," said Liza.

"Good point," Davidson agreed. "And audiences love sequels. Look at the Twilight franchise."

"So the female is the Wall Street player?" Prince asked.

"No, she's married to the Wall Street player," John said, and looked straight at me. "I've already read the sequel. It's terrific."

King and Prince exchanged a glance, then King said, "Can we get a copy of the e-book, Sam?"

"You bet."

"Got your iPad handy, Brian?" Liza asked.

He slipped an iPad mini from the bag slung over the back of his shoulder. "Always."

"Here comes *The Suite Life*."

"Fantastic," King said.

During this exchange, waves of anger rolled off Paul. He emoted such hostility that I was sure everyone at the table felt it, especially John. The corners of Paul's mouth tightened, his lips rolled together, fury burned in his eyes. I ignored him and kept glancing surreptitiously at John, trying to memorize his face, all the beautiful details. Something about him was familiar, but I didn't know what it was.

Our meals arrived. Paul ordered two more drinks during the meal and started acting like Don Draper in *Mad Men*. Voice too loud, laughter too boisterous. But at least with Draper, his muse was usually apparent. Paul's muse had crawled into a cave for a nap.

After we'd eaten, everyone except Paul ordered a cappuccino; Paul ordered another drink. John and I chatted about books and stories, and I discovered he was well versed in Joseph Campbell's work. Like me, he'd been riveted by the PBS interview Bill Moyers had done with Campbell in the library at George Lucas's Skywalker Ranch not long before Campbell had died. Both of us had seen it some years after the interview had aired.

"He defined the hero's journey," John said. "After I watched that interview, I did a movie binge of *Stars Wars* and *Indiana Jones*, *E.T.*, and some other Lucas and Spielberg films. I'd seen all of them before, but never like I had during that binge. They embody the essence of mythology and archetype that Campbell talked about."

I was riveted not only by what he'd said but by his words and the tone and texture of his voice. I had done exactly the same thing after I'd seen that interview.

"Campbell's tot'ly overrated," Paul muttered, words slurring.

I ignored him. King said, "*Overrated?* Damn, Paul, Campbell was one of the most brilliant thinkers on the planet."

Paul, properly chastised, simply sat there and pouted as he sipped his drink.

After coffee, Liza announced that she and I had to get moving. By then, Paul was six sheets to the wind, and Prince and Davidson said they'd get him home. No telling what kind of soap opera *that* drive would be. I was grateful I didn't have to make the drive with them.

"He's been having some bad problems with his son," King remarked, watching as Davidson and Prince steered Paul toward a waiting limo.

"Even when your kids are adults, they're still your kids," Liza said.

The only thing John said was that he was pleased we'd finally met. We didn't shake hands, but our eyes held briefly, with that same intensity I'd experienced earlier. Then he and King walked off up the street together, and Liza and I crossed the street to where she'd parked her car.

She and I didn't speak until we were in the car. It was as if we thought that someone might be listening—Hollywood's version of the NSA, sensitive satellites or drones launched by the studios or the gossip rags. Paranoid? Yes. Prudent? Probably. But once we were inside, the windows sealed shut against intrusion, we both burst out laughing.

"Oh, my God," Liza gasped. "They loved you, Sam. I knew they would. And once John Steeling said he'd read *The Suite Life*, it suddenly became a viable project for them."

"Do you know him? John?"

"Never met him before. While they were chatting, I Googled him. A level-one Google search didn't reveal anything about him further back than eleven years ago, when he financed the Sundance winner *American Splendor*. The screenplay was nominated for an Oscar. In 2005, he put up a shitload of money for *Brokeback Mountain,* and after that became a phenomenon, it put him on the map as a financier. Beyond that, no clue. At first when I saw you two eyeing each other when you were returning from the restroom, I thought you knew him."

"He felt familiar to me."

"Karma, hon. Maybe it's a past-life thing. Whatever. In *this* life, he has the ear of the studio execs. Maybe more than the ear. He seemed to be pretty thick with Brian and George. And even Paul didn't know about him. Did you, uh, trade email addresses, phone numbers?"

"No. Nothing."

"Well, you'll hear from him. I saw how he looked at you. Everyone did. Especially Paul. My God, he got so shitfaced, Sam. I'm sorry he's having problems with his son, but he shouldn't be taking it out on you."

"Yeah, no kidding. I'm just glad we didn't have to drive him home. So when you said I'll hear from John, was that the 'tad psychic' part of you speaking?"

She knew I was teasing her, but instead of laughing, she suddenly turned serious. "Listen, Sam. I need to know something. During lunch, I saw this spirit around you."

"A spirit? You mean, like, a ghost?"

"Yes." She proceeded to describe Grandma Ruth, who had died long before Liza had come into my life. "Does that sound like her?"

"You've seen her photo on my mantel."

"True. But there's no photo of her cooking you breakfast, of your mother stumbling around drunk. Right? Am I right?"

"Your point?"

"Grandma Ruth was with us at that lunch. Sometimes she was to your right, other times she was standing next to John. I don't know what that means, but maybe you do."

Not really. Not yet.

Her description of herself as a "tad psychic" suddenly slammed into a category that I called *Well, fuck me*. "What was she wearing?"

Liza described my grandmother's favorite outfit when

she was cooking latkes by the stove: a floral housedress. I sat there nearly choking on the description. Did the universe have any more weirdness to dish out before I ran, shrieking like a banshee, into the late-afternoon sun?

I smoothed my hands over my wrinkled skirt. "Listen, there's something you should know, Liza."

"Oh, shit, this sounds like confession time."

And because I'd had two glasses of wine and had been blown away by a man I'd just met, I told her about Vito's appearance. I thought she might swerve off the road or slam on the brakes in the middle of traffic. Instead, she swung a sharp right, into a parking lot. She pulled into a space, turned off the car, and looked at me.

"*The* Vito?"

"Uh, yeah. As far as I know, there's only one."

"Does Isabella . . . ?"

"No way. I wouldn't let him near her. I put him up at the Malibu Motel and bought him a one-way ticket back to New York."

"You shoulda called me, Sam. You shoulda told me. I would've set the bastard straight."

"I handled it myself. He's gone."

"He'd better be gone. Your dad fits into your bio as a dead guy, not as a man who's alive."

"What bio?"

Liza flexed her fingers against the steering wheel, stared out the windshield. Everything about her just then seemed hard, set in stone. Her wedding ring, a rock of three or four carats, glinted in the sunlight.

"Appearances, Sam. Everything in this town is about appearances. I'm fifty-three years old. Every eight weeks I get collagen injections that make me look a dozen years younger. My mouth is filled with twenty grand of dental implants. I spend twelve hours a week in the gym—weights, Pilates, yoga, treadmill, rowing machine. I'm a vegan.

"I know nearly everyone in this town who's worth know-ing, the power brokers. I'm an *image*. I'm bullshit, okay? But that image earns me ten to fifteen percent of whatever I sell and an income in the seven figures. And right now, I'm sell-ing you." She paused. "But the difference between me and the other bullshit artists in this town is that I can't sell what I don't believe in. And, honey, I believe in *you*. Your story. Your talent. So if your old man has come back into your life, this is something I need to know. It's something that *Entertainment Weekly* or *People* might find worthy of a cover story. Or not. Your call. It all depends on the image you want to project."

I absorbed everything she said, as Liza was busy typing away on her iPhone, and churned it through my tired brain, and said, "*Not*. Forget it. Vito isn't a part of *this* story, except on film."

She looked at me then, and I saw only relief in her ex-pression.

"Can I ask you a question?" I said.

"Always."

"Besides the money, what's in this for you?"

She burst out laughing. "Are you kidding? You know how many women are in the position that I'm in? I can count them on one hand: Kathryn Bigelow. Debra Granicks's *Win-ter's Bone,* which starred Jennifer Lawrence before she was huge. Granicks's star rose when Lawrence was nominated for that part and went on to become the beloved Katniss of *The Hunger Games.* Suzanne Collins wasn't just the author of the books; she was an executive producer. Then there's Amy Pas-cal, who actually heads a major studio. But none of them do what I do, Sam. I'm a connector, a networker, a thread that unites a lot of people in various areas of the industry."

"At what personal cost, Liza?"

She didn't answer immediately. She gazed out her win-dow, her lip quivering, and when she looked back at me, her eyes welled with tears. "My marriage has collapsed. Tom's having an affair with a woman twenty years younger and thinks I'm clueless. It's a mess."

I put my arms around her, letting her cry. "What're you going to do?"

She pulled back, dabbing at her eyes with some Kleenex, and shook her head. "Nothing. Not yet. But I've been stashing money away in my own accounts so he can't touch it. Not that he needs my money, he earns plenty. But since the spouse is entitled to fifty percent in California, I'm being careful. I've worked too long and too hard to have some bimbo twenty years younger than me sweep in and enjoy the fruits of *my* labor."

I suspected there was a lesson in all this for me, too. "Look, however the whole thing shakes out, Liza, you'll land on your feet. You will always land on your feet—it's how you are."

"Damn straight, I will." She smoothed her hands over her clothes, then slipped out her iPhone. "You've got an interview with *Entertainment Weekly* next Wednesday, and they'd like to do it in your home or in your office. *People* wants to do a photo shoot with you and Jenean Conte. And, honey, you with that gorgeous raven-black hair, those sultry eyes . . . You'd be perfect for a cover shot. They've already spoken with Jenean's publicist, and she's on board. We just need a firm date."

Her abrupt transition from the personal to the professional startled me. "You need to teach me how to do that, Liza."

She winked; she knew exactly what I meant. "Sistah, if we stick together, no men are going to screw us over."

Amen to that.

"So, you good with these two interviews?"

"Absolutely."

"And there are more in the pipeline. Onward, my friend. Ever onward."

With that, she put the Mercedes back in gear, exited the parking lot, and pulled back into traffic.

chapter

FOUR

I didn't hear anything from Paul for the next few weeks and didn't miss the drama or the negativity he had so recently stirred up in me. I hoped he'd gotten the hint that my feelings toward him had changed so we could avoid a confrontation. I didn't want to be in a relationship with him, I didn't want to sleep with him, and I knew that at some point I would have to say these things to his face. But not today. So for now, I let it be. Besides, I suddenly had a lot of other stuff on my plate.

The interview with *Entertainment Weekly* went well. It was held at our office, with Liza, Marvin, and Clara there, too. I talked to the interviewer for more than two hours—mostly about Brooklyn and how I'd written the novel. They were going to feature the novel and get quotes from King, Prince, and Paul, and the article was supposed to run next week. As Liza said, "Prepare yourself, Sam. Once this piece and the *People* article are published, folks from your past are going to be popping out of the woodwork."

Great, as long as those people didn't include Vito, Tony, and any of the Brooklyn Boys.

The day before the *EW* article was published, Jenean Conte and I met at my house, with a writer and photographer from *People*. She arrived early, which gave us a chance to chat over coffee.

In person, she was strikingly pretty in an offbeat sort of way. Everything about her physical appearance seemed excessive—she probably didn't weigh even a hundred pounds, her eyes were a bit too large, her mouth a bit too seductive, her nose a bit too long. But somehow it all worked. I had the distinct impression that she didn't spend a lot of time primping, getting manicures, or having botox injections. Well, she was too young for the latter, her flawless skin the kind that every woman over thirty-five envied. She seemed completely comfortable in her own skin, something I'd never mastered.

Even the way she dressed was about comfort—black cotton slacks with a beautiful blue top that matched the color of her eyes, sandals, gold peace-symbol earrings. I liked her immediately.

We sat out on the back deck, in the cool morning air, the rust-colored canyon wall rising behind us like a monolith from some ancient past. "So, Sam, besides your daughter and writing, what are your passions?"

"Finding true love."

As soon as I said it, I regretted it. It sounded absurd, like something a woman in a nineteenth-century romance novel would say or Rapunzel herself in the tower—and, hey, the woman in the novel would say it more poetically. But Jenean got it immediately. "Well, hell, isn't that what we all want? The perfect guy. Great sense of humor. He's madly in love with you, loyal, he'd never cheat on you. He's hot, passionate, great in bed. He's kind, loves your pets and your kids, isn't a freeloader, and how about if he's a great cook to boot? Did I leave anything out?"

"He's your other half."

"Well, yeah. There's that." She twisted her long brown hair behind her head and sat back, her expression contemplative. "Your soul mate."

"Right."

She let her hair fall back to her shoulders, a thick, shiny cascade. "You finish each other's sentences."

I nodded.

"There's hardly any need to talk because you understand each other so completely."

"Yes."

"Are you also business and creative partners?"

"That would be awesome, an extra bonus. But he's not my clone." I thought immediately of John Steeling. "He's different enough so that we complement each other." He seemed to drift in and out of my mind lately, ever since our last encounter.

Her head bobbed, and she pulled out an iPad mini and stylus and made some notes. "You think our soul mates actually exist?"

"I sure hope so."

She laughed. "Yeah, me, too. But you know what?" She leaned forward slightly, and in a hushed, confidential tone, said, "You and I, talking about soul mates . . . you know how many people would say we're hopeless romantics?"

"Most people."

"I'd rather be a romantic than a cynic."

"Same here. You dating anyone special?"

She rocked her hand from side to side. "Sometimes." She mentioned an actor whose name wasn't familiar to me. "But in this town, it's hard to meet guys with substance."

"Yeah, tell me about it."

"I like this thing you do with your hands, Sam."

I wasn't aware that I did anything with my hands. "What thing?"

"Your hands are expressive, always moving."

Not surprising. I'm half Italian. But I suddenly felt so self-conscious about them, I nearly tucked my hands under my thighs to still them. "I don't even notice it anymore."

"Your grandmother. Tell me about her."

"She was my support system, my cheerleader. She told me to write myself out of this story and into a better one. So I did."

"My God, I love that line. I just love it." She tapped furiously on her iPad, then looked up and glanced around slowly. "I'd say you've written yourself way out of Brooklyn and into an American dream."

"Did you read *The Suite Life*?"

"Finished it last night."

"Well, I'm here in this American dream because my husband took out a large life insurance policy that I didn't know about. He died nearly two years ago."

She'd probably made millions during the course of her short career. Just the same, her eyes widened. "Wow," she breathed. "Incredible. Do you think he had some sort of precognitive feeling that he would die young?"

When you lived as hard as Alec had—driving yourself relentlessly, robbing yourself of good meals, enough sleep, and a peaceful lifestyle and hitting yourself hard with HGH, so you could keep up with it all, you probably didn't need precognition to know your days were numbered. When I said all that, she stared at me for a long, uncomfortable moment.

"That's sad," she said finally. "People burn themselves out for all the wrong reasons. Every time I finish a movie, I treat myself to a trip to some remote place where I don't know the language or the customs. It forces me to be fully present, to be really aware of what's important. Do you have something like that?"

"Yeah, my daughter."

"Just so you know. I heard that *Brooklyn Story* is true. I don't care one way or another. To me, it's just a terrific story. But if that comes up in the interview, you'd better know what you want to say."

"Thanks for the warning."

Speculation abounded on the Internet about all sorts of things, but the question about whether the *Brooklyn Story* was memoir or fiction seemed as if it should be pretty far down on anyone's list. And it was mostly fear of reprisal from the Brooklyn Boys that prompted me to write the book as fiction. Sure, I cared about what people might think—people out here in L.A.—but fear was at the root of my reluctance to call it a memoir.

The sliding-glass doors opened, and Marvin stepped out. "Hey, Sam, Jenean. The writer and photographer from *People* are at the gate. If you two are ready for them, I'll let them in."

"We ready, Jenean?"

"Sure."

"Okay, let them in, Marvin," I said, as though they were a pack of wolves.

"Done." He slipped back inside the house.

"Have you been interviewed by *People* before, Sam?"

I shook my head.

"Then there're a couple of things you should keep in mind. If we get on the cover, it'll be fantastic for your novel and for the movie. It means the article will be a couple of pages instead of a few paragraphs that you read in the bathtub. This magazine makes bestsellers and puts people on the map, okay?" Her thumb popped up. "That's number one. Number two . . ." Her index finger joined her thumb. "We *engage* them, we *play* to them, we give them some juicy quotes, we *tease* them. Got it?"

"Got it," I replied, and hoped that I did.

"Otherwise, they're in control and may start asking questions that we don't feel like answering."

The reporter was male and the photographer female, both in their early thirties, I guessed. Rick and Ria, an ambitious duo. He was all smiles, a public relations marvel who made you feel like you two had been best buds your entire life. *Tell me your secrets*, his smile whispered. *You can trust me.* And he almost won me over until he asked, "So tell me, did your dad really hit your pregnant mother with that car jack?"

"It's a novel, Rick. That means it's fiction."

"Well, yeah, but I hear it's all true."

We were in the kitchen when he said this. Rick was sitting at the table, his iPad in front of him, and I was slicing up some strawberries and cheese for a platter of snacks. For all I knew, he was looking at porn on his iPad. Ria was out on the deck with Jenean. "Heard from whom?"

"Paul Jannis, who else?"

"He optioned a novel, not a memoir." And why had Paul taken it upon himself to tell the media?

Rick shrugged. "Hey, novel or memoir, it's all the same. Writers write what they experience. Did you know that Cormac McCarthy lived under a bridge for a while? I mean, honestly, this guy won the Pulitzer, and he's living under a *bridge*?"

Another bridge, another story.

"You know who he is, right?" Rick asked when I didn't say anything.

"*The Road,*" I replied. "One of the most depressing dystopian novels I've ever read. But I couldn't put it down."

"Me, neither."

I walked over to the table with the platter of snacks and sat down. I leaned close enough his way to hear him sucking at a strawberry. "So tell me, Rick. If something is true, how does that change your reporting?"

He laughed nervously and drew back. "Are you kidding? It's the difference between five hundred words and fifteen hundred, between an article and a cover story."

"Really."

The light streaming through the windows danced in his eyes. I had seized his attention. "Well, here's the thing, Rick.

If I told you it was all true, I might find myself with broken kneecaps, a broken jaw, a severed spinal cord. I might find myself in a wheelchair. So it's fiction. Got it?"

And there it would stay, I thought, unless I heard from Father Rinaldi that the Brooklyn Boys were thrilled they would hit the big screen. He'd always had his ear to the ground, and he had known everything about everyone. But fat chance of that. I didn't even know if the priest was still alive.

"Uh, yeah. For sure."

"And please don't quote me on that."

"You'd better talk to Paul. He's been telling people all over town that the story is true."

Interesting. No wonder I hadn't heard from him. He'd been too busy getting even because I hadn't allowed him to speak for me. He wouldn't call it getting even, of course. He would tell me that a movie based on a true story had greater box office appeal. Maybe it did. But I couldn't risk it. For all I knew, the Brooklyn Boys were alive and well, and if and when they saw the movie, they might decide to get even. Everyone was busy getting even.

"Thanks for the tip, Rick."

Jenean and Ria joined us then, and Ria took some photos of Jenean and me together out on the deck, in the kitchen, then walking together down the driveway, two women deep in conversation. As we walked, Jenean asked, "How'd it go?"

"Great. Except that Paul Jannis has apparently been telling everyone that *Brooklyn Story* is a memoir."

"That's what Paul told my agent last week when they spoke. He said he thought it might help me really get into the part in a more profound way." She laughed. "He obviously doesn't know much about how actors immerse themselves in their parts. Like I said before, it doesn't make any difference to me whether the story is true or not. I'm captivated by the character."

So had Paul called up the agents and managers of everyone who had been cast in the film to let them in on the big fucking secret? Had he let John in on the real scoop, too?

"Hey, have you met John Steeling?" Jenean asked.

"At lunch the other day. Why?"

"He's nuts about your book."

"How do you know him?"

"I just met him several days ago. Apparently, he's investing a chunk of change in the film, and King and Prince have given him considerable say about things."

"Is that normal?"

"I honestly don't know. I've never paid too much attention to the financial workings of studios. I always figured that when they have big-name directors and stars on board—Spielberg, Lucas, Streep, De Niro, DiCaprio, Willis, Lawrence—they've got banks lining up, eager to loan what they need. If studios are anything like producers, then they're loath to use their own money."

It sounded cynical but was probably realistic. As a fledgling production company with limited funds, we weren't exactly leaping at the chance to put out a quarter of a million for a script—even when we loved it—if we didn't already have interest from a studio, network, or cable station. And we hadn't been approached by any banks eager to extend loans.

"So when you met John, what did you talk about?"

"The character of Samantha. He wanted to know how I perceived her, flaws and strengths, her inner world, really specific questions. He said he had studied my films—not *seen* them, but *studied* them, like some AFI student, right? Or like a critic. And he said that after studying my films, he felt I'm the perfect actress for the character. I had the distinct impression that if he'd felt otherwise, I would've lost this role."

"Really? You think he has that much clout at Gallery?"

"It sure seems that way to me."

We stopped at the end of the driveway, and Ria asked us to walk back uphill for some additional shots. "I want a couple of profile shots," she called. "Of the two of you conversing."

Well, that was easy, as long as Ria was out of range. Jenean and I turned, facing each other. She whispered, "John wants De Niro in the film. Did he tell you that? Maybe as one of the priests."

"Which priest?"

"Probably Rinaldi."

"His part's not very big."

"I think that's the point. De Niro in a small part. I don't know, they'll figure it out. He has also approached Susan Sarandon about playing the grandmother. Even if we only get one of these people, this movie is going to be off the charts."

"With you in it, Jenean, it's going to be off the charts."

Her laughter was quick, fluid. "Thanks for the compliment, but there's no way in hell I compare with the likes of Sarandon and De Niro."

"Do you know Camilla Batiste?"

"Met her. I think she's perfect for the role of the mother."

"Me, too."

I was trying to wrap my head around Sarandon as Grandma Ruth. I still remembered her as the young beauty in *The Hunger*, the movie based on the novel by Whitley Strieber. Sarandon, seduced by that stunning vampire, Catherine Deneuve; I could still see that scene. Paul hadn't told me any of this. But maybe Paul didn't know about De Niro and Sarandon.

As soon as I thought that, I wondered why I was always so quick to give the men in my life the benefit of the doubt.

Ria got the shots she wanted, and Rick had a couple more questions for the two of us. He said the article would be in the next issue. Then he added that he was hoping it would make the cover despite the fact that it wasn't based on a true story—*wink, wink*.

Those winks troubled me. I had serious doubts that Rick would keep his word.

When they'd all left, when it was just Marvin and me in the living room, I gave him the *Reader's Digest* recap of what I'd learned. He rolled his eyes. "Christ, what a jerk he is. Look, I'll go to Isabella's swim meet after school and drive her home. You go tell Paul the Asshole to pound sand. Hell, he probably makes huge donations to the right-wingers who vote against gay marriage."

I actually didn't know anything about Paul's politics. We didn't talk about national politics, only about Hollywood politics. But it wouldn't surprise me if Marvin was right. "You think I should text him?" I asked. "See if he's free?"

Marvin looked at me like I was nuts. "Hell no. Don't give him any warning. Drive over to his office."

Confront him, put him on the spot, face-to-face, that was what Marvin was saying. Not exactly my forte. But maybe it was time to change the status quo.

Before I left, I changed clothes. Off came the interview outfit and on went the designer jeans that hugged my hips and made me look skinnier than I was, 115 pounds on a five-foot-four frame. I wore a short-sleeved blouse, a blue print beauty with a scoop neck that showed some cleavage, and a pair of expensive sandals as black as my handbag. Let him regret what he'd done. Let him drool. Let him lust. Let him hunger for me.

In my head, I heard Diana Ross's "It's My Turn."

Jannis Productions was in a two-story building tucked away in the Hollywood Hills. Paul owned the building, had inherited it when his mother passed away some years back.

It had been his childhood home, then his mother's writing studio—she had been an accomplished novelist—and was one of three structures on the five-acre property. No gate, no guards, just drive on in and wing it. I liked that about him.

But I realized that I didn't like much else about Paul and that I'd been hiding that fact from myself for weeks.

His assistant, his right-hand guy, Jim Flannigan, actually answered the door. Jim was an Irishman with red hair and a million freckles. "Sam!" he gushed, and hugged me hello. "What brings you into the Hills?"

"Five minutes with Paul."

He slung his arm over my shoulders and walked me into the comfortable living room, a place where visitors slipped off their shoes and put them in a tidy lineup against the wall. Very Asian and hygienic.

The floors in Paul's house, coquina tiles with inlaid bits of shells and coral from ancient times, were spotless. A cleaning crew, I guessed. A daily cleaning crew. And servants, though not as many as there were in *Downton Abbey*. He wasn't quite at that level. Or if he was, I didn't know about it.

Flannigan grabbed two bottles of Metromint water from a bucket of ice just inside the hallway, then showed me to a comfortable chair in the living room. Two other men were hanging around—beefy guys, bodyguards. The taller one, Donaldson, nodded hello. The other man, Olmoso, had a scar that crossed his right cheek and reminded me of some character actor in a bad movie. He didn't acknowledge my presence in any way. It was as if I were invisible to him. Or maybe he just had a grudge against women.

Flannigan and I settled in the living room, in opposite chairs. He crossed his legs, right foot swinging back and forth, hands laced in his lap. "You must've heard, right?"

"Heard what?" I asked. Donaldson and Olmoso left the room and moved like shadows through the hallway.

"Luke escaped the rehab place. He assaulted two guards; one of them is in the hospital."

Huh? A twenty-four-year-old kid was in a rehab place for his addiction to a specific game, and he suddenly became a violent criminal? Something didn't compute here. "What the hell were they doing to him?"

Flannigan suddenly looked uncomfortable. He leaned forward, helping himself to a pretzel from a bowl on the sculpted redwood coffee table. "That's just the thing," he said quietly. "That's exactly what I said to Paul. Does this facility function like some of those gay-conversion places? Where you beat up effigies of your mother? Where you're punished if you don't toe the line? What the hell, right?"

Since Flannigan was gay, I could see how this might be something of a concern for him; he, along with Marvin and every other gay person in Hollywood, was quite vocal against the Michele Bachmans and Rand Pauls of the world. Flannigan had been with his partner for more than a decade, longer than most heterosexual couples I knew. And Marvin and his former partner in New York had been together fifteen years before his partner left him for a younger man.

"Paul's ex must be freaking out," I said.

"So is Paul. I think he's realizing that he wasn't much of a father to the kid. Turns out that Luke owes the game nearly a hundred thousand that he put on fraudulent credit cards. Not good." Flannigan shook his head and bit into another pretzel. "Not good at all."

"Who's Paul with now?"

"The owner of the rehab place. I think he's trying to talk him out of pressing charges."

"Maybe I should come back . . ."

"No, no, no," he said quickly. "Stay put. Let me tell him you're here. He needs to see a friendly face."

I wasn't feeling too friendly. I was pissed off and ready

for battle. I was primed for confrontation, an out-of-the-box thing for me. But the situation warranted it. I couldn't have Paul calling people in Hollywood to tell them *Brooklyn Story* was actually a memoir. That was for *me* to decide.

A few minutes later, a short, harried-looking man rushed out of Paul's office; ten minutes after that, the door opened again and Flannigan motioned me to come in. I was relieved when Donaldson and Olmoso didn't follow me. Relieved that it was just Paul and me, that even Flannigan didn't stick around.

When I saw the expression on Paul's face, all the fight bled out of me. He grabbed my hand like a drowning man clutching a rope and pulled me against him, into that scent of aftershave and maleness, our bodies pressed together like sheets of paper. I couldn't utter a word against him, couldn't lash out at him. I felt like sobbing.

Luke was like some alter ego of Paul—the venue was different; iPads hadn't existed when Paul was his son's age—but the issue was the same. Addiction. Paul's addiction was power. Luke's addiction was weird, something you'd find only out here, in the country of illusion. But the bottom line was that Paul's son had broken out of his prison, assaulted some guards, and committed credit card fraud, and now Paul, like any good father, was trying to make it right.

Except that I didn't know squat about good fathers. Vito was hardly a stellar example. Alec had provided well for Isabella, and sometimes he had even *engaged* in her life, helping with math homework, science projects, English compositions. He hadn't gone on class field trips. He had hugged her good-bye in the morning and hello in the afternoon. That was about it. If he were still alive, things might have been different. Even he had known that our daughter was truly a gift from God.

Maybe Paul hadn't been a good father to Luke at all.

What did I know about the father-son dynamics in their relationship? Nothing. It wasn't as if we'd lain around after making love and talked about our kids, the kids we'd had with other people. It wasn't as if we'd ever talked to each other about anything other than the business of Hollywood.

"Christ, Sam," he murmured against my neck. "What the hell should I do?"

I stepped back from him. His breath, warm against my neck, stank of booze. "Make it right, Paul. And to begin doing that, stop drinking before noon. That would help the situation."

He ran a hand over his bald head. "My horrible ex has called five dozen times since she heard about this."

"Yeah, so? It's not about you. Or her. It's about Luke."

He looked—what? Surprised? Shocked? No, he looked stunned by what I'd just said. Then a dark roiling anger poured across his face, took root in his eyes. "Who the hell are *you* to judge *me*?"

Hanging on the wall directly behind him was the vintage movie poster for Hitchcock's *Vertigo*, which was exactly what I felt right then. I put some distance between us . . . slowly. I had seen this kind of rage before in Tony, in Alec. I knew that if I moved abruptly, a clenched fist might follow.

"Look, I'm not judging you, Paul. I'm just telling you what I see. That's all."

"Well, you want to know what the hell *I* see in *you*, Sam? An ambitious broad with talent that doesn't care what it takes to get to the top in the industry. I see . . ."

He never finished his sentence because I snapped, "I'm done here," and threw open the door and headed out. Really? I was sleeping my way to the top of *what*? With *whom*?

Before I could leave the room, he lunged at me, threw his arms around my waist, and we both crashed to the floor and rolled.

I shrieked for help, shrieked for Flannigan, beat my

fists against Paul's back, struggled to free myself. The door exploded open, and Flannigan and Donaldson and Olmoso rushed in and pulled Paul off of me. I stumbled to my feet, my heart racing, pounding, and stood there for a moment with my hands clenched, trying to draw air into my lungs.

"Get outta here, Sam," Flannigan said, as he and Donaldson pinned Paul to the floor, holding him against it the way a trainer holds a feral dog.

"He's going to bite me? He's got rabies?" I spat.

"Just go," Flannigan said, his voice so thick with exhaustion that I suddenly felt sorry for him.

The exhaustion I heard in his voice told me he dealt with this bullshit daily, that he wasn't just Paul's assistant—he was the man's moral compass. Flannigan was probably the one who tucked Paul into bed when he was blasted out of his mind.

"You tell him that if he makes another call to *anyone* about how *Brooklyn Story* is a memoir, not fiction, I'll sue his ass and make sure he doesn't have anything to do with the movie. Tell him that, Jim. Make sure he's sober enough to understand it. And he and I are *done.* Be sure he's clear on that. Paul, did you hear what I just told Jim? We are *through, done, finished.*"

On the floor, Paul writhed and fought the men who held him down. But I knew he'd heard me.

I marched through the door and on out into the other rooms until I was outside, moving swiftly toward my car. Before I reached it, Flannigan barreled after me, shouting, "Sam, hold up. Please."

I stopped. "I could file assault charges against him, Jim."

"Look, he's got problems with his son, financial problems, and a major drinking problem. Please don't compound the trouble by filing assault charges. Breaking it off is the best thing you can do."

"Which I just did."

"I guess he thinks he owns you because he discovered you."

"No one owns me and no one discovered me. God did all that." I gave his hand an affectionate squeeze. "But thanks for explaining, Jim. I appreciate it. Please make sure he understands that he and I are done."

"Don't worry, Sam. I'll make that clear."

chapter FIVE

In early May, two things happened: principal photography for *Brooklyn Story* was delayed until May 11, and DeMarco Productions optioned its second script for fifty grand. The script Clara and Marvin had brought to my attention. It was the second book in a trilogy about spirits who have learned to seize the living so that they can enjoy the pleasures of physical life. When they seize the living, they are able to use that physical body for anything, but they are mostly interested in sex.

Even though a love story was folded into this script, it wasn't *my* kind of love story. Yet, I recognized the commercial value. With the popularity of zombies and vampires, of werewolves and shape-shifters, this script offered a new, different take on the whole idea that the dead aren't really dead.

Marvin and Clara were immediately on it, querying individuals at networks and cable channels. They received several requests for the script. It was my gift to them, a chance to work on something that didn't involve *Brooklyn Story* and the mafia boys. But it meant that my fund for these kinds of projects was fifty grand less that it had been a day earlier. However, if shooting began according to the schedule King and Prince had set up, I would receive a nice payoff for *Brooklyn Story* when principal photography began.

Then I realized that check would go directly to Paul, not to me, and that *he* would be paying Liza, who would take her cut and pay me. It wouldn't surprise me if he delayed the payment to get even for what had happened at his house. But legally, our contract said that his production company had to pay within five days of the receipt of the money.

On the twenty-first, *Entertainment Weekly* hit the stands, and a day later, so did *People.* In *EW,* my interview was buried in the middle of the magazine. But it was the cover story in *People,* with a captivating photo of Jenean and me walking across the Brooklyn Bridge—that part of it was Photoshopped. Rick had kept his word—sort of.

Toward the end of the article, there were a few lines about how "some people involved in the film" believed *Brooklyn Story* was actually a memoir, not a novel, but that "the author denies it." I figured Paul was "some people." And at this point, did it really matter?

Within a few hours of *People* hitting the stands, the office phone and my cell were ringing constantly and hundreds of emails had stacked up in my in-box. Marvin and Clara weeded out the legitimate calls and emails from the crank stuff, and by midafternoon, we had a handle on things. I realized I needed a publicist who could sift through all this and help me make smart decisions about which talk shows and interviews were worth my time. Liza, naturally, was my first choice. We agreed to meet at Blu Jam for a late lunch.

I arrived before she did and sat at the same table where I'd first laid eyes on John Steeling. While I waited for her, I went through some of the email on my iPad and was shocked to find a note from Priti Sarma, who had been my closest friend years back, when I first met Alec.

She had emigrated from India with her family and, during the course of our friendship, had taught me about her country's culture and customs. She had first introduced me to Buddha and the Hindu faith and used to attend Mass with me occasionally at Our Lady of Victory back in New York City. She had gone back to India to get married, and hearing from her now, so close to the start of filming of *Brooklyn Story*, felt like a fortuitous gift.

> Sam! I saw the article in People! I'll be in L.A. soon, opening a textile biz w/my hub. Let's re-connect! I've so missed you!

Her optimism and enthusiasm for life came through in that brief email, and I suddenly missed our long talks, missed everything about her. I emailed her and gave her all my phone numbers. Moments later, a text message came through:

> Am so proud of u!

She said she was deeply sorry to hear about Alec's death and hoped that Isabella was adjusting. She suggested we Skype soon and reminded me that the time difference between L.A. and India was about thirteen hours. I told her we could schedule a time when we could both talk freely.

When I glanced up from my iPad, I thought I was hallucinating. Brian King strolled up the sidewalk with John Steeling. Neither of them had seen me yet, and it gave me a chance to really look at John. He was a beautiful man, and once again, I felt that strange familiarity, that niggling certainty that I knew him from somewhere.

He and King wore dark cotton yoga pants, sandals, and dark T-shirts with NAMASTE written across the front in white letters. Both had yoga bags slung over their shoulders. I knew there was a yoga studio nearby and found it interesting that these two men apparently had taken a yoga class together. How much Hollywood business was conducted in yoga studios? In gyms? On jogging tracks? Maybe it was time for me to join a gym or sign up for some yoga classes.

Or to start running, to become a female Jim Fixx, and run my zillion miles a week.

Then John spotted me and moved toward me, his smile widening, those intense eyes burning into me. Once again everything around me paled and faded away. It was just him, a handsome man who seemed so familiar, slipping between tables, past customers, his eyes never leaving me.

"Samantha," he said. "So good to see you again."

My heart thudded like an old engine badly in need of repair. "Nice seeing you again, too, John. Looks like you and Brian are headed to a yoga class."

"Just finished it."

King jogged over. "Congrats on the *People* article, Sam. We've been getting calls all day about it. May we join you?"

Oh, no, of course you can't join me. Ha. "Sure. Liza should be along any minute."

Almost as soon as I'd said the words, Liza came barreling around the corner, phone pressed to her ear. She was dressed more casually than usual, so I guessed she'd been working from home today. When she saw me, I read her astonishment in her body language. She quickly ended her call and slipped her phone into her bag.

"Well, gentlemen, to what do we attribute this pleasant surprise?" she asked when she reached us.

"Yoga," King said.

"Destiny," John said, glancing at me.

I felt those eyes peering inside me, moving through me with the power and force of a living, sacred thing. I didn't know if King or Liza noticed it. They were chatting away and ordering from the waiter. I finally wrenched my eyes away from John's and looked down at the menu, my heart hammering so loudly I was sure that the others could hear it.

I ordered a grilled chicken wrap and iced tea and allowed myself to tune in on their chatter. Liza, King, and John were deep in conversation about the shooting schedule, which had been delayed by several days, another detail Paul had neglected to tell me.

Actually, I hadn't spoken to Paul since that scene at his place, so of course he hadn't told me squat.

"Why the delay?" I asked.

"Paul's son has to be in court, and he wants to be there," King replied. "We don't really need him on the set opening day, but we don't want to rob him of being there. Our principals said it's fine with them. It gives them another few days to prepare."

Would they feel that way if I'd told them what had happened at Paul's house? Or would they just think of me as some drama queen diva?

"When it comes to the courts, our kids need all the support they can get," John remarked.

"Do you have kids, John?" asked Liza.

"A twenty-five-year-old son. He's in grad school at NYU's film school. And if he were in trouble, I'd drop everything to be with him."

"Honey, you don't look old enough to have a twenty-five-year-old son," Liza remarked.

He laughed and ran his fingers through his beard. "If I shaved this thing off, Liza, you'd see the wear and tear." He looked over at me. "So how's the response been to the *People* piece?"

"Overwhelming." I tilted my head toward Liza. "I'm hiring her as my publicist so I don't do anything stupid."

King nodded, and his glance at Liza, I noticed, indicated interest in her that went beyond her abilities as a publicist. "No one in this town is smarter than Liza when it comes to publicity. No one."

"You are," Liza shot back, pointing one of her manicured nails at him.

"Ha," King laughed.

"Has Oprah called?" John asked.

"Now, *that* would be something," I replied.

"Well, maybe we can make that happen," he said. "I'll invite her to Frank's Pizzeria for some of the best pizza on the planet."

Did he really just say that? Frank's Pizzeria was a place in the old Brooklyn neighborhood where my friends and I used to hang out after school. There were no scenes about Frank's in *Brooklyn Story* or even in *The Suite Life,* so he couldn't have read it in the books. He had lived in Manhattan, of course, and he might know of it that way. Still, the remark struck me as odd. John was a Hollywood power broker, not exactly the kind of clientele you'd find at Frank's.

"You know Oprah?" Liza asked.

John's smile hinted at undiscovered universes. "Not yet."

"John may have as many VIPs on speed dial as you do, Liza," said King.

"Well, hon," Liza said with a quick wink, "we should combine lists."

"How do you and John know each other?" I asked King.

He laughed. "Back when he sold real estate in Manhattan, he saved my ass by advising me not to buy a certain penthouse. Then, long story short, our financing for an indie movie a dozen years ago fell apart, and John stepped in and saved the day. He was living in L.A. by then."

"Heroic," Liza drolled. "The hero's journey, à la Joseph Campbell."

Joseph Campbell again, I thought. It was something that Priti, with all her wisdom, would term a synchronicity—a meaningful coincidence. And according to Priti, synchronicities could be signposts, guides, warnings, confirmations. They apparently happened more frequently when your life was in transition, in the midst of some major shift. This one seemed to be saying: *Pay attention, Sam. This John Steeling is different from all the others. You may not know it yet, but you will.*

"Business," John said. "It was strictly business, not a

hero's journey. Brian offered me a percentage I couldn't refuse."

"I hear that Brian does that when he wants something or someone badly enough," Liza remarked.

"What?" King said. "Who'd you hear that from, Liza?" King asked.

"Honey, I've got my sources."

Once again, I sensed something moving swiftly between the two of them, a current that went beyond work.

"It sounds like she has sources you don't know about, Brian," remarked John. "Maybe Gallery should hire her."

And King leaned toward Liza and touched her arm. "We should talk about that, Liza."

Liza played it coy and cool. "Aw, I don't know, Brian. Your offer would have to be exceptional for me to relinquish what I have."

"Exceptional," said John, "is Gallery's business model."

I wondered if John was getting a percentage on *Brooklyn Story,* but didn't have the nerve to ask. Besides, what difference did it make? I would supposedly get the money stipulated in my contract with Paul, and everyone would go home happy.

Unless Paul withheld my money.

Unless Paul had spent the money. Flannigan had said Paul was having financial problems, so what if . . .

Unless, what if . . . I cut that thought off. It was part of the old loop. Best not to go there at all. I stole another look at John. *His eyes,* I thought. His eyes were the part of him I recognized.

Had I dreamed about this man? I remember reading a story about a woman who had dreamed of the man she'd married five years before she'd actually met him. In the dream, it was his eyes that had captivated her and his eyes she remembered when he sat down next to her one afternoon on a city bus. This sort of thing happened to other people but had never happened to me.

Or, if it had, I hadn't been paying attention.

Just then, my phone barked—yes, barked. An Isabella text message.

John looked under the table, around at the other customers. "I heard a dog."

"That's, uh, my daughter's text tone. Excuse me." I got up and walked away from the table to read her text.

Mom, am in head-mistresses office. Guy here claiming to be my grandfather Vito. Who is this person?

"Shit." I tapped frantically.

Do not go w/him. Stay right there. Am on the way.

Screw Vito. He'd never gotten on that flight to New York. He'd used that money I'd given him to hang out in L.A., doing whatever someone like him did in this city. And now he was at my daughter's school and was claiming to be her grandfather so that he could—what? Drive her home?

Yeah, right. Drive her in what? A cab?

Kidnap her? Hold her for ransom? *Get outta here. Fast.*

I hurried back to the table. "I hate to eat and run—"

"Your order hasn't even arrived," Liza exclaimed.

"Box it up for me, will you? There's a problem at my daughter's school. I need to get over there."

"Is she okay?" King asked.

"Is the school in lockdown or something?" Liza asked.

And from John: "Anything we can do to help?"

I answered all three of them: "Yes, no, and no, but thanks."

Nope, not unless you know how to deal with Sicilians from Brooklyn who beat their wives and abandon their families and then show up more than forty years after the fact to claim a cut of the pie. John's eyes held mine for a brief moment.

"Call me," Liza said.

I hurried off toward my car.

You hear about this kind of thing, read about it on the Internet, on the front page of your daily newspaper, if you still get one.

Enraged father shoots son in schoolyard and turns gun on self.

Enraged boyfriend . . .

Mother drives car into lake with kids inside . . .

Crazy grandfather . . .

Okay, you don't see too many headlines about nutty grandfathers shooting their grandchildren. Or kidnapping them. Or harming them in some way. But maybe Vito's intention wasn't to kill. Maybe he intended only to intimidate, to threaten me through Isabella until I agreed to pay him off. How much money would keep him away from us forever? How much would it take?

I couldn't place a value on my daughter's life, but I was pretty sure he had a figure in mind. Ah, Vito, you schmuck, you bastard. *How much? How much do you want?*

Liza had asked if Vito was part of my living bio. He wasn't. But here he was at Isabella's school, doing who the hell knew what, a part of my *living bio* in spite of my best efforts to get him out of L.A.

I screeched to a halt at the curb in front of the school and saw three police vehicles parked in front, too. I grabbed my purse and leaped out of the car.

I ran toward the front door, anxious to see Isabella, throw my arms around her, hold her. My shoes slapped the old ceramic floors, and, yes, those slaps were loud. They echoed. They sounded hollow, despairing. The big, ugly black-and-white clock on the wall told me nearly thirty minutes had passed since Isabella had texted me.

I sped through the hallway, and there, outside the principal's office, stood my daughter, my beautiful daughter,

pacing like some caged animal while the principal, Sister
Anne, stood nearby, talking frantically on her phone. Then
Sister Anne turned and saw me, probably looking as crazed
as Tippi Hedren in some scene from *The Birds,* and she
ended her call and hurried toward us.

"Ms. DeMarco . . . ," she called.

Isabella ran over to me, threw her arms around me. I
hugged her tightly, hugged her so close I was pretty sure
one of us would be deprived of oxygen before anything else
happened.

Sister Anne was a plump, stern woman wearing a simple
but dull dress and no head covering. She glared at us, at
Isabella and me, as though public demonstrations of love
were forbidden in the corridors of this school. Her predeces-
sors had carried out corporal punishment with all the relish
of the executioners at Salem. I could see this woman with
one of those horrid rulers that had whacked down against
knuckles, bare asses; and bile surged in my throat.

"What the hell's going on here, Sister Anne?"

"Please, keep your voice down."

"Keep my voice *down*? My daughter texted me in a
panic. What has happened?"

"That maniac"—she stabbed her finger toward her
office—"*in* there, claims to be your father, Isabella's grandfather. He burst in here, and when the security guards tried
to escort him off the campus, he became unruly. I . . . was
forced to call the police."

"My father is dead," I snapped, then looked at Isabella.
"Stay here."

I stepped away from her and opened the door to Sister
Anne's office, where the circle of cops around Vito parted
like the Red Sea. Vito was handcuffed to a chair and looked
like shit warmed over.

"Samantha," he burst out, trying to leap up, but the
cuffs held him back. "Tell them who I am!"

Oh, sure, Vito. I'm going to do that now, here, so you can harass us some more and create profound misery in our lives. Nope. Sorry. That isn't going to happen, pal.

"Ma'am, do you know this man?" asked one of the cops in the circle.

Did I? Even though he was my father and I had his DNA, even though I thought of Judas, I shook my head. "No."

"Sam!" he wailed.

"Please," I said to the cops. "Get him out of here."

The taller cop nodded. "With pleasure, ma'am." Then he looked at Sister Anne, who stood in the doorway. "Are you pressing charges for trespassing?"

"Definitely," Sister Anne replied. "For trespassing and every other law he broke."

"This is bullshit!" Vito yelled. "She's my daughter! Tell them, Sam. Tell them the truth!"

"You're demented," I said, and hurried out of the office, Vito's shouts pursuing me.

Isabella and I moved down the hall and slipped into one of the empty classrooms. "It seemed like he knew you, Mom," Isabella said.

"He's a crazy old man, love. He probably read about me in the *People* article that came out today."

I hated lying to her, but I refused to open this door now. Or ever. I was determined that her life would be free of Vito and the other toxic elements of my childhood. I didn't want her subjected to what I had gone through.

I turned toward the window, walked closer to it, and watched the police haul Vito away. He struggled and fought them, his skinny body jerking this way and that, his hair flying around.

"I bet he's a celebrity stalker or something," Isabella remarked. She stood next to me, watching. "Will they Baker Act him?"

"Maybe." Three days in a padded cell might convince

Vito that there was nothing in L.A. for him, that he should return to New York and forget about his get-rich-quick scheme. "I hope so. He needs help."

The classroom door opened, and Sister Anne waddled in, her expression of disapproval set in stone. "We simply can't have this kind of disruption at our school, Ms. DeMarco."

Oh, really now. She wasn't going to get away with *that* comment. "Frankly, I'm rather appalled by your lack of security. How did that crazy old man get on the school grounds? How'd he get into the school?"

"I'm, uh, not sure." Flustered now, she smoothed her hands over her dress. "But you can be sure we'll conduct a full investigation."

"I certainly hope so. With school shootings happening all over this country, you should have instituted safety precautions long ago." I slipped my arm around Isabella's shoulders and steered her out of the room and up the hall toward Sister Anne's office so she could retrieve her backpack.

"I feel sorry for that guy," Isabella said softly.

My daughter's capacity for compassion far surpassed mine. I felt sorry for him, too, but not sorry enough to acknowledge him as my father.

During the drive home, Isabella asked me to stop at the grocery store so she could pick up a copy of *People*. While I waited in the parking lot for her, I thought of those two Brooklyn numbers Kelly had given me for the calls Vito had made from the Malibu Motel. I slipped the piece of paper from my wallet, stared at them, uncertain, hesitant, and, yes, at some level, terrified. Then I popped open the glove compartment.

I removed a disposable cell phone that I'd bought when I'd first moved out here. Liza had advised it. *For those calls you don't want registered anywhere.* I'd never used it before. I tapped in the first Brooklyn number. It rang twice, then a woman answered, her voice tired and husky from the twenty thousand cigarettes she'd smoked over the years. "Providence House, Rachel speaking. How may I direct your call?"

"Hi, I'm trying to get in touch with Vito Bonti."

"And you are . . . ?"

"A friend."

"Yeah? Well, Vito's friend, I haven't seen him since he lit outta here with cash he stole. *My* cash, from *my* purse. You can tell him I filed a report with the cops and he can go straight to hell."

She disconnected.

I punched in the second number and let it ring a dozen times. But there wasn't any answer—not from a machine or a human.

I turned the phone off and buried it under some papers in the glove compartment. I went online with my phone and located Providence House—2518 Church Avenue. I knew that neighborhood. I remembered the delis and focaccerias. Church Avenue bordered Jewish territory in a primarily Italian area in Brooklyn, so it was, as I liked to call it, a healthy mix of culture.

Things had to be pretty bad for Vito if he'd stolen money from someone who worked in a homeless shelter. Maybe that was how he'd gotten out here—probably not on a plane, but on a train or bus. I started to feel sorry for him again, briefly considered bailing him out and telling Isabella everything. But I slammed that door shut.

My phone belted out "Made to Love" by John Legend. The text message was from him: I loved that song and ironically the text was from him, only fitting for him to have this ringtone.

Everything ok w/your daughter?

I hadn't given him my number, so he must have asked Liza for it.

Yes. Thanx. On our way home.

R u free for dinner Fri. nite?

Friday, Friday, holy shit. I suddenly felt like a teenager who had been asked out on her first date. Sweat sprang from the pores of my hands; my heart did an odd little jig. *Yes, yes, I'm free on Friday.* Except that I wasn't. Isabella was having a sleepover, six buddies from school. I texted him as much and his response was quick:

Saturday? Sunday? Monday? Tuesday? Name the day.

Saturday. Better.

On Saturday, she was going to be at a sleepover at Lauren's house.

Fantastic. See u on set Thursday. Talk then.

"Awesome," I whispered.

The passenger door opened, and Isabella slipped inside. "You're grinning. What's going on?"

"I have a date Saturday night!"

"Really? With who?"

"This guy connected with the film."

"That's so cool, Mom. I'm happy for you. But what about Paul?"

"We're not dating anymore, love. I broke things off."

She gave my hand a quick squeeze, then set the magazine flat on her lap. "Now, let's see what *People* has to say about you and *Brooklyn Story*." She flipped the magazine open to the cover story.

chapter
SIX

Finally, on May 11, shooting started, and Marvin and I drove out to Gallery Studios.

The studio was an anomaly for Hollywood. It didn't offer visitor tours, didn't have some huge sign outside that screamed, *I'm here, I'm here,* and if you were driving past it, you probably wouldn't have any idea what it was.

Tucked away in Laurel Canyon, amid the towering, ancient rust-colored rocks, the property covered more than three hundred acres. Yes, that was small potatoes compared to the two thousand acres that made up Skywalker Ranch, Lucas's place north of San Francisco. But to a girl from Brooklyn, where your neighbors practically lived inside your bathroom, it was an incomparable paradise of space.

"You're kidding, right?" Marvin leaned forward over the steering wheel, his eyes sweeping across the vast expanse beyond the curving driveway. "I mean, really. What the hell kind of money buys *this*?"

"A lot more than we've got."

He sat back. "In some ways, Sam, this kind of wealth is almost obscene when most of the world is going hungry."

I knew what he was saying. It was the sort of wealth Alec and I once had, before Wall Street went belly up, and we blew through it faster than he earned it. But back then, world hunger and the planet's dwindling resources barely registered on my radar. I tithed to my church, gave to various charities, helped people I knew who were down on their luck. But when confronted with huge, practically insurmountable inequities and suffering, I felt helpless. What could one person do to alleviate it? After I received the insurance money, I donated half a million of it to a Feed the Hungry organization and would do so again at the end of this year. Even so, it didn't seem to put much of a dent in the magnitude of hunger and poverty globally.

Priti had described the vast and terrible poverty in India. I had seen it in Africa, in the Caribbean, in South America. When you went hungry, not much else mattered. When you had to eat mud cakes to stay alive, as Haitians had after the earthquake in 2010, everything else fell away.

I knew that Gallery had established a foundation that donated enormous amounts of money to victims of natural disasters, money that helped them to relocate, to put their lives back together. Yes, it was a lucrative tax write-off for them, but I also think Gallery did it because the people in charge had social consciences.

Gallery's enormous profits enabled them to tackle subjects in documentaries that addressed problems that we, as a human collective, as a planet, were facing in the coming century. Two of these films—one on climate change and one on alternative fuels—had won Golden Globes. And earned practically nothing at the box office.

As Kurt Vonnegut used to say, *So it goes.*

Marvin parked in the tree-shaded lot at the side of the main building. I recognized Liza's Mercedes and Paul's BMW, but not any of the other cars. As we headed toward the front steps, an electric cart came around the corner of the building, King at the wheel.

"Hey, Sam, Marvin, hop on board," he called, and drew

to a stop beside us. "We're shooting in studio four. George emailed you the breakdown of scenes we're shooting today, right?"

"Yeah, he did," I said. "The kitchen scene with Grandma Ruth, making potato pancakes and blintzes. And the mother, Joan, stumbles in, hungover."

"Wait till you see Sarandon. Her ability to transform herself is astounding. And Camilla as Joan is incredible. And then there's Jenean, who is simply remarkable."

He was so uncharacteristically chatty that Marvin's brows shot up. *WTF? Who wound him up?* "A great cast, a great studio, and a fantastic director. What else can any novelist ask for?" Marvin said.

"A good producer," King said, with a slight smile that indicated he knew Paul and I were no longer seeing each other.

"Ah, right," Marvin agreed.

King drove the cart along a hard-packed path that curved and twisted through trees and beds of flowers, past a swimming hole. Thick branches hung over it, and ropes had been slung over several of the branches, an invitation to leap and swing and drop into the glistening water.

"We should write in a scene that can be shot there," I said.

King laughed. "Jenean said exactly the same thing."

The woods thinned, and the path took us up a shallow hill, where a large Victorian house stood like something out of a fairy tale. Tremendous trees formed a semicircle around it, as if embracing it. Half a dozen electric carts were parked in a small, shaded gravel lot on the right. The only vehicle was a large van with GALLERY STUDIOS written across the sides in vibrant blue letters.

"Wait till you see the set, Sam," King said. "Our art director did a fantastic job of duplicating the apartment in Brooklyn."

Way back when Paul first optioned the book, I had written up descriptions of the interior of the apartment, as shabby as it was; of a local café where my friend Janice and I used to hang out; and of other places in Brooklyn. I suspected those notes had gone to the art director.

We followed King into the house. A lot of people mulled around in the living room, helping themselves to a spread of food on a large wooden table. The crew. They all looked to be in their twenties, wore jeans, had iPhones sticking out of their shirt pockets. They had an easy, casual air about them that I had never mastered—not in my twenties, not now.

"Hey, guys," King called out. "I'd like you to meet the author of *Brooklyn Story,* Samantha DeMarco, who also wrote the screenplay, and her assistant, Marvin Castelli.

A chorus of hellos and welcome rang out. A petite blonde came over and introduced herself as Renée Tennerin, the art director. "I loved your book, your notes were fantastic, and I hope you'll give me pointers on how my staff and I can improve the set." Then she looked at Marvin. "And you're Samantha's buddy from *The Suite Life,* right?"

Marvin looked embarrassed. "Uh, yeah."

She winked and leaned close to us and whispered, "There's some buzz about optioning the second book and the third one, when it's out. Is the new one nearly finished?"

Hardly. I had written exactly two paragraphs. "It's a long way from finished. Since I moved out here, I've been busy with my production company."

"Oh, right." She rocked back on her heels. "I heard you just optioned a rather intriguing fantasy screenplay."

"I have to thank Marvin and my other employee for that. They both have a great sense of story," I said.

She and Marvin started chatting, and because I was suddenly famished, I slipped away toward the banquet of food. I picked up a plate and moved through the line, helping myself to a bit of everything—crepes, omelets, shrimp in some delectable rice concoction, baked plantains, vegetarian wraps, and on and on. It was like grazing my way through a shopping trip at Whole Foods, but a whole lot better.

Just as I was about to dish some paella onto my plate, the hairs on the back of my neck stood straight up. I raised my eyes, and there, on the other side of the table, was John, his plate heaped with as much food as my plate held. He glanced at me, at my plate, back at me, and laughed.

"You're too petite to be able to eat all that."

"Ha. I have a monstrous appetite." *In more ways than one.*

"Want to eat outside? The weather is perfect, and they aren't shooting right this second."

"Are there tables outside?" Did it matter? I would eat on the sand with this man, sit on concrete in the blazing sun with him.

"We'll make one," he said with a quick laugh, and added a helping of salad to his plate.

Minutes later, we were sitting on the ground, our backs up against the trunk of this huge tree. "This studio always has the most incredible food," John remarked. "Honestly, just look at the variety."

He held his plate out, like an offering, like some ancient ritual to a mythological deity. For a moment or two, I couldn't wrench my eyes away from his hand. It was large, larger than any hand had a right to be, and beautifully formed, the fingers symmetrical, the nails perfectly cut, the skin smooth and beautiful. It was easy to imagine that hand on my body, igniting a hunger I hadn't felt for a long time.

"Paella is one of my favorites," I said, looking down at my paper plate, picking up my fork and scooping up a bite of it. "Even if it isn't Italian."

"I love Cuban food. I love Cuban coffee. I love Cuban everything. I've begun to think I had a life in Cuba in the pre-Fidel days, you know, when Che was doing his revolution thing."

He talked fast, as if he felt the urge to say whatever he had to say before something came along and changed the dynamics.

"A past life as one of Che's main guys?" I asked.

"Yeah, something like that. Or maybe Che himself? Now, *that* would make an interesting script."

Priti had talked a lot about reincarnation, and at one point a few years back I considered going to a past-life therapist for a regression. Stuff had interfered, though, and that regression remained on my bucket list. "Do you speak Spanish?" I asked.

"I do. Took a year of it in college, then quit because it . . . I don't know, this sounds weird, but it all came back to me. I didn't need the class to speak the language."

His eyes. I knew those eyes. Recognized them. Knew that somewhere in the past, those eyes had pierced mine. But I couldn't find the specific memory. Maybe I was delusional.

But what about that reference to Frank's Pizzeria? Had that been delusional?

I picked away at the food on my plate. The cool breeze blew around us, through us, and I pulled my lightweight jacket more tightly around my body and zipped it up. *"Parli italiano?"* I asked. Do you speak Italian?

He rocked his hand from side to side. *"Un po'."* A little. "Very *un po'*," he added with a laugh.

As we sat there in our slice of warm sunlight, I kept stealing glances at this man, struggling to find a memory of him. I knew it was there, buried somewhere in the past, but I couldn't find it. The problem was that I had cut myself off from so much of my Brooklyn past that chunks of my memories were probably gone forever. It struck me as ironic that I was mulling this over when, inside that studio, my past was being filmed.

"What?" he finally asked, and met my eyes.

"I can't shake this feeling that we've met before."

"In this life?"

I laughed. "Yeah, in this life. It'll come to me."

"Maybe I've got a doppelganger."

"The other day you mentioned Frank's Pizzeria. It's in my old Brooklyn neighborhood. I used to go there in high school. How do you know about Frank's?"

"Must've read it in one of your books."

"It wasn't in either of my books."

"Then I must've been there at some point when I lived in Manhattan." He finished off the last bite of food on his plate, set it on the ground, changed the subject. "Isn't that swimming hole something? I told Brian and George there should be a scene added at that swimming hole."

"I thought the same thing when I saw it."

Marvin hurried over to us. "Hey, shooting starts in five minutes. You two going to watch?"

"Wouldn't miss it," John said, and picked up our paper plates and tossed them in a nearby trash can.

The studio looked so much like the kitchen of my childhood that I felt almost suffocated by the past. The air even smelled the way that kitchen had smelled so long ago—of potato pancakes and blintzes. Susan Sarandon was the spitting image of Grandma Ruth—silver hair, wrinkles and all. And Jenean had somehow transformed herself into my much younger self. Watching them was like time traveling.

"That no-good Italian ran out on your mother," Sarandon said, her voice so Brooklyn and Jewish I was astounded. "What could she do? I tell you, my Samelah, you marry a Jew, you hear me?"

Jenean rolled her eyes. Her hands moved as she spoke. "Oh, so a Jewish guy will never leave me. Right, Grandma?"

"Right. They stay with the family. Look, now you have no father. He punished you, too, see?"

"Yeah, well, I'd rather have been abandoned by him than learn firsthand who the hell he really was."

Vito. I suddenly felt really uneasy watching this scene, reliving those moments in the Brooklyn kitchen, knowing what I knew now about Vito. Why hadn't he just stayed out of my life?

"Watch your mouth," Sarandon snapped. "Don't get like your mother, always swearing and cursing through the house. Consider yourself lucky to have prospects." Sarandon flipped one of the pancakes and glanced at Jenean. "So, bubelah, any boy got your heart yet?"

"I'm waiting for the right one, Grandma."

"Good. You don't want to do what your mother did. Don't be in such a hurry that you give milk without making them buy the cow first. Oy! Your mother, she never listened to me, and look where that got her!"

Sarandon wiped her brow with the back of her hand, then blew strands of hair off her forehead. "Did you write today?"

"Yes, I did."

"*Machayeh*. I'm proud of you. Write yourself out of this story and into a better one."

On the other side of the room, I saw Paul lean in close to Carl Davidson, the director, and whisper to him. Liza, who stood nearby, glanced at them, then at me, and winked as if to say, *Don't worry about them. It's your story.* Davidson nodded and gestured at someone I couldn't see. A moment later, Camilla Baptiste stumbled into the kitchen, lighting a cigarette stuck in the corner of her mouth, her hair disheveled, her clothes wrinkled, her feet bare. She looked so much like my mother that goose bumps erupted on my arms.

"No one ran my bath," Camilla whined through a haze of smoke.

A black hole opened in the pit of my stomach. Maybe it hadn't been such a great idea to be on set. Camilla was such an exact duplicate of my mother that all these negative feelings I'd had in my childhood now rushed back and nearly overpowered me. Yet the scene was too rushed. In real life, there had been a lag, my mother hadn't appeared that quickly. In real life, on that morning, her eyes had opened so slowly it was as if they had been glued shut and she had to pry them apart. In real life, she had lit that cigarette before she had even gotten out of bed. And in real life, she'd been coughing up blood by the time she had stumbled into the kitchen.

I waved my arms, the signal King and Prince had told me to make if I disagreed with how a scene was being filmed, and Davidson called, "Cut!" Then he marched across the studio, his long, thin arms swinging at his sides like pendulums. "What is it, Sam?"

"It's too fast," I said. "We need to see Joan in the bedroom as she wakes up. She's hungover. Or still drunk. She lights the cigarette before she even gets out of bed." That scene hadn't been in the book, but it had been in the script, and Davidson—or someone else—had deleted it. "We need to see her haggard face, her coughing fit as she sits at the side of the bed. She looks like hell, hair disheveled, the lines in her face are really visible."

"That's not enough action," Davidson said, his wiry body twitching, pacing, restless.

"I love it," Sarandon said.

Davidson rolled his eyes. If he'd been a smoker, he would have lit a cigarette just then and puffed furiously. "Susan, no disrespect intended, you're Grandma Ruth, not Joan."

"No disrespect intended, Carl," she replied. "But you're a director, not an actor. This is the kind of scene where an actor climbs into the character's skin. It's a scene that helps define that character."

"It's also how it happened," I said.

Davidson's shoulders twitched. *He* was Mr. Creative, and the rest of us were simply the pawns he moved around as he saw fit. "Look, I don't think—"

"We need that bedroom scene." John spoke up. "It tells us everything we need to know about Joan Bonti."

And that was that. The scene was rewritten and shot again. I felt Paul's eyes on me, burning through me. *What're you doing, Sam? Don't interfere. Can't you see what I've done for you?* those eyes seemed to be screaming. *See the stars I've recruited for your movie, Sam?*

I ignored him and watched as the scene unfolded the way I had originally written it, the way I had lived it. Who were we if we weren't true to our stories?

In this retake, we saw Camilla transformed into the woman my mother had been on that day. And when she stumbled out into the kitchen, she moved toward the stove with all the gracelessness of the drunk she had been. "Who's gonna run my bath?"

Run it yourself, I felt like screaming.

"Bubelah, run your mother's bath," Sarandon said, sliding the potato pancakes onto a plate. "She's *feelnish git.*"

Jenean took Camilla's hand. "C'mon, Ma. I'll run your bath." Jenean waved away the cigarette smoke, then did something I had never done: she jerked the cigarette out of Camilla's mouth, hurried over to the sink, and ran water over it.

I started to say something, but decided that I loved what she'd just done. It showed a streak of rebellion, a rebellion that would also be apparent in one of the scenes they'd added to the script as a flashback. In that scene, my mother had brought home some new guy, and because I hated it when she did that, I peed on the carpet in her bedroom. Like a dog. I kept doing it until one of her men caught me in the act.

I knew I wanted to be on set when they shot that scene.

I knew Jenean would capture the horror of that moment for me, when the man caught me peeing on my mother's carpet. I knew she would capture the essence of my revenge. But right now, the longer I watched, the shittier I felt. It was like a mathematical axiom. It was as if all those negative feelings from the past were making me ill.

I turned toward the door, then moved through it, out into the main area where lunch had been set up. I went over to a huge metal bin filled with ice, helped myself to a bottle of water, and headed for the exit, suddenly so overwhelmed with tumultuous, unresolved emotions about my childhood that I felt like puking.

I stumbled down the steps and wove toward the tree where John and I had eaten. A sob exploded from my mouth, tears coursed down my cheeks. I practically ran away from the house, out past where the cars were parked, into grass and flowers. My knees buckled, and I went down, sobbing.

If Rick from *People* saw me now, he would know just how true *Brooklyn Story* was.

What would my life have been like if Vito had stuck around? Or if my mother and Grandma Ruth had left and he had raised me? Of if Tony hadn't gone to prison? These alternate paths my life might have taken abruptly opened up inside me, shooting off into their own space and time like threads in a spider's web. Pluck one thread and I would be there, in *that* Samantha's life, in *that* Samantha's body. But where was the thread to the life I so desired?

"Sam? You okay?"

John stopped next to me, and for the longest moment I just stared at his shoes, New Balance running shoes. I studied the way the cuff of his jeans brushed the tops of those shoes. I managed to nod and started to push to my feet, but he took gentle hold of my arm and helped me up. I finally looked at him.

"It's all just a little close to home," I said.

His hand moved away from my arm. "Brooklyn leaves scars. I understand. Let's take a break and walk over to that swimming hole."

"Hey, John, Sam."

We glanced around as Paul trotted toward us, his bald head covered with a cap that was pulled down low over his eyes. His sunglasses held perfect reflections of John and me, and I was struck by how good we looked together.

"What is it, Paul?"

John's voice held a certain tension, a what-the-hell-do-you-want kind of tension, and I could tell from Paul's body language that he heard it. "Just, uh, that Sam's getting paid a fee for every day she's on the set, and that's where she should be right now."

"Excuse me, Paul," I snapped. "But I haven't even seen a check yet for the exercise of the option. First day of principal photography. That's today."

John frowned. "That check went out to you last week, Paul."

He looked embarrassed and stammered, "Really? It's probably still with my accountant. I'll make sure you get the check by tomorrow. Direct deposit, Sam. My apology."

"Good, now that it's settled, we'll be back in a bit." John touched the small of my back as he turned away from Paul.

I knew that Paul stood there as John and I started walking; I could feel his eyes boring into my spine, felt the rage pouring off him. "He's pissed," I said quietly.

"Anger issues. It's not unique to Hollywood, but it's more prevalent out here."

Yeah, you might say that. I even felt the moment when Paul stopped staring at us, at me; it was as if the weight of excessive gravity had fallen away from the air. "Definitely."

"Look, I don't want to interfere if you and Paul are still—"

"We're not."

He didn't ask what had happened. I liked that. John didn't pry. But even if he'd asked, what would I say? The relationship had been killed by an accretion of small, telling things—he was possessive, he presumed to speak for me, when he drank things got ugly, and, most of all, he thought he controlled me. That last part shocked me. I'd never thought of it in quite those terms before, but it was true.

Paul had discovered me; therefore, he owned me: that was his thinking. It was the way men undoubtedly thought in Neanderthal times. *I saved her, she's mine.* In Jean Auel's first book, *Clan of the Cave Bear,* which later became a movie with Daryl Hannah, this "ownership" was expressed clearly when the protagonist's mate told her to "assume the position," or something to that effect. She'd fallen forward on her hands and knees, her naked butt raised in the air, and he'd taken her like that, from behind. Taken her without regard to her pleasure, her body, her being. *He owned her.*

As we started walking over grass, I stopped and removed my shoes, a pair of fashionable black flats. Thank God, Christian Louboutin made those little show-stopping gems. I stuck them in my bag and pressed my bare feet against grass as soft as an infant's skin. My toes vanished in the softness, my dark blue nails peeked up through it like little imps. "I love the color blue."

"So do I. We now have something in common." I smiled.

"I think we have more in common that you think." John stared at me, those blue eyes piercing through me.

"My God, you sure make it feel unbelievably good," John said. "I hardly ever went barefoot as a kid."

"Kinda hard when the only grass is the size of a postage stamp."

He tore off his shoes and socks, tied the laces together,

and draped them around his neck. "Race ya." We took off across the field, through the magical California light, laughing like fools.

He was fast, as nimble as Superman. I almost expected him to suddenly flap his arms and lift into the air. I used to be a fast runner, but I hadn't been doing much physical exercise since we moved out here and I felt it—a shortness of breath, a tightness in my chest, a burning in my muscles.

The swimming hole came into view, a kid's fantasy with those rope swings swaying in the breeze, the huge trees embracing water that reflected the vast sweep of sky. At the tips of the ropes were burlap bags stuffed with hay or cotton so you had someplace to sit as you swung.

John reached the hole first and leaped at one of those ropes; he swung way out over the water, whooping with delight. "C'mon, Sam," he shouted. "Leap and swing."

I found one final burst of speed, dropped my bag in the grass, and leaped at the other rope. It swung wildly out over the water; my hands started slipping, and in my head I heard strains from the theme music of *Jaws*. I couldn't remember the last time I'd gone swimming. Suppose I no longer knew how to swim? How deep was this swimming hole, anyway? If I slipped off the rope and plummeted into the deepest part of the water, I might drown. Shit, *drown*.

No way. Not now, as my life was just starting to shape up rather nicely.

I swung my legs up, up, and wrapped them tightly around the burlap bag. The rope seemed to be gathering speed and momentum, the shore blurred, John swung past me in the other direction. A thrill zipped through me.

"Pump your legs to keep the rope moving, Sam," he yelled. "So we can leap back on shore."

He made it look easy. But when I pumped my legs, nothing happened, the swing started slowing down. I pumped harder, nothing. Then, suddenly, John swung toward me, reached out, and grabbed hold of my rope, pulling it so close to him that our legs pressed together.

"Relax into it," he said. "You're trying too hard. It's like you have to become the rope, the breeze."

"Sounds Zen," I quipped. "The Zen of rope swinging."

He leaned toward me and his mouth brushed mine, a light, cool touch that I felt in every pore of my body. "I'm going to give you a hard push, and as the rope swings back toward shore, just leap off."

"Got it." I still imagined myself floundering out there in the middle of the water, my body unable to remember the basics of swimming.

"Hold on tight, Sam."

I clutched the rope, and suddenly I felt like I was sailing through space and time. I dropped my head back, peering up into the belly of the blurring skies, the blurring branches and leaves, green and blue melting together into a rapturous collage of color.

I realized I was laughing, that John was laughing, and our laughter rang out through the sunlight and shadow, a promise that the best was yet to come. As my rope swung back toward shore, he shouted, "Jump now, Sam!"

But my speed was slowing again, so I let my legs drop and pumped them hard and furiously, working up enough speed so the rope flew out over the shore. And then I let go.

I landed on my hands and knees in a bed of cool moss and seconds later, John landed beside me on his hands and knees. We looked at each other, both of us laughing again, and then he rolled onto his back and folded his hands under his head and I did the same.

"I could stay here all day," he said.

I could still feel the touch of that kiss. "Same here. When I was growing up, I used to daydream about spots like this."

He turned his head, looking at me. Our eyes locked. In

that moment, I felt some long-forgotten memory struggling to escape the box into which it had fallen years ago. Brooklyn . . . something about Brooklyn and this man.

What I felt just then must have shown in my expression because he frowned. "What? What is it?"

"I'm just trying to figure out why you seem so familiar to me. And, I'm sorry, but your explanation about Frank's Pizzeria just doesn't cut it."

He started to say something, but we both heard a car racing up the road, the horn blaring, and sat up.

Paul's car.

He leaped out of his car and strode toward us, everything about him angry. Before he reached us, another car screeched to a stop behind his vehicle. Prince got out and trotted after Paul.

"Hey, Paul," Prince shouted. "Hold on, man."

"This doesn't look good," John muttered.

"No shit."

But it was becoming typical for Paul. How had I ever been so blinded by him? And felt I owed him for optioning my novel?

"Stay here, Sam," said John.

He strode away from me, and for a moment I stood there, as motionless as a fly on a wall. Male bravado? *Been there, done that, screw it.* I didn't need male bravado. I wasn't some damsel in distress waiting to be rescued. If I could write my way out of Brooklyn, then I could sure as hell make it clear to Paul that we were done, finished, the end. It was obvious that Flannigan hadn't given him the message that day and Paul had been too wasted to hear what he didn't want to hear. Just what I needed—another obsessed Tony Kroon on my hands. This had to end.

I hurried to John's side. He seemed surprised that I hadn't hung back. "Thanks, John, but no one has to fight my battles for me."

"I feel like decking the asshole."

"It would just make things worse."

We were close enough now to Paul and Prince to hear their exchange.

". . . fire your ass if you can't control yourself, Paul."

"How about controlling *her*?"

"We're talking about *you*," Prince snapped.

"Fuck off, George. And you can't kick me out as producer. "I've got a contract—"

"Contracts can be broken." Prince's voice: sharp, firm. "What's it going to be?"

"What's the problem?" John asked when we reached them.

Paul spun around, seething. I could almost imagine him foaming at the mouth like a rabid dog. He stabbed his finger toward me. "*She's* the problem. She fucked her way into this entire gig, she—"

"Time for you to shut up," John said, his voice quiet but like ice, and started to move toward Paul, his hands fisted.

I touched his arm, stepped closer to Paul. "I'm only going to say this once. You were so drunk that day at your house when you tackled me that you must not have heard what I said, Paul. But Flannigan heard it, and apparently he never told you that we are *done*. You and I are *history*. You don't own me; you don't control me. I can't make it any clearer than that."

Prince looked embarrassed.

John looked pissed.

And Paul? He looked stunned by the news, as though he couldn't quite wrap his ego around the fact that he—the great producer Paul Jannis—was being dumped by a woman. And that he was being dumped in front of witnesses. That was probably what stunned and humiliated him the most.

Then that dark, moiling rage poured into his eyes, taking shape like some massive shadow. I suddenly understood that Paul was actually two people, and his darker self had subsumed the other self, swallowed it whole.

He burst out laughing, a loud, unnatural sound that echoed beneath the canopy of the trees, mockery. "You poor sucker, John. I knew that day at the restaurant that she had the hots for you. This is how she operates. This is her MO. She'll use you until you're no longer useful to her and then toss you aside like a piece of Kleenex. You'll see. You'll find out how it is."

I felt the tension rippling through John's body and knew he wanted nothing more than to punch Paul. Instead, he ignored Paul and looked over at Prince. "Hey, George, can we get a lift with you?"

"Sure thing."

Prince turned to head back to his car, and for a long, terrible moment, Paul, John, and I just stood there in silence, the air so thick and dark I found it difficult to breathe. Paul was no longer laughing. Daggers shot out of his eyes, and they were tipped with poison.

John grasped my hand and, walking past Paul without acknowledging him in any way, we followed Prince to his car. Paul was left standing alone in the sunlight.

As we got into Prince's car, I glanced out at Paul, still standing there, staring after us, as motionless as a pillar of salt. In that moment, I felt a sudden and terrible certainty that he might try to kill me. His humiliation; rage; unresolved issues with his son, his ex-wife; and the mess he'd made of his life had slammed together in a way that made me the person responsible for his misery.

Couldn't Prince see that?

But Prince didn't say anything, didn't make any reference to what had happened. Maybe he had seen far worse in the past. Maybe this was business as usual in Hollywood and didn't warrant comment. Maybe he felt it would be intrusive.

I sensed that John felt disturbed by it, but he didn't say anything, either. Then again, it wasn't his fight. If that was the reason for his silence, then great. It meant he thought I could fight my own battles. Or it meant that Hollywood was where nuance reigned supreme, and no one called anyone on anything because, if you did, you jeopardized your own ass.

But in jeopardizing your own ass, money was usually at stake. That wasn't the case for John. He had money *and* clout.

As we got out of the electric cart, John said, "George, maybe it's time to fire Paul."

"He won't do anything more," Prince said. "Trust me on that. He knows he's close to blowing it."

Right then I understood that if Gallery broke their contract with Paul, it would cost them dearly. It always came down to money. Profit.

"Are you thinking the film would be compromised?"

"We'll talk about it later," Prince said.

Later. When I wasn't around.

chapter

SEVEN

Isabella's friends started arriving for the sleepover around five that Friday afternoon. Within minutes, they were all outside on the patio, sitting around the pool, music blasting from a CD player. Isabella and I had laid out a banquet of food that they could pick at all night if they wanted, and the fridge out there was jammed with bottled water, juices, and more snacks. Isabella's bedroom and the den had sliding-glass doors that opened to the patio, so they wouldn't even have to come through the house.

Marvin, Clara, and I were sitting around the kitchen table, going through the script and making notes about the breakdown of scenes for next week's shooting. After what had happened with Paul at Gallery Studios, I had been back to the set just once, when neither he nor John was there. My dinner with John was tomorrow night, and my anticipation grew by the hour. Tomorrow, Liza and I were going shopping; I didn't feel confident about my own judgment when it came to an outfit for dinner with John.

I hadn't heard much from him since that magical hour at the swimming hole. I hadn't heard from Paul, either, not that I expected to, and Vito seemed to have dropped out of my life for good. Just as I thought that, my cell belted out "Made to Love" by John Legend. It seemed to be the

John-and-Samantha theme song for the moment. Marvin and Clara glanced up from the script. They knew what that ringtone meant.

"Well?" Clara said. "Aren't you going to find out where he's taking you for dinner tomorrow night?"

"Suppose he's canceling our dinner date?"

Marvin rolled his eyes. "Gimme a break, Sam. I saw the way he looked at you. He's not canceling any dinner date."

I got up, unplugged my phone from the charger, clicked on his text message.

How's the sleepover going?

Noisy!

My son & his girlfriend came into town. You mind if they join us for dinner tomorrow?

Sounds good.

Dress casual. Place w/tables on the beach. Will pick u up @6:30.

Perfect.

"Okay, what restaurant in Malibu has tables on the beach for dinner?" I walked back to the kitchen table.

"Beats me." Marvin circled something in the script.

"La Playa," Clara said. "I've never eaten there, but I've heard the food is fantastic. I think the place is owned by a Chilean couple."

Beach, parking lot, swimming hole, a picnic table: it didn't matter to me where we ate.

The sliding-glass door suddenly slammed open, and Isabella and Lauren stood there dripping wet, their eyes glinting with joy. Lauren was blond to Isabella's dark hair, and was an inch or so taller, with dimples in the corners of her mouth when she smiled.

"Mom, we're going to walk down to the beach, okay?" Isabella asked.

"We'll be careful, Ms. DeMarco," Lauren said.

"Take your phones with you. Be sure to wear shoes. That path to the beach has a lot of rocks. Be back by dusk."

"Right-o!" Isabella said.

Right-o? Where had that come from?

As Isabella and her buddies all headed to the beach, I stepped out onto the patio to put together a platter of munchies for Clara, Marvin, and me that included a bowl of salad and some leftover pizza. As I was carrying it back into the house, my phone pealed. No number IDing the caller showed on the screen. I hesitated, but curiosity, of course, prompted me to take the call as I put down the food.

"DeMarco Productions."

"May I speak to Samantha, please?"

"Who's calling?"

"Luke Jannis."

Paul's son. What was I supposed to do with *this*? I'd met Luke several times—over dinner, a brunch, and once at Paul's place, where Luke had shown me Mystery Manor, downloaded it onto my iPad, and guided me through the first six or seven levels. At the time, I didn't know enough about the game to understand how anyone could be addicted to it. I still didn't know since I'd never played again.

"Luke. What a surprise." I walked toward the far end of the pool so that I wouldn't be overheard. "What's going on?"

"I . . . I . . ." His voice broke.

"It's okay, Luke, take a couple of deep breaths. Then talk to me. Tell me what's going on."

I opened the sliding-glass door that led into my office,

went over to my altar. I lit my three candles—and asked only for wisdom about how to deal with Luke, Paul's lost son.

"He threw me out," Luke said. "He threw me the hell out."

I didn't know that Luke had moved back home. "The last I heard, Paul was in court with you." I squeezed the bridge of my nose, could feel tension building in my skull. "Can you fill me in?"

And he did, chapter and verse in legalese that sailed over my head. But the bottom line—the human line—was that he needed a ride to his girlfriend's place and could I help him out, please? Please?

Call your mother, dude. Call Flannigan. Call your messed-up old man. But I couldn't say any of it. "Sure, as long as she doesn't live in San Diego."

He laughed, a small, broken sound. "She's, like, twelve miles away. She can't pick me up because she's at work."

"Where're you?"

He was waiting at a gas station several miles up the road.

I hung up, told Clara and Marvin what was going on, said I'd be back shortly, and asked if they'd stick around till then? Keep an eye on things? They said sure, no problem, but Marvin looked irritated and followed me out of the kitchen.

"Sam, there comes a time when you have to draw a line, establish boundaries. He's not your kid. Paul needs to deal with this."

Marvin didn't know that I'd turned my own father away from the gate at the bottom of the driveway, that I'd had him arrested at my daughter's school. There were some things you didn't tell even your closest friends.

"He's a kid with a shit for a father. I don't mind doing this. I'll be back shortly." I swept my purse off the hallway table and left.

En route to the gas station, I called Liza and explained what was going on. I was so sick of drama, all drama. Yet I wondered if at some level I craved the drama because of the contrast it offered. Was it a psychological aberration, an addiction like Mystery Manor was for Luke? Was I that messed up? Had my past damaged me irreparably?

Liza said she would make some calls, find out what was what. When I turned into the gas station, Luke was sitting on the curb between two vacuum machines, a backpack at his feet. He was emailing or texting on his phone. The headlights struck him, and he looked up, a handsome young man with his father's wide jaw. His eyes and hair were the color of walnuts.

He stood, swung his pack over his shoulder, and I got out and walked over to him. "Hey, Luke. Where's your car?"

"He wouldn't let me take it. He . . . he said that until I can make the car payments, he's keeping it. It's his."

"How'd you get here?"

"A taxi."

"How come you didn't have the cab drop you off at your girlfriend's place to begin with?"

"I didn't have enough money to get over there." He sounded embarrassed. "I haven't worked since before I went into rehab."

We walked to my car, the night air wrapping around us, soothing me, but only briefly. Moments later, I pulled out onto the highway.

"Can't your dad loan you some money?"

He laughed, but it was a hollow, bitter sound. "Yeah, sure. He could. But he won't. He says his money is all tied up in investments, movies, yada, yada. Actually, his money is tied up with attorney fees and his ridiculously trumped-up lifestyle. He slapped twenty bucks on the table and threw me out."

"What's happening with your court case?"

"Dad, uh, paid off the rehab facility, and they dropped the charges. But my attorney says I'm probably going to do time for the credit card thing."

"*Thing?* You mean the credit card fraud?"

"Yeah." He twisted in the passenger seat like a restless little kid. "My life is pretty screwed up right now. Then again, that's nothing new. I've been screwed up since I was born. My whole family is a mess." He glanced at me, his smile forced, his face vampire pale.

"Where's your mother?"

"San Francisco, living with some guy."

"Can she help you out?"

"Sure. But she won't."

Pathetic. Maybe people should have to be licensed to become parents. Not that I'd always done such a great job, but I was learning. And I hoped that what I was learning would ensure that Isabella would never turn out like Luke, a poster child for the dysfunctional Hollywood kid.

Luke gazed out the passenger's-side window. "After I got arrested, my mother called my old man relentlessly, blaming him for everything. He's pissed because he had to hire a lawyer, pay off the rehab place, and she didn't help out with any of those bills. Then again, she doesn't have that kind of money. Neither does he, not really." He shrugged, then keyed in the address for his girlfriend's place on the dashboard GPS. "I can get a waiter job at the place where my girlfriend works."

"When is your court date for the fraud charge?"

"A couple of months, my attorney said. No firm date yet. I'm out on bond. That's the other thing that pissed him off. He had to put up the bond money, and it was substantial."

I didn't ask how much. But I suspected the bond money and Paul's other recent expenses explained why I still hadn't gotten the money he owed me.

For a few minutes, we didn't say much. The silence felt weighted, uneasy, and I sensed that Luke had more to say. "Did you manage to get everything you needed from the house before he tossed you out? Clothes, your computer, whatever else you needed?" I asked.

"Yeah, Jim Finnegan helped. He drove me to the nearest shopping plaza and I took a cab from there. I don't think he wanted to leave Dad alone."

I felt something coming in what he was about to say, and I knew it wasn't going to be good. I braced myself inwardly.

"My dad really has a grudge against you, Ms. DeMarco. It comes out when he's been drinking, which is most of the time now. Tonight, I walked into his office and found him loading and unloading a gun, a nine-millimeter. When I asked him what the hell he was doing with a gun, he pointed at a photo of you on the wall, then aimed and fired, and said that if he couldn't have you, no one else was going to have you, either. That's what set this whole thing off. He and I had a really bad argument about how screwed up he is, and that did it."

That image of Paul shooting at my photo was so vivid, I nearly drove off the road. "My God, he hates me that much?"

"He hates himself that much, Ms. DeMarco. Also, you gotta understand that his ego is huge. No woman he's been in love with has ever dumped him. Other women have, but no one he has loved, at least not that I know of."

The female voice in the GPS instructed me to turn left and continue for another half mile to the next turnoff. I couldn't get that image out of my head, Paul shooting at my picture on the wall. Target practice. *Bang, bang.* Two shots to the center of the photo's forehead. *You're dead, Sam.* Anxiety twisted through me. It was one thing to live with this sort of anxiety during the Tony years, when it was business as usual. But I was no longer that same person, and I disliked the familiarity of this anxiety, this coil of fear in the pit of my stomach.

"Don't be surprised if he does something to sabotage the movie," Luke said. "He won't call it that, he may not even be conscious of what he's doing, but that's what it'll be." He shook his head and ran his hands over his jeans. "There's a huge, dark shadow inside my dad."

I knew all about those dark shadows in people—my mother, Vito, Tony, Alec, Paul. Was there something like that inside John? I didn't sense it when I was with him, but in the past I'd been wrong about people about whom I felt it was best to assume there might be.

"My friend Jake is staying at my girlfriend's place, too. After he nearly died from some STD he picked up and then went back to rehab and was released, his father threw him out. Your daughter's lucky she has a mother like you, Ms. DeMarco. Compared to a lot of Hollywood types, you're the most normal person I've met in a long time."

I appreciated the compliment, but if I was *normal*, then nearly everyone around me was nuts.

"I appreciate your honesty, Luke."

"You needed to know all this," he said. "Maybe you should hire a bodyguard."

"Was Jim Finnegan at the house when your father fired the gun at my photo?"

"Yeah. He barreled into the den, expecting to find dad or me dead. When he saw your photo on the wall, riddled with holes, he told my dad he needed professional help. They had a huge argument, and Jim stormed out of Dad's office and told me to get my stuff, that he'd drive me to the shopping center."

"You have arrived at your destination," the GPS announced. I pulled over to the curb on a tree-lined street of apartment buildings.

Luke dug into his jacket pocket, withdrew twenty bucks. "For gas. I lied about not having enough money for a cab over here. He lent me a hundred bucks. I just wanted you to hear all this, in person."

I gently pushed his hand away. "Keep it. I'm really grateful you took the time to tell me all this, Luke."

He smiled sadly, fitted the strap of his pack over his shoulder, opened the door. We traded cell numbers, then he swung his legs out. Just then, the door to the apartment building opened and a tall, thin man hurried out. "Hey, Luke."

"Hey, man." Luke motioned him over to the car. "You need to meet a normal parent."

I stepped out of the car, and when Luke introduced us, Jake thrust his hand across the Prius roof. "Nice to meet you, ma'am. Luke talks about you a lot."

"Nice to meet you, too, Jake." He was a cute kid with curly dark hair, but so emaciated he could've been a refugee from Auschwitz. "Luke says your dad tossed you out?"

He shrugged. "Yeah. Me and Luke, we're a couple of orphans. But I've got a job, and it's going to be okay."

"If you guys need anything, Luke has my number."

"Thanks, Ms. DeMarco. We appreciate it."

Lost souls. I sat there watching them climb the steps of the apartment building. Before they disappeared inside, Luke turned and waved.

I understood I had made the right decision about Vito, about keeping him away from Isabella. Bad enough that she'd lost her father, but it would be even worse if Vito was in our lives. All the toxicity and venom that Paul had unleashed on Luke would be like a spring day compared to what Vito's presence might do to my daughter.

Liza called back as I drove away from the building. "Where're you now?" she asked.

"I just dropped Luke off. Why?"

"Well, I had a rather disturbing conversation with Flannigan. He thinks that Paul is in total meltdown and that you should take steps to protect yourself. Those were his exact words, Sam."

A chill licked its way up my spine. "Luke said the same thing." I told her about my conversation with him.

"Christ, Sam. I'm going to call King and Prince and let them know about this."

"No, don't do that. He wouldn't try anything on the set, in front of industry peers." Except that wasn't quite true. He'd exploded in front of Prince down by the swimming hole.

"A rational man wouldn't. But it sounds like Paul's no longer rational. If he tries to pull anything again, Sam, get a restraining order against him."

"Prince would then look at me as someone who had compromised the film."

"That means it would cost Gallery money to fire him. Paul must have gotten something to that effect in his contract with them. I'm going to mention this to Brian. He's more grounded than George. Flannigan wants to quit. He's looking for work elsewhere. He's had it with Paul and has worked for him for sixteen years. I told him I'd hire him in a heartbeat."

Exhaustion nearly overwhelmed me. "Let's talk about it tomorrow. What time should I meet you to go shopping?"

She understood and didn't press the issue. "Meet me at ten," she replied, and named a shop in downtown Malibu.

That night, I lay awake thinking about what Paul might do, freaking myself out. A hundred different scenarios played out in my head, all of them equally real, viable. Were Liza and I—and Luke—the only ones who saw Paul as dangerous? George Prince seemed to think that Paul would behave because he knew he was walking on thin ice. I didn't know what Brian King thought. It wasn't as if he'd said anything to me. John certainly understood where Paul was coming from, but he was an investor in the movie, not a co-owner of the studio, and he didn't make hiring and firing decisions. He made *suggestions*.

I heard the girls out by the pool, splashing around and laughing, and suddenly imagined Paul entering the house through the pool area, mowing down Isabella and her friends like one of the Charles Manson crazies. It terrified me more than the fact that after he mowed them down, he could rush into the house looking for me.

He wouldn't be able to drive through the gate, but if he was determined enough, he could scale the wall. We didn't have a dog, and I suddenly wished we did. Some huge, ferocious Rottweiler would do, for starters.

I quickly got out of bed and moved through the house, making sure the doors and windows were locked. I couldn't engage the security system because the girls were still going in and out from Isabella's room to the patio. But I flicked on the outside security lights and turned on the security camera at the gate.

Think you'll scale the wall when you're bathed in light, Paul?

Damn unlikely. I had lived with this kind of paranoia and fear during the years with Tony and his fists, and I hated it. But my situation now was vastly different from what it had been back then. I was older, wiser, and, yes, rich.

I could hire bodyguards and a security company to keep an eye on my property and Isabella, too, if that was what it took. I refused to cower in fear this time around and didn't intend to allow any man to make me feel diminished or fearful.

Just the same, I allowed my body to absorb the cool night air, and looked around. Was Paul hiding in the bushes? Nuts, but there you had it, the way your head could play tricks on you when fear entered the picture.

Marvin came out of the guesthouse, no doubt wondering why all the security lights were on. I realized they probably shone through his bedroom window and felt bad that the lights had awakened him. He spotted me and trotted over in a short robe and bare feet.

"What's with all the lights, Sam?"

"A bout of paranoia." I recounted what I'd learned.

His eyes widened, and he ran his fingers through his hair, glanced down toward the gate, then at me. "You should let Brian know all this. He can fire Paul even if Prince won't."

Should I? I didn't really know at this point. I was so badly shaken by what Luke had told me and so pissed off that I had become the object of Paul's meltdown, I doubted if I was thinking straight. "Wouldn't that just give Paul another reason to detest me? Wouldn't it make me look like some sort of diva?"

"Who gives a shit how it makes you *look*? The point is to protect yourself."

"Marvin, I think Paul is in deep shit financially. If he's fired from the film, I may never see that option money."

"What good is option money if you're dead, Sam?"

It was that word, *dead,* that followed me back into the house.

Dead—not afraid, not diminished, not humiliated or controlled, but *dead.*

Buried.

Six feet under.

I dimmed the security lights, except for the ones that shone directly on the gate, then sat at the kitchen table sipping hot tea, mulling over my options. I brought out my iPad and went online and Googled Malibu security companies. Nothing leaped out at me. I decided to ask Liza about it tomorrow. She would know whom to hire—for the house; for Isabella, so that she was never confronted again by Vito; and for me.

Despite the fact that Isabella and her friends had stayed up half the night, they were ready by nine the next morning when Lauren's mother, Becka, came by to take them to her house for the rest of the weekend.

"Thanks so much for having them over last night," Becka said as she came into the house. "It gave Ben and me a chance to finish the script for the last show of the season. And, wow, it's good!"

Their TV show had been called *Breaking Bad* meets *House of Cards,* an accurate description for a riveting sixty-minute drama on Showtime about a powerhouse couple in the TV business. Marvin, Liza, and I had watched the first two seasons.

The three of us came away convinced that it was all true—that Becka and her hub were the powerhouse couple, that he had a drug problem, that infidelity was the norm in their marriage. In fact, their agent was on Liza's speed dial, and he confirmed it. Their lives were the creative fodder for the show.

But whenever I was around their daughter, I doubted it. Lauren was . . . well, *normal,* at least as normal as you could be in Malibu if your parents worked in the entertainment industry.

"Well, they were great. They didn't sleep much, so if you're lucky, they'll fall out at eight tonight. You'd think they would get tired of sleepovers, but they don't!"

"Malibu moms," Becka said with a quick laugh. "Trading our kids for weekends. This is what we do."

"You bet. Is your show going to be picked up for another season?" I asked as we walked into the kitchen.

"We think so. Our audience isn't quite up there with the final episode of HBO's *Game of Thrones,* but we're close and just have one more episode to the finale and we've got ten million viewers."

"That's fantastic, Becka."

She beamed, and for a moment there, I could easily imagine her as the character in her and her husband's TV show, a knockout woman in her late forties who oozed seduction. "You know what I find intriguing, Sam? Malibu consists of a twenty-one-mile-long strip of coastline. Our population is pushing thirteen thousand. And just about everyone here is connected somehow to the entertainment industry—TV, movies, music. I don't know much about the music business, but for TV and movies there are just a handful of studio execs who green-light projects. Maybe a dozen total. Those dozen people are why you and I and practically everyone else in Malibu are here. That's a hell of a lot of power, isn't it?"

"Sort of scary, actually. The Malibu Kingdom."

Becka was a tall, slender blonde who looked like a surfer girl on an old Beach Boys album cover. She was in her late forties, but like so many women in Malibu, didn't look a day over thirty-five. She moved with the grace of a dancer and seemed so certain of herself and her place in the world that I envied her.

"Too much power," I replied. "It's probably why some of them go bonkers."

"So *many* of them," she said.

I handed her a mug of fresh coffee, and she plopped herself down on one of the stools. "Hey, I heard that shooting started on *Brooklyn Story*. That must be exciting."

"It's great. Well cast."

"Paul Jannis is the producer, right?"

I nodded.

"Are you still seeing him?"

"Nope."

"Smart girl. I heard he's been having some major trouble lately." She lowered her voice, as though she were afraid the walls had ears. Hell, maybe they did. Maybe Paul had my home bugged. "Financial problems, kid problems, booze problems—the usual stuff you encounter around here."

"Yeah, he seems to be having more than his share lately."

Becka stirred cream into her coffee. "I knew his wife. She and I worked on a show together ten or eleven years ago. She was a good writer, with an ear that was equally good for comedy and drama. I liked her. But never liked him much. Anyway, one morning she came to work with a black eye, said she'd run into a door or some other ridiculous story. Not too long after that, she filed for divorce."

The things you learned over coffee, I thought. "His son was in rehab for addiction to a video game and credit card fraud."

Becka laughed. "Christ. Only in Malibu do you hear about stuff like an addiction to a game. But with a father like Paul, it's not surprising. Just be careful, Sam." She pressed her hands against her slender thighs and pushed to her feet. "Now, let me gather up the girls and get out of your hair. Hope you've got something special planned for tonight."

"A date, actually."

I felt silly saying it, *a date*, like I was eighteen years old. But Becka's eyes lit up. "Good for you. It's hard enough living here as a married couple."

Uh-oh. I was sure she was about to tell me the TV show was real, that all of it was true, that she was an adulterer and her husband was an addict.

"But as a single mother, it can be really tough," she went on. "Anyone I know?"

"John Steeling."

She frowned slightly. "Steeling, Steeling, the name's familiar." She snapped her fingers. "Wait a minute. *The* John Steeling? The financier?"

"You know him?"

"Not personally. But I hear his pockets are deep, and some of the major studios have been tapping him for financing. Like he's a bank. He may be buying a percentage of Gallery Studios. Did you know that?"

This woman was a treasure trove of information. "No, I hadn't heard."

"Girl, you need to keep your ear to the ground. What you *don't* know can be your downfall in this town. Now I've got to round up the wild ones."

I met Liza at a breakfast place in downtown Malibu. As usual, she was dressed to kill in Armani and had at least twenty projects she was working on simultaneously, most of them accessible through her trusty iPad or phone. The speed at which this woman lived astounded me.

"I've got three recommendations for security companies, Sam," she said as I slid into the booth across from her. "I just sent you an email with the info."

"You think that's the route I should go?"

"Bet your ass, honey. That's the first step. You've got Isabella to think about." She leaned forward. "Paul's son and his longtime assistant think he intends to harm you. What other confirmation do you need? If you feel uncomfortable about hiring a personal bodyguard, then at least hire some security people to keep an eye on your property. And maybe you should get a big dog with a ferocious bark and an even more ferocious bite."

"Maybe I should go to the police."

"And tell them what? He hasn't broken any laws. Yet."

Frankly, the idea of dealing with cops made me nearly as uneasy as Paul did. Back in Brooklyn, in the Tony days, we avoided cops. Even though Malibu wasn't Brooklyn and the cops were probably accustomed to the strange problems that celebrities had, it still left a bad taste in my mouth. I would sound like a crybaby. *My ex-lover and the producer of the movie based on my novel has been using my photo for target practice.*

Yeah, sure, lady. Get back to us when he does something really nasty.

It wasn't like Paul was OJ. Or Charlie Manson. Or even Tony.

"I'll start with the property. And maybe a dog."

"Great." She sat back, rubbing her hands together—her beautifully manicured red nails glinting in the light—and looked me over. "Casual or dressy?"

"In between." I handed her my phone so she could read his text message.

"Ah, okay, perfect. I know just the place to start."

Most women love to shop. I used to be one of those women. But when Alec and I went bankrupt, I pretty much stopped shopping and all personal shoppers and accounts in the fancy department stores went out the window and good riddance. It didn't define who I was, it never does. It's hard to justify thousand-dollar sunglasses when your bank account has suffered a major meltdown.

My bank account these days, though, was still healthy, despite the fact that Paul owed me half a million. I could afford a new outfit, a new pair of shoes, a new purse, a manicure and pedicure, and a visit to Malibu's premiere hair salon. And it felt good and satisfying because it was *my* money—not my grandmother's, not Tony's, not Alec's, but mine.

Since I had been on both sides of the financial tracks, I had a deep appreciation for the twenties and fifties and hundreds that passed from my hands to a clerk's. It felt good to shop, to enjoy what I had earned.

Four hours after Liza and I set out on our shopping expedition, I had spent over two thousand bucks. I'd also learned that Liza was filing for divorce and that it was true about John buying a piece of Gallery Studios. Liza said John was negotiating for a 35 percent cut.

"And," Liza added as we left the hair salon, "King offered me a job heading up their public relations department."

"Awesome! Did you accept it?"

"I sure did. He'll be paying me an outrageous salary to do what I basically do now, and my soon-to-be ex won't be entitled to any of it. I told him I can start anytime, but I don't want him to pay me until my divorce is final. My soon-to-be ex is already going to scoop up half of my net worth, but he won't be able to touch what Brian will be paying me."

"Karma's a bitch."

The instant the words were out of my mouth, I glanced up to search for my car in the lot, and I saw Paul coming out of the breakfast place where Liza and I had eaten this morning. He was with an older, gray-haired man. Banker or attorney, I guessed. Both of them were dressed casually. Paul didn't look crazy. He just looked like another guy in Malibu, chilling on his day off, having a bite to eat with a friend. Not a care in the world.

And then he spotted Liza and me and made a beeline toward us. A fast beeline.

"Shit," I muttered.

"Yeah, I see him. Just keep walking."

We kept walking, and Paul kept moving toward us and finally shouted, "Hey, Sam, Liza. Hold on."

We didn't stop. We reached Liza's Mercedes, and she said, "Hop in, Sam. I'll drive you to your car."

I slipped into the passenger seat, and she locked the doors and started backing out of the parking spot. We were acting like a couple of frightened women pursued by a cannibal. Or a rapist. Or worse.

Paul reached the car before Liza had completely backed out and slammed his fist against the passenger door. My door. "Hold on, Sam, Liza," he shouted. "Hold on for a minute."

I lowered my window. "What the hell, Paul."

Rage poured out of him. "Who do you think you are, driving my son anywhere?"

"He called and asked me to drive him somewhere. He needed help, and since you wouldn't give it to him, he reached out."

I pressed the button to raise the window again, but Paul grabbed the glass, his long, thick fingers gripping it as though it were a living thing, and shook it. The window kept going up, and he continued shaking it, shouting, "You bitch, you can't interfere with—"

I threw open the door so fast and hard that it whacked him in the stomach, and he stumbled back, gasping for air. "Leave me alone, Paul, or I'll get a restraining order against you."

"You . . . you can't do that. I"—he struggled to catch his breath—"haven't broken any laws."

"Bullshit. You're stalking me. You attacked me in your house. You threatened me. And you haven't paid me what you owe me."

I got quickly back into the car. "Let's get outta here, Liza."

"It'll be a pleasure, honey." And she slammed her foot

against the accelerator and the Mercedes took off, a dark bullet that flew through the parking lot away from Paul, past his gray-haired companion who trotted toward him, and out onto the road.

What explanation would Paul give his companion? *She stole money from me; she slept with my son; she, she, she . . .*

Liza glanced over at me. "Call the security company, Sam. Paul's definitely gone around the bend."

By the time we pulled up to the gate at my place, I'd spoken to the security company and arranged for someone to come by tomorrow afternoon. But how was this going to work, exactly? Security cameras installed at the gates? Armed men patrolling the grounds? Gigantic Rottweilers racing along the fence and howling at every car that passed?

The idea didn't fit with how I imagined Isabella and me living out here. But the alternative—Paul rampaging across my property brandishing a weapon—wasn't particularly appealing, either.

I pressed the remote on my key chain, and the gate slid slowly open. As we rounded the first curve, I could see two cars outside the guesthouse—Marvin's and a blue Ford truck. *Interesting,* I thought.

"Hey, that's Flannigan's truck," Liza exclaimed, then frowned. "What's *he* doing here?"

"He and Marvin know each other, but I, uh, didn't know they knew each other well enough to visit."

Liza laughed softly. "You know what? Flannigan and his partner split up last week. They were together as long as he had worked for Paul. I think this is fantastic! And if he accepts my job offer, he'll be working for us! For Gallery! Paul's going to have a freakin' fit."

The two of us collapsed into giggles. But a shadow loomed in the back of my mind. I worried that all these changes, which essentially isolated Paul from the rest of us, from his former pals at Gallery, might push him over the edge completely. And in retaliation, he would lash out at me.

By five-thirty, a full hour before John was due to pick me up, I was a bit nervous, but so excited to see him. I stood in front of my bedroom mirror, critiquing the way I looked, which I rarely do. I was checking out my hair, even my manicure; dark-blue nails—hey, it was the color I loved and obviously so did he.

Even as I tore through my closet, searching for something else that was casual and classy, a small, soft voice in my head whispered, *That's the old tape you're playing, Sam. The one where you never look good enough, you never speak well enough, you're never smart enough.*

I was barely aware of that voice. All I could think of was that shoes didn't match handbags, that handbags didn't match the flowing Bohemian blouse I'd bought, or the black jeans. I was so caught up in that old loop that I couldn't see myself as I was now: a changed, better person.

A new woman.

But how changed was I, exactly? Something inside of me—some vibe, some quality others sensed—still attracted the kind of scene that had played out repeatedly with Paul and twice with Vito. If change began within, then maybe I needed therapy. A shrink. Counseling. Could counseling help me break this inner pattern? Could anyone or anything?

I pressed my fists against my eyes, so irritated with myself that I wanted to scream, shriek, pull a Scarlett O'Hara and throw myself across my bed. Dramatic, ridiculous.

Sam, diva drama queen.

Considering the money I'd spent and the time crunch, this outfit would have to do.

When the doorbell rang at six, I nearly panicked. He

was half an hour early? But when I opened the door, there stood Marvin and Flannigan, looking quite pleased and happy with themselves and with each other. They both took one look at me, and Flannigan let out a low, soft whistle. "Damn, Sam, you look . . . stunning. You look like—"

"A movie star," Marvin burst out.

"You guys just being nice?"

"Honest." Marvin crossed his heart. "I've never seen you look this good, Sam. Never. And we've known each other how long?"

"Okay, I believe you. So the outfit works for a casual dinner on the beach?"

"Perfectly," Flannigan replied.

"Now tell her what just happened," Marvin said excitedly.

"Let me guess," I said. "You're going to work for Liza, who is going to work for Gallery Studios."

Flannigan's eyes widened. "You already know!"

I hugged him. "Welcome to the team of good guys, Flannigan. We're all entering a whole new chapter in our Malibu story."

chapter NINE

There was a moment when John and I were walking out to his car that I felt Grandma Ruth's presence. It was as if the air on my right side were suddenly lighter, clearer, and I could hear her whisper in my head: *Is this the boy who's gonna get your heart, bubelah?*

I stole a glance at him, at John, his dark hair pulled back in a ponytail, his beard threaded with gray, his profile in the evening light like that of an Olympian god. Malibu rogue. I imagined he could wear almost anything and it wouldn't diminish the essential core of how he looked. I also imagined him with short hair and no beard. What would he look like? Who would he be? I wanted to really see him.

"I heard a rumor today," I said.

"Only one?" he laughed.

"Same rumor from different people."

"Ah, then it must be true." He opened the passenger door of his Prius—same year as mine, but a different color, silver instead of white—and swept his arm toward it like some footman in *Downton Abbey*. "Hop in, lovely lady."

The inside of his car smelled new, of leather and meticulous care. There wasn't a speck of dust on the dash, no dirt on the floor mat, no spots on the windshield. Beneath the scent of leather were other odors that were more complex, suggestive of a certain maleness, an essential mystery: *Who is John Steeling? Where did he come from?*

I had Googled him, just as Liza had done the day we'd met, and hadn't found anything more than she had. It was as if he'd simply appeared in Hollywood a decade ago.

"What's the rumor?" he asked.

"That you're buying thirty-five percent of Gallery Studios."

"That's the plan."

"What prompted it?"

"Brian and I have been talking about it for weeks. But what really pushed me was how George reacted to that whole thing with Paul by the swimming hole. I realized that I didn't have the right or the power to fire Paul's ass. Now I will. Brian will retain forty percent of the company, George will have twenty-five percent, and I'll have the rest."

"Given the money you've been investing in their movies, it makes sense."

"I also have great respect for the way the company is run. They're honest, they pay their employees well, and they make quality stuff. Gallery has room to grow—I like that. And Brian has a deeper sense of social conscience than a lot of the players out here who basically just pay lip service to charities and causes."

"I think it's fantastic. You'll be a great fit for Gallery. And now Liza has been hired, too, basically doing what she does now. She'll head up their publicity department."

He flashed a sly smile. "And she has hired Jim Flannigan."

I lightly slapped his shoulder. "You already knew all this."

"Brian, George, and I talked about it last week."

Once we were out on the road, John seemed distracted and finally blurted, "Sam, has Paul paid you yet?"

Uh-oh. So Paul was the distraction. "No. I think he's having financial problems."

"That doesn't give him an excuse not to pay *you*. You could sue him for breaching the terms of your contract with him."

"I try to stay away from lawyers."

"Look, I set George straight about Paul, that if they fire him, I'll pay whatever is stipulated in his contract."

"Don't do this because of me, John. It would just piss him off and give him more reason to hate me."

"It's not just about you. We want the filming to go smoothly. Paul is toxic, and that energy can infect the entire process of making the movie. The bottom line is that we can fire him as producer if he keeps the money."

I didn't want to talk about Paul. I was burned out on the subject, fed up with it, done. I changed the topic by asking John about his son. His face lit up when he talked about Nick and his fiancée, and I just let the sound of his voice flow over me, through me, and found it enormously calming.

"How long will they be here?" I asked.

"Just until tomorrow." He looked over at me again. "They really wanted to visit the set and watch some of the filming, but both of them have midterms. I told him that when we shoot in Brooklyn, he and Nina can visit the set all they want."

"When do you think the Brooklyn shoot will happen?"

"My guess is June."

"You mind if I ask you a personal question, John?"

"Ask away."

"What did you do before you ended up in Hollywood? I mean, I know you sold real estate in Manhattan, but was that the main thing you were doing before?"

"A lot of things. But selling high-end real estate in Manhattan is how I made most of my money. After I advised Brian not to buy that penthouse in Manhattan, he told me to get out of the stock market before everything crashed. And I did."

"Why'd you advise him not to buy?"

John looked amused. "You always ask so many questions, Ms. DeMarco. You are very inquisitive, my lady."

"These days I am. But I don't mean to be inquisitive."

"Of course you do, Ms. DeMarco." He smiled wide. "My advice was really a gut feeling. The asking price was ridiculously high; I knew Brian wanted to turn it around in a few years, and I just felt he would lose money. Turned out I was right. The people who finally bought the place paid the high price and then couldn't sell it when the market took a dive, and it ended up in foreclosure. I came out to L.A. to see Brian, had some money to invest, and put it into one of his films."

"That's quite a journey."

"It's had its twists and turns, that's for sure. You mind if I ask you a personal question?"

"Ahh, your chance to be inquisitive, Mr. Steeling," I laughed. "Ask away."

"Your books, all the stuff you write about. Was it all true?"

"You already asked me that back when we met."

"Yeah, I know."

In the past when people have asked—like that Rick guy from *People*—it annoyed the shit out of me. Now that John had asked twice, I was thrilled. Go figure. "Yes. Next question."

"How'd you survive that kind of childhood?"

"My grandmother, a lot of hope, and the belief that I could write my way out of Brooklyn."

"Is Tony still doing time?"

"As far as I know. Or ever want to know."

"And your husband actually ended up in a psychiatric ward?"

"Yes."

"But he still had the smarts to make his insurance payments."

"He loved his daughter. I think that was his motivation. Even after our marriage fell apart, I couldn't leave him because of Isabella. I felt it would mess her up."

"Because your own father abandoned the family."

"Right. What about you? Are your parents still alive?"

"I never knew my birth parents. I was adopted when I was six months old. My adoptive parents have both passed on."

"Were they good parents?"

"Nope."

He said it with a hardness in his voice that suggested bitter memories, so I didn't pursue it.

"What about your father?" John asked. "Has he ever contacted you?"

Interesting. My moment of truth. How much did I want to confide in this man? It was one thing to lie to Isabella to protect her. But if I lied to John, what would I be protecting? An image of myself? My Hollywood image? What kind of bullshit was *that*?

I didn't have an image. I was who I was because of what I had experienced, and Vito was a part of that experience. But suppose John told King and Prince the truth about my father, that he was alive, had harassed me twice, and that I'd had him arrested? Would they cancel the movie because of it? Of course not. But the real issue was whether or not I trusted John.

What's it gonna be, bubelah?

"One night back in April, this haunted, scrawny man showed up at my front gate and announced that he was my father," I said, and the rest of the horror story tumbled out.

John listened without interrupting. He didn't even

interrupt when the story about Vito melted into recent confrontations with Paul. By the time I'd finished talking, we were in the parking lot in front of La Playa, and John just sat there staring straight ahead, his hands gripping the steering wheel.

"Look, I'm telling you this so you understand who I am. My history with relationships pretty much sucks, and a shrink would probably say it's because Vito abandoned my mother and me. Maybe there's some truth to that. But I'm working on overcoming it, and the steps I took in dealing with Vito have helped. With Paul . . ." I shook my head. "I don't know. That's part of an inner pattern, too, I guess. I attract men who aren't what they initially seem to be."

"Paul's an asshole, Sam. Don't blame yourself for what's happened with him. When I came on board with this film and met him for the first time, I told Brian that he was the wrong producer for *Brooklyn Story*. But Brian feels a particular loyalty to Paul because he brought your novel and screenplay to Gallery. If Gallery does *The Suite Life,* which I think they will, it will be after I'm part owner. So you can be sure Paul won't be producing it." His hands dropped to his thighs. "And I think you handled Vito well. Has he been in contact since his arrest?"

"No. Hopefully, he went back to New York."

"Hungry?"

"Starved."

He leaned toward me then, touched the side of my face, and kissed me. "If I weren't so damn hungry, I could sit here all night with you."

As if in response, my stomach rumbled. We both laughed, got out of the car, and walked toward the restaurant, holding hands. A simple thing, but I liked it. His hand was warm and large, and made my hand feel like a small, sleepy creature nestled inside of it. For some strange reason

I had a sense of peace and safeness with him. Again, that familiarity. It never left when I was around John.

La Playa looked like a large beach shack—just one wall where the S-shaped bar was, and everything else open to the elements. The last of the evening light spilled across the water and sand where a dozen tables were set up. Music played softly in the background, a catchy, Hispanic rhythm that made me want to tap my feet.

John gave his name to the hostess, said we were expecting two more people; she showed us to a table for four on the beach, beneath a pair of palms. A waiter came over immediately with menus, a bucket of ice that held four chilled bottles of Metromint water, and a basket of warm rolls.

"This is gorgeous." I slipped off my shoes, ran my toes through the warm sand.

"I bet you just slipped your shoes off."

"How'd you know that?"

"Because I did, too. If you look around, you'll see that nearly everyone does that out here. My theory? It's the kid inside of us that just can't resist doing it."

"Before I left Brooklyn, I could count on one hand how many times I'd gone to the beach."

"Brighton Beach, right?"

"You got it. And it sure as hell didn't compare to *this*."

"Not many beaches do." He opened two bottles of water, filled our respective glasses.

Beneath the table, his toes brushed mine, then moved in a little closer, brushing them again, moving away, a little dance of toes that felt strangely and deliciously intimate. Now his toes were caressing the tops of my feet.

"Something seductive about sand, isn't there?" he asked.

"Very."

Our eyes held in that way they had the first day I'd seen him in that café. Then the moment was broken when a handsome young couple—Nick and Nina—strolled over to the table. Nick looked like a younger version of his father—longish hair, a neatly trimmed beard, the same intense eyes, but he stood about two inches taller. Nina was a slender five seven, with wavy blondish-brown hair and skin so olive toned it was like the color of a saddle. When she smiled, dimples appeared at the corners of her mouth.

"I'm such a fan," she gushed as John introduced us. "Just loved your two books. So Brooklyn and Wall Street!"

"Thanks so much."

They sat down, the waiter returned, and John ordered a bottle of Sassicaia. "It sounds like they've got a great cast for the movie," Nick remarked. "Does it get any better than Sarandon, Batiste, and Conte? Wow."

We traded set stories. Nick and Nina talked about a documentary they were working on, about being in film school, how they hoped to move to L.A. when they graduated. They were young people with big dreams, and their enthusiasm was infectious. I couldn't wait to get back on set Monday morning.

The waiter returned with our wine and a plate of tapas, and John's toes came looking for mine again, and inscribed a secret language on the top of my feet. It felt erotic until either Nick's toes or Nina's brushed against ours. I quickly moved my feet back, closer to my chair.

It hadn't taken John long to figure out how to play me. Even though my body craved his, I didn't want to sleep with the man yet.

The tables around us were now filled, customers spilled out from the bar onto the sand, the bar was jammed with people, the music got louder. When John started to refill my glass of wine, I shook my head. I had spent way too many dinner parties with Alec during which four-hundred-dollar bottles of wine had been consumed like water. *Been there, done that, no, thanks.*

"Do you have any idea where the restroom is?" Nina asked.

"Nope. But let's go find it."

"Be right back, guys," Nina said as we got up.

"Oops. My shoes."

I slipped my sandals back on, grabbed my purse, and Nina and I made our way through the crowd in search of the restroom.

Maybe it was the two glasses of wine I'd had on an empty stomach, but the press of bodies, the music, the laughter, and chatter suddenly reminded me of a dinner Alec and I had had in the very early days of our relationship. We had eaten like gluttons and had drunk Tattinger champagne, plus several bottles of wine, and talked for hours. In the end, what difference had any of it made? In the end, I was just one of his many possessions. The only difference was that I was kept in a much grander and more expensive way.

Where did John fall in this picture? Was he going to turn out to be a power maniac with a raging appetite and fierce temper? It seemed unlikely right this second, but what the hell did I know? I'd made so many mistakes in the past that I felt I could no longer trust my own judgment about men.

Nina and I finally found the restroom, a door out back, behind the bar. As far as restrooms went, it was pretty cool—dolphins and palm trees painted on the concrete walls and some cool slogans. My favorite was the opposite of Murphy's Law: *If anything can go right, it will.*

Nina pointed it out and exclaimed, "That's my motto!"

Most of the time, at least with men, my life had pretty much proven that Murphy's Law was the norm—*If anything can go wrong, it will.* So I decided my new norm would be the first slogan, Nina's motto. I repeated it to myself: *If anything can go right, it will.* I repeated it silently in my mind, like a prayer to the Blessed Mother, to Buddha, to Christ, to whoever was listening.

"Nina, do you think it really works like that? That your motto is how your life unfolds?"

We were standing at the sinks when I asked this, and her pretty brown eyes met mine in the mirror. "If it's your deepest belief, then yes. If it's just something you say because it sounds good, then no. A belief is something you feel. Here." She brought her fist to her heart. What you say comes from here." She touched her temple. "You see what I mean?"

"Not really," I replied.

Nina turned to face me, her expression earnest, her model's body taut with tension. She placed her hands on my shoulders. "Sam. We all carry emotional baggage. For some people, that baggage sculpts and defines their lives forever. But for other people, that baggage falls away when they realize that our point of power lies in the present. *Now*. It's the only certainty. This instant. This breath."

I just stood there, blown away by her words. I mean my faith was solid, without it I would not be where I am today, but she was half my age and so far beyond me in wisdom that I was speechless, which I rarely was. "That's how you break past patterns?"

Her arms fell from my shoulders; she reached into her handbag and withdrew a brush. Then she turned to the mirror and drew the brush through her hair. "My uncle first raped me when I was twelve. It continued until I was fifteen. He was my dad's brother, a real shit of a human being. Fortunately, my parents believed me, and my uncle is now doing twenty years in a Connecticut prison. But it took me a long time to turn my beliefs around."

"How'd you do that?"

"Read, attended seminars, blogged, went to film school. Internally, I could feel things shifting. And then I met Nick and realized I'd had to go through everything I'd gone through so that I would be in the emotional and spiritual space where a relationship with someone like Nick would even be possible."

"What do you think of his father?"

"Love him. He and Nick have a great relationship. Even when John did time, he and Nick . . ."

Blood pounded in my ears. I didn't hear the rest of what she said. *Did time?* John had done time? Shit, for what? I couldn't ask for details because she would realize this was the first I'd heard of it. So I tried not to look surprised. I tried to act as if I already knew that he'd done time. I wished the pounding in my ears would stop.

John lied to me.

He's like all the others.

Then we were moving out of the restroom, back into the crowd toward our table and dinner. But I had lost my appetite. I was instantly and totally sober. I just wanted to go home, back to my sanctuary, and curl up and sleep.

We navigated our way through the growing crowd of customers, and before we reached the beach, I spotted two men and a woman standing by our table, talking to John and Nick. My heart nearly stopped. Prince, Paul, and Jenean Conte.

As we approached the table, Paul glanced around and glared at me. I didn't look away from him, didn't cower, didn't give any indication what I felt just then, which was unmitigated anger that he kept showing up wherever I was. "Hey, you all," I said.

Jenean and I hugged hello. I introduced her, Prince, and Paul to Nina. Nina didn't know anything about my history with Paul and invited them to join us. This elicited a snarky smile from Paul, who was already looking around for some chairs to pull over.

"Thanks," Jenean said. "But we can't. We're meeting Susan and Camilla to discuss some scenes in next week's shooting. You're going to be on set, aren't you, Sam?"

"Wouldn't miss it," I said.

A waiter came over and told Prince their table was ready.

After a chorus of courtesies, Prince herded Paul and Jenean to their table, four removed from ours. Paul glanced back just once, his eyes shooting daggers at me.

Yeah, fuck you, too.

John stared after him, his mouth as flat as a dash, his expression as inscrutable as stone.

Our meals arrived, the dinner chatter went on, but I didn't say much. My mind was stuck on the fact that John had done time and had never mentioned it. I wondered what he'd thought when I'd confessed I attracted men who weren't what they initially seemed to be.

That would have been the moment when he could have said, *Listen, Sam I want you to know that I did time.* But he hadn't.

Now and then, as I picked at my meal, barely tasting it, I felt Paul glancing our way and wondered if he realized just how close he was to unemployment. I decided right then and there to tell Brian King that I hadn't been paid, that Paul had breached his contract. I suddenly didn't give a shit if he was fired.

"Oh, my God," Nina said. "There's Susan Sarandon and Camilla Batiste. Sam, how weird is that? Sitting at that table are the women who're playing Grandma Ruth, Joan, and Samantha Bonti. Your novel has leaped to life."

I looked over at the table, and, yeah, it was unnerving. Sarandon saw me and waved, then Camilla turned around, and they got up and came over. Both women were recognizable, and even though celebrity sightings were fairly common in Malibu, they drew looks from other customers.

John introduced the women to Nick and Nina, who were obviously starstruck. Then Camilla said, "Sam, Susan and I have a question."

"Several questions," Sarandon said. "But you first, Camilla."

"What kind of cigarettes did mother Joan smoke?" Camilla asked.

"Marlboros," I replied.

"I knew it," Camilla said. "Paul kept insisting she smoked Lucky Strikes."

"Paul didn't do his research," John remarked.

"Okay, my question," Sarandon said. "What's the most outstanding quality about Grandma Ruth?"

I didn't have to think too long about that one. "She allowed her granddaughter to make her own choices and her own mistakes but remained a constant source of encouragement."

"Wow," Sarandon said. "That's perfect. I also like that she understood how messed up her own daughter was and that she was determined to buffer her granddaughter as well as she could from growing up to become her mother."

"Next week we're shooting the scenes after Samantha gets her first kiss from Tony, the morning afterward, when Sam is dying to have a private conversation with her grandmother about Tony. But her mother is up and wants to know who she was talking to on the phone," John said.

Camilla put her hand on her hip and in a perfect mimic of my mother's voice, said, "I heard ya talkin' on the phone." She paused. "What the hell is he doin' sleepin' his life away?" She paused again. "Remember that scene, Sam?"

Vividly. "You've got the Brooklyn thing down pat, Camilla."

Sarandon winked and drew her fingers through my hair. "Now, bubelah, you find yourself a nice Jewish boy."

"Wow," Nick exclaimed. "And you've got the Jewish grandmother schtick perfect."

How lucky was I that these two women were playing Grandma Ruth and my mother? "You two are the best," I said, and got up and hugged each of them.

I knew that Paul watched the whole scene and that it pissed him off.

"Well, we'll leave you guys to coffee and dessert," Susan said. "See you on Monday, Sam."

"Maybe we should skip our midterm exams, Nick," said Nina. "I'd rather be on the set."

What ensued was a sort of argument between Nick and Nina, probably triggered by too much wine, about whether they should stay an extra few days and miss their midterms. Nina said yes, but Nick reminded her it would cost them an additional two hundred bucks if they changed their tickets now. Nick won.

While this mini argument was going on, John's toes sought mine again, but I pulled my feet back toward my chair. *Not interested, pal. You're a liar. I've had enough lying men in my life.*

He felt my withdrawal—he'd have to be completely oblivious not to—and he gave me an odd look, one of those WTF? looks that men give women when they realize they've messed up but aren't sure what they've done. Through coffee and dessert, no one said much of anything. Nina was pissed at Nick, Nick was pissed at Nina, I was pissed at John, and John was just bewildered.

When we finally left the restaurant and walked out toward the parking lot, all I wanted to do was get home to the silence of my sanctuary and, like the old man in the nursery rhyme, pull the blanket over my head.

Since Nick and Nina had come in their own car, we said our good-byes in the parking lot, then John and I headed toward his car on the far side of the lot. We walked in utter silence beneath a shockingly clear sky strewn with stars. He finally spoke first.

"Did I do something to tick you off, Sam?"

A direct question. That was good. Points in his favor. Since he'd thrown open the door with that question, I walked through it. "It's not anything you did. It's what you neglected to tell me." I spoke with sincerity, trying to give him the benefit of the doubt.

We stopped next to one of the solar-powered street-lamps and stood there in a circle of light like the orphans we were. He thrust his hands in the pockets of his jacket, frowned, and studied the ground at his feet. When he finally raised his head, he said, "Let me guess. Women's restroom. Nina said something about my having done time. She figured you knew."

Maybe he was a tad psychic, like Liza. "How'd you know?"

He shrugged. "It's the only thing that makes sense."

"John, you coulda said something after I made my little confession about the kind of men I attract. What were you thinking?"

"It just didn't seem to be the right time or place. My story is complicated and long-winded."

"I'd be happy with a *Reader's Digest* version."

He gazed off to his right, where Nick's car was pulling out of the lot, Nina's waving hand visible outside the window. Then he looked at me straight on. "Frank's Pizzeria. You and I were there together at least twice."

My mind didn't race into the past, it leaped there.

"Bobby Santos," he said. "Does the name ring any bells, Sam?"

The Santos family had lived eight houses down from us in Brooklyn. Santos senior ran a money-laundering operation for the mafia; I had pieced together that much over the years. There were three sons—and Bobby had been the youngest. Bobby, whom I had kissed beneath a bit of mistletoe at some New Year's Eve party where Tony had vanished long before midnight. I vaguely recalled that Tony had returned in the middle of the night, in what was essentially the new year, and was enraged that I had left.

I got a fist in the face for it the next day.

But I never forgot that kiss from Bobby Santos. Or, at any rate, my body apparently had never forgotten. *That* was why John had seemed so familiar to me.

"*My God,* Bobby Santos and the kiss under the mistletoe."

"I never forgot it."

"Oh, my God," I muttered, and got into the car.

He scrambled in behind the wheel. "Sam, let me explain."

"Leave me alone." Forget the toe dance, forget that his mouth had inflamed mine hours earlier. Forget all that. Right now, he was a liar no better than Tony, than Vito, than Alec. "I'm done. Please just take me home."

I felt something from him, something swift and powerful, a tsunami of emotions that seemed to seize him, shake him, and shred him to the bone. I wasn't sure how I could actually feel such a thing, but I did. And it changed something deep inside of me—but my change was slow and cautious. This was a man I had known for thirty years. How did I not know him? How is he here? And why is he here? These were my questions that I needed to have answered.

chapter TEN

From La Playa, it was a twenty-minute drive to my house. But there had been an accident on the Pacific Coast Highway, a multiple-car pileup with fatalities, and John and I sat there together in his car for a long time before either of us said anything.

I felt as if I had been cast in a really bad movie, one of those grade-B Japanese films from the 1950s, where a monster of some kind would suddenly appear at my window, its face pressed up to the glass. And then all hell and chaos would be let loose, a kind of Pandora's box of horror scenes that had all been done somewhere before but could still shock you senseless.

I was thirsty. I wanted to sleep. I wanted to get away from John. I needed to be alone to absorb this. But he began to talk—about his childhood, about who Bobby Santos had been. And his voice captured me and whisked me away, back to Brooklyn.

"We laundered everything. Drug money. Prostitution money. Assassination money. Wall Street pyramid scams. It was Wall Street that paid me the most, next to the later—real estate—which legitimized me. The pump-and-dump schemes. We laundered money for local gangs and cartels, and for international outfits. We were your first stop, probably your only stop. I started working for my father when I was fourteen, delivering messages. I'm now in my forties. I got busted when I was twenty-one for selling drugs and was sentenced to eight years. I did six. My time was hard and I went to jail for a charge that I barely had anything to do with. There's nothing easy about prison. If I'd been busted for the Wall Street stuff, I'd probably still be doing time. Fortunately, I stashed away a lot of my profits, and I took that money, changed my name, and paid my way through college. Then I went into real estate. You know the rest."

I did? And what was that? That he had saved Brian from buying a Manhattan penthouse that would lose money? That on a trip to L.A. he'd invested money in one of Brian's movies? That was it? End of story?

"And that's it? You're a changed man because of six years in prison?" What happened in those six years behind that cell door? How does one redeem himself?

"I'm a changed man because of Nick. I married his mother as soon as I got out; she got pregnant almost immediately, and when Nick was five, she had an affair with her boss. We got divorced. We had joint custody except that he spent most of his time with me because she couldn't be bothered."

Traffic inched ahead. I stared out my window, struggling to understand why some people bothered having children at all. Why had my mother and Vito had a kid? I was undoubtedly a mistake, but how many children were mistakes? How many children where the result of lust triggered by too much booze or too many drugs?

Paul's son, Luke, had been conceived during a long weekend in Barbados that he barely remembered, during one of his early jobs as a producer. At a cast party, they'd gotten smashed on champagne and margaritas, he'd told me, and had screwed on the beach. Six weeks later, his wife had learned she was pregnant. When Luke was two, they'd gotten divorced, and Luke had bounced back and forth between mom and dad. *Now look at him,* I thought. The trajectory of his life was nothing for a parent to brag about.

And what about Isabella? I had tried my best to be a good parent, but sometimes your best wasn't good enough because you got caught up in your own shit. I regretted that she'd had nannies when she was really young; I should have been there more. My best parenting probably started after Alec's death. Pathetic, but there you had it. It all came back to my thought that perhaps people should be tested for parenting in the same way they were tested for any profession or skill. Yeah, it sounded fascist. But I believed it was also true.

I broke out of thought as John started talking again. "It was my eighteenth birthday. And every year the same thing would happen. We had a cake at my home and all the family—sometimes forty of us—would pack the little place. They would light my candles and my dad would run over and take them out and place one single black candle in the center of the cake and tell me I wouldn't live past this year. That year, he told me I wouldn't see nineteen. 'You'll be dead and your mother will wear black for the rest of her life,' he said. I moved out a month later and had nothing more to do with him. So I know about deadbeat dads firsthand."

I realized that I'd made so many misjudgments about men in the past that I didn't trust my own instincts. "I don't want to talk about this. I just need to sleep."

My head tipped against the passenger's-side window, I shut my eyes, and after a while, the car moved forward at a normal rate. I found comfort in the noise the tires made as they sped up the highway, in the scent of the Pacific, even in the dampness of the rising fog.

Ah, bubelah, Grandma Ruth seemed to whisper in my ear. *Don't be so hard on yourself. As you always say, shit happens; just deal with it.*

John roused me when we reached my front gate, and I fumbled in my purse, searching for my keys and the remote. I wondered why the security lights at the gates hadn't come on. They were supposed to be automatic. The gate slid open noisily, slowly, and I was suddenly alert and aware of the fact that John might want to come in, that he might want to stay the night.

As we rounded the curve in the driveway and passed the guesthouse, there weren't any lights on inside and no sign of Marvin's or Flannigan's cars. I began to feel deeply uneasy. And it wasn't just about what John might be expecting. This feeling went deeper, concerned something else. The moment I reached the front door and inserted the key in the lock, I understood my feeling. The door simply swung open, and I knew someone had been inside my house, my sanctuary.

"Did you leave the door unlocked?" John asked.

"Are you kidding? I'm from Brooklyn."

I pushed the door all the way open, and we walked inside.

The hallway looked as though a cyclone had torn through it, stuff scattered everywhere; clothes and food and random stuff that had been crammed into drawers and closets now lay scattered across the floor. The kitchen was a disaster, water overflowing in the sink and spilling over onto the floor, so we sloshed through several inches. Dishes, pots and pans, and silverware lay strewn from one wall to another. The cabinet that held glasses looked as if it had been pummeled by a bat, the wood smashed, the glasses reduced to smithereens.

I ran down the hall to my office. My wonderful library had been destroyed: books everywhere, their covers torn off, their pages ripped apart. The perp had even tried to burn some of them, leaving scorch marks on the tile floor, the stink of smoke riding the air. I didn't check the smoke detectors, and even if I had, it wouldn't have mattered because whoever had done this had opened the windows so that the smoke would drift out.

My computer—an iMac—looked like a refugee from a disaster, its screen smashed, its motherboard exposed. All of my flash drives and external hard drives lay scattered in bits and pieces across my desk. I had a flash drive that I always carried with me, but I couldn't recall when I had last backed it up. The only positive thing I could think of was that I always emailed my documents to my multiple email accounts, then opened them on my office computer. The laptop in the guesthouse would be intact, unless the perp had broken in there, too.

I threw open the closet door, dropped to my knees, swept office supplies out of the way, and slid off the panel of flooring that hid my stash.

My stash of photos, my stash of money, the stash that would get me through anything short of a nuclear blast. All here, thank God.

But my altar, humble as it had been, had been destroyed, the statues smashed, the candles forever extinguished, my offerings reduced to memory, nothing more. A photo of Grandma Ruth had been torn apart, the frame on the floor, now cracked and broken, beyond repair.

In nearly every room, there was damage and evidence of rage and derangement. Even in Isabella's room. I knew Paul was behind this, knew it with every fiber of my being, and pressed my fists against my eyes to hold back a torrent of tears. When had he done this? Before he'd gone to La Playa? It had to have been then—he had arrived later than we had, much later. *You fucker, you sick fucker.*

My hands dropped away from my face, and I took a long, slow look around my daughter's room. *Remember this, Sam. Next time you're about to make an excuse for Paul, remember this.* Her bed frame had been destroyed, her chest of drawers had been ravaged, her closet had been turned into a nightmare of empty hangers with clothes puddled everywhere. My bed, my comfortable king, had a knife sticking up out of the middle, impaling a printed note that read: *Do not pass GO. Do NOT collect two hundred buckaroos.*

Monopoly. Paul and I had played Monopoly a couple of times with friends. But how could I prove he had done this?

At some point, John apparently had called 911, and now sirens shrieked through the neighborhood. I assumed that John opened the gate and the front door for them because when I finally went out into the living room, he was speaking to a short, muscular man in a Malibu police uniform.

"Lieutenant Gotti, this is Samantha DeMarco."

Gotti? Really? His name was *Gotti*? Who said the universe didn't have a sense of humor?

"Evening, ma'am. Mr. Steeling filled me in on the basics." His blue eyes wandered around the living room, pausing here, there. "Do you know yet if anything was stolen?"

"I . . . I haven't had a chance to check. The level of destruction . . . is . . ." I shook my head.

"Do you have any enemies, ma'am?"

I nearly choked. *Well, hey, guy, where the hell would you like me to start?* "Probably."

"Have you received any threats recently?"

"Threats?"

"Through email, hang-up calls . . ."

"There's a note impaled in my bed with a knife."

"What's the note say?"

I told him. Gotti held an iPad as he asked questions, and kept tapping it, entering information. "Christ," he muttered. "Sickos come in every variety. Does anyone live in the guesthouse above the garage?"

"My assistant, Marvin Castelli. He isn't home right now."

"Was the guesthouse broken into?"

"No," John replied. "I checked as I was calling nine one one."

"So the guesthouse was unlocked?" Gotti asked.

John shook his head. "I peered through the windows and didn't see anything out of place."

The forensic team—four men and two women—came into the living room, and Gotti directed them to start at the other end of the house. One of the men whistled as he took in all the destruction. "Wow, someone's got an ax to grind."

"A psycho," John said.

"And is it just the two of you who live here?" Gotti asked us.

"John doesn't live here. It's just my daughter and me. She's spending the night at a friend's."

"Do you have security cameras on the property, Ms. DeMarco?"

"No." But by tomorrow night I would. I should have done that sooner, but a part of me had felt that if I'd had security cameras installed right after Isabella and I moved here, then I might attract circumstances that would require them. Ha. Looked as if I'd attracted the circumstances regardless. In fact, right about now, armed guards sounded even better than security cameras or a ferocious Doberman. Hell, maybe I'd have bars put on all the windows and metal grates installed over the doors.

Tap, tap, went Gotti's fingers. "How many remotes are there for the front gate?"

"Three. Marvin, my daughter, and I each have one."

"And they're all accounted for?"

"As far as I know."

"Any spares anywhere in the house? Maybe in your car?"

"No. But anyone could climb over that gate."

"Are there security lights at the foot of the driveway, around the gate?"

"Yes. They're supposed to come on automatically, but

didn't. I thought it was odd, but we didn't stop to check the bulbs. Maybe the bulbs burned out." But even as I said this, I knew that wasn't the case.

Gotti snapped his fingers and called to one of the forensics people. "Joe, get someone down to the gate to dust for prints, specifically on the security lights. It's a long shot, but let's go for every long shot we've got."

"On my way," Joe said, and headed for the front door.

"It's going to take several hours for the forensics team to go through everything, ma'am," Gotti said. "You're welcome to stay in the house, but my advice is to use the guesthouse till we're done."

"There is one thing you should know," I said. "You asked if I had enemies. A man, a producer, has been stalking me."

Gotti's eyes lit up. "His name?"

"Paul Jannis," John said.

In my head, I saw my half million dollars sprout wings and fly away, like some stupid scene from a cartoon.

"Your relationship to Mr. Jannis?" Gotti asked.

"He optioned my novel and screenplay and is one of the producers on the film that's being shot by Gallery Studios," I replied. "We, uh, were dating for six weeks or so, then split up recently."

"I see."

Yeah, he probably did. He probably saw a lot of this kind of madness. "I'd like to get a few things out of my office and bedroom before you start."

"Sure thing, ma'am. Please be sure to change passwords on your bank accounts and any other private financial information. Same with your email addresses."

"I don't have a computer anymore. That's going to be difficult to do right now."

"If you own an iPad, do it from that."

"There's a computer in the guesthouse. I can do it there.

You think the person who did this took information off my computer first?"

"It wouldn't be the first time."

I turned away, but Gotti suddenly said, "Ms. DeMarco, we're going to be dusting for prints. I'll need a list of names of the individuals who have been in the house in the last month."

"Paul Jannis is at the top of the list. I'll email you the other names before you finish up here."

In my bathroom, I gathered up a few toiletries and stuffed them into a backpack. I gathered up some clothes, added them to my pack, then went into my office and cleaned out the hiding place in the closet floor. I put everything—photos, cash, jewelry—into the pack. One slow glance around the room told me a few of the books might be salvaged, but not much else.

I felt so overwhelmed by the extent of the destruction that for long moments I just stood there, struggling to understand the sort of rage that would prompt someone to do this.

Tony had been capable of this kind of rage. Alec, too. But Alec's rage had been kept under wraps most of the time and had sneaked out only when he'd felt cornered. Then there was Vito. And Paul. I knew—a deep-down sort of knowing—that I had done the right thing when I told Gotti that a producer had been stalking me. John was ready to fire Paul once his deal was cemented. Liza could make her recommendations to Brian, but the bottom line was that she was simply the newest employee and didn't have any clout about who was hired or fired. In the end, until John became a partner, the decision for firing Paul was left to Brian King and George Prince. In other words, a fifty/fifty chance. But now that I'd given Gotti his name, Paul would be questioned, he would be a suspect. Perhaps that would tilt things in favor of *firing*. Maybe it would overcome the factor called *profit*.

"You ready?" John asked, coming up behind me. "The forensics team wants to get started."

I nodded, grabbed my pack, and navigated the field of debris. My phone rang; Marvin's name came up in the window. I took the call.

"Sam, thank God you answered. I was thinking the worst. I'm parked at the gate, and the cop out here won't let me in. What happened?"

"The house was broken into. I'll tell the lieutenant to have his guy let you in. I need to stay at the guesthouse while forensics does their thing."

"Good enough."

John and I hurried into the living room, where I told Gotti the situation with Marvin. He took care of it immediately. We traded cell numbers and email addresses, then John and I continued on outside. "Well?" he said. "Paul or Vito?"

"Paul."

"Then he must have done it before he went to La Playa. I'm sorry you had to go through this, Sam."

"Me, too. I appreciate that you stuck around. I don't do well with cops."

He chuckled. "Me, neither. But, hey, he's a Gotti. It almost made me feel like I was back in Brooklyn."

We both laughed—for a moment we were united by this inside joke. We were in the car then, headed to the guesthouse. Lights shone at the bottom of the hill, lights from the police vehicles, and I could see Marvin driving through the gate.

"If you need help cleaning up your place tomorrow, just holler. I'll get Gallery's cleaning service out here."

"That'd be great, thanks."

He pulled up in front of the guesthouse, stopped. "Sam, I . . ."

"Let's just take things a day at a time, okay?" I slipped

my arms around his neck, hugging him. "I just need some time to process things." *Yes, like process this man that is suddenly back in my life from thirty years ago, but is also my main source of financing for my dream. Yeah, I'd say a lot to process.*

"A day at a time is better than not seeing you again."

"Thank you for the lovely dinner, John. And it was wonderful meeting Nick and Nina."

"Let me know about the cleaning service."

"I will. I'll text you tomorrow. Thanks."

I got out of the car just as Marvin drove up. He hopped out and hurried over, then John honked and waved and drove down toward the gate.

"The house is a wreck, Marvin."

"So what. At least you're okay. C'mon, I'll fix you a strong coffee or a drink or whatever you want."

"And then I've got to spend hours changing passwords on all my accounts."

The guesthouse was spacious enough for both of us, two bedrooms and a loft where Marvin had set up his office, a small living room and kitchen with a great porch that overlooked the Pacific. That was where we sat, sipping cappuccinos and catching up on everything that had happened. While we talked, I went to work on my iPad, changing passwords, making a new password list.

I finally told Marvin about Vito, and he didn't seem the least bit shocked by what I had done.

"I wouldn't have been that gracious, Sam. Do you think . . ." He waved a hand vaguely toward the house.

"No. It was Paul. I'm sure of it."

"Some of the stories Flannigan told me about him are appalling."

"But appalling in the sense of what he did to the inside of the house?"

"You mean, is Paul a psycho?"

"Yeah, I guess that's what I mean."

Marvin ran his palms over his shorts. "When he's been drinking, he apparently can be."

"I gave his name to the investigating officer."

"Good."

"But a part of me feels as if I've kicked a guy when he's down. And suppose he wasn't the one who broke into the house? Suppose it wasn't Paul *or* Vito? Maybe I've got an enemy I don't know about, someone who despises me so much that he felt compelled to invade and violate my home?"

Marvin mulled this over in that way he had, his eyes fixed on his coffee mug, his forehead thrown into a chaos of wrinkles. "Look, you don't have a mean bone in your body. You just got dealt a really shitty hand in terms of parents, and it has had repercussions in terms of the kind of men you attract. But that's a pattern that can be broken, Sam. And maybe you broke it tonight when you told the cop about Paul. Maybe it got broken when you met John."

"If Paul goes completely over the edge, am I going to have to buy bulletproof vests for Isabella and me? Will I have to hire personal bodyguards? Will he come after Isabella? Is he that kind of psycho, Marvin?"

"If he's responsible for the damage inside the house, then he's already gone over the edge."

My cell rang again. It was Lieutenant Gotti. "Ms. DeMarco, Liza Corrlinks is at the gate. Do you know her?"

"Yes, you can let her in."

"It's going to be a long night, ma'am. We probably won't be outta here till four or five a.m."

"Okay, thanks for letting me know, Lieutenant Gotti."

"Gotti?" Marvin snickered. "A cop named Gotti? Are you kidding me?"

"Yeah, pretty weird. He probably never hears the end of it. Liza's on her way in. Did you call her?"

"Nope. Maybe John did."

I walked outside to greet Liza as she pulled up in her Mercedes. "Holy crap, Sam. I was on my home and decided to swing by your place, and what the hell do I see? Cops everywhere. What's going on? What happened?" She hooked her arm through mine, and we walked toward the guesthouse. "Are you okay?"

So for the second time in a few hours, I went through the whole story. By Monday, the break-in would probably be reported on the police blotter of the *Malibu News,* and everyone in town would know what had happened. King and Prince would know about it.

But the truth was that I probably wouldn't get to the set on Monday. It would take time to get everything put away again, to buy furniture to replace what had been damaged, to install new locks in the door, to have the security company wire the house and the property with cameras or whatever it was they did. My home would become a kind of prison, a surveillance nightmare.

And that pissed me off.

Maybe it *was* time for me to speak directly to Paul, to confront him when he was sober, when we were in a crowd, at a café, or even at the studios. Yes, maybe there. If he exploded, it would be witnessed by everyone—the entire cast and crew and by King, Prince, and John. Maybe it was time for me to goad him in full view of the people with whom he worked, so that everyone could see the monster inside Paul, what his son called the *big dark shadow.*

My imagination seized on this scenario and ran with it. And suddenly, in my head, I could see Paul pulling out a weapon, the same one he'd used to shoot at my photo, and opening fire on the cast and crew. And then another Aurora or Sandy Hook might play out, a tragedy triggered by a psycho.

How could I have been so wrong about yet another

man? Weren't there signs right from the beginning that I should have heeded—and hadn't?

Paul Jannis should have been named Paul Janus, the two-faced Roman god in mythology who ruled beginnings and transitions and was usually depicted with two faces. One face supposedly faced the future, the other peered into the past.

But to me, Janus meant *two-faced.* I'd had this thought about Paul rather frequently, that he was actually two people, with two distinct personalities living inside of him. He was like the character Joanne Woodward had played in *The Three Faces of Eve*, suffering from multiple-personality disorder.

And maybe, like the Woodward character, the schism in him was so profound that one personality didn't have any idea what the other personality did. If Paul were responsible for the destruction in my house, the Paul who—when he couldn't get his way through charm and money—used brute force, if he himself had actually done it, then the personable Paul—the successful producer and Hollywood power broker—might not even know what his darker self was capable of. The personality split could be that complete; he could be suffering from what used to be referred to as multiple-personality disorder and was now called dissociative-identity disorder.

In people who were afflicted with this disease, the schism between the personalities was so total that one personality could have diabetes while the other didn't. One could be allergic to penicillin while the other wasn't. Each mind and consciousness ruled each body and its physiology, chemistry, everything. With that disease, Paul Jannis the charmer wouldn't remember that Paul Jannis, the Darth Vader side of the equation, had destroyed my house.

And that thought terrified me more than anything else. Hollywood's level of dysfunction was so great that many of the people here couldn't recognize mental illness even when it was shoved in their faces. A guy like George Prince could have that conversation with Paul down by the swimming hole—threatening to fire him if he didn't shape up—but in practically the next breath, he could remark that firing Paul would compromise the film. *He wasn't connecting the dots.*

Liza and Marvin connected the dots, for sure. They were New Yorkers. And John, also a New Yorker and an ex-mafioso, connected the dots. Was that the fundamental difference here? As Lauren's mom, Becka, had pointed out, Malibu was basically a twenty-one-mile shoreline inhabited mostly by people at the very high end of the entertainment industry. Their perceptions and values, their worldviews, weren't like those of us from Brooklyn, whose childhoods had been about food stamps for some, owning stolen jewelry and delivering goods for the mob.

I had taken action against Paul tonight. And I didn't intend to stay away from the set. Why should I?

I felt liberated by the plan. In the past, with Tony, with Alec, even with Paul, I had tried to ignore what was going on, hide my head in the sand, look away in the hopes that the problem—whatever it was—would disappear. And of course the problem had never disappeared. It had only grown larger, more pervasive, until it had blown up in my face.

No more.

By Sunday evening, my property was wired with hidden cameras. Tomorrow morning, security personnel would begin a twenty-four/seven patrol outside and around my property. It was the direct result of my poor judgment about men and wasn't what I'd imagined for Isabella and myself. But, as the saying goes, better safe than sorry.

John had dispatched the cleaning company that Gallery used, and the crew had done a masterly job restoring order to my sanctuary. At the moment, Isabella and I were making lists of furniture, dishes, and other items that we needed to replace.

"I don't need a new bed frame, Mom. I like having my bed on the floor. It's kind of Zen, you know?"

"We can go totally Zen and buy some bamboo furniture and redo the wallpaper, change the flooring, whatever you want."

"I'll go online and see what I can find. Oh, I almost forgot to remind you. There's a teacher's in-service day tomorrow. No school. Can I come to the set with you?"

How had I forgotten that? I usually circled holidays and teacher in-service days on my calendar so that I could spend time with Isabella. "That'd be fantastic!"

"Will I get to meet your new guy? Will he be there?"

"He's not my new guy." Yet. "We've had only one date. But, yeah, he'll be there." And Paul probably would be there, too. Even though Isabella had never come out and said she disliked Paul, I knew that she did.

"I'll check him out and give you my assessment, Mom." She grinned as she said it, then turned back to her iPad and began checking Web sites for furniture ideas.

I watched her for a moment, her lustrous hair flowing like a dark river down her back, her long, nimble fingers tapping away on her iPad. Isabella, my greatest joy, always and forever.

I went into my office, now sparse and sparkling clean. The crew had hauled away the debris of broken furniture and shattered glass, and my floor was now so clean I could eat off it if I felt like it.

I spent the next hour fiddling around with the security system, synching the video feed to my iPad. The feed was private. But if the house security system was breached, the company would know about it and would alert the police, who would be here within minutes unless they received a call from us saying that the alarm had been tripped accidentally.

Even though my iMac had been destroyed, I decided that my MacBook Air—which was at the office—could fill in and get the job done. I would just bring it home with me every night.

Marvin and Flannigan dropped by, and I showed them both how to use the system and engage the alarms, which had also been installed in the guesthouse. "Are these security guards going to be armed?" asked Flannigan.

"No." I didn't want guns around my house and property.

"Then if someone tries to get in, what do they do?" Marvin asked.

"They call the cops."

"If Paul was behind this break-in," Flannigan said, "or did it himself, then being at the restaurant will be his alibi. He may have sent Donaldson or Olmoso to do the dirty work."

Maybe. But in my bones, I knew Paul had done it.

"You were his moral compass, Jim."

"Ha. He rarely listened to me. I was just the dude who cleaned up after him when he was six sheets to the wind."

"Are you going to feel weird about being on the set with him there tomorrow?" Marvin asked.

"Weird?" Jim ran his fingers through his thick copper-colored hair. "No. I'll feel relieved that he's not my problem anymore. And I'm deeply grateful to you two and to Liza for giving me options."

Monday morning, we were on the road by eight, just Isabella and me in my car, and Flannigan and Marvin following us in his car. Since Liza's car was in the garage, we swung by her place to pick her up.

For her first day on the job as King's new PR person, she was dressed casually chic, a look that she had perfected and that would fit right in with the way everyone else dressed at Gallery.

"Wow, Liza, you look fantastic," Isabella said as Liza got into the car.

"Isabella, hon, wonderful to see you. I'm so excited you finally get to come to the set! I'll show you around, introduce you to everyone."

"I'm going to love this," Isabella said. "And I brought my swimsuit so I can try that swimming hole Mom told me about."

"Well, since it's a teacher's in-service day all over the county, maybe there will be some other kids around," Liza said. "Brian has a sixteen-year-old son."

As they chatted away, Lieutenant Gotti called with an

update: forensics hadn't been able to lift any clear prints off the security lights. "But we'll find him, Ms. DeMarco. It just may take some time."

"I understand. And thanks for the update, I appreciate it."

"You bet. By the way, while I was updating my notes on the break-in, I came across a file about an arrest that involved an older man who trespassed at your daughter's school and then harassed her."

Shit. "Yes. What about it?"

"Well, I followed up on it, thinking that maybe he was the perp who broke into your house. After his arrest, he was evaluated psychiatrically, then Baker Acted. He spent three days in a psychiatric ward, and was released. One of the nurses at the facility actually drove him to the airport, and he presumably got on a plane and went home."

Presumably. That word worried me. Vito was a slippery devil, and if there had been a way to sneak out of the airport, he probably had done so. "Do you know if the nurse actually escorted him to check-in and saw him board the plane?"

"I don't know. I'll find out."

"I'd appreciate it, Lieutenant. I just don't want any repeat performances."

"Can't say that I blame you. We have his prints on file, though, so I'm going to run them against whatever we got from your house and see if anything shows up. I'll be in touch."

"Have you spoken to Paul Jannis yet?"

"Yes, I did. He has an alibi, says that he was at La Playa, having dinner with members of the cast, that you even saw him there."

"Where was he before he got to La Playa?"

"In conference with his attorney about his son's problems."

"Did the attorney confirm that?"

"Yes."

Then the attorney is lying to cover up for him, I thought.

"But don't worry, Ms. DeMarco. He's on my radar."

"Thanks again, I appreciate the update."

At Gallery Studios, we parked to the side of the main building. We were early enough so that there were still electric carts lined up in the lot, keys in the ignition, for cast and crew to use to drive themselves to studio four. The five of us crowded into one of them, and Liza drove us along that hard-packed path that led past the swimming hole.

A light fog swirled across the ground, and the air was still cool enough so that the area around the swimming hole was deserted. But once the air warmed up, I was pretty sure that would change, particularly if there were any other kids on the set today. Maybe John and I would come down here for a repeat performance of our last visit.

And maybe not.

Now that I knew the truth about who he was, I wasn't sure what I felt about him—an enormous, visceral attraction, yes—that hadn't changed. Even thirty years ago, I'd felt that. I'd felt a visceral attraction for Tony, Alec, and Paul, too. But there had to be something more than hormones. I would like to blame all my past mistakes on hormones, but I knew that wasn't the case.

"What scenes are they shooting today?" Liza asked. "I didn't get a chance to look at the script notes you sent me, Marvin."

"The Sunday-night date with Tony, the apartment scenes. Then in studio two, it's going to be the club scene at Platinum. Renée sent me some photos of the set, and it looks so genuine you'd think you were in Brooklyn. And there're thirty or forty extras today in the Platinum scenes."

"Does the club still exist?" Flannigan asked.

"Yeah," I replied. "But now it's a strip club."

Flannigan laughed. "Well, that's what thirty years will do, right? I mean, just look at all the changes we've seen in our lifetimes. The Internet changed everything. Isabella hasn't even lived in a time without cell phones and the Internet, without Facebook and all the social media."

"No Facebook?" Isabella exclaimed. "No iPhone? No iPod? No texting? How boring would that be?"

Marvin passed me his iPad with the photos the art director had sent him, and suddenly I was back there on that night with Tony, anxiously wondering how the hell I was going to get into the club since I was underage. But Tony had fake ID that said I was Priscilla Montiglio, twenty-two years old. Her photo didn't look much like me. Not a problem for Tony. He had known the fat bouncer, who had glanced at the ID, smirked, unhooked the velvet rope, and ushered us into the noise and smoke and surrounding darkness.

I remembered that "Love Machine" by the Miracles had been blasting through the place. Guys in tight pants and nylon shirts unbuttoned halfway down their chests gyrated to the music with girls whose breasts bulged out of tiny halter tops. They all wore high-heeled platform shoes. It was like something out of *Saturday Night Fever*.

Tony had led me past the bar and along the edge of the dance floor to a restaurant area, where we'd sat with Richie and Vin and their dates. I remembered how much I detested Richie. He had recently beat up my closest friend, Janice, and here he was at the club with another girl.

But that was the mob's MO with women. Take Vin Priganti. His family had overseen the mafia activity in Brooklyn, and everyone had known it. You didn't cross Vin. His father, Tino, had built an empire on gambling, theft, loan-sharking, and prostitution. And the torch would pass eventually to Vin, so when he had issued a command to his peers, everyone jumped into action. He was a pig through and through.

I wondered what had happened to him, to all the Brooklyn Boys. If any of them were still alive, would they recognize themselves when the movie came out? Probably not. They hadn't really seen themselves as *bad guys*. They were just doing what their fathers and grandfathers ten times removed had done before them. It was like a trait passed down genetically from father to son.

"Looks amazing, doesn't it?" Marvin said.

"Renée's incredible," I replied. "Maybe Gallery should keep her on payroll for all their film and TV work."

"I'll suggest it," Liza said. "But I bet Brian is already thinking about it."

"Hey," Isabella said, "can I get hired as one of the extras?"

"You can ask," I replied.

"They'd probably love it," Liza remarked.

As we pulled up in front of studio four, I noticed that one of the cars parked in the lot was a 1972 black-and-beige Toyota, the exact vehicle that Tony had owned, that he'd driven to Platinum's that night. "Is that car   "

"It is," Marvin said with a laugh. "Hey, Gallery does things right, all the way down the line."

I could almost see my younger self in that car, thrilled to be with the handsome Tony Kroon, but wanting to say something to him about what his buddy Richie had done to my friend Janice. I hadn't because I'd promised Janice I wouldn't, so I had made an inane comment that I'd never forgotten: *Hey, do they really have dikes in Holland?*

Ya mean lesbos?

His reply should've been a dead giveaway about the sort of person he was. But I was just fifteen and hopelessly naïve. Now it was thirty years later, and in spite of Tony Kroon and Vito and all the rest of them, I had written myself into a better story. The story wasn't perfect yet. It was a diamond in the rough that I would continue to polish and work at until it was exactly the way I wanted it.

In the studio's front room, a spread of food had been laid out, breakfast stuff so varied it would satisfy any palate. The cast and crew were milling around, and Liza immediately started working the room with Isabella, introducing her to everyone.

My daughter was starstruck when she met Jenean, Camilla, and Susan. Within moments, though, the three women were plying her with questions about school and her interests and whether she wanted to write, too. Then they herded her through the breakfast line. Marvin and Flannigan were talking to the crew. I started to get into the breakfast line but spotted Kelly, from the Malibu Motel, and hurried over to her.

"Kelly, it's so good to see you." We hugged hello. "How're you doing?"

"Just great, Sam. I can't tell you how fantastic it is to be out of that clerk job. I'm so excited about this movie."

"Are they shooting a Brooklyn-girl scene today?"

"They might. Mr. King said it depended on how well things go this morning. He asked us to come in just in case. If not today, then this week sometime." She lowered her voice. "Any news about Vito?"

"Yeah. We'll catch up, okay? I need to get a bite to eat."

"Sounds good."

I slipped into the breakfast line behind Isabella. "Mom, they're all so *nice*," she whispered. "After we eat, before the shooting begins, they said we can take some photos together outside."

"Fantastic, love."

"Does Susan look like Grandma Ruth did?"

"With makeup. And she has her personality down perfectly. You'll see."

"Thanks for letting me tag along."

Across the way, King, Prince, and Paul emerged from another room. Paul looked to be in good spirits, laughing at something one of the other men had said. Then he saw me, and his laughter dried up faster than rainwater in a desert. I glanced down at the food and helped myself to scrambled eggs and bacon and a biscuit smothered in honey.

I could feel Paul's eyes on me as I followed Isabella through the line, adding slices of cheese and fresh fruit to my plate. Scalding eyes. Eyes that shot those poison daggers at my spine.

"Let's eat at one of the tables outside," I suggested to Isabella.

"Great."

The picnic tables were a recent addition, and because the weather was gorgeous, they were all filled. Renée Tennerin, sitting with one of the artists in her crew, waved us over. I introduced Isabella to both women, and Renée introduced the artist, Barbara.

"Marvin showed me the photos of the Platinum set, Renée. It looks exactly as I remember it."

"Wonderful. It took some Googling to find old photos of the place, but once it's dark and the music is rockin'—and the extras are wearing those *Saturday Night Fever* clothes—it'll be like the original Platinum's was teleported here."

"You think they'd let me be an extra?" Isabella asked.

"They might," Renée said.

"I heard that a couple of the extras were no-shows," Barbara said.

"You know how to dance?" Renée asked.

"Sure."

Renée snapped her fingers. "Like, boogie on down?"

"Definitely."

Isabella snapped her fingers, brought out her iPod and a mini speaker, scrolled to a song, and was suddenly on her feet, dancing, swinging her hips, her feet moving rhythmically, her dark hair flying. Renée and Barbara started clapping, and pretty soon, so did everyone else. Isabella was so into the dancing that she moved with her eyes shut and didn't realize she had such a large, enthralled audience. When she was done, everyone cheered and clapped, and she glanced around, obviously thrilled. She gave a quick little bow, then disconnected the speaker and put it and the iPod back in her bag.

"Hey, Brian," Renée called, "Some of the extras were no-shows. Do you think Isabella can fill in?"

King, Prince, and John—where had *he* come from?—apparently had seen the whole thing, and King flashed a thumbs-up. "You're hired, young lady. Renée, after she eats, get her over to costumes to be fitted. We can email the paperwork later. Welcome to the troupe, Isabella."

Just like that, my beautiful daughter had become a member of the cast of extras for the scenes at Platinum's. How was that for Hollywood magic?

John made his way toward us. He looked good enough to eat, decked out in jeans that fit him perfectly, a blue Polo shirt. His eyes met mine, then he greeted Renée and Barbara. "Got enough room for one more?"

"Of course," I said, and slid over on the bench to make room for him between Isabella and me.

"That dancing was awesome, Isabella." He extended his hand. "I'm John Steeling."

"Thanks, Mr. Steeling. Nice to meet you."

"I'll be emailing all the paperwork to your mom."

"Wow, this is so cool," she said. "My friends are never going to believe this. But if it's a club, I need to look like I'm twenty-one, right?"

"Makeup will fix you up," Renée said. "Don't worry about that. In fact, as soon as you're finished eating, Barb and I will walk you over to costumes and makeup."

Within minutes, John and I were alone at the table, the two of us on the same bench, his thigh touching mine. I realized, again, that I wouldn't be here now, in this moment, if Paul hadn't optioned my book and given me the chance to write the screenplay. I was grateful. But the bottom line was that he was just a more sophisticated version of the men I'd known in Brooklyn.

"Did you get your house squared away?" John asked.

"Pretty much. We have to replace some furniture and dishes, that sort of thing. The cleaning crew was great, John. I really appreciate your sending them. The house has never been so clean."

"Brian and George both know about the break-in at your place." He paused. "And Brian asked if you'd been paid yet. And so did George."

"What'd you tell them?"

"The truth. I told Brian that I want Paul fired, that I'll cover what he owes you."

"What'd he say to that?"

"He asked me why. I told him everything. And then he said that Paul will be gone by the end of today."

I started to say something, but just then Prince, standing on the steps, shouted, "Okay, people, listen up. We're going to start shooting in studio four in fifteen minutes. After that winds up, we'll have lunch, then shoot in studio two. If you don't have a copy of today's script notes, raise your hand and we'll make sure you get a copy."

As John raised his hand, my phone vibrated, and I slipped it out of my back pocket. A text message. From Paul.

Can we talk privately?

I glanced around the crowd, looking for him, and spotted him sitting with members of the lighting crew. He was busy texting and wasn't aware that I was watching him.

No.

He glanced up a moment later, and so did I. He glared at me; I shrugged. He looked down at his phone again and another text came through.

R u sleeping w/him?

I didn't dignify the question with a response. I knew he was watching me, so I deliberately leaned in closer to John and whispered, "Has your deal with Gallery gone through?"

"We signed the papers yesterday. Why?"

"Just curious. I'm glad this is working out for you and for them. It seems like a good fit all the way around."

"You ready to go to Brooklyn, Sam, for the shooting there?"

"It'll be weird, but, yeah, I'm ready. You have new dates?"

"Not yet. The—"

"Excuse me," Paul said, suddenly appearing behind us. "I'd like to speak to Sam privately."

I glanced at him, stood, grabbed my bag. "I've got nothing to say, Paul. Leave me alone."

I started walking away to join the crowd of crew and cast that was headed back inside the studio. But Paul rushed up behind me, seized my arm, spun me around. "Did you tell King you hadn't gotten the rest of your money yet?"

I wrenched my arm free. "Did you break into my house and wreck everything?" I shot back.

"Did I *what*?"

"You heard what I said."

"Why the hell would I do *that*?"

"How should I know? Why the hell do you keep stalking me? Confronting me? Isn't it obvious that I don't want anything more to do with you? That we're done? That there's *nothing* going on?"

"*Nothing going on?*" he snapped. "There's plenty going on. I *discovered* you. I *own* you."

His words wiped out my guilt. Before I could say anything, John grabbed Paul by the back of his shirt and jerked him away from me. "You don't grab her arm like that, asshole. She said to leave her alone. Got it?"

Paul, flustered and pissed, pushed John away from him. "Get lost. This isn't your business."

Aw, shit, I thought.

"It's very much my business," John snapped. "You owe Sam half a million bucks. You've breached your contract with her."

"Who the hell do you think you are, Steeling? You don't work for this studio, you don't—"

"I'm now one of the owners." John swept past him, his expression unreadable, like stone, and hooked his arm through mine. As we moved away from Paul, John said, "I think we're done out here, Sam."

"*We* may be, but Paul isn't," I said softly.

"He is. Trust me, he is."

But just as we reached the front steps to the studio, Paul barreled into John from behind, body-slammed him like some NFL player. John pitched forward, I stumbled away from him, and John and Paul both crashed to the steps, rolled to the ground, and fought like a couple of feral dogs. Carl Davidson, the director, and a couple of the line producers ran over to them, shouting and waving their arms, trying to pull them apart.

Even though John was taller than Paul, far more fit, and outweighed him by at least thirty pounds of muscle, Paul—in his adrenaline-fueled rage—clung to him like Velcro. They rolled and punched each other, and Davidson finally managed to grab the back of Paul's shirt and jerk him back far enough from John so that John's legs trapped Paul against the ground, and his massive hands gripped the sides of

Paul's head and jerked it upward, toward his own face. He hissed, "I'm saying this just once. Back off."

Then he vaulted to his feet, and Paul fell back against the ground and just lay there, his nose bloody, his lip cut and bleeding, his hands fisted, his eyes wild. He started laughing, a weird, hysterical sound, and his fists pounded the ground.

"She's that great in the sack?" Paul shouted. "Wow, I definitely missed something."

John tensed. I felt it in his muscles, his cells, his very being. I was that tuned in to the presence of a man with whom I'd never been intimate. How could that be?

"Ignore him," I said quietly. "We're not in Brooklyn."

Davidson and the line producers stood nearby, and members of the cast and crew were watching from the windows, the open doorway, the sidelines. Overhead, birds flew past, a murder of crows, cawing loudly. Suddenly, I saw Paul in my peripheral vision, rushing toward John. Paul crashed into him from the side, John pitched to the right, rolled, and Paul hurled himself on top of him and began to pummel him with his fists.

Now people poured out the front door of the studio, King and Prince in the lead and Liza not far behind them. King grabbed Paul, yanked him upward, and King clasped him by the shoulders.

"You're done, Paul. You're done on this film."

Paul's arms swung to his sides as though he simply couldn't maintain the necessary strength to do otherwise. He blinked hard. "You . . . you . . . can't *fire* me."

"I just did. Gather up your shit and get off this property."

Liza dropped a pack at Paul's feet. "Here's your stuff."

"*You,* Liza? You're just a broad in her fifties who thinks she's got clout, but you're just pathetic. Maybe more pathetic than Sam."

Liza reacted with more fury than I'd ever seen in her.

She stepped toward Paul and slapped him across the face. "You're an asshole, Paul."

With that, Paul snatched up his pack, wiped his arm across his bloody nose, and stalked off toward one of the electric carts.

I felt numb, and relieved.

There's a Hawaiian Shamanic chant—called Ho'opono-pono—that made its way around the Internet after one of the major oil spills, and it ran through my head now:

I am sorry.
Please forgive me.
I love you.
Thank you.

I repeated it to myself several times and suddenly understood its full meaning. We must forgive ourselves first. Without that forgiveness, we're just a conglomeration of experiences. Rootless. Directionless. So as I watched Paul hurry to his car, I *forgave* him, *thanked* him, felt enormous gratitude for the changes he had ushered into my life. I *honored* the fact that I was here now because of Paul. But did I *feel* these words, this prayer of forgiveness? If I didn't feel it, *genuinely* feel it, then the prayer was just empty syllables.

I knew Paul was responsible for the break-in at my house. I also knew that something within me was attracting circumstances and situations similar to those I'd experienced in Brooklyn. It was the Bonti part of me that probably needed intensive therapy—although true love might do the trick, too!—and all that the Bonti in me wanted just then was a bit of peace.

Once we were inside the studio, people came over to me and expressed their relief that Paul had been fired. Apparently, others on the cast and crew had had confrontations with him, too, but hadn't said anything at the time because he was the producer.

I felt enormously relieved that others had seen this side of him before, that it wasn't just me, that it was something inside of Paul, unresolved issues, power issues, money issues, a messed-up son, a bad marriage, a messed-up childhood, who knew? *Issues*. But the main issue was that Paul had never learned to take responsibility for his own actions and decisions.

A shrink would have a field day, no doubt, with most of the people who worked at this studio—or in the Hollywood entertainment business. Toss a bunch of creative types together and you were sure to find all the Jungian archetypes—heroes, villains, martyrs, saviors, psychopaths, geniuses.

But Paul still scared me. Paul frightened me more than Vito, Tony, Alec, than all of them put together. And that was saying something.

John's arm came around my waist, and he pressed his face into my hair and whispered, "Swimming hole this afternoon? After the scene at Platinum's?"

"A date," I whispered back, and he moved away from me, through the crowd, to get the shooting under way.

TWELVE

The filming of the scenes at Platinum's in studio two were so awesome, I nearly forgot about the ugliness earlier with Paul. I didn't experience the emotional angst I'd felt during my first day on the set, when they'd filmed the early scenes with my grandmother and mother. Part of the reason was that my daughter was stunning as one of the extras.

Makeup had turned her from a teenager to a twenty-one-year-old woman, and she danced and wowed everyone who was watching. It sort of freaked me out that in just a few years she would be going off to college and building her own life. And a few years later, she would be as old as she was supposed to be now. Five years. Where would *I* be in five years?

At one point, Liza was standing next to me and whispered, "You're seeing five years down the road, right? But don't fret. Isabella will be fine. Even more of a lovely human being than she is now." She gave my arm an affectionate squeeze, then added, "You aren't going to believe this, but Brian King asked me to dinner tomorrow evening."

"My God, that's fantastic!"

"I feel like a teenager. Butterflies in the stomach. Like that."

"I have a really good feeling about this, Liza."

"We'll see." She paused. "I used to think there weren't any nice men left in this town. I'm now reconsidering."

"Me, too."

We looked at each other, and the current that passed between us then was that linking soul sisters. She high-fived me, and we both struggled not to laugh out loud.

There were two takes of the scene at Platinum's, and several breaks, and when we finally wrapped for the day, a dozen pizzas arrived at the main building. The whole cast and crew sat outside at the picnic tables, in the splendid late-afternoon air.

Isabella, Liza, King, King's sixteen-year-old son, Brent, John, and I were at the same table. As I listened to the laughter and conversation, I realized this group was a kind of family, kindred spirits whose immediate goal was to bring my novel to life. My gratitude to these people, all of them, was so profound that I nearly wept for joy.

"Hey, Sam," John whispered. "This will last for a while. Want to watch the sun set at the swimming hole?" He touched my leg as he said this, his large, powerful hand warm against my thigh, and I suddenly hungered for that hand against my bare skin, for his mouth against mine, for our bodies fitting seamlessly together. And it wasn't just hormones or that visceral attraction. There was something else at work with this guy.

"Sounds perfect." I told Isabella that I'd be back in about thirty minutes and that she should just enjoy herself.

But she didn't need any encouragement from me. It was obvious that she was enjoying herself and that Brent was interested in her. He was a good-looking kid, a younger version of his father. He and Isabella were both competitive swimmers, and, yeah, he'd seen her dance. It worried me, this boy thing, this hormonal thing, particularly when I thought back to when I was about her age. At fifteen, I had lost my virginity to Tony Kroon. I understood that, despite

Isabella's Catholic school education, maybe it was time for a visit to Planned Parenthood.

John and I slipped away from the others and quickly realized it was too far to walk, so we took one of the electric carts to the swimming hole. He drove like a Manhattan cabbie, as though there were a wall of traffic he had to negotiate. The cart bounced over the hard-packed path—beneath a vast sky with blue melting into soft golds, streaks of orange—and veered into the trees.

He tapped the brake, the cart stopped, and he slipped his arm around my shoulders and drew me gently against him. "I've been wanting to do this all day," he said softly, and kissed me.

If life was composed of perfect moments strung together like lights on a Christmas tree, then this moment was certainly one of them. His mouth was warm against mine; his hands cupped the sides of my face, thumbs caressing my skin. My arms went around him, and his fingers strolled through my hair, as if to memorize its texture and even the shape of my skull.

My senses exploded wide open, and I was suddenly aware of the scent of his skin, his hair, his clothes; and of the smells in the air around us, the trees and the greenery and the water. Birds sang from the branches, a celebration of spring. When I drew back, the shadows cast by the trees surrounded us, embraced us, creating a cocoon of privacy.

"C'mon, let's walk down to the swimming hole," he said.

He took my hand, and we moved down the slippery path. The air here smelled loamy, rich, of moss and damp grass, and of the earth. I paused to remove my shoes. I wanted to feel this richness against my bare feet. He took off his shoes, too, and stood for a moment, wiggling his toes against the softness.

"In Brooklyn, I never went barefoot much," he said.

"But since I moved out here, I go barefoot every chance I get."

"I know what you mean." I pointed at my toes. "Look."

My toes slipped and slid through and under moss, wet grass, fallen leaves. The closer we got to the swimming hole, the damper the earth became, so that when we finally reached the edge of the water, our toes were black with mud. We laughed at the silliness of it all, how we were like a couple of city kids out in the country for the first time.

We moved farther up the bank, where the ground was relatively dry, and stretched out on our backs, arms folded under our heads, and peered upward, through the branches. The incident earlier today with Paul stood between us; I could feel it like a concrete wall. I lifted up on one elbow. "You're on Paul's shit list now, John, and I'm really sorry that I'm the cause of that."

"He's disliked me since the day we met. You're just the catalyst. And being on his shit list doesn't worry me. I've dealt with much worse. My concern is Paul coming after you. Psychos don't need a reason to do what they do, that's the disturbing thing."

"The security company I hired and the stuff I had installed on my property will make his coming after me a lot more difficult."

"More difficult, yeah, but not impossible, especially if you're anywhere but at home. Psychos usually find their way around obstacles. And unless you sue him, you probably won't see a dime of what he owes you."

"*Sue* him? That would probably cost me in legal fees what he owes me. Or it would cost me even more." I shook my head. "Besides, my aversion to lawyers is nearly equal to my aversion to cops."

"Did Liza review your contract with him?"

"Liza negotiated it. She got me one percent of gross."

"Good. That'll come directly from Gallery now."

I told him what Paul's son had said about his father using my photo for target practice. "And *that* worries me."

"Shit. Do you own a gun?"

"I'm allergic to guns. I figure that if you own one, then you may attract circumstances in which you'll have to use it."

John turned his head, looking at me, a smile tugging at the corners of his mouth. He touched the tip of his index finger to the tip of my nose. "Smart lady. I agree with you completely." *I do remember when we were younger and Tony was in the picture, that crazed murderer, mafia henchman of mine, and John liked me, a girl could tell, but he wouldn't dare act upon such a feeling or even look at me wrong. To a guy like Tony that's a sign of disrespect and there would be high consequences to pay, so he stayed away. Now here he is again. Fate has this funny way of showing up unexpectedly.*

He, too, lifted himself up on one elbow, and traced the contours of my face with a blade of grass; then he drew me toward him, his mouth meeting mine, his hand against the small of my back. Then we were lying on our sides on the cool ground, our tongues dueling. My fingers slipped through his thick dark hair, his hands traveled slowly down my back, over my hip, and I was so turned on that I felt like tearing his clothes off then and there.

We rolled across the grass, through light and shadows, laughing and touching each other, until we were nearly at the edge of the swimming hole. He covered my throat in soft, gentle kisses, as though he were inscribing a secret language against my skin. My skirt had hiked up and when his hand found my bare thigh, his fingers ducked beneath the hem and then between my legs.

I gasped at his touch, and he kissed me deeply, passionately. I felt his hardness against my leg and wanted him inside of me. I didn't care where we were—nothing mattered except the exquisite sensations he ignited in me. I knew this wasn't just hormones or chemistry; it went deeper than that. What I felt toward him was starting to bloom, blossom. Pretty soon, this feeling would be as huge and lush as those banyan trees I'd seen in Florida, gigantic beauties with roots so thick and deep they could withstand even hurricanes. He rolled my panties down and slipped his finger inside of me, moving it slowly, delicately, over and over again until I started groaning, my back arching. He drove me right to the edge, then suddenly we heard laughter somewhere close by and scrambled to our feet like a couple of guilty teenagers.

We laughed as we straightened our clothes, buttoned buttons, zipped up zippers, and laughed more as I stumbled around trying to pull my panties back into place. We ran toward the cart and tumbled inside, giggling so hard we both had tears rolling down our cheeks.

John turned the cart around just as a cart with Marvin and Flannigan appeared. Right behind them were Liza and Isabella, and behind them were King and Prince and Renée. We all waved to one another, and John and I joined the line of electric carts. I was still reeling from what had happened, from what I'd felt, and my heart hadn't yet settled down into its normal beat.

"You going to be on set tomorrow?" John asked.

"Probably not. I've got tons of emails and calls to return and more scripts to go through. Clara has pretty much been running the place by herself since shooting started."

"You free for dinner anytime this weekend?"

"I'll have to find out what Isabella's plans are." It sounded coy, but it was the truth. "I'll let you know."

"I'll fix you an Italian dinner like you've never had before."

"That sounds fantastic. I just realized I've never seen your place."

"It's pretty simple. Just a two-bedroom bungalow in the hills above Malibu. What kind of wine do you like?"

"Rosé."

"Rosé it will be. Any preference in Italian food?"

"I've never had an Italian dish that I didn't like. Do you actually cook?"

He laughed. "Yeah, I actually did a lot of cooking in prison for all the guys on my tier. Why? Is that rare in men or something?"

"Very rare in my experience of men. Most of the men I've known figure that cooking is women's work."

He clicked his tongue against his teeth. "Too bad. Old thinking. I actually learned to cook in the joint. We had job assignments, and that was mine. I got so good at it that the superintendent started using me for lunches and suppers when we had outside visitors."

It was as if we were now catching up on the minutiae of each other's lives, squeezing the details in between everything else.

"What about you, Sam? What do you enjoy?"

You. "I try to enjoy everything I do, but I particularly love being with Isabella, walking on the beach with her in the evenings. And I love to write. When I was younger, I could sit for hours and write. Now I'm usually so busy that I'm lucky if I can write for a few minutes every day. Not complaining, though. Running a production company is just a different expression of the creative process. What else do you cook?"

He laughed. "White clam sauce with linguini is my specialty. The sautéing of the garlic makes it perfect."

The line of carts slowed as we approached the main building. The actors were already waiting outside, and I suddenly wondered if any of them had seen John and me rolling around on the grass by the swimming hole. Had we been visible from the road?

As we all exited the carts, King called out, "Hey, everyone, listen up!"

Liza, Isabella, and Brent joined John and me. My daughter was glowing. She and Brent talked quietly, and I sensed their mutual attraction. Liza noticed my watching them and leaned in close to me and whispered, "Chill, Sam. He's a nice kid. Just like his dad."

Easy for her to say. She'd never had a daughter, and her three sons were adults.

"Okay, we're going to finish the Brooklyn-girl scenes this week, and if we don't need any retakes, then we'll head to Brooklyn next week," King said. "And we'll be ahead of schedule. Good job! Anyone have questions?"

"Where're we staying in Brooklyn—do we know yet?" asked someone in the crew.

"The Greenwich Hotel in Tribeca. It's close to Brooklyn and will be super-convenient to the shooting locations."

Murmurs of *fantastic* and *awesome* rippled through the crowd.

"Should we make reservations now?" asked Renée.

"Liza's going to take care of our travel arrangements," Prince said. "Our goal is to leave midweek and spend six or seven days there. We'll be shooting every day. Either George or I will get you the script notes for the scene locations before this weekend. As always, if you have questions or concerns, call or email me."

"One more question," said Camilla. "Will we have makeup and costume trailers or what?"

"We've reserved two penthouses. One of them will be for meals, makeup, costumes, everything. Then you'll travel to the locations by private bus." King glanced around the room. "Anything else?"

No one said anything.

"All right, then, let's get moving," King said.

The group broke up shortly afterward, and John and I went our separate ways. I wondered what Brooklyn would be like for both of us, what it would it be like to be there together again, even if back then we had known each other only long enough for a New Year's Eve mistletoe kiss.

As we reached the car, I turned my phone on—the first time I'd done so since the shoot had begun that morning—and found a text message from Priti, announcing that she had arrived in L.A. two days ago.

Can we meet tomorrow for lunch? Am so excited to see u!

Blu Jam. Noon. It'll be great to see u!

She texted back that the time and place were perfect and she would be there. As I slipped behind the steering wheel, another text came through, this one from John.

You are my stunner!

I smiled with satisfaction.

"Mom, Brent invited me to a party at his place on Sunday," Isabella said, sounding breathless. "Can I go?"

"What kind of party?"

"It's his birthday. His dad and grandparents will be there."

"So will I," Liza said. "Brian asked me to join the family."

"It sounds like fun. Sure, you can go."

"And Lauren's having a sleepover Saturday night. Can I go to that, too?"

"You're turning into a social butterfly, hon," Liza said.

"The sleepover's fine, too."

And it would give me a night with John.

After we dropped Liza off, Isabella and I picked up some Thai takeout and headed home. We just loved the pad Thai noodles. It reminded us so much of New York City.

She was chatty, my daughter was, and was also doing her Facebook thing, posting photos of herself with the cast and as an extra. Her generation practically lived on Facebook. If you had a boyfriend, it wasn't really official until you announced it on Facebook.

But from the start, I'd insisted that she use an abbreviated version of her name to make it more difficult for celebrity stalkers to find her—or me. Most of the parents I knew in the entertainment business insisted that their kids do the same thing. So on Facebook, Isabella was Bella D and I was Sam D, listed as her mom. Safer.

When we approached the house, I was pleased to see that the security lights at the gate had come on. I also spotted the security patrol and blinked the headlights, as I had been instructed to do. The patrol car blinked its headlights in response and pulled alongside me in the driveway. A middle-aged man stuck his head out the window.

"Evening, Ms. DeMarco. It's been quiet here."

"Quiet is good. Thanks so much. Mr. Castelli should be here shortly."

Isabella pressed the remote-control button, the gate slid open, and I drove uphill toward the house. The security lights around the property and outside the guesthouse and the main house were also on. Bright but not too bright, and they could be dimmed from the main panel inside the house.

"Maybe we kinda overdid it with the security stuff, Mom," Isabella remarked as we got out of the car.

"Maybe. But I don't want a repeat of what happened the other night. I'm starving, how about you?

"Famished."

We hurried into the house with our takeout, and while Isabella set out plates, I downloaded the video feed from the security cameras to my iPad. As we ate, I went through the feed, slowly, looking for anything unusual. About an hour ago, the security camera aimed at the road just outside our gate revealed a car moving slowly in front of our property, slowly but not slowly enough to attract the attention of the security patrol. I froze the image, zoomed in on it.

Paul's car.

You armed, Paul? Going to shoot up the house? Shoot me as I sleep?

I moved quickly through the house, checking doors to make sure that they were locked, that the security system was engaged. I was pissed that I had reached this place yet again, where I had allowed a man, any man, to instill such fear in me.

The next morning, I dropped Isabella off at school and walked into the office minutes before nine. Clara was meeting Marvin at Gallery, so I had the place to myself. There were twenty-two messages on the answering machine, nearly a hundred emails in my in-box, and a stack of mail that had been delivered on Saturday. I settled behind the front desk with a mug of strong coffee and a pastry from the bakery down the street, and dived in.

When Isabella and I had first moved out here and I'd opened my production office, I had set up the office email address on my phone as well. But within three months, I was receiving so much email that it seemed I was constantly on my phone, answering mail. I decided to pick up work stuff only on the computer. Now I regretted it. Last night, some emails had been sent to the company address from ladyofguadalupe@gmail.com.

Lady of Guadalupe was a church in Brooklyn where I had found solace and peace from time to time, and where we would be shooting location shots. Father Rinaldi, the priest at the church, had welcomed my infrequent visits and my numerous questions, drew parallels between biblical parables and my troubles, and always listened and offered counsel without any strings attached.

The wonderful thing about the priest was that he

hadn't cared what my religious beliefs were. He didn't try to convert me. He was simply there for me, supportive, caring. So whoever had sent these vile emails had taken one of my best memories and tried to corrupt it.

Email #1: Pretty soon, the world will know just what a bitch you are.

Email #2: You can't hide from me. I watch you constantly.

The inside of my mouth flashed bone dry. Paul? Vito? Or did this go even further back, maybe to Tony Kroon or one of the Brooklyn Boys? I started to delete all of them, then picked up the phone and called Lieutenant Gotti's cell phone. He answered on the second ring. "Gotti here."

"Lieutenant Gotti, it's Samantha DeMarco. I just received a couple of threatening emails through my company's email account from what I suspect is a bogus Gmail account. Is there any way you can find out who owns the account?"

"From Google? Ha. Not likely, unless I go through the Department of Justice or the NSA, and that might take years. Would you forward them to me?"

"I'm doing it right now."

"Good, stay on the line while I look at these." Seconds ticked by that amounted to less than a minute. Gotti muttered, "Pretty lame stuff. Don't worry about them, Ms. DeMarco. But if you get anything else, let me know."

I squeezed the bridge of my nose and wished I were at the swimming hole with John. "What do you suggest I do?"

"Don't delete them. If that email address isn't already connected to your phone, please synch them up now so you can pick up your email as soon as it comes in. If you get any more of these, forward them to me immediately."

"Okay."

"Does your daughter have a cell phone?"

"She's sixteen. Of course she's got a cell phone."

"But is it with her at school?"

"Yes, but she can't use it except at lunch hour."

"Does she get email through her phone?"

"Yeah, but I don't know how often she checks it. She's more the texting and Facebook type. Why?"

"Look, whoever broke into your house probably lifted a lot of info off your computer before whacking it into the next world. It's likely the perp has your and your daughter's electronic info. I hope you changed your passwords."

"I did, but . . . there was a lot of info on the computer that didn't need passwords."

"Like phone numbers, you mean. And Facebook tags. And twitter tags. And . . ." He paused. "You know, people talk about how the Internet has facilitated our lives, but I just don't see it. Mostly, it's just complicated my work and my life. Text your daughter, Ms. DeMarco, and definitely forward any other emails to me immediately."

"I will. Thanks, Lieutenant Gotti."

"One more thing. Is your security system installed?"

"Yes. And a patrol twenty-four/seven."

"Has anything unusual shown up on your video feed since you had the equipment installed?"

I thought of Paul's car, clearly visible in the zoom, and planned on mentioning it. The image didn't prove anything other than the fact that he'd driven by my place. On the other hand, if Paul was behind this—and after losing his job, he might be, I had to keep that in mind—then I needed to be honest. So I told Gotti what I'd seen, and he asked if I could send him the feed. I said I would. I could access the feed from any computer.

"By the way. I spoke to that nurse who drove Vito Bonti to the airport. She says she dropped him off at the curb. She assumed he got on the plane."

Shit. Assumed. "Thanks for checking."

"I also spoke to Paul Jannis and his attorney. Both men

are sticking to their story. Conference, then La Playa. I'm not backing off from the investigation."

"Just curious, Lieutenant Gotti. Do people kid you about your last name?"

He laughed. "I never hear the end of it. I actually met John Gotti before he died. There was a case I was working on out here that seemed to be connected to him, so I flew east to talk to him. His cancer was pretty advanced then, but he loved having an audience, and I was all ears. We actually tried to figure out how we might be related. Gotti isn't a very common name. I think we finally pegged that we might be cousins eight times removed. Something like that. He was a very strange man, and Brooklyn is a very strange place."

Amen to that.

"I read *Brooklyn Story*, Ms. DeMarco. And last night I got about halfway through *The Suite Life*. I have to ask. Between us, how much of it's true?"

I hesitated but not for long. "Between us? You'll swear to that? I won't suddenly find an interview with you on some entertainment blog? Or in a magazine?"

"My word."

"It's all true," I said. "Every last word of it."

I texted Isabella, forwarded the emails to Liza and John and to the new personal email address I set up. Isabella must have left class for the restroom or something, because she texted back almost immediately.

> Got weird text message earlier today. Didn't open attachment. Am forwarding & then deleting from my phone.

The text came from an area code I didn't recognize. When I clicked on the attachment, it was a very fuzzy photo of John and me, rolling through the grass at the swimming hole.

No way was I going to forward this to Lieutenant Gotti. I clicked the sucker into the trash and then sat there, fuming. Threatening emails and the photo: Didn't they add up to Paul? I was certain the emails were from Paul, but it was possible the photo had been taken by one of the extras or even a member of the crew. I let that thought sit for a moment, but didn't feel anything one way or the other.

I finally understood that the biggest impediment in my relationship with John was our violent pasts. Both of us having healthy appetizers into the mafia world as kids, then entrees into the Wall Street world as adults. Now the sweet part, the dessert; Hollywood. It was all starting to taste better than I ever imagined. This was recipe enough for a meal of a lifetime.

When I finally calmed down, I went into the restroom and splashed cold water on my face. That helped. I stood at the sink for the longest time, just staring down at the porcelain, waiting for an idea, a plan, a strategy, something. Nothing occurred to me. My phone buzzed and rang and sang. I didn't slip it from my back pocket.

After a few minutes, though, I peeled my hands away from the edge of the sink, pulled out my phone, and sent the image to John with a note.

While we died and went to heaven, the nasty gnomes were out & about.

By the time I arrived at Blu Jam, that photo had started appearing on the Internet. I knew it because I had spoken to John and Liza, King and Prince, Jenean, Susan, and Camilla. The consensus was that I should ignore it. No comment.

I suddenly wondered how celebrities—real celebrities like George Clooney and Julia Roberts, stars of that ilk—could stand all the scrutiny they received.

chapter

THIRTEEN

Priti Sarma looked just as I remembered her, a pretty woman with finely chiseled features and gorgeous black hair. We hugged hello, and as always she gushed with compliments about how good I looked, how wonderful it was to see me, how I hadn't changed one bit since we'd last seen each other. She ignored the bags under my eyes, the new lines at their corners, the threads of gray in my hair. Priti saw only the best in people.

We sat outside, just Priti and me—no studio execs, no Liza, no one in the industry, no men—and caught up on each other's lives. "My husband wants to expand our textile business to this country, and he thinks L.A. and New York are the best places to do that."

"Have you found a location yet?"

"I'm working with a Realtor. We think somewhere along Melrose would be good. Tap into the entertainment industry."

"I can help you out with that once you get settled. Is your husband joining you here at some point?"

"As soon as he finds a manager for the business at home."

Once our meals arrived, Priti leaned forward, her glowing eyes twinkling. "So, any special guy in your life, Sam?"

I didn't want to just sit there and talk about myself, so I gave her the abbreviated version of events, the high points—Vito, Paul, John. VPJ: it sounded like a Fortune 500 company or something. But she was so intrigued by it all that I ended up telling her about the break-in, the threatening emails, even about the fuzzy photo of John and me that had hit the Internet.

Samantha Bonti DeMarco, drama queen: that was how it sounded to me, but that wasn't who I was. Priti's expression turned sympathetic. "Sam, Sam," she said softly, "you need a man whose capacity for love is as great as yours. And you're going to find him. Maybe this John is the one. But regardless of who your true love turns out to be, when you get married, I'm making your wedding dress. And you are coming to India for your wedding."

A song went through my head about finding true love: John Legend's "You & I." That man sure knew how to say *I love you* in a song—that was for sure. A wedding in India sounded divine; the romantic in me could already envision it. But at the moment it seemed that I was just as far from a wedding anywhere on Earth as I was from a wedding on Pluto. "It just seems so easy for other people to find their soul mates, Priti. I don't understand why it's been such a challenge for me."

"Everyone has challenges, Sam. If you're destined to meet your soul mate in this life, then it will happen. I believe that in between lives, soul mates agree to come in at a particular time and place, to meet, to partner. Sometimes we recognize the person immediately. Other times it has to build. That's how it was for my husband and me. That's how it was for my parents."

Maybe, all these years, I'd been trying too hard, eager to see something in the man of the moment that simply wasn't there. I still believed that it all went back to my being abandoned by Vito, to his hatred of me before I'd even been born. But wasn't forty-five years kind of long for the unconscious to hold on to a particular pattern?

"Have you read Eckart Tolle's *The Power of Now*, Sam?"

I shook my head. "My reading the last several months has consisted of scripts and script notes."

"You should read it. In a nutshell, see, Tolle says that *now* is the only thing we have. *Now. This instant. This breath.* We can't change the past, and the future isn't here yet. We should try to live more in the moment. I know it sounds facile, but I've been putting his principles to work in my own life, and I have to tell you, I'm much happier because of it."

"But you're a naturally happy, optimistic person, Priti."

"So are you, if you'd give yourself half a chance. I used to have bouts of anxiety. Like when I'd fly. In the past, the night before a plane trip, I would be up half the night worrying about whether the plane was going to crash. Or get hijacked. Fear, my pending trips were always dominated by fear, what if this happened, what if that happened. . . . Every time there was something in the news about a plane crash, I would cancel any upcoming flight, forgo my trip, and lose what I'd paid for my ticket. But when I heard about a recent crash before making this trip to the States, it didn't affect me at all. That's the difference Tolle's book has made for me." She slipped her iPad out of her bag. "You have your iPad with you?"

"Always. Why?"

"I'm gifting you this book."

"Thanks, Priti, but I can buy it."

"You have great intentions, Sam, you always do; but life gets in the way sometimes. I'm sending it."

As she tapped away on her iPad, I brought mine out and thought about what she'd just said. It was true. I always had the best intentions—with my attitude, my daughter, my work, men I met, my life. But somehow, those intentions were all too often disrupted by drama, and my energy was spent trying to make right what had gone wrong. Then my best intentions went south.

Another pattern, I thought.

I picked up the book, and as it downloaded onto my Kindle app, I glanced up—and saw Paul and Luke headed along the sidewalk, toward us. They weren't speaking. They walked fast, and neither of them looked happy to be in the other's company.

Luke, in particular, was ragged; his good looks were worn down, like the surface of a stone long exposed to the elements. He might have been a homeless person who hadn't had a good meal or a shower or a night's sleep in a real bed in days. His jaw was unshaven; his jeans and shirt were soiled. And Paul was pissed—I could see it in his fisted hands, in the way he moved.

The irony struck me. Seeing them now, just after the comment Priti had made about my best intentions, prompted me to wonder if the universe was tossing me a challenge. *Can you hold on to your intentions? How are you going to react? With fear? Are you going to worry about what might happen if he sees you?*

Luke saw me first, said something to Paul, and gestured at a shop behind them. Paul, obviously irritated by Luke's request, abruptly turned around and hurried off toward the shop. I realized Paul hadn't seen me, and Luke had created a distraction so that Paul wouldn't see me. Now Luke made a beeline toward our table.

"Ms. DeMarco." He glanced at Priti, then back at me. "Listen. He's making me return to rehab."

"How can he *make* you?" I asked. "You're over twenty-one."

"He threatened to have me arrested for who the hell knows what. But I want you to know that dad is in total meltdown. All he talks about is revenge against you. He blames you for his getting fired from the movie."

"He needs to look within himself," Priti remarked.

It was delivered with such seriousness, with such benevolent intention, that I nearly laughed—not at her, but at the thought of Paul even grasping what it meant to *look within*. Luke seemed taken aback by her comment.

"Uh, no offense, ma'am, but that's not going to happen. My dad has zero capacity for self-reflection."

"I appreciate the warning, Luke. But if he's that hotheaded, you really shouldn't let him see you talking to me."

"Listen to us." He threw out his hands. "Even when he's not around, he's dictating what we do and don't do."

It was true. "You're right. So pull up a chair, join us."

He immediately looked frightened. "I . . . I can't do that. It would jeopardize you. Both of us. You need to go inside. I . . . don't know what he'll do if he sees you out here."

"He's not going to do anything with those cops around." Priti motioned toward a couple of cops on bikes, headed up the sidewalk toward us. "Not unless he's blind or crazy."

"You don't know how nuts he is," Luke murmured, glancing back nervously.

"Did he break into my house, Luke? Did he say anything about that?"

"He wouldn't tell me even if he had. He doesn't just blame you for getting him fired. He blames you for everything that's happened to him in the last six months. He thinks you're, like . . . a curse, an ancient curse, that was the phrase he used."

"An ancient curse."

As the words rolled off my tongue, I imagined where Paul had gotten that phrase—maybe from *Romancing the Stone* or from *Indiana Jones and the Last Crusade* or from *The Mummy*. Sure, I was an ancient curse. Granted, there were days when I felt plenty ancient, when my joints creaked and complained and I felt like some mummified skeleton. But that was all in my head, not in my body, not for another forty or so years.

"And . . . he's still got that gun," Luke finished.

"He carries it on him?" Priti exclaimed.

Her horrified expression made it utterly clear what her culture's take was on concealed weapons and on guns generally.

Paul suddenly appeared, a blur of speed, and rushed up behind his son, grabbed him by the shoulder, and yanked him back so hard that Luke stumbled over a chair behind him and crashed into a table. Glasses, plates, and silverware clattered to the ground. Paul leaned into our table, his cheeks flushed with anger, and got right in my face.

"You don't talk to my son, Sam, got it?"

I drew back, stumbled to my feet.

Priti leaped up and waved her arms in Paul's face. "Hey, hey, hold on a minute. Your son came over here."

"Lady, I don't know who you are, and this isn't your business. Luke is *my* son, Luke is—"

"Back off, Paul," I snapped, pushing away from the table and hurrying over to help Luke up.

"You okay, Luke?"

"Yeah." He lifted his arm, revealing a cut on his elbow from which blood flowed freely. "I've had worse."

Paul grabbed my shoulder and spun me around, and I wrenched back and threw up my arms to break his hold on me. "Get away from me," I shouted.

Other customers now stared at us, pedestrians moved out of the way, waiters hurried toward us. The cops rode up, leaped off their bikes, and the taller one insinuated himself between Paul and me.

"Move back, sir," he barked.

Paul didn't even look at the cop. He simply glared at

me, his eyes so hateful and crazy that I was terrified that, if I made an abrupt move, he would pull out his gun and shoot me.

"I said, *move back*," the cop repeated.

"Yeah, fine, fine, I heard you. I'm moving back." Paul raised his hands, patting at the air as if the cop were a wild animal he hoped to placate. "She's the one who started this." He stabbed a finger at me, marched over to Luke. "C'mon, Luke. We're outta here."

"I'm not going anywhere with you," Luke yelled, and held up his bleeding elbow. "You just shoved me into that table, you . . . you're a lunatic, a . . . crazy, fucking lunatic. . . ."

"You little prick." Paul lunged at his son, swinging his fists, and punched Luke in the stomach; he kept pummeling him, shouting that he was an ungrateful shit.

The officers sprang toward Paul and wrestled him to the ground. *"You can't do this, what do you think you're doing, hey, hey, you can't . . . ,"* Paul shouted. He kicked and fought and struggled like some beast from hell that was allergic to the light. *"Do you know who I am? You can't . . ."*

I hurried over to Luke, his face the white of Wonder Bread, and helped him over to our table. "Shit, he's a maniac," Luke whispered, watching as his father continued to struggle against the cops. "He'll kill me if I go with him, I know he will, he isn't thinking straight. . . ."

Tears rolled down his cheeks, and his eyes filled with such pain that I wanted only to gather him in my arms and comfort him. Priti grabbed a handful of napkins, soaked them with water, handed the wad to him. "Hold this against your elbow, Luke. That's right."

By giving him a task, she had distracted him from what was going on yards away from us. A waiter hurried over with some towels and a first-aid kit. Sirens shrieked through the air, and moments later, two police cruisers screeched to a stop at the curb.

Three cops leaped out and ran over to the other two officers, who were still trying to subdue Paul, a wild man fueled by rage and adrenaline. It took all five cops to hold him down, his cheek squashed against the sidewalk, and cuff him. Two cops jerked him to his feet and pushed him forward, toward the cruiser. Paul continued shouting, trying to wrench free. His face had turned strawberry red; his eyes bulged in their sockets. His head snapped around, and he screamed, "Luke, call my attorney, call—"

He was shoved into the back of the cruiser, and I couldn't hear the rest of what he shouted. The tall cop returned to the table. His name tag read SERGEANT ROLLINS. "Do you need medical attention?" Rollins asked Luke.

"I . . . I don't think so."

Priti and I went to work on Luke's elbow, using items from the first-aid kit. Rollins pulled out a chair and sat down with us. "I'll need your names and some information."

"I'm . . . Luke Jannis. That lunatic you took away is my father, Paul. Paul Jannis. He was threatening Ms. DeMarco. He . . . he uses her photos for target practice . . . he's nuts, he's . . ."

"Okay, Luke," the cop said, nodding, jotting rapidly in a notebook. "I understand. And your age?"

"Twenty-four."

"Ms. DeMarco, what's your relationship with Paul Jannis?"

"We dated for a while, but it ended weeks ago."

"I see."

I knew that he did. He'd probably heard this story hundreds of times before. It was undoubtedly such a common story in Hollywood that he had several choice words that he jotted down for it. Something like *ex-lover's revenge.* Or: *Relationship meltdown.*

"And your relationship with Mr. Jannis?" he asked Priti.

"None. I'm just having lunch with my friend."

"And your employer, ma'am?" He glanced at me again.

"I'm self-employed."

"DeMarco Productions," Priti added.

Luke said, "My father optioned her novel and screenplay. He was the producer on the movie until he got fired."

Rollins nodded, jotted more notes. "Ah, okay." The picture apparently was becoming much clearer for him. "Is the movie in production?"

"Yes." I nodded. "With Gallery Studios."

He asked for our cell numbers, addresses, and our driver's licenses. "I need to radio this in. I'll be right back."

As he hurried over to one of the cruisers, I saw Paul craning his neck in the backseat of the second cruiser, trying to see what was going on. I suddenly felt that the next time we ran into each other, he would kill me.

"Do you have a place to stay, Luke?" I asked.

"Yeah. Same place. With my girlfriend. He . . . he stormed in there this afternoon because he . . . got another credit card bill for . . . Mystery Manor purchases . . . but that bill . . . it was old, from before my rehab. I . . . I got a job, I'm making money. . . ."

"I'll get you to your girlfriend's place," I said. "But if I were you, I'd find another place to stay for a few days, someplace your dad doesn't know about."

"Yeah, I can do that. Jake's got his own place now. It's small, but I can sleep on the sofa."

The cop returned, handed our licenses back to us. "Ms. DeMarco, when I ran your license, I found that Lieutenant Gotti had flagged your name. I phoned him, and he told me about the break-in to your home over the weekend. I explained what had happened here, that Mr. Jannis is in custody and will be charged for resisting arrest and for assault and battery of his son. He suggested that you get

a restraining order against Mr. Jannis. If you give Lieutenant Gotti a call, he'll get the process started. He's going to
be speaking to Mr. Jannis in person, too, and will set him
straight on a few things."

"I'll call him. Thanks, Sergeant Rollins."

One of the employees was now sweeping up the shards
of dishes and glasses that had crashed to the floor when
Paul had shoved Luke. Rollins stabbed his thumb toward
the mess.

"They may charge you for the broken dishes, Mr. Jannis.
If you'd like, I'll speak to the manager and make it clear that
they should recoup the damage from your father."

"Thanks. Thanks very much." Luke sounded surprised
that a cop—that anyone—would offer to do that for him.

Rollins went inside. "You hungry, Luke?" I asked.

"Famished."

"Well, let's get you something to eat," I said, and Priti
flagged down the waitress.

Priti and I drove Luke to his girlfriend's place first so he
could pick up his belongings, then we headed into downtown Malibu, where Jake lived. I felt sorry for Luke, sorry
that Paul was his father, that Paul had struck him, that Paul
was so damaged.

Paul always sought to place blame on someone else for
whatever happened to him. He refused to take responsibility for his own actions, his own choices. But neither Luke
nor I were the cause of his meltdown; we were just catalysts,
triggers for his rage, for that dark shadow in him. Paul had
no one to blame but himself for what had just happened.
I suspected Gotti would tell him as much, unless Paul's
attorney bailed him out before Gotti even arrived at the
station.

No telling what would happen once Paul was bailed
out. That thought troubled and scared me.

When we pulled up in front of Luke's friend's apartment, a nice place near the beach, Luke leaned forward from the backseat and slung an arm around my shoulders, then Priti's. "Thank you so much for everything. If it hadn't been for you two, I don't know . . . what he might've done."

"Stay safe," Priti said.

"And keep in touch," I told him.

"I will." He held up his iPhone. "He can't cut off service on this one. I just bought it, had some money saved from my job. Here, I'll text you the new number." He did it quickly. "And, Ms. DeMarco, please stay out of his way. Unless they Baker Act him, his attorney will spring him outta jail by this evening."

"I understand, Luke. And thank you for the warnings. Let me know if he tries to find you or contact you, and I'll let Lieutenant Gotti know."

"Okay, thanks."

He got out and walked up to the building, his shoulders sagging like those of an old man. The bone-white bandage on his elbow was only today's scar. The other scars, from earlier, didn't show.

I rubbed my hands over my face, suddenly wishing that I was anywhere but here. A beach in the south of France. The mysterious island of Chiloé in southern Chile. In Paris. In Africa. In Costa Rica. Anywhere but here, just like the movie of the same name.

"Sam?"

My hands fell away from my face, and I glanced over at Priti. "Yeah?"

"I think it would be really smart if you could get out of town for a few days. The, uh, dynamics in all this are disturbing."

Ya think? And then, to my utter horror, I started to cry, to sob. I hated to cry in situations like this, when I undoubtedly looked like some helpless female—that silly woman in the old Snidely Whiplash cartoons, tied to a railroad track as a train barreled toward her, hoping some guy would gallop in to her rescue.

Gag.

"I came out here . . . to find a dream, Priti. But it seems it's . . . it's just been one nightmare scenario after another. There's . . . something in me that attracts this bullshit, the violence, these men who are so . . . so eaten up with the need for power. And it's not just that they want to control me, they want to control everything. Look at Paul's relationship with his son . . ."

"What relationship? Luke is like his abused puppy." Priti slipped her arm around my shoulders. "You're too hard on yourself, Sam."

"Am I?"

"Of course you are. We've all made bad choices at one time or another. We all have these messed-up patterns in ourselves. The trick is to break the pattern, somehow. I mean, c'mon, you wrote yourself out of Brooklyn. You've said it yourself. You wrote yourself into Manhattan and then out of Manhattan and into Hollywood. You've lived the contrasts. You know what you want, what you deserve. You can write yourself into anything. Just *do it.*"

Priti, my cheerleader.

Priti, always in my court.

She even handed me a wad of Kleenex so I could dry my eyes, blow my nose. Then I turned the key in the ignition and slammed my car into gear and tore away from the curb in front of the apartment building. I sped toward Melrose, where Priti had left her car, popped a Whitesnake CD into the player, cranked up the volume. *"Here I go again on my own . . . down the only road I've ever known,"* blasted through the car.

Priti lowered the windows and the wind whipped through, sweeping away the detritus of the past, sweeping away the issues and the men and the bullshit, until there was only this moment, this second, this breath. Priti and me, laughing our asses off.

Late afternoon. I was sitting by the pool with a glass of rosé. The dusky sky was cloudless, the air was cooler, birds sang as though their hearts were swollen with joy. The afternoon light struck the towering canyon wall, turning it a burnished copper. And way above me, gulls shrieked, winging their way elsewhere for the night.

Beyond me, the property seemed fluid, vivid colors spreading out in every direction, waves of green rolling all the way to the gate and the fence at the bottom of the driveway. I drank it all in, my slice of paradise.

I'd been reading Tolle's book and was beginning to understood now what Priti had been talking about. I wondered if I'd ever lived fully *in the moment.* As a young girl in Brooklyn, I was always trying to write my way out, one eye perpetually glued to the future. During my marriage to Alec, there had been some living-in-the-moment times, but mostly it seemed I had worried and fretted about *what ifs. What if* Alec didn't slow down, *what if* he didn't take better care of himself, *what if* he took up with another woman, *what if, what if, what if* . . .

In other words, I had spent so much time anticipating the future, worrying about it, planning for it, that I had probably missed thousands of *nows,* tens of thousands of moments I could never recapture. It was time to live in the now, I craved it so.

So I set aside my iPad and padded over to the sliding-glass door that opened into Isabella's room. She and Lauren were sitting on her bed, doing homework, their intense concentration so deep they didn't even glance up. I drank in the sight of them, then turned and drank in the sight of this gorgeous property.

Gratitude.

Lights burned in the guesthouse, where Marvin and Flannigan were, the security people patrolled the property outside the gate, the security lights by the gate shone brightly. Right this second, barefoot and relaxed, I was free—free of drama, free of bullshit, free to be whoever I was at this point in time.

Priti was right. I needed to get out of Malibu, and not just because of Paul. I was beginning to feel corralled, controlled, like some carefully calibrated machine. During my years with Alec, I had felt like this many times and had found that a change of scenery always helped. It didn't solve the fundamental problem, but it shifted my focus.

I finally turned on my phone again, and it pinged and pinged as text messages and emails came in. I really wasn't in the mood to scroll through endless messages of any kind, but when I glanced down, I saw messages from Liza, John, Priti, Jenean, and from Prince and King.

We r headed 2 brooklyn day after tomorrow, King wrote. Pack your bags, folks, and contact Liza for details about travel.

Six days, people!!!!!! wrote Prince, his six exclamation points making it sound like Brooklyn was up there with London, Athens, Rome.

Isabella would go with me, of course. She would get to see her grandmother, her uncle, Alec's family. It would be the first time we'd been back since Alec had died. A new start, a new chapter, and a journey back to the roots of *Brooklyn Story*.

The timing on this intrigued me. Here I'd been thinking about how badly I wanted to get away, and suddenly that was exactly what was going to happen. How could I manifest my other desires that quickly? How had desires and events come together so seamlessly?

This meant I now had an immediate goal: packing for

the trip, tending to details that had to be handled before we could leave.

Six days to visit the past in all of its strange and bewildering glory. Was it enough time to allow myself to release those darker memories so that I could move forward without these destructive inner patterns?

chapter

FOURTEEN

Our trip to JFK was riddled with setbacks, delays, schedule changes. Our flight was delayed for a couple of hours, and while we were waiting in the passenger lounge, Carl Davidson emailed everyone the latest script changes for the scenes that would be shot in Brooklyn. Then he came over and sat down next to me. "Let me know, Sam, if these changes are okay with you."

"Sure thing."

"And I want you to know that I think Paul should've been fired a long time go. He created trouble for a lot of the cast and crew, but everyone was afraid to speak up because he was so tight with George. The dynamics are much different now that John is a partner."

"Thanks, Carl. There were points when I was beginning to feel like I was a curse or something."

"The curse was Paul." He got up and moved, in his frenetic way, across the waiting area to one of the shops.

When we were finally en route, I felt so incredibly good that it was easy to put the ugliness with Paul behind me. John sat on one side of me, Isabella on the other—how could I possibly ask for more? In fact, the cast and crew took up the entire business section on the Boeing 777, thirty-five of us, and the mood was upbeat and rollicking. The five-and-a-half-hour flight flew by.

As the plane made its final approach, I spotted central Long Island, a glorious spread of emerald green and houses attached to each other. The contrast excited me. Even though I loved Malibu, I was a New Yorker through and through and didn't realize until that moment how homesick I'd been. I could feel the pulse of the city's frenetic energy radiating upward from the streets below. I could almost hear the constant din of traffic, the chatter of voices, and the clattering of trains over subway tracks. I could almost taste the spring air. I could almost taste the greasy zeppole at the 18th Avenue Feast in the heart of Benson-hurst. What a joy it would be to reenact that!

Then we were on the ground, and excitement surged through me. I was home.

A private bus took us from JFK into the city, to the Greenwich Hotel in Tribeca. It was a gorgeous building, the color of dark copper, on North Moore Street and Greenwich. There were eight floors, seventy-five thousand square feet, eighty-eight rooms and suites, and no two of them were alike. *Travel & Leisure* called it the crown jewel in De Niro's Tribeca holdings, which included the Tribeca Film Center, Tribeca Cinemas, and Nobu and Tribeca Grill restaurants.

The hotel featured two sumptuous penthouses that were two thousand and twenty-five hundred square feet, respectively. When Alec was at the height of his career, we had stayed here on several occasions, usually in the larger penthouse. I remembered asking Alec how much the place cost, but he refused to tell me. *Don't worry about it. We can afford it.*

Now I knew it cost nearly six grand a night.

What I particularly loved about the Greenwich was the vast range of cultural influences in the furnishings and spaces: everything from hand-loomed Tibetan silk rugs to English leather settees to the Paris-inspired courtyard. The beds were to die for—Duxiana from Sweden. In the bathrooms, you found hand-laid Moroccan tile or Italian Carrara marble. The Shibui Spa had a shiatsu room, a traditional Japanese bathing room with a large tub, as well as a fitness area with hemlock floors. The Shibui also featured a lantern-lit swimming pool and lounge. As the hotel brochure pointed out, the pool and lounge were under the roof of a two-hundred-fifty-year-old wood-and-bamboo farmhouse that had been reconstructed by Japanese craftsmen for the hotel.

This Old World charm was carefully balanced and complemented with twenty-first century technology—Wi-Fi, high-def TVs, iPod-docking stations, laptops. The suites even had iPads. In other words, everything here was first class. The moment you stepped into this hotel, you were transported. To me, it was the perfect place to be, yet private—so close, yet so far away from Brooklyn. The only thing that separated us now was that glorious bridge.

Liza had booked Isabella and me into the fireplace corner suite, which had a sitting room, dining area and wet bar, huge bathtubs and a walk-in shower, a working fireplace, and everything else we could possibly want for the next several days. John, Liza, King, and Prince had suites down the hall from us, and Susan, Camilla, and Jenean had the penthouse. The rest of the cast and crew had interconnecting rooms. King had also reserved the smaller penthouse for meetings and meals.

After Isabella and I had showered and changed clothes, we met John and Liza in the lobby and hopped a car for a short ride to Brooklyn. I didn't want to take the train. I needed to drive over that bridge again. I needed to feel that energy. And, most of all, I needed to cross it once more to get to the final destiny of my dream, the film.

It felt good to be in Manhattan again, to spot familiar

shops and stores, landmarks from those years I spent with Alec. But I was glad to be in Malibu, even as fractured and strange as it had felt recently.

John asked the driver to let us off in Bensonhurst. "There's a great pizza place in this neighborhood," he said.

"Let me guess," I said. "Frank's Pizzeria!"

He laughed. "But first, we've got another stop to make. A surprise."

"Very mysterious," Liza remarked.

"I love mysteries," Isabella said.

But I knew where he was headed.

Sure enough, we stopped in front of Our Lady of Guadalupe, the church where I had so often found solace and peace during the tumultuous years earlier in my life, the years of the Brooklyn Boys.

Liza saw the name and snapped her fingers. "Hey, we film here tomorrow morning."

"You got it," John said.

As the four of us walked into the cool silence, I almost expected to see Father Rinaldi, the old priest who had spent so much time with me. The two of us used to sit in one of the pews, talking quietly about God and faith. And when my relationship with Alec had been new, the priest and I had even talked about that.

It felt odd to think of my younger self talking to a priest about the intimate details of my life. I knew I wouldn't do such a thing now. But Rinaldi had been a kind of counselor for troubled teens, and I suspected my earlier journey would have been much more difficult without him.

"Wow," Liza murmured. "Look at these gorgeous stained-glass windows. Can't you just see it? It's going to be perfect for filming. The weather tomorrow is supposed to be sunlight and New York grand." She suddenly frowned, reached into her voluminous handbag, and pulled out the script notes for tomorrow. She paged through them quickly.

"I knew it. There's nothing in here about who's playing Father Rinaldi!" She glanced at John. "John?"

His eyes twinkled. "A secret we've kept under wraps quite well, don't you think?"

"Another surprise?" Liza drolled.

"Yeah?" I said.

"C'mon, Mr. Steeling, tell us who," Isabella said.

"De Niro."

Liza squealed and clapped her hands like a little kid. "My God, that's fantastic!"

I was floored. "Really?" I remembered someone had mentioned the possibility of De Niro as a priest, but I'd long since forgotten it. "How in the world did you . . ."

"He's in town, knows we're staying at the Greenwich, gave us a break on the price, so I made a call."

"Awesome," Isabella said. "And I'm going to miss meeting him? That is *so* not fair."

"Maybe your grandmother can pick you up later in the morning. I'll give her a call and arrange it."

The plan was that she would spend the day with Alec's mother, sister, and brother, who would take her anywhere she wanted and spoil her rotten for twenty-four hours. But how often did you get to meet De Niro? We would work around it. I was sure Alec's family would understand.

I went over to the candles and lit three: for my mother, for Grandma Ruth, and for Alec. I stood there for a few moments, drawing the peace and silence around me like a shawl, a cape, a cocoon, and was astonished that I could still feel such peace in a church.

John came up behind me, touched my shoulder. He gestured at the three lit candles. "Mother, Grandmother, Alec."

I nodded.

He gave my shoulder an affectionate squeeze. "Ready for pizza?"

I turned, and for a long moment we simply looked at

each other, our eyes locked, both of us remembering those incredibly sensual moments down by the swimming hole. "Thank you," I said softly.

"My pleasure, Sam."

He clasped my hand, and we headed down the aisle to the front of the church, where Liza and Isabella were ogling one of the many exquisite sculptures. "Pizza time, ladies."

"I'm famished," Isabella said.

"Ditto," Liza echoed.

"Anything Italian sounds fantastic to me," I said.

Frank's Pizzeria wasn't far, and the evening was perfect for walking. John and I held hands, an electrical current racing between us. We were behind Liza and Isabella, and at one point, he slipped his arm around my shoulders, leaned toward me, and kissed me. "I love being here with you," he whispered.

"That makes two of us."

"And I love that I can return here on my own terms. You know what I mean?"

"Do I ever. It's kind of liberating."

We had both grown up poor, had dealings with the mob. He was actually a self-made man who had basically disappeared from everyone's radar by moving out to L.A. We both had known more than our share of violence. To think about where we had come from and who we had become was incredible. Now we, a couple of orphans, were part of the Gallery Studio family, were with that family in the place where we had grown up and come of age. Pieces were sliding together beautifully. I still could not believe that this man was back in my life after so many years. Sometimes while your eyes are half-closed, love manages to open them wide.

At Frank's Pizzeria, we ordered a large pizza with all the trimmings, a round of Brooklyn Lagers for the grown-ups, and lemonade for Isabella. John regaled us with stories about working on Gallery's movies and some of the comical mishaps that had occurred. We were all in stitches.

Marvin texted me that he and Flannigan were in Brooklyn—where were we? I told him, and moments later, they walked in and joined us. "I've been showing Jim our old haunts around here," Marvin said.

"It's definitely not Malibu," Flannigan said with a quick laugh. "But it's all about a kind of Old World charm. I like it."

"A Brooklyn convert," I remarked.

"Well, not exactly. I'm still a California guy at heart, but there's something wonderful about walking around in real neighborhoods that have trees and sidewalks and kids playing in yards and parks. Is your son coming to the shoot tomorrow, John?"

"He and his girlfriend. They were going to join us tonight, but they're tied up with stuff on campus."

"Did you tell them, Mr. Steeling?" Isabella asked. "About tomorrow's surprise?"

"Nope."

"What surprise?" Marvin asked.

Isabella looked at John. "Can we tell them?"

"Can you guys keep a secret?" John asked.

Marvin and Flannigan leaned forward. "Our lips are sealed," Flannigan said. "Spill the beans, John."

"De Niro."

"Oh, my God," Marvin gasped. "To play the priest, right? Father Rinaldi?"

"That's it."

"I can so see him playing the part," Marvin said.

"Will he sign autographs?" Flannigan asked.

"I can see it now," I laughed. "De Niro surrounded by all the Gallery groupies who request his autograph, ply him with questions, ask him to pose for photos . . . He might quit before we start shooting!"

"We promise we won't be that bad!" Flannigan said, and crossed his heart.

John rolled his eyes. "Yeah, yeah."

I liked what I saw of John that evening, a fun-loving, personable man who seemed to understand the landscape of the human heart in a way that no other man I'd known had ever grasped. He redeemed himself at every level. As though his past experiences had never occurred. In spite of what he had endured in his life—abandonment by his blood parents; his adoption into a mafia family, where he'd been inducted into the underworld at a young age; the time he'd spent in prison—he had emerged from the darkness as a changed man. It was the archetypal Plutonian journey into the dark underworld. But he had crawled out on the other side and made something of himself.

It was the classic hero's journey that Joseph Campbell had written about, upon which all wonderful stories were based. In terms of storytelling, the journey had been broken down into succinct steps, and whenever any of us read a script, we looked for these steps:

The hero is introduced in his ordinary world.
The call to adventure.
Refusal of the call.
Meeting with the mentor.
Crossing the threshold.
Tests, allies, and enemies.
Approach.
The ordeal.
The reward.
The road back.
The resurrection.
Return with the elixir.

In his personal journey, John had been resurrected already. I figured he was nearing the final step. What would the elixir be for him?

In many ways, we had been living on parallel tracks, and now those tracks had intersected. We were both a couple of underdogs who had come out on top. But perhaps each of us was missing the essential ingredient—true love.

During a moment when everyone was riveted by a story that Flannigan was telling, I asked John how he had met De Niro. He smiled. "The truth sounds like fiction, Sam."

"Hey, you're talking to the queen of truth as fiction. Try me."

"In 2008, I was involved in the sale of the Greenwich Hotel. I was living in L.A. by then, working with King and Prince, but my real estate license was still active in New York, and one day, I got this random call. . . . I flew back to New York that night and showed him the place the next day."

"Just like that?" I snapped my fingers. "Is that how stuff usually happens in your life?"

"Not before I went to prison. But now, more so. He and I hit it off years ago, and we shared similar interests, similar backgrounds. Over dinner and drinks, he described his vision for what he wanted to do with the Greenwich. And he achieved what he set out to do. Anyway, a few days after that dinner, we had a deal."

"I like that he had a vision and sculpted it."

"Don't most of us try to do that?"

"I think so. But we don't always succeed."

"When we do, though, the reward is incredibly gratifying. The commission I made on just that deal has facilitated everything since then. I invested the money well, and it grew." He paused and touched my thigh. "This movie, Sam, is going to be incredible. Paul's outta the deal, we have a solid script, terrific talent in the cast and crew, and we're working with a fantastic studio. What could possibly go wrong?"

The moment he said those words, the superstitious part

of me recoiled in horror. If I'd learned nothing else over the years, it was never to tempt fate by asking what could possibly go wrong. When you did that, Murphy's Law tended to spring into action.

Not long ago, out in Malibu, I saw a sign that really kicked Murphy's Law in the ass. It read: *If anything can go right, it will.* That was also Nina's motto.

My resolve was to try to live by those words.

When we returned to the Greenwich, we ran into King, who asked us to have a drink with him. Isabella said she wanted to Skype with some friends, so I gave her the key and she went up to the room. Since Marvin and Flannigan begged off, too, it was just John and me, Liza and King in the hotel bar.

I thought how wonderful it was to be here, not worrying about Paul suddenly appearing like some monster in a fairy tale. With three thousand miles and his stint in jail separating us, it seemed unlikely that Paul would be a problem, at least not while we were on the East Coast.

It was in that moment that I recognized the enormous tension and stress I'd been functioning under since early April, when things had started falling apart with Paul. I could feel it across the back of my neck, through my shoulders. I thought about John kneading my shoulders, massaging them, those large, powerful hands of his working the tension out of my muscles. And I fantasized about how his hands would feel against my bare skin, what kind of lover he might be.

"Sam?" Liza snapped her fingers in front of my face. "Hey, hon, you were a zillion miles away. Rosé for you?"

"Perfect."

"What was it like returning to Our Lady of Guadalupe?" King asked.

"Like time traveling," I said. "I almost expected to see

Father Rinaldi and me sitting in one of those pews. It's a weird feeling."

"I suppose John gave away our surprise, huh?"

"He sure did," I said.

"It's hard keeping something like that under wraps for too long."

"I did my best," John said.

"You definitely did, John," Liza remarked. "I remember way back in April someone had mentioned the possibility of De Niro as the priest, but no one ever said anything else about it, and I forgot about it. And I wasn't paying attention to the full cast list."

"It wouldn't have mattered," King said, then whipped out a folded copy of the cast list and held it up. "Father Rinaldi." He pointed at the name. "TBA. To be announced."

My back was to the door, so when King suddenly gestured at someone behind me, I glanced around—and gaped. Father Rinaldi came through the door, waved at the bartender, said hello to a couple of the waitresses, and made his way toward our table.

De Niro. It was De Niro. And he looked so much like Father Rinaldi, he could pass for his twin. Dark clothes, a clerical collar, graying hair. Rinaldi's hair had been coal black, but I liked him with that touch of gray. The enigmatic smile and sphinxlike expression, though, were pure De Niro. When John introduced us, I was speechless.

"I enjoyed your book, Samantha. And your script. It's a pleasure to play Father Rinaldi." He paused. "So. Do I pass the look-alike test?"

"Absolu-lutely," I stammered. "I . . . you fooled me. I thought he'd risen from the dead."

De Niro laughed and slapped his thigh. "Risen from the dead. Love it." He pressed his palms together in an attitude of prayer and gave a small, mock bow. "And now, child, for your confession . . ."

We all laughed, and King asked, "Can you join us?"

"Love to."

He pulled out a chair and sat down at our table, and I felt overwhelmed by—what? That he was De Niro? But at the heart of it I was deeply grateful to all of these people—from the studio executives to the actors and crew members who were bringing my story to the screen, breathing life into events and individuals who had helped mold and shape me. How many people have that kind of opportunity?

"So tell me," De Niro said, "about Rinaldi's hand gestures, his expressions. Did he talk slow or fast, or just like an Italian guy from Brooklyn? Did he have any habitual facial expressions? A tic? A quick smile?"

We spent the next fifteen or twenty minutes talking about the priest, and I was surprised at how vivid my memories were of him, even all these years later. Just as Jenean had sat and talked with me, observing my hands movements and the way I spoke, so was De Niro using this conversation to work himself into the physical person Rinaldi had been.

Before De Niro left, John snapped a couple of photos of all of us at the table, then a photo of me with De Niro. Isabella probably would never forgive me for not calling her to come downstairs to meet him. But she would get her chance tomorrow at the church, if not before.

"So, what about this, Sam?" De Niro ran his fingers through his hair. "Should I dye it black or do you think the gray works okay?"

"The gray looks great. I like the idea of Rinaldi as prematurely gray."

"Gray it is, then."

When De Niro finally got ready to leave, he asked if we were all comfortable in our rooms and if the staff could help us out in any way. John and King walked with him across the room to the door, and Liza leaned toward me and whispered, "Do I look okay?"

"What? You always look more than okay, Liza. Why? What's going on? What're you talking about?"

"Fuck, I think I'm having a mini panic attack. Brian asked me back to his room for a nightcap. I . . . well, I feel kinda weird about, you know, sleeping with him. I mean, I'm in my fifties, I—"

"Liza. Enough already. You're the fittest woman I know. You go for it, girl."

"Sam, I think that he's just in his late forties, that he—"

I laughed. "Honestly? Does it matter if you're—what? Four or five years older than he is? Men never worry about that. Why should women? Look at Susan Sarandon, dating a guy thirty years younger."

"Wow, I'd forgotten about that. Good point." She sat back, worry bleeding from her expression. "I went through so much shit in my marriage, Sam, that I guess I'm kinda gun-shy now."

"I get that completely."

"You and John . . . have you . . . ?"

"No. Just rolling around in the grass by the swimming hole."

"Who do you think took that photo?"

"I'd like to point the finger at Paul. Maybe he was hiding in the bushes nearby or something. But I'm pretty sure he was escorted off the studio property."

"Yeah, he was."

"Maybe it was one of the extras. It doesn't matter. It's not like we're fodder for the paparazzi."

"And about John and you . . ." She spun a perfectly manicured finger in the air and winked.

"I'm, uh, looking forward to it."

Liza laughed.

As John and King made their way back to the table, my phone buzzed. I glanced at it, saw a text message from Paul's son.

Dad is out, headed to NY.

"Oh, no." Waves of apprehension tore through me.

"What?" Liza asked.

I handed her the phone.

"Maniac," she muttered. "Let Brian and John see that. Maybe we need some security guards around the shoot tomorrow."

"Good idea." I was beyond giving Paul the benefit of the doubt. I'd already done that once too often.

When the men returned to the table, I handed King my phone. "Take a look, Brian."

He glanced at the text message and passed the phone to John without saying a word. John read it, gave me the phone, and the two men exchanged a glance. "Well?" John asked.

"Paul doesn't have a copy of the shooting schedule for Brooklyn," King said. "Just the same, I'll take care of it."

"He knows where our shooting locations are in Brooklyn, though, Brian. He has seen the script notes; he made suggestions about the locations," John said.

"As long as he doesn't know when we're shooting where, it shouldn't be a problem. But let's not leave anything to luck."

King pushed away from the table and walked out of the room, John striding alongside him.

I texted Luke a thank-you and asked when his father had left L.A. He replied that Paul's flight would leave at midnight Eastern time, which meant he would be here sometime tomorrow morning.

Does he know where you're staying? Luke asked.

I had no idea. "Liza, when you made the arrangements for our staying here, did Paul know about them?

"Nope. But he may figure it out. He knows Brian's tastes. He knows Brian has stayed here before. But unless he has reserved a room here, he won't get past the front desk."

"Maybe we should warn the front desk?"

"Brian's probably doing that already."

I texted Luke again.

Did yr dad tell u where he'll be staying?

No. He never does. Only reason I know he's leaving is because he got my # from Jake's mom & called & asked me 2 give him a lift to the airport. Can u believe that shit? I didn't take the call.

U ok?

As long as I stay away from him, I'm fine. Take care—& if u see him, take cover. Seriously.

Take cover.

I fully intended to.

I knew Paul was nuts, but at that moment, I didn't really grasp just how psychotic he'd become.

Later, alone in the elevator, John slipped his arm around my shoulders and gently pulled me closer to him. "Not to worry, Sam. Even Paul, as relentless as he is, won't be able to get through the barricades tomorrow. Even to film at and around the church, we had to get permission from the local bishop and from the city council. The block will be closed during filming, and Brian just hired some private security guards. The Brooklyn cops will also be there."

"That's a relief."

He touched my chin and raised my face ever so gently and kissed me. I melted into him. His hands traveled slowly down my back, and a current of desire swept up my spine. "You and I need some time alone," he whispered. "Serious time alone."

There was nothing pushy in what he said, nothing controlling or manipulative as there had been with Paul, with Alec. John's words were about desire.

"How about tomorrow night?"

The elevator doors opened, and an elderly couple stood there, both of them looking as if they were decked out for a state dinner. "Evening," the man said with a twinkle in his eyes, as if he remembered a scene like this from his own life.

"Evening," John murmured.

We swept past them, snorting and snickering, and as soon as the elevator doors shut, sealing the elderly couple inside, we burst out laughing. "You know how you make me feel, Sam?"

"How?"

"Like you're the only woman in the world to me. Even if it took thirty years to find you again."

He kissed me good night at the door and I floated into the suite, the taste of him lingering on my mouth. His words between kisses were what mattered most to me. Three decades was certainly worth the wait.

FIFTEEN

Breakfast the next morning was in the penthouse. Isabella and I arrived a few minutes late because I was on the phone with Alec's mother, rescheduling Isabella's pickup time so she could meet De Niro. She'd seen the photos of De Niro that John had taken and hadn't quite forgiven me for not calling her to come downstairs to meet the man. I figured the photo of De Niro and me would be up on her Facebook page shortly, if it wasn't there already.

King and Prince had set out a virtual feast for the cast and crew. Isabella and I went through the line, helping ourselves to breakfast goodies from half a dozen cultures. We sat next to the huge picture window with John, Prince, and Renée. The view was spectacular.

Tribeca spread out before us, light spilling across the busy streets below, transforming the neighborhood into some sort of magical dimension where anything was possible. The sky was a magnificent shade of blue, utterly clear, and seemed to fit over the Manhattan skyline as perfectly as a dome. Sitting up here—at this particular table, at this particular moment in time, with these particular people—filled me with enormous gratitude.

I had read in many self-help books that the most important emotion we could experience, next to love, was gratitude. The more gratitude we felt, the more readily we attracted other experiences, situations, and people for whom we could be grateful.

And after reading Tolle's book, I'd decided that part of my new "program" for myself would be practicing gratitude consistently, daily, in every way, and not just when I lit candles to the Blessed Virgin, the Archangel Michael, and Buddha. It meant that when I felt this surge of gratitude, as I did now, I should focus on it, appreciate it, turn it inside out and explore the texture and reality of the feeling. I should memorize its contours and shapes, its nooks and crannies. I should explore this emotion so completely that I could conjure it even in the moments when I didn't feel it, when it seemed impossible to be grateful for anything.

So as I gazed out at this fantastic view, I appreciated it with my entire being. What woman wouldn't want to be in my shoes?

"Everyone rested up?" Prince asked.

"I feel great," John said. "I slept the entire night through. And that rarely happens."

"Same here," Renée and I said simultaneously, then looked at each other and laughed.

"Maybe jet lag adjusts sleep patterns rather than disrupting them," Renée remarked.

Considering the text from Luke, I actually hadn't expected to sleep as well as I had. But since I'd spent the last few weeks in a state of almost constant anxiety about this situation with Paul, I was probably suffering from adrenal exhaustion or something.

Prince, as if reading my mind, said, "Brian told me about the text from Luke's son, Sam. I can assure you there won't be a problem."

"I understand he called the hotel last night to make a reservation," John said. "The front desk told him the Greenwich is fully booked."

Interesting, I thought. "Is that true—is it fully booked?"

"Nope," John said.

"I hope he doesn't find it suspicious."

"Look, if he comes into the hotel and makes a scene, he'll be arrested," Prince said. "Simple."

Except that, with Paul, nothing was ever simple.

Before we finished eating, King stood on one of the steps leading up to the second floor of the penthouse and waved a copy of the script. "If you all could get out your copies, I'll quickly go through which scenes we're going to film today and their locations. When we're finished here, a bus will be waiting downstairs to take us into Brooklyn."

Most of us had iPads. I turned mine so that both Isabella and I could see it. As King spoke, I jotted notes on a pad of paper about the locations: Our Lady of Guadalupe and Sally's, a coffee shop where my friend Janice and I used to hang out. I wondered if the place still had the best chicken sandwiches for miles around. Probably.

Before Isabella and I had moved to California, we had gone to Sally's one afternoon, the first time I'd been there in a decade. When we had walked into the coffee shop, I'd experienced that time-traveling feeling. The worn black-and-white ceramic tiles were still there, and so were the stainless steel stools with the red leather cushions. Even the booths beyond the counter, where Janice and I used to sit, were still there. It was as if Sally's had gotten stuck in a time warp.

"Sally's, that's where we went, Mom," whispered Isabella. "How cool."

The neighborhood where I'd actually met Tony Kroon had been changed for shooting purposes. Those scenes would be shot tomorrow morning, in a public park lined with food stalls, where two hundred extras would be strolling and laughing and enjoying the perfect weather. The shoot in the park had required several permits from the city bureaucrats and we had only three hours to do it.

"Questions, anyone?" King asked.

"Just a detail," Liza said, waving her arm. "Lunch will be at one p.m., at Sally's. We were going to cater it to save time, but Sally insisted they can have everything cleared in ten minutes once we've eaten. The menu is Greek, and according to those in the know, the food is fabulous. Our shooting there should wrap up between five and six. You're free for the evening, but you should all be downstairs at nine tomorrow morning to take the bus into Brooklyn. Shooting will start at ten. All of you in the crew who are setting up the stalls in the park for the shoot tomorrow morning should be ready to roll at the unforgivable hour of six-thirty."

A collective groan went up from the crowd.

"The good news is that the weather is forecast to remain perfect, with temps in the sixties."

Around lunchtime, Alec's mother and sister would meet us at Sally's, and they would pick up Isabella and head out for the day and night to enjoy her dad's family. It was all going to work out beautifully.

"Anything else from anyone?" King asked.

Silence.

"Then let's head downstairs and out to the bus."

On the bus, John and I sat together in the back. We talked about the script, the locations, about some of our recollections of Brooklyn from the years we'd lived here.

As we talked and the bus rolled toward Brooklyn, I kept thinking how all of my life I had wanted to wear a wedding ring that truly symbolized a union between two people. I had thought that was what my ring had meant when Alec and I were married. But after our finances went south, he took it off my finger and sold it, a testament to what the marriage had become.

"You're a million miles away, Sam," John remarked.

"The past is still alive here in Brooklyn."

"Yeah, I know what you mean." He took my hand and planted small, delicate kisses on each knuckle. "But the future is alive here, too."

His eyes met mine, held them. In that moment there on the bus that was taking us into our pasts, my fear that John would turn out to be no different from the other men I'd known collapsed in on itself. I could feel it, feel the gigantic inner shift. John had never tried to control me, had never presumed or taken me for granted, had never told me what to do or not do. In fact, he had bent over backward to accommodate me, and the repercussions of my bad choices in men. Right then, I knew I was falling in love with this man and that, in his eyes, I was glimpsing the beauty of his soul.

"If we were alone," I whispered, "I'd do a striptease for you."

He looked surprised, delighted, and as swept up in the moment as I was. "If we were alone," he whispered back, "we would spend several days in bed. We would take our meals in bed. We would write ourselves into a story so grand there would be no end to it."

"If we were alone," I continued softly, tracing his knuckles with the tip of my index finger, "I would devour you from head to toe."

His eyes widened. "If we were alone, I would swallow you whole."

"If we were alone, I would tell you my deepest dreams and desires."

"If we were alone, I would reveal my soul to you."

Our eyes held a moment longer, then we both cracked up, doubling over with laughter.

The bus turned, John motioned toward the window, and I glanced outside. We were on the road that ran in front of the church, outside a barricade of cops and orange traffic cones, and were waved through it. Throngs of curious bystanders lined the road. Paul could be hiding among them, I thought, and felt unnerved at the prospect.

Then the bus turned down an alley alongside the church and pulled up behind it. To our right were picnic tables shaded by trees with shiny green spring leaves. Birds sang from their branches. To our left was the rear entrance of the church. No security back here.

We piled off, and I was surprised to see John's son and his girlfriend get out of a car and hurry over to us. They hugged us both hello, and I introduced them to Isabella. Nick and Nina fell into step beside us, gushing with excitement about watching the filming, meeting the cast, the whole nine yards. And John was obviously delighted that they'd made it.

As we approached the rear entrance, a tall, gray-haired priest moved toward us, and for a moment, I thought that I was hallucinating, that he wasn't real. Then he stopped in front of us and said, "Samantha!"

"*Father Rinaldi?*" I whispered. "Oh, my God . . ."

He laughed and hugged me hello, and waves of emotion crashed over me. I nearly cried. "But how . . ."

"It's still my church. When the producers requested permission to film here, the bishop told me about it, and as soon as I heard it was *Brooklyn Story,* I knew I had to be here."

I quickly introduced him to Isabella and John and the others, and for a few minutes we all stood out there in the warm light, talking. Then he drew me aside. "I just want to reassure you, Sam, that there won't be any reprisals from the old Brooklyn Boys against you because of the movie. The word in the neighborhood is that everyone is thrilled they're going to hit the big screen. Most of them have read your novels, too. So don't ever hesitate to admit the story is true."

"Of all the things you might have said to me, Father Rinaldi, this is the best."

"Good." He slipped his arm through mine, and we walked to the door. De Niro stood just inside the door, decked out like Father Rinaldi, and ushered us all into the church. "So Father Rinaldi," De Niro said. "Do I pass the muster?"

Rinaldi laughed. "Absolutely."

When De Niro saw Isabella, he held out his hand. "It's a pleasure to meet you, Isabella. You're the spitting image of your mother."

"Wow, thank you, Mr. De Niro. And you're a convincing-looking priest!" She whipped out her phone. "May I take a photo of the two of us together?"

"Definitely."

He slipped his arm around her, and Isabella held her camera out in front of her and snapped three pictures. "Do you, uh, mind if I put them on Facebook?"

"Facebook, Twitter, Instagram—do the whole thing. And text them to Brian, okay? He has my number. We'll use them to advertise the film."

They laughed and high-fived each other, and we moved on into the church. Habit prompted me to dip my fingers into the bowl of holy water. I blessed myself, then continued deeper into the church.

The crew began setting up their equipment, and Father Rinaldi, Isabella, Liza, and I slid into the last pew, where I had often sat during my visits to the church. One of the scenes that would be shot today was when Rinaldi and I had sat in that very pew and he had asked me how my writing was going. I could remember the conversation so clearly— and not because I'd just looked at the dialogue in the script. I could remember the aroma of Rinaldi's aftershave, the way he combed his hair, the intensity in his eyes, and the tone of his voice. This man was like the faith I never had. He was a rock for me.

So, you have a new boyfriend, he'd said that day.

It hadn't been a question. Rinaldi had known everyone and everything in our corner of Bensonhurst. He would have been in the mob if he hadn't become a priest, I was sure of that much. I wondered how some men ended up on Tony's path and how others, like Rinaldi, ended up on a spiritual path.

Tony, I had told him.

That strapping young blond man.

Yes!

The same young man who cuffed a boy at Outer Skates yesterday?

Yes. And I remembered the sinking feeling in my stomach that Rinaldi even knew about that. I knew how the incident looked to the priest, how it colored his opinion of Tony.

And that's the type of person you should be with, child?

He's just like everybody else, Father. Only different, too, you'll see.

I tapped Rinaldi's arm. "Do you remember that day as clearly as I do? When we sat here and you asked how my writing was going?"

"Of course I do."

"Your encouragement meant a lot to me, Father Rinaldi."

Thinking back about that conversation now, hearing it in my head, I was struck mostly by my own naïveté, my youthful hope that Tony Kroon spelled true love. Had I really been that brainwashed by my life in Brooklyn, by such a gross lack of expectation? This lack of expectation probably had been the very impetus I had needed to write myself out of Brooklyn.

I see a lot. And I hear even more. I don't like a lot of what I hear. I don't want you to get hurt.

I won't, Father.

I have faith in you, child. And he had glanced toward the statue of Mary at the front of the church. *And I have faith that our Blessed Mother will watch over you.* The moment he'd uttered those words, I knew he sensed my own connection to the Blessed Mother.

As it turned out, Rinaldi had been right about Tony Kroon. He had known what kind of shit Tony was. He had known and tried to warn me. But I was driven by hormones, a need to be loved, to be accepted, and to belong somewhere, anywhere.

I often wondered how my life would be different if I'd never met Tony, what unimagined paths I might have taken. For that matter, what path might things have taken if I'd never met Alec? Would I have had Isabella with another man? Was the soul bond between a mother and her child so powerful that she would have come to me regardless of who her father was?

These questions were the kind I had asked for as long as I can remember, in the privacy of my own mind. These inner dialogues had fueled my imagination as a writer and enabled me to at least articulate what I was feeling and to get it down on paper. I had kept voluminous journals over the year and still had them.

Some people carted furniture around with them from place to place, or photo albums or their favorite shoes. But my personal history was in those journals, and maybe someday in the distant future, when I was very old and looking back over my life, those journals would help me recall some detail that age had stolen from me. Or perhaps they would sustain me in some other way. One of my future projects was to have the journals turned into computer files so they could never be lost, so I wouldn't have to worry about the paper turning yellow.

As the shooting began, John, Nick, and Nina joined us in the pew, and we all sat spellbound, watching Jenean and De Niro doing their thing. They were both masterly actors. She had captured my younger self so perfectly, it was as if she had zipped herself up inside my skin and bones. She even talked like I did, fast, and had my hand gestures down pat. She moved as I did, flicked her hair with her hand the way I did. Spooky.

Just as it had been disturbing to see her playing those scenes with my mother and Grandma Ruth, it was now eerie to watch her play my younger self, that self who had been so conflicted about everything and so deeply insecure. Jenean had captured that insecurity in her expressions, her eyes, in the tone of her voice, in her very presence.

Just as De Niro/Rinaldi was telling the younger Sam that he didn't like what he'd heard about Tony Kroon, the rear door of the church suddenly exploded open. A thin, haggard man with a scraggly beard and soiled clothes stumbled inside, shouting, *"I'm her father, I have every right to be in here, I'm her fuckin' father."*

What the hell. Vito? Here? Now? How? What hole had he crawled out of? How had he known where to find me?

Since no one knew if Vito was armed, and because he sounded as if he'd just escaped a nuthouse, bedlam erupted inside the church—people shouting, four cops racing in after Vito, more security personnel pouring in behind them. Vito was a wild man, a madman, waving his skinny little arms, yelling—just as Paul had yelled during that terrible scene in front of Blu Jam. Cameramen and other members of the crew scrambled to get out of Vito's way.

I was so shocked that I was paralyzed, incapable of movement, barely breathing, while everyone else around me shot to their feet, dived for cover, got out of the way. Vito moved like the wind, and kept shouting and waving his arms, wild with rage, hatred, ferocity. It was like a scene from a nightmare, one of those horrid dreams from which you suddenly awaken, covered in sweat, your heart hammering, its vividness so real that you're sure the dream has followed you into waking life.

He got halfway up the aisle before one of the cops tackled him, and they both crashed to the floor, Vito shrieking, kicking, biting. It took three cops to hold him down, while a fourth cop cuffed him.

"You broke my hand, you bastards," he shrieked.

My paralysis shattered. I shot to my feet and moved toward him, my father, Isabella's grandfather. Waves of revulsion swept through me. I was mortified and ashamed that my daughter now knew the truth, that the crazy, scrawny man who had confronted her all those weeks ago at her school was here now, screaming the same thing he had then. I couldn't wrench my eyes away from him.

And then Vito spotted me, saw me walking toward him, rapidly. *"Bitch, you bitch! Tell them who I am! Tell them the truth!"*

Seeing me seemed to infuse him with adrenaline, and he somehow managed to break away from the cops and stumble toward me, his hands cuffed behind him so that he moved awkwardly, like some grotesque, mutant spider scrambling toward its prey. His shouts echoed in the cavernous church, bounced off the walls and between the stained-glass windows, between the towering statues of the Blessed Mother and Christ, from one station of the cross to another, from one confessional to the next. A travesty. A sacrilege.

It infuriated me that he had burst into a place of worship and into this sacrosanct bastion of peace and harmony from my childhood. This church was one of the few places in my childhood where I'd felt safe. And then he stopped, and I stopped; we were only a yard apart.

"Tell 'em, Sam!" he shrieked. *"Tell 'em who I am!"*

I was aware of Vito's erratic, ragged breathing, of the cops shouting, of people still scrambling to get out of the crazy man's way. Tears flooded my eyes. Everything around me faded into a blur. The only thing that existed was Vito's tragic, haunted face—the rheumy eyes, the unshaven jaw, the flaring of his nostrils, the spittle caught in a corner of his mouth.

"Tell them, Sam, tell them who I am," he shouted again.

His words echoed inside my skull.

Tell them!

The world screeched into a slow-motion nightmare, my eyes bored into his. His nostrils flared again. One of his legs shot out and narrowly missed kicking me in the stomach. Then two cops tackled him again, and the three of them fell into one of the pews, Vito still shrieking and screaming, kicking and biting like a rabid dog. His face burned as red as a radish, the tendons in his neck stood out like cords of rope, his eyes bulged in their sockets. I knew this image of Vito would stick with me for the rest of my life.

The cops finally restrained Vito once more and jerked him to his feet. They pushed him out of the pew, into the aisle where I was standing.

"Tell them who I am," he hissed, blood blooming in a corner of his mouth and streaming from a gash over his left eye. *"I'm your father, admit it, say it, tell them, tell them. . . ."*

His words throbbed in my ears. Why was it so important to him that I tell anyone who he was? Was it public recognition that he craved? A public acknowledgment? What the hell *did* he want from me?

I let him have it. I said it exactly as I saw it. "You're not my father. You're the man who slammed a car jack across my mother's pregnant belly, who used to beat her senseless, who abandoned his family, who left us so poor we went on public assistance. Because of you, we needed food stamps to eat. Because of you, my mother drank herself into a stupor every night. Because of you, all of us were damaged. That's who you are. That's the only thing you are. That's the only thing you ever were and the only thing you ever will be."

I took great satisfaction in the fact that he was shocked into muteness, that his haunted eyes looked as though they would pop out of their sockets, that his mouth fell open. In the silence, in the utter, fragile silence that spread throughout the church, his gasp sounded preternaturally loud. I knew he never expected me to say what I'd said, to reveal the truth about what kind of man he was, to expose him in such a public way. Never mind that he had burst in here to demand that I acknowledge him. Never mind that he probably had expected me to fall to my knees in front of him, sobbing with gratitude that he'd found me, that he'd entered my life again.

What total bullshit, Vito.

Then I swept past him and headed for the nearest door.

The instant I stepped into the deserted alley, I burst into tears and covered my face with my hands. Now everyone knew the truth. Everyone—even Isabella—whom I had tried so hard to protect from him, from his toxic being.

A part of me desperately yearned to feel compassion for Vito. I wanted to go back inside the church and put my arms around him and pat him on the back as though he were a small child in need of comfort.

But how do you forgive the unforgivable?

Forgiveness was a spiritual practice advocated and taught by Christ, Buddha, Gandhi, Martin Luther King Jr., and many other spiritual teachers. Years ago, Priti had told me a Tibetan Buddhist story that came to mind now about two Buddhist priests who ran into each other some years after they'd both been released from prison, where they had been ruthlessly tortured by their captors.

The first monk asked the other monk: "Have you forgiven them yet?"

The second monk drew back in horror. "Never! I'll never forgive them!"

And the first monk remarked, "Well, I guess they still have you in prison, don't they?"

I was like that second monk. I had never forgiven Vito, Tony, Alec, or even my mother. Not really. I liked to believe I had, but deep down, the core of resentment had remained for all these years, festering, flaring up, maintaining the endless internal loop, the pattern, the *vibe* that ultimately had attracted Paul.

After Alec's death and the insurance money that had enabled Isabella and me to move to Malibu, it was as if God, the universe, some greater force, had tossed one more challenge my way. Paul. *Let's see how you deal with this.* And as long as it kept happening, it meant the pattern hadn't been broken.

In a sense, Paul was the embodiment of Vito, Tony, Alec. He was the darkest embodiment of their collective soul.

Even though I couldn't bring myself to run after the cops and forgive Vito to his face, I whispered, "I forgive you, Vito. I forgive you."

If words have power, then these words would ripple through the invisible net that Priti believed connected us all and he would feel them, wouldn't he? He would understand, wouldn't he? He would change, right?

That wasn't the point. I couldn't change Vito. My forgiveness couldn't change him. He had to forgive himself, just as I did.

The door behind me opened and whispered shut, and my daughter's arms reached around me, holding me tightly. We stood there like that for several long moments, until the rhythms of our breathing became one. Then she pulled back and looked up at me with those wide, beautiful eyes, her father's eyes. "I understand," she whispered. "I understand why you didn't tell me the truth that day."

I hugged her, kissed the top of her head, and inhaled the scent of her hair, her youth, the tangible reality of my daughter, the greatest gift of my life. "I . . . I just couldn't allow him to poison your life the way he did mine. Some people are just so consumed with rage, it takes over their lives. That's how I think it is for him, love."

And for Paul.

"I know, Mom, I understand." She stepped back, wiped at my tears with her hand. "They took him away, and he shrieked and fought them the entire time. The whole thing was pretty sad."

Sad, pathetic, tragic. But not for Isabella or for me.

"Have they started filming again?"

"In a few minutes."

The door opened once more, and John and Liza came out, their expressions concerned, worried. "You okay?" John slipped his arm around me.

"Yes." Not *maybe,* but a resounding *yes.*

"And here we thought Paul was going to show up," Liza remarked.

"Ironic, isn't it?" John said. "You prepare for one thing and something else happens."

"Life," Liza remarked. "You can't anticipate everything. You can try, but the best-laid plans and so on . . . We're just glad you're okay."

"We should have had security at the rear of the church," John said, as if thinking aloud. "I'm not sure why we all overlooked that."

"Who would think that a madman would come through the back door of the church?" Liza asked, then touched my arm. "Let's take a walk. "It's a gorgeous day. We could use some fresh air."

"You two go on," Isabella said. "I'd like to watch the rest of the filming."

John leaned forward, kissed me quickly. "Isabella and I will save your seats."

As they turned away to go back inside, I heard Isabella say, "So you like my mom, huh?"

John glanced back at me and winked. "I'm crazy about her."

"She's a great person, you know."

"So are you," John said.

"I hear you're pretty awesome, too."

He laughed. "Well, that's good to know."

"We sound like a mutual admiration society," she said.

"Hey, that's not a bad thing, is it?"

Isabella laughed. "I guess not. So what do you think . . ."

I didn't hear the rest of what my daughter said because she and John vanished through the rear door of the church. Liza and I just looked at each other, and she burst out, "Wow, my God. He's a keeper, Sam."

Yeah, I thought so, too, and nodded. "But a part of me keeps wondering if he's too good to be true."

"I'm so with you on that." She lowered her voice as we walked through the alley toward the rear of the church. "I stayed with Brian last night. He . . . he thinks I'm amazing. Can you believe it? In all the years I was married, my husband never once told me he thought I was fucking amazing. Never."

I gave her arm a quick squeeze. "But you are. Brian sees the same things in you that I see. How great is that?"

"It's wonderful. But, Sam, I don't want to be one of those women who needs a man's approval to feel whole. It's not what I'm about. I mean, Brian's exciting and an incredible lover and he's oozing with class . . . but maybe it's too soon. Maybe I need to be by myself a while longer, to . . ."

"Enjoy the moment, Liza. That's all we've got; it's the

only thing that's certain. This second, this instant." *Thank you, Tolle.*

She started laughing. "I could be saying this to you, Sam. Do you realize that? Even though you were dealt a shit like Vito for a father, you've got great people in your life *now*. That's what's important."

She was right.

We emerged from the alley and the air filled, suddenly, with the songs of birds, the coos of pigeons, the ring of distant laughter, and a flurry of butterflies we startled from the bushes. Behind the church, we sat down at one of the picnic tables, in a pool of warm light.

"I just want you to know something, Sam. If I'd been in your shoes inside that church, I probably would've slugged Vito. You handled it incredibly well."

"I wasn't consciously *handling* anything. That's what's weird. At first, I was paralyzed, then I felt infuriated that he would burst into a church like that, yelling obscenities. And then I felt . . . humiliated."

"Naw, the core of who you are can't be damaged by Vito, Sam. The best thing that ever happened to you and your mother was that he left when he did. His function in the bigger scheme of things was to supply DNA. That's it. And I think he knows it, and it just galls him to realize that the child he abandoned grew up to make something of herself in spite of him."

"But I realized I needed to forgive him."

"Sometimes in order to do that, the past has to be exorcised. And right now"—she tapped her temple—"that part of me that's a tad psychic is telling me that's what this whole thing in there was about. Some pattern has been broken, some internal thing."

She was right. I felt it. In a sense, the filming of *Brooklyn Story* was a kind of purging. I was laying my past to rest, and slowly but surely I was finding my way into a future untarnished by everything that had infected my earlier life. John was evidence of that.

I hugged Liza. "Thank you for always being there for me."

"Honey, I feel the same." She gave me a high five. "Soul sisters forever!"

SIXTEEN

As the bus pulled up in front of Sally's coffee shop, I spotted Alec's mother and sister on the sidewalk. Punctual. It meant they were really excited to see Isabella.

"You want to eat at Sally's or with your grandmother?" I asked Isabella.

She glanced through the window, watching them, then looked at me. "I haven't seen them in, like, nearly two years, Mom. I should eat with them."

I kissed the top of her head, grabbed her pack off the floor at her feet, and handed it to her. "Got your phone?"

"Check."

"Your iPad?"

She rolled her eyes. "Check."

"Your—"

"Check, check, check." Then she whispered, "I'm sixteen, okay? Not five. But I love you anyway!"

Filomena, Alec's mother, was a large-boned woman, yet slim and trim, and had aged since I'd last seen her. Her chin-length blond hair was threaded with gray, and new lines had appeared at the corners of her eyes. But she greeted us as she always had, with bear hugs and the quiet elegance that defined her. And Gianna, Alec's sister, was overjoyed to see us, especially Isabella, with whom she had always been close.

We chatted for a few minutes there on the sidewalk outside Sally's, then Isabella hugged me good-bye, slung the strap of her pack over her shoulder, and said she'd check in later in the day.

The three of them walked off with their arms linked, their laughter echoing in the air, and I stood there alone, watching them, a void opening in my heart. She was just going to be gone overnight, I reminded myself.

But I immediately projected forward to the day she would leave for college, and I knew I would break down in tears then, just as I had the day I'd dropped her off for her first day at kindergarten. Once you were a parent, you were always a parent. It didn't end when your child turned eighteen or twenty-one or thirty or forty. Always, your child was your child.

It didn't mean I had to project.

Liza came up behind me and touched my shoulder. "Hey, lunch is ready."

"There goes my baby," I murmured.

"Sam. It's for one night."

"Yeah, I know. But suppose the world ends between now and tomorrow morning?"

"Oh, my God." Liza rolled her eyes. "Seriously?"

"No. Just thinking out loud."

Liza stood beside me, gazing after them. "When my oldest son went off to college, I used to lie on his bed at night, inhaling the smell of him on his pillow, and sob myself to sleep."

I laughed. "I hope I'm not going to be *that* bad!"

"When my second son left for college, I didn't cry as much. When my youngest departed, I didn't cry at all. It gets easier. They're always your kids, the best part of who you are; that never changes. But it gets easier to let them go."

I realized I was not accomplished at *letting go*. But I knew the words, understood the sentiment: *let go and let*

God . . . I knew about surrender, about stepping back and allowing a higher power to direct the flow of events. It seemed that I knew a lot of words and phrases like that, but all too often the words didn't penetrate, didn't sink in deep enough.

We went inside the Greek coffee shop, and I was immediately struck by how Sally's existed in a permanent time warp. Nothing had changed since Isabella and I had been in here two years ago—the stainless steel counter stools with red cushions, the black-and-white ceramic floor tiles, even the booths beyond the counter. In fact, not much had changed since I'd first stepped in here more than thirty years ago.

Sally and her staff had prepared an amazing spread of food—feta cheese salads, humus with pita, fried chicken sandwiches, and even my favorite, moussaka. I went through the line with everyone else, helping myself to a little of everything. We all squeezed into booths and tables that still faced glass display cases that showcased doughnuts, pies, Greek pastries. "Play at Your Own Risk" by Planet Patrol started playing on the jukebox. It was like this faded sound in the background had brought me right back to the old days. It was picture-perfect. For the next thirty or forty minutes, the place rocked with tunes from the seventies and eighties, laughter rang out, and I truly believed these people were my extended family. I felt safe and secure enough with them to be who I was.

When the filming started, it was a scene with Jenean and a young brunette named Anna DiAntonio, who played Janice, my closest friend at the time. As John and I watched from the sidelines, I once again remembered that day vividly, how Janice had grabbed a couple of menus propped up by the condiments and passed me one.

"Order whatever you want, Sam. My treat."

"I have some money, Jan."

"No ya don't."

"I will as soon as I turn sixteen and get that job in the book-store."

"Then you'll be saving for college. You can pick up the tab at those fancy places in Manhattan you'll be taking me to when you're a big shot."

I still recalled how Janice never once made me feel poor, how there was never any doubt in her words when she referred to my dream of being a writer, a dream I'd shared with her. There had been people like that in my life from time to time, people who believed in my talent, in me, and I understood how fortunate I was that I had those kinds of people in my life now.

At the time this conversation took place between Janice and me, I'd had only three bucks in my pocket.

"I'll have a Coke and some fries," I said.

"No way," Janice replied, and opened my menu. *"I'm starved, and I'm not goin' to eat alone. Besides, we have a lot to talk about."*

"That guy you mentioned?"

"I had to check it out first with Richie. He's okay with it, and Tony's available."

"I already told you I wasn't interested."

"Your mouth says no, but your eyes and budding breasts say something else."

At that point, John elbowed me gently in the side and mouthed, *Did she really say that?*

I covered my mouth with my hand, snickering silently, my head bobbing.

These days, Janice was happily married, had four kids, and lived in Florida with her husband, who was in the import/export business: women's clothing. The journey she'd taken from the past to where she was now in her life was living proof that anyone can escape his or her past.

John slipped out his phone and tapped away. A moment later, my phone vibrated. He'd sent me a text message.

When we wrap here, how about dinner?

Sounds great!

We looked up simultaneously and in his eyes, I saw the promise of a magnificent night ahead.

The scenes shot in Sally's required several retakes and some rapid script doctoring. When we finally wrapped, it was nearly six p.m. Everyone looked exhausted but happy.

"Okay, people, great job," King said to the crowd. "We reconvene tomorrow morning in front of the hotel at nine, except for the art and maintenance crew, who will be setting up the stalls for the annual Festival of Santa Rosalia. Sam, could you be on site at eight, just to take a walk through with Renée to make sure it looks the way it should?"

"I'll be there," I said.

John touched the small of my back and guided me out the front door and onto the sidewalk in front of Sally's. It was still light out, the air was cool but not cold. I zipped up my lightweight jacket.

"Car?" John asked. "Or should we walk?"

"Where're we going?"

"My Brooklyn hideout."

"Really? You actually have a hideout?"

"Bought it a few years ago. I love Malibu; I love California. But my roots are here."

"But if you have a hideout here, why're you staying at the Greenwich?"

"Because you are," he said, as though it were the most obvious thing in the universe.

We walked several blocks to this adorable, out-of-the-way mom-and-pop pizzeria that was attached to what looked like a small two-family house. Very old-school Italian, and mostly what I grew up with in this neighborhood. I loved it immediately as I watched our elongated shadows moving along the sidewalk with us. "Do you ever wonder about them?" I suddenly asked, and pointed at our shadows.

John laughed and slung an arm around my shoulders. "The shadow people. When I was really young, I used to see them a lot. I remember one time my mother and I went to some neighborhood park, nothing special, just a slide, swings, a merry-go-round. I was maybe five or six. And I kept seeing something in my peripheral vision, something . . . quick, fleeting, a dark form. It intrigued me. And when I mentioned it to my mother, she told me this really complicated story about the shadow people. How they live in a dimension parallel to our own, a two-dimensional existence."

"Like the characters in that book *Flatland*."

"Yeah, similar to that. But the way my mother told the story, it freaked me out. In retrospect, I think her version of the shadow people referred to the mafia."

"I think they're magical. Watch."

We stopped there on the sidewalk, pedestrians flowing around us, and I cupped his face in my hands and brought my face very close to his and whispered, "Now look at them."

We both glanced down at our shadows. Their bodies were pressed so tightly together that no light shone between them. And because our faces were so close, it looked as if we were kissing, but we weren't. His eyes slipped back to mine. "Spooky shit, Sam."

"But spooky good. They have their own lives."

He kissed the tip of my nose and slipped his fingers

back through my hair, and we hurried on through the lengthening shadows, our hands clasped. Once when Alec and I were out walking, I drew his attention to our shadows on the sidewalk and said, *Do you think they have their own lives separate from us?*

He'd looked at me like I had lost my mind. *What the hell, Sam. They're shadows, that's all.*

But didn't infinite possibility lie in our perceptions? If we couldn't think outside the box in which we'd been raised, where would any of us be? Still living in caves.

We stopped outside the house, and John opened the door. We climbed two flights of stairs. I felt strangely nervous—butterflies in my stomach, sweaty palms, tongue-tied. I might as well have been seventeen years old again.

Since I had never seen his place in Malibu, I had no idea what to expect of this hideaway in Brooklyn. Maybe he was into deep purples and shades of black, maybe I would find mold on the food in his fridge, his furniture in tatters, his bedsheets soiled, his laundry room piled high with refuse from other trysts. Maybe he was an S&M freak with whips and chains in the bedroom. Maybe this, maybe that. After all, what did I really know of this man other than the persona he showed to the world and a kiss under a mistletoe thirty years ago?

Then the door swung open, and I walked into a spacious, twilit apartment with high ceilings, skylights, hanging planters that billowed with ivy and ferns, wooden floors, impeccable furnishings, a place that whispered, *Take off your shoes, have a bite to eat, chill, relax, kick back, you are home.* John pressed a button on the wall, and some sexy, smooth Barry White music floated through the room. It sounded faded, like at Sally's earlier, but was he trying to get me in the mood? I certainly was already.

He opened terrace doors to reveal a beautiful garden with lounge chairs. It appeared to be a hidden oasis in

Brooklyn. John seemed to enjoy ducking away from people, from the world. He was a private kinda guy, and I loved that most about him. I noticed the wall-to-ceiling bookcase that must have held several hundred books, all of them neatly upright and probably organized according to author, subject, a John decimal system. I noticed a lot of war, Roman Empire, and old Bibles. The wraparound sofa, a rich, walnut brown, looked comfortable enough to sleep on. More books were stacked neatly on the stone coffee table. A colorful throw rug in the center of the room invited you to plop down and time-travel to . . . well, wherever your imagination could take you.

The largest wall held a high-def plasma TV that also served as a computer screen.

"Thirsty?" he asked.

"Parched."

"Hungry?"

"Starved."

"Delivery or should I cook?"

"Your choice."

He thought a moment, then ducked into an open kitchen with granite counters, cedar cabinets, and a rack shaped like an infinity symbol that held bottles of wine. He cut up some Parmesan cheese and put out some olives from the refrigerator and laid some thinly sliced pieces of prosciutto on the plate. I enjoyed watching his hands move with ease. I enjoyed watching him and appreciated the simplicity with which he moved around the kitchen. Most men I'd known were clumsy in a kitchen and seemed to regard the room as a woman's domain.

He poured the wine and tapped his glass against mine. "*Salud*, to Brooklyn. To the present."

"To Brooklyn."

As I sipped the delicious wine, I felt as if it might be a magical potion, the kind of thing a woman in a fairy tale would drink before she turned into a princess. Or a goddess. "This is fantastic, John."

"Like you," he said, holding up the glass, and our eyes locked.

I sipped again from my glass and thought it was probably the best thing I had ever tasted in my life, indescribable, silk sliding down my throat, through my bones, all the way to my toes. "What, is this like some sort of aphrodisiac?" I blurted.

"I think of everything, my Stunner, ahead of time. My mind is always going and never forgets, especially one as beautiful as you. I have never forgotten you. I always knew we would meet again, even if it did take this long."

"I'm still in a kind of shock, Bobby Santos." I poked him in the chest. "I think I actually like your new name better. John Steeling. It rolls off my tongue."

He laughed. "Lemme see what else I can rustle up in terms of food. This stuff will knock us flat on our asses if we drink it too fast on empty stomachs."

I sipped, paused, paused, sipped again. "What can I do to help?"

"Set the table and be beautiful as you are?"

"Perfect." I started opening drawers, moving around the kitchen, carried a couple of plates and some utensils over to the kitchen table.

He eyed the contents of the fridge, shook his head, opened the freezer, and began removing packages of food. "Okay, our choices, Sam. I don't have the ingredients I need to make any of my favorite Italian dinners. But we've got the workings of a fantastic Tuscan salad—and a pizza."

"Who supplied the fresh stuff for the salad?" I was imagining a wife hidden in the closet. "And who waters the plants?"

"An Asian woman who is, I don't know, probably in her late seventies. She lives downstairs and takes care of the place for me. Every so often I call her and give her a list of stuff I need, and she goes shopping for me. She cleans twice a month and comes in every few days to water my plants."

"So you have a place that functions on automatic."

"Several places."

"Yeah?" I poured water into the glasses I'd placed on the table. "Where else?"

I expected him to name places like the south of France. Monaco. Tasmania. Auckland. Instead, he named San Francisco and Santa Fe, places I'd never been. "Why those cities?" I asked as he chopped up veggies to put on top of the pizza.

"San Francisco may be the best city on the planet, and from there, I can explore northern California, and I love wines. Santa Fe has a thriving art scene and is close enough to Anasazi ruins. But my favorite is Santiago, Chile. I get there only once or twice a year."

"All cities that start with S. What's that about?"

"*S* is the initial that captured my heart early on in life, so I follow things that I love. I try to do whatever feels right at the time. Living in a concrete room can teach you that."

Twenty minutes later, our pizza was done, and we had opened another bottle of wine. "What's Chile like?" I asked.

"Gorgeous, varied, and parts of it are mystical. Like the island of Chiloé. There's a—"

"A ghost ship there," I said, interrupting him. "I read about it somewhere. The *Caleuche* . . . yeah, I think that's what it's called."

"On Chiloé, they believe that ghost ship exists. They believe in mermaids. The place is enchanted, I'm sure of it. I took Brian with me once. We agreed it would be a great location for a movie." He laughed. "All we need is a script."

"When have you had the time to buy all these properties?" The question was crass and none of my business, but an answer seemed important, at least in some deeper sense. Maybe everything he was telling me was bullshit, right? It wouldn't be the first time.

"A couple times a year I take a few weeks off. That's when I've bought properties in the past." He popped the last bite of pizza into his mouth and sipped at his wine.

I touched his arm. "Show me the rest of your place," I said.

"You have to see the coolest thing yet." He motioned for me to follow him. "No one else has ever seen it. The renovations were just completed last week."

The exquisite thing wasn't his bedroom, per se, but started *in* his bedroom, in a corner: a tight, spiral iron staircase that led to the roof. Half of the roof was a garden where he grew herbs and bamboo.

"Wow, this is impressive. But who tends the garden?" I asked.

"The Asian woman."

"Does she have a name?"

"Yes, Asian woman." We both chuckled.

"Lalyie. She is lovely, I'm blessed."

"So your hideouts hum along without you." In all those places he'd mentioned where he owned homes.

"Yeah, something like that."

"What do you pay them? No, wait. I'm sorry. That's none of my business."

John just laughed. "You always have so many questions?"

"Inquisitive."

"It's refreshing. Most people are more interested in talking about themselves." He was standing in a slice of sunlight during this exchange and looked breathtakingly handsome as his hands patted the air. "Okay, let's see. I employ a dozen people to take care of my homes when I'm gone and to stock the places before I arrive. I pay my employees well and am grateful for them. The only place where I hold a mortgage is on my place in Malibu, for tax purposes."

"Uh, okay. I wasn't really asking you for an accounting, John, I was just wondering about . . ." *The way you live. Who you are.* "I was just curious about how it all works."

"After those years in prison, when I didn't have control over any facet of my life, when it was the same routine day after day, I enjoy making choices that make me feel good. Does that sound selfish?"

"*Selfish?* No way. It sounds like all of us should be living our lives like that."

"C'mon, I'll show you the other part of the roof."

I followed him to the other side of the roof, where four cobblestone steps led to a small tinted-glass dome. It was a beautiful room that held a perfectly round bed with an African motif—quilt, rug, pillowcases. There were plants everywhere, so it possessed an unmistakable lushness that scented the air. Next to the bed was a gorgeous cedar nightstand that held a bark wood lamp and several neatly stacked books. Against one wall was a pint-sized fridge, a teak dresser, and a closet. Another door led to a bathroom.

"Your man cave," I said with a laugh. "It's fantastic."

He pressed a button on the wall; the dome darkened, and the bark lamp as well as several others came on, emitting a light so soft I could feel it against my skin. I set my drink on the nightstand and shed my jacket. I could not believe how he had this under the radar, how hidden away this space was. In the depths of a Brooklyn street, and he did so much to it. I could also tell how John never forgot where he came from, still keeping some sort of roots here. Just his name. That was forgotten.

He set his drink on a nightstand on the other side of the bed, and the dome now blacked out completely. I wasn't sure that I liked the tinted darkness. But I definitely liked what I saw as he unbuttoned and removed his shirt—a tattoo of Christ next to an image of the Brooklyn Bridge. "Wow," I whispered, running my hand over it. I couldn't believe the artwork or the man who had done this to his chiseled body. To be able to ink all your beliefs onto your body was, to me, a beautiful form of expression. Not all men can display it as such.

Then he turned, showing me his back. The tattoo of the Archangel Michael stood next to a tattoo of a Blessed Mother. The artwork was exquisite, detailed, breathtaking. I was blown away that all the things I believed in were on this man's body. "Every morning, I light three candles," I said quietly. "To the Blessed Mother, Michael, and Buddha—that's all you're missing from this wonderful exhibit."

His eyes widened. "Really, Samantha?" I loved it when he said my full name aloud.

"Paul used to make fun of me for doing that. He told me religion doesn't have any place in Hollywood."

"Religion probably doesn't, but spiritual practices definitely fit into Hollywood." Then he cupped my face in his hand and drew me down against him, against the bed, and our clothes slipped away from us like water. The sheets were pure white and the fabric ever so soft. I melted into them. He drew the top sheet over us, and it fluttered down against my skin with exquisite softness. His hands moved over my body with unbearable gentleness, and yet it felt as if they emitted an electrical current that pulsed from my head to my toes.

"My God, you are beautiful," he whispered, and kissed my eyelids, the tip of my nose, the corners of my mouth, my breasts; and his hands slipped under me, over me, between my thighs.

We rolled, laughing, across the inviting sheets, our bodies pressed so tightly together that it was impossible to tell where my skin ended and his began. I pulled back at one point and ran my hands over his chest, over the intricate tattoos, and I wanted to know in detail about each one and its origin. "Tell me about these," I murmured, sliding my fingertips over the ink on his skin.

He rolled onto his side, head propped up with one hand, and started talking, telling me how each tattoo had come about as his free hand slipped over my body. "My Blessed Mother was before I went to prison. It represents faith and hope. Michael is my protector, my warrior; and Jesus, well, he's pure love. And, of course, the bridge was who I was and where I've been, and I can never forget that . . . it led me back here to you, my Brooklyn girl, my real-life Rapunzel, who was always filled with bags of love, even when we were kids. Remember you were the one who grabbed me under the mistletoe, always on the attack."

He explored me like Magellan exploring a foreign country, a new land, learning the valleys and peaks, the planes and angles of this new place.

Now he paused, and his mouth moved to where his hand had been, toying with my nipples. His tongue slid down the center of my body, circling my navel, inscribing a secret language against my belly and igniting a fire against my skin that burned hot and furiously.

He rocked back onto his heels, slipped his hands under me, and then his mouth moved between my legs. When his tongue touched me, I groaned and gripped his shoulders, the sensation so overwhelming that my body arched, hungry for more. His fingers slid inside me, and his tongue kept darting, flicking, tasting. My groans seemed to fill the dome, echoing, bouncing off the glass walls. I moaned loudly as I came, my body twitching, my nails sinking into his skin.

"Oh, my God," I moaned. "Not so fast . . . stop . . . don't stop . . . never stop . . ."

He brought me to the edge again and again, pausing just before I came, then held me there at the precipice, his mouth against mine, kisses between words, my hands groping at him, at his hardness, desperately wanting him inside me.

"Not yet," he said, his voice husky with desire.

He gently turned me onto my stomach; I lifted to my knees, and his hands ran over my ass, fastened to my hips. I felt his hardness against me and reached back, stroking him, trying to coax his penis inside of me. But his fingers slipped into me from a different angle and stroked long and hard, and I moaned into the pillow. His tongue slipped down my back, as if counting the steps in my spine, and I somehow rolled onto my back once more. He hovered just above me, his eyes locked on mine.

"I . . . I . . ."

"Ssshhh," he said, and kissed me again, his hands everywhere at once.

"Wait," I said, and took him in my mouth, and he groaned as his fingers knotted in my hair.

Then we rolled again, and he moved between my legs and his tongue teased me, flicking, darting away, driving me insane with desire. My body was slick with sweat; he licked it off my belly and lifted my hips and fastened his mouth against me. He stroked me with his finger, then his tongue, then both at once, and I began to shake and groan and didn't just fall over the precipice, I plunged. I screamed; I was sure I screamed, but his mouth covered mine and took my scream into himself.

Then he was inside of me, and we moved against each other, our bodies slapping together, our rhythm was perfection. I felt our inexorable power, a force of nature that could move mountains, change the course of rivers, and flip the planet on its axis. I lost track of time and space, lost track of everything.

We lay together beneath the tinted dome, in the soft light that might have been the glow of stars or of the moon, our fingers clasped. And we talked and made love again and talked and talked.

"I'd like to stay right here for the rest of my life," he said.

"We'd starve."

"Nah, we'd call the deli up the block and have them deliver whatever we need."

"We'd get fat."

He laughed. "Okay, so we could get up now and then and walk through Brooklyn."

"We'd have to shower now and then, too, you know."

He laughed and slipped his arm around me and glanced at the clock on the nightstand. "Holy shit, Sam, it's four in the morning."

"No way."

John got up and pressed a button that turned the dome transparent. The room filled with starlight. "Gorgeous, isn't it?" he asked.

"Incredible. But how can it be four a.m.?"

"We were abducted by aliens." He slipped back under the covers. "That's the only explanation."

I pulled the sheet over us and stifled a yawn. "Well, if it was aliens, I'm glad they abducted the two of us at the same time."

He slipped his arm under my shoulders, drawing me closer to him, and I instantly fell asleep.

The sun woke us a few hours later. I realized I didn't have even a toothbrush with me. I would have to go by the hotel to change clothes and freshen up before heading over to the park.

"We'd better get moving." I swung my legs over the edge of the bed, and he wrapped an arm around my waist and drew me back.

"One more minute," he whispered, and buried his face

in my hair. I turned and kissed him. The heat rose between us again, and I finally pulled back, traced the shape of his mouth with my finger. Then I vaulted off the bed, swept my clothes off the floor, and floated toward the bathroom.

Thirty minutes later, we were outside, moving along with the pedestrian traffic, the early-morning light spilling across a neighborhood as familiar to me as my own skin. But everything looked different. I felt as though I had been transported to some other world, a dimension of such magic and beauty that the air tasted new and fresh. Even the hum of traffic and noise sounded changed, almost musical.

"Ever since that day I saw you at Blu Jam," he said, "I imagined us walking along this very street after having spent the night together, knowing that the world would be transformed for me."

Was he really saying this? It was as if he'd just read my mind. As if he'd just stepped inside me and scooped out my thoughts and articulated them. This man knew everything I was thinking. "I feel like I woke up in a new life or something."

He laughed and squeezed my hand. "Same life, new story. When I first read your novel and then your script, I was blown away, Sam, by the honesty of what you'd written. So many of the women I've known have been deceptive and conniving, especially in Hollywood. Brian had emailed me the script and asked me what I thought. As soon as I'd finished reading it, I called him and told him that Gallery really needed to shoot this movie. An hour later, we had a deal with Paul."

Paul. During the night John and I had spent together, I'd completely forgotten about Paul, the monster in the shadows. And the nasty confrontation with Vito had been pushed out of my mind. Bliss, I realized, was possible even in the midst of chaos. Or maybe it grew out of chaos.

"I wonder how our lives would have been different if

something had developed between us after that first kiss all those years ago."

He shook his head. "I wasn't the person I am now. It wouldn't have worked. Besides, we're here now, that's what's important. In spite of all the bullshit the two of us have lived through, we found each other, Sam, once again."

He touched my chin, turning my face toward him, and kissed me. The crowd of pedestrians flowed around us, and once more I was transported, swept away like some lovesick teenager being kissed for the first time.

When we broke apart, he said, "You make me forget where I am."

"That's the nicest thing anyone has ever said to me. I feel the same way, my John Steeling."

He looked delighted and surprised and let out a gleeful roar. We hurried on through Brooklyn, through the morning light, our strides easy and quick, as though we were walking on air. Then John called for the car that took us back to the Greenwich.

SEVENTEEN

When we arrived at the park, the entire area had already been closed off for the shooting. Two dozen stalls were lined up in neat rows from one end of the park to the other. They would be selling food, crafts, statues of Santa Rosalia and other Catholic saints and icons. Some booths would feature games and raffles, and the place would be rocking with music. A DJ was setting up at the far end of the park, and I knew that one of the songs that would be playing was Cher's "Half-Breed."

The two hundred extras hired for this shoot spilled through the park. Some would play vendors in the stalls; others would be visitors at the festival. One scene would include Janice and me at a coin-toss booth, where you pitched a nickel into the center of a glass ashtray to win silly stuffed animals. A spotted giraffe, a black bear, a lion with a fuzzy mane, or a gangly-legged zebra with a yellow bow tied around its neck: I remembered all of this so vividly, it was like it had happened yesterday. It was as if, somewhere, my younger self still thrived and flourished.

The coin toss had been especially popular with the guys, who enjoyed showing off for their girlfriends. That day thirty years ago, I remembered, Janice had worn a red halter top and khaki chinos, and I had worn tapered lime-green pants and an off-white tank top that covered my modest breasts and tiny waist. The day had been muggy—not the perfect weather we presently had.

One of the scenes that would be shot this morning would involve Father Rinaldi—De Niro—who would be selling raffle tickets at the church's booth. He would spot us and wave us over. In real life, as Janice and I had moved toward him, we had talked about what a hot-looking guy he was. And he really had been a handsome man, tall and lean, with dark hair that was perfectly cut and a broad smile.

It's a shame such a hot-looking guy isn't available, Janice had said.

Tell me about it.

I could do him.

Janice!

Wouldya blame me?

We both had burst into giggles, silly teenage giggles, the kind of giggles you would hear at slumber parties or during long, hot afternoons in the summer when we hung out together at someone's house. When we reached the booth, Rinaldi had asked if we were enjoying ourselves.

How's your mom, Sam? he'd inquired.

It seemed to be common knowledge in the neighborhood that my mother had some problems. Or maybe it was just that Rinaldi knew more about his parishioners and their families than anyone had a right to know.

So-so.

I'll keep her in my prayers, Rinaldi had said.

Thanks, Father.

And Rinaldi had touched my shoulder and remarked how he hadn't seen me in church for a while. I had assured him I would be back soon, and he'd pressed a raffle ticket into my palm and told us to go have some fun.

Janice and I had melted away into the crowd, and she

had started looking around for Tony. *I guess Tony's not here yet*, Janice had remarked.

Maybe you missed him in this wall-to-wall crowd, Janice.

Not a chance. Believe me. Meaning that Tony Kroon was such a handsome hunk, no woman in her right mind could miss seeing him.

We had spotted Dara, one of Janice's classmates, in the crowd, being played by one of the extras. She was a voluptuous blonde—from a bottle, of course—who had been dating Vin. It was common knowledge on the streets that he beat up on her as often as he fucked her. I had started toward her, I remembered, but Janice had held me back. *You know how Dara flaunts it, and I want you to meet Tony on your own.*

What's the matter? Aren't we hot enough?

The oddest thing about these recollections, about how I was going to see them played out by actors and actresses, was that none of them affected me now. Even though I understood that these scenes were straight out of my life, I didn't experience the same angst I'd had when I'd first seen Susan, Jenean, and Camilla acting out those scenes in my old Brooklyn apartment. Maybe Liza was right that the filming of *Brooklyn Story* was a kind of purge.

John touched my elbow. "I'm off to find Brian."

"See ya around, handsome."

He laughed, bussed me on the cheek, and moved off through the crowd. I spotted Liza and Father Rinaldi near the food tent, where the cast and crew would be eating breakfast shortly, and I made a beeline toward them. Rinaldi hugged me hello. "I meant to catch up with you yesterday before you left the church, Sam. I just want you to know that I'm proud of the way you stood up to Vito."

"I had to, Father Rinaldi."

He gave my shoulder an affectionate squeeze. "See you out there, Sam." He gestured toward the sea of actors.

The expression of Liza's face was almost comical. I knew that she knew John and I had become lovers. That "tad psychic" part of her sensed it; that was how connected she and I were.

"You . . . look different," she remarked.

"Ya think?"

"Ha. I *know*."

"It changed something inside of me, Liza. Is that possible?"

"Possible?" She laughed. "Honey, you're absolutely glowing. I'm so happy for you."

I hugged her. "Maybe we both had to come full circle back to Brooklyn to find real love. Or does that sound hopelessly corny?"

"Who gives a shit how it sounds. I think it's true, and who woulda thunk it? C'mon, let's get a bite to eat. I'm famished." Then in a softer, confidential tone, she added, "Having sex half the night left me with a ferocious appetite!"

Once again, the spread of food was amazing: lard breads and frittatas—my favorite—and muffins, and half a dozen types of Italian pastries and espresso. There were even dishes that would be found in some of the stalls: calzones and sausage-and-pepper heroes. Those dishes used to be made by Papa Tucci, and on the day Janice and I had been at the festival, I'd wanted to buy both of them but didn't have the money.

Despite the fact that it was barely eight in the morning, I helped myself to both now, grateful that I could afford a full-time cook who would prepare those dishes for me daily, if that was what I wanted. Money may not buy happiness, but when you grew up as poor as I did, money certainly bought you a degree of freedom. Someone, maybe it was Priti, once remarked that my life had been filled with stark contrasts that enabled me to feel immense gratitude for what I had. It was true.

We sat at a table with Marvin and Flannigan, both of them in high spirits, chatting about the sightseeing they'd done after the shooting at Sally's had wrapped. I could tell that something good was developing between them, and I was happy for them both. What was it with this return to Brooklyn/New York stuff, anyway? Had it helped the three of us—Marvin, Liza, and me—open up in some way? Had it enabled us to tap into and manifest our deepest desires?

King stopped by our table, and I noticed the way he touched Liza's shoulder. "Ladies and gents, we're about ready to get under way here. Another ten minutes or so. Sam, do we have things set up correctly?"

"I walked through when John and I got here, Brian. It looks pretty much the way I remember it. Even the food." I gestured at my plate.

"Great. Perfect. We'll start the shooting with that scene where you and Janice see Father Rinaldi. Bob has to catch a plane in a couple of hours, so we want to do that scene first."

"Sounds great," I said.

Then King ran his fingers through Liza's hair, a slow, delicate caress. "Does this woman have gorgeous hair or what?"

Liza looked flustered, but said, "Honey, flattery will get you everywhere."

King laughed and motioned to his right, where John and Prince were entering the tent with Nina and Nick. "Hey, John's son made it. Good enough. The stars must be aligned or something." He walked out into the center of the tent to address the cast and crew. "Okay, people, listen up. We'll have exactly three hours for this shoot, so let's make the most of it. Everyone got their script notes?"

For the next ten minutes, he went through the script, explaining which scenes would be shot.

John, Nick, and Nina joined us at our table, and at one

point Nina leaned toward me and whispered, "I want you to know that I've never seen John happier. I think you're the reason."

"That's awesome to hear. He makes me feel the same way."

"He's such a great guy—Nick and I have been hoping he'd meet someone who deserves him."

"Did you know his ex?"

Nina wrinkled her nose as if she'd bitten into something bitter. "She was way before my time, but I met her once when she came to see Nick. A really pretty woman, but one of the most negative human beings I've ever been around. Nick refuses to have anything to do with her now. When John started making a lot of money in real estate, she tried to take him to court to collect back alimony or child support or something. Thing is, there was never any agreement about child support *or* alimony because John had full custody of Nick. Go figure. People do some pretty strange things when money is involved."

She was preaching to the choir. Vito was proof of that.

"Well, Nick's lucky that his dad makes up for what his mother lacks."

"That's for sure."

A few minutes later, the cast and crew left the dinner tent and moved en masse out into the park. Throngs of bystanders had gathered outside the barricades to watch the filming. Word had undoubtedly gotten around that some *big* stars were filming. We were a celebrity-obsessed culture, after all, and it wouldn't surprise me if some of those bystanders had come equipped with pen and paper to garner autographs. There was a police presence, just like yesterday outside the church, but it didn't seem as substantial.

Liza, Nina, Nick, and I stood on the east side of the park, well out of the way, and when the cameras started rolling, I watched with delight. My younger self from three decades ago was now headed to the big screen. Some of the extras were supposed to be mob boys who kept an eye on things.

Bottom line, the Feast of Santa Rosalia—also referred as the 18th Avenue Feast—was their celebration as well, an expression of the Italian heritage that united this Brooklyn neighborhood even now. The people who lived here reveled in their traditions and the opportunity to exhibit their collective pride. The differences and disputes that existed within and between families were forgotten during this weeklong feast.

I spotted John on the other side of the park with Prince, Carl Davidson, and Barbara, the artist we'd met at Gallery who worked with Renée. They huddled together in what appeared to be some sort of heated discussion. *But about what?* I wondered. Everyone had agreed on the scenes that would be shot, and even though many elements in my original script had been changed over time, the changes were for the better. Had the art department screwed up somewhere with the stalls? Was that it? Or was it some other detail about which they disagreed?

My phone vibrated, and when I glanced down at it, there was a text message from Lieutenant Gotti.

Just rec'd results from forensics. We have 3 sets of prints from inside and outside the house. Yr intruder Paul Jannis. APB out on him now. His son says he's in NY. You're there, right?

Yes. Brooklyn. Filming.

Be careful. As soon as he returns to LA, we'll bring him in. Will keep u posted.

Thank u so much!!!

"Here goes the DJ," Liza said, leaning into me, and

suddenly the speakers boomed with Cher's voice singing "Half-Breed."

The music blasted across the park, seductive and so beautifully rhythmic that even bystanders were swaying to the tune. The day that song actually had played, I'd been thinking how often I'd been told that my hair was like Cher's. In those days, it had cascaded down my back, almost to my hips, an ebony river, and I had taken great pride in it. After all, who had better hair than Cher? And at the moment I'd had that thought, the song had boomed from the PA system, just as it was now.

Janice had wrapped her arm around my waist, as Jenean was doing to the young woman playing Janice, and we had sung along with Cher and several others. Music had been a large part of my childhood in Bensonhurst. We had enjoyed dancing in time with the upbeat tempo of a new sound and had known every word to every popular song.

As my past played out in this scene, something registered in my peripheral vision, something out of place, something that didn't belong.

My head snapped right, left, but I didn't immediately notice anything unusual. The number of bystanders had swelled, probably because of the music, but I didn't see anyone attempting to shove his way into the filming area. People were snapping photos with their phones, and I was sure that some pictures of De Niro and the other actors were already on Facebook and Twitter and zipping through the virtual world as text messages.

Liza touched my arm, and I glanced at her. She pointed upward, where four sparrow hawks flew in wide circles over the park, as if they'd been drawn by the music, the crowd, the aroma of food. Weird. In all my years of living in this area, I'd seen only one hawk within the city limits, and it had been living in the eaves of the Dakota. After Lennon's death, it vanished.

When the Imagine tribute to Lennon had been erected in Central Park, a hawk had been sighted frequently, circling the monument and occasionally landing on it. No one knew, of course, whether it was the same hawk that had been living in the eaves of the Dakota. But in my mind, the hawks were one and the same. In my mind, that hawk *became* Lennon's spirit, his soul, watching over his former home, his wife, his tribute, his legacy.

Sounds I couldn't immediately identify erupted from somewhere in the crowd, then screams tore apart the air. I couldn't tell if the screams came from within the park or outside of it, beyond the physical and human barriers. People dived for the ground and scrambled behind trees and leaped into the road. They raced away from the park, hurled themselves behind cars and buses.

And then I saw him, saw him as Cher belted:

Half-breed, that's all I ever heard
Half-breed, how I learned to hate the word

Paul. His bald head gleamed in the glare of the sunlight as he walked quickly and purposefully toward John, Prince, Carl Davidson, and Barbara. He didn't run, didn't do anything to attract undue attention to himself. He wore jeans, a denim jacket, and jogging shoes, and wove his way through the crowd of extras with a focused determination.

When he broke into a sprint, he shouted something I couldn't hear and waved a gun, a large gun, larger than any gun had a right to be. He fired shots into the air, and the sounds reverberated through the park, above the volume of Cher's voice, and sped out into the larger world, a reminder that terrorists weren't just Middle Eastern guys with box cutters who hijacked airplanes and crashed them into the World Trade Center.

Bedlam exploded through the park, worse than anything

in the church yesterday. Not only were there more people diving for cover, but they'd heard the gunfire, they'd seen the gun, they knew he was a madman.

I didn't realize I was racing toward John until Liza grabbed my arm and jerked me back. She shoved me to the grass and threw herself over me, screaming, *"Stay the fuck down, Sam, don't move, don't breathe, stay down!"*

People ran past us, screaming, sobbing, terrified. They crashed into stalls, overturning them, spilling food and crafts and statues of the saints and the Blessed Mother, which shattered on impact. Barbecue grills slammed to the ground, spewing hot coals everywhere. Shelves toppled, cameras and sound equipment shattered, and everywhere, the horrendous, panicked screams and the endless shrieks of sirens.

I pushed Liza off me and scrambled to my feet and tore toward the other end of the park. Paul now fired into the crowd, one more nutcase with a gun and an ax to grind—except that he wasn't just some random madman. He had worked with the cast and crew, had known many of these men and women professionally for years, had been a producer for this film. These facts didn't connect in any way with the crazy man I saw now. I understood just how deeply Paul's mind had cracked.

As I raced toward them, cops swarmed into the park, SWAT teams in full gear. My head drummed, my heart hammered, I could no longer see John. I ran faster, faster, my arms tucked in at my sides, my shoes pounding across grass, concrete. I dodged overturned stalls, leaped over a couple huddled on the ground next to a trash can, jumped across overturned barbecue grills and shattered religious icons. I tripped over something and pitched forward, and my arms shot out to break my fall.

I struck the ground and my arms buckled, but I rolled and somehow vaulted to my feet and kept on running. The music had long since stopped, the shrieks and cries and shouts of a panicked crowd filled the air. Sirens screeched nearby. It took me several lifetimes even to get near the area where I'd last seen John. Everything now moved in slow motion—every sound drawn out, like an animal writhing in agony; every flash of color scorched paths through my brain; every movement was an urgency that propelled me forward faster, faster.

Then I was there, and John and Prince lay on the ground, bleeding, groaning, and Paul stood over them, clutching his gun, screaming senselessly. He was oblivious to the cops rushing in on either side of him. His back was to me, and I was closer to him than any of the cops. Red poured across my vision. I didn't think. I saw John bleeding, injured, and simply reacted.

I screamed something unintelligible and crashed into Paul from behind, body-slammed him so hard he never knew what hit him. He stumbled forward and lost his grip on his weapon, and we both struck the ground, rolled. My fists pummeled his chest, his head, and my nails clawed at his face.

"*Fucker,*" I screamed. "*You fucker.*"

His knee jammed upward into my stomach; my head snapped back, and he threw me off him and struggled to his feet. I grabbed his ankles and held on like Velcro. He pitched forward and slammed into the ground so forcefully that I heard the clunk of his head as it hit, and then he went still.

I could barely lift up from the ground. I tasted blood in my mouth, felt the sticky warmth of it oozing down the sides of my face. My ribs burned with pain. I had trouble breathing, heard a strange rattle in my own lungs. I crawled toward John on my hands and knees, my eyes fixed on all the blood, pools of it around him and Prince, and I started praying, making deals with God, the Blessed Mother, Buddha, whoever might be listening.

Please, please, don't let him be dead. If you let him live, I will . . . I will . . . I will . . . what? What the hell kind of deal can you make with God? To be a better person? To be a more forgiving person? To give your money and clothes and all your belongings to charities? To live in abject poverty like Mother Teresa?

These thoughts raced through my head as I crawled toward John, toward the man with whom I'd made such exquisite love for most of the night. The man who now looked to be bleeding to death on the ground, in this grand and beautiful park where my past had been reenacted in such precise detail.

This wasn't supposed to be part of my Hollywood story.

Just as I reached John, as I slipped my hands under his head and sobbed uncontrollably, cops moved in on either side of us. Someone grabbed my arms, jerked me to my feet, cuffed me, and shoved me forward, away from John.

"What the hell!" I shouted, struggling to free myself. *"What're you doing? I'm a bystander, for God's sakes. I didn't do this, I'm injured . . ."*

"She needs medical treatment," someone snapped. "Get her to the ambulance, take off her cuffs, moron!"

My vision was strangely blurred, so I couldn't see who gave the order. But my cuffs fell away, I stumbled toward an ambulance, cops gripping my arms, holding me up, and I was unable to understand what was happening, unable to hold my head erect. My ribs screamed, my head pounded; blood still rolled down the sides of my face. I tasted it on my lips.

I knew that I was injured, that John and Prince had been bleeding all over the ground, that Paul was responsible. That was all I knew. I couldn't think straight, couldn't connect one coherent thought to another.

Where was John?

Mercifully, I blacked out.

• • •

When I came to, I was in the ER, on an examining table, and my arms and legs were restrained. I couldn't move; I ached all over; my head felt like little gremlins were inside of it, hammering nails into my skull. I had trouble breathing. I desperately needed to know where John was, how he was, how any of this had happened, if he was . . . dead.

Dear God, please, not that.

Even though I was physically restrained, my voice was fine, and I bellowed, *"Hey, someone, get me outta here!"*

A nurse quickly appeared, a pretty little thing in a crisp white uniform, her blond hair drawn back into a ponytail. "Ms. DeMarco, if you could calm down, please, we—"

"Calm down? Calm the hell down?" I sobbed, shouted, struggled. "I need to know . . . about John. About Prince. About the people who were shot. Please, my God, please tell me what's going on."

The nurse patted my forearm, spoke softly, gently, her voice a soothing balm. "Hey, it's okay. You were restrained out of precaution, okay? You have six stitches in your right temple, eight stiches in your chin, and a fractured left rib. Your left wrist was broken and will be in a cast for six weeks. Do you understand what I'm saying, Ms. DeMarco?"

What? What?

I nodded, blinked back tears, stared down at my left wrist. At the cast. It was lightweight, a pale blue, and suddenly, the skin beneath it itched terribly. "Y-yes," I stammered. "Did you . . . understand my questions? About . . . the others?"

The nurse, whose name tag read PEG CISCO, RN, said, "Yes." As she checked the IVs that ran into my left arm, she continued. "I'm not supposed to say anything about the other patients. But . . . I understand your need to know." She removed my restraints, picked up an iPad mini, tapped the screen. "John Steeling and George Prince are still in surgery. What are the names of the other people you need to know about?"

I couldn't remember. My mind had been wiped clean. I was suddenly Arnold Schwarzenegger in *Total Recall*, my brain washed of memories of my trip to Mars.

Think, you know the answers.

"A woman in the . . . art department . . . Barbara . . . I don't know her last name. And one of the . . . assistant directors. Shit . . . he has the same last name as a president . . . Lincoln, his last name is Lincoln."

I rubbed my free hands over my face. The cast felt strange, an intruder, and the itch beneath it persisted. I tried to stick my finger under the cast to scratch at my skin, but it didn't work very well. Peg handed me a pen. "This always works best." She tapped away on her iPad again. "Barbara . . ." Peg glanced up. I knew from the shadows in her eyes what she was about to say. "She . . . didn't survive. The other man . . . Dave Lincoln? Is that the right name?"

"Yes. Yes, that's it."

"He's still in surgery and is expected to survive."

I squeezed my eyes shut, struggling not to cry, sob, scream, or leap out of bed.

And then it hit me. The four hawks. They were the omens. I didn't know how such a thing was possible, but I remembered what John had said about the murder of crows he'd seen the day he was released from prison. The crows had proved to be positive omens for him. The hawks, not at all. Four hawks, and at least four injuries or deaths to people associated with *Brooklyn Story*.

"What . . . other injuries?" I whispered. "On the set?"

More tapping on her iPad. "Just the four. Some people were injured trying to get out of the park, but not critically. Scrapes, bruises, stitches."

I couldn't hold back tears, floodgates slammed open,

all the Catholic guilt rushed in. The kind of guilt that you couldn't dodge in the confessional, the kind of guilt that left the priest reeling and doling out penances of several dozen Hail Marys and more dozens of the Lord's Prayer, and who the hell knew what else. My soul was fucked, that was how I felt.

My fault. Because of Paul. If I'd never slept with him, if I'd never ended it with him, if, if, if . . .

So much of my life had been predicated on *if* or *what if*, and right now, it was the only thing I could think about. *What if* I had done things differently, behaved differently toward Paul? *What if* I hadn't ended it with him? Was this my *Sliding Doors*?

If that version of events had happened, was there running parallel to this universe one in which no one had died today? Where I was still with Paul? If so, then on this alternative path of personal history, John and I had never become lovers; I had never known the exquisite joy I'd experienced overnight in his strange outdoor dome.

The things I knew were spit in the wind when compared to what I *didn't know* about anything.

"Ms. DeMarco?"

"Sam." I blinked and focused on her, the nurse, Peg Cisco. "My name's Sam."

"Sam. Okay, Sam. Do you need to use the bathroom?"

Yeah, now that she mentioned it, my bladder was filled to bursting. "Yes."

"Are you hungry? Thirsty?"

"Definitely."

"What's the date?"

That depended on how long I'd been blacked out. Since I didn't know what time it was or how long I'd been out, I gave her a range of dates. I was apparently correct, because she then asked who the president of the United States was.

Another cognitive question. "Obama."

She flashed a smile filled with dazzling white teeth. I apparently had passed some sort of test. "Excellent." She helped me sit up. "Let's get you into the bathroom. I'll order some food."

Peg helped me to the bathroom. Even though my legs weren't injured in any way, I had trouble putting one foot in front of the other. I had trouble stringing my thoughts together in a sequence of time. But when I finally formed a question in my mind, I blurted it. "The shooter. Can you tell me . . . about him? His . . . status?"

She tapped again at her iPad. "Name?"

"Paul Jannis."

More tapping. "Still in surgery."

"For?"

"Blunt head trauma."

Shit, that was me; I had done that.

"And gunshot wounds."

"But he . . . had the gun."

"The cops were armed." We reached the door of the bathroom. "You need help inside?"

The cops were armed. That translated as: *The cops shot Paul.*

"Sam? Hey, hello?" Peg said. "Do you need help getting to the toilet?"

I shook my head. I was forty-five years old and felt like I was twice that age. But damned if anyone was going to help me take a piss. "I'm . . . fine. I need a shower."

"Just be sure to wrap plastic around the cast so it doesn't get wet. You'll find a plastic bag on the shelf above the sink."

I gripped the edge of the door frame, pulled myself into the bathroom. Shut the door. Then I grabbed the edge of the sink, made my way to the toilet, and collapsed onto it.

I snapped a towel off the rack, pressed it over my face, and sobbed. I wept for the dead, the injured, all the victims of my bad choice in men. Every part of me ached, throbbed, and all I wanted to do was crawl into a cave somewhere and drift into a dormant state, like a bear in winter.

I sat there until my bladder was empty, my tears dried up, until I had nothing more to do than to get off the toilet, strip off my hospital gown, turn on the shower. I made sure to pull the plastic bag over my cast.

I didn't know how long I stood under the hot spray, but when I stepped out, I felt as if I had washed away most of the inner stuff that made me feel soiled, guilty. I pulled on the hospital gown, dried my hair and body, opened the door.

There was Peg, my caregiver, my connection to the larger hospital world.

"When can I get outta here, Peg?" I asked.

She looked at me, this pretty young blonde who was probably in her late twenties, nearly young enough to be my daughter. "They want to keep you for the night. Your vitals are good; your injuries aren't life threatening. Let us take care of you for the night, Sam."

"Can I have visitors?"

"You bet." She slipped my phone out of her pocket, passed it to me. "This sucker has been dinging like crazy."

I gripped the phone, wove my way back to the bed, collapsed onto it. Someone had delivered a meal of hot soup, Jell-O, a piece of buttered whole-wheat bread. I was famished and started shoveling the food in my mouth.

"I can let them in two at a time," Peg said.

I nodded, pulled the sheet over my body, glanced at my phone, at the dozens of text messages and emails. My vision blurred, all I could think of was John; of how much blood I'd seen; of his being in surgery, fighting for his life. "Can you keep me posted . . . on John Steeling and the others?"

"Of course. I'm on for twelve hours today." She tucked the sheet in around my feet. "You'll have a room shortly, within the hour. Your first visitors are here, Sam."

The first person to walk into my ER area was Isabella, then Liza. I burst into tears and kept right on crying as they hugged me, as they sat with me, as my daughter and my closest friend and I prayed for John, for Prince, for all the others who had been injured. And in the end, we also prayed for ourselves.

EIGHTEEN

Since my room on the third floor was private, I was permitted to have visitors twenty-four/seven, so Liza and Isabella stuck around most of the day. They brought me updates. But other than the fact that everyone was out of surgery and in ICU, not much had changed. John hadn't regained consciousness and remained in critical condition.

They left that evening. Liza had assured me she would get Isabella back to Filomena's place for the night and then would pick her up in the morning before I was released. I tucked my freshly charged cell next to me on the bed, strangely grateful that I was in the hospital for the night because I was closer to John here than I would have been at the hotel. Nonetheless, I lay there feeling anxious about him. Why hadn't Peg the nurse been in to give me a recent update? Did that mean he'd taken a turn for the worse and she didn't know how to break the news?

My anxiety deepened. I turned on the television, and the local news was about the shooting rampage in the park.

"The names of the deceased haven't been released yet, pending notification of next of kin," said the female newscaster on CNN. "The shooter is presently in the hospital, under police guard, and hasn't been identified. But we do know he's a white male in his forties who was associated with the filming of *Brooklyn Story*. Two of the victims, John Steeling and George Prince, underwent surgery this morning for multiple gunshot wounds and are in critical condition."

Critical. I texted John's son.

How's your dad doing? Any word?

His response was immediate.

No word yet. Glad u r ok. Liza gave us update. Nina & I will be at the hospital till we know something. Will keep u posted.

K. Thanx.

I pressed the heels of my hands against my eyes, dimly aware of the newscaster's voice droning on about the shooting, the movie. She mentioned the lineup of actors and actresses in the film, talked abut the novel upon which the movie was based. I heard my name. Under any other circumstances, hearing my name on CNN would have thrilled me. Now it left me feeling cold and cursed, like the wicked witch in every fairy tale I'd ever read.

"Brian King, CEO of Gallery Studios, which is filming *Brooklyn Story,* is about to issue a statement."

I glanced up at the screen, raised the volume. King looked haggard, older. He wore the same clothes he'd had on this morning—jeans, a work shirt, moccasins. His jeans were splattered with blood.

"On behalf of my colleagues at Gallery Studios, our thoughts and prayers go out to the families and loved ones of our beloved friends who were injured and killed in this rampage. We'll be issuing further statements about the time and place for memorial services. Thank you."

"Mr. King," shouted a reporter. "Can you tell us how this tragedy will impact the filming of *Brooklyn Story*?"

King's haunted eyes peered out at the reporter, and he shook his head. "Right now, I have no idea. Our primary concern is the healing of those who were injured and attending to the families of the victims. Thank you for your time."

He turned and walked back inside the hospital, and I sat there, tears coursing down my cheeks, blaming myself. *If I hadn't . . . if Paul hadn't . . . if, if, and fucking if again.*

"Sam?" Peg the nurse hurried in. "Not much news. Mr. Steeling and Mr. Prince are both still in critical condition. I'm about to sign out for the night, but I wanted to check back with you first. Can I get you anything?"

"What were his injuries?" I asked.

Peg's frown told me she was uncomfortable divulging that information. "I really shouldn't . . ."

"Please?"

She held my gaze for a moment longer, then brought out her iPad, scrolled through it. "Are you sure you want to know?" she asked.

"I'd rather know than sit here the rest of the night gnawing my knuckles."

"In layman's terms, he had a severe injury to his right shoulder that will require extensive physical therapy when he's released. The joint had to be replaced. He also sustained a gunshot wound to the stomach that caused internal bleeding and required surgery. His blood pressure continues to drop, suggesting that he's still bleeding internally, and his temperature is spiking, indicative of a bacterial infection. He's on IV antibiotics and is being monitored carefully. He's heavily sedated on morphine."

"My God," I whispered.

"Honey, he's young and physically fit. That's on his side. And he had excellent surgeons."

But was it enough? "May I see him?"

"His son is in with him now. ICU allows only one family member at a time, and since you're not family, you wouldn't be able to get in." She hooked me up to the blood pressure machine, brought out a thermometer, did her nurse thing.

"What about Mr. Jannis?" I asked.

"He's in a coma."

"Am I going to be able to get outta here tomorrow?"

"You should. Your vitals look good. You want something to help you sleep?"

"The only way I'm going to be able to sleep is if I can see Mr. Steeling."

Peg regarded me for a long moment, then picked up a pad of paper off the nightstand and scribbled something on it. She tore a sheet off the pad, folded it, handed it to me. "No can do. I'm sorry. I won't be in until the three p.m. shift tomorrow. Let's trade cell numbers, okay?"

So we did, and her text made me smile.

I'm a huge fan of yr work. Read the note.

"You take care, Sam. I can't wait to see you at the Oscars."

Without another word, she left the room, and I unfolded the note she'd given me. *He's in room 424, one floor up. Go around 11 p.m., when shifts are changing. There's a nurse's uniform and a stethoscope in your closet. Speak to him. He'll be able to hear you.*

I slipped her note inside my bag, then threw off the sheet and swung my legs over the side of the bed. As I stood, I felt much steadier than I had earlier, and padded over to the closet. Sure enough, a nurse's uniform hung from a hanger, and it looked to be about my size. Liza had brought over a change of clothes and shoes for me, as well as toiletries, a hairbrush, and a hair dryer. I shut the closet door and glanced at the clock on the wall.

Ten p.m. The countdown to eleven had begun.

• • •

At ten-thirty a doctor dropped by, asked the usual questions about how did I feel and was I ready to get out in the morning. He said my vitals looked good and yada, yada. I just wanted him to leave so I could put on the nurse's uniform and head upstairs to see John.

"If I'm in such good shape, why was I admitted for the night?" I asked.

"Mainly for observation."

I kept watching the hands on the wall clock, one of those big, ugly clocks I associated with classrooms in middle school. Black numbers, black hands. *Ticktock, ticktock.*

"Am I going to be able to get a good night's sleep in here?" I asked. "Or is someone going to come in and wake me every two hours?"

He was going through a checklist on his iPad and looked up, amused. "Every four hours someone will be in. But they won't need to wake you. In fact, I'll make a note to that effect."

Ticktock. Please leave now. He'd been here for six minutes. The minute hand moved again. Seven minutes. *Ticktock.*

"I'm delighted you're doing so well, Ms. DeMarco. And I'm sorry for the loss you and your friends suffered today."

"Thank you."

"You'll be released around ten tomorrow morning."

Eight minutes. *Ticktock.*

He made some more notations on his iPad, then finally left. I waited a few moments to make sure he wouldn't return, then leaped out of bed and hurried over to the closet.

I grabbed the nurse's uniform and my own shoes, a pair of Scratchers with memory foam soles, and slipped into the bathroom. Fortunately, the cast was on my forearm and didn't impede my ability to bend my arm. I changed quickly. The uniform fit remarkably well, and I wondered where Peg had gotten it. Was there, somewhere in the bowels of the hospital, a wardrobe department like there was on a movie set?

I brushed my hair, gathered it back into a ponytail. That seemed appropriate for a hospital. I hadn't seen any nurses here who wore much makeup other than a touch of lipstick and mascara, so that's what I used. The one item I lacked was a name tag. Hopefully, with the shifts changing and people arriving and leaving, no one would notice.

I pulled on my Scratchers, grabbed my phone, noted the time: 10:57. Perfect. I put the phone into a pocket in the uniform and hurried toward the door. The shoes, with their memory foam padding, felt good against my bare feet. It was like walking on clouds, on air. In these shoes, I could do anything, be anyone, I could somehow bring John back to me.

I cracked the door open, peered out. Elevator or stairs? I spotted an EXIT sign at the end of the hall. Stairs it would be.

Deep breath, check the hall once more. Believe, Sam, believe.

I slipped out the door and walked right—quickly but not so fast that I drew attention to myself. I was nearly to the EXIT sign when an elderly man stuck his head out the door. "Nurse, could you please give me a hand with something?"

I started to tell him I had an emergency situation at the end of the hall. But he looked so small, thin, and frail, his shoulders hunched over as if beneath a terrible weight, that I went over to him. "Sure, what do you need, sir?"

He hobbled over to the closet, one hand gripping the back of his gown to keep his naked butt from showing, a knobby finger on his other hand pointing at a suitcase on a top shelf. "Can you reach that?"

"I think so." The suitcase weighed almost nothing at all. I pulled it down and set it on the nearest chair.

"Thanks so much. I'm getting out tomorrow, and I need to be packed."

I hear ya, friend. "Do you need anything else?"

"Yeah, to be about forty years younger." He glanced back as he said it and gave a small, embarrassed laugh. "But not to worry. That's not your department."

"Ring the nurses' station if you need anything else, sir."

On my way out, I noticed his room number was 324; that meant John's room was directly above it, near the stairs. Guidance, I thought. I was being guided. No telling how much time I might have wasted looking for his room. I figured that ICU, like the obstetrics areas in most hospitals, was actually a cluster of rooms, and I hoped that I wouldn't be prevented from entering the ward.

I hurried on, past several nurses and orderlies headed in the opposite direction, and no one gave me a second glance. Just the same, I was relieved when I slipped into the stairwell. I stood there for a moment, back against the door, anxiety eating away at me.

Stethoscope around my neck. Phone on vibrate. What else? I felt like some kid sneaking out to meet her boyfriend after everyone had gone to bed. Ridiculous. It wasn't like I was breaking any laws.

I heard voices but couldn't tell if they were above or below me. *Move.* Up the stairs, struggling to maintain a normal pace.

Did the rooms in ICU have video cameras?

A little late to worry about that, Sam. You know you're going in there regardless.

A nurse and an orderly trotted down the stairs toward me, chatting and laughing, and I simply nodded and kept on moving, as though I had every right to do so. You would think I was planning a bank heist or something.

I reached the top landing, pulled the door open just a little, peered out. Half a dozen visitors sat in chairs that lined the wall on either side of the doors to ICU. They probably were waiting to see loved ones. Several hospital employees were visible, hurrying up and down the corridor.

I walked out into the hall as though I belonged here, as though I worked here and knew what was what and who was who. No one challenged me.

Believe.

I headed right into the ICU unit and immediately heard the beeps and hums of machinery from half a dozen rooms in the area. Two nurses were at the station, and neither of them even noticed me. I moved straight toward room 424 and slipped inside.

The twilit room threw me. It was like entering some Neptunian world, something in the ocean's depths where sunlight barely penetrated. As my eyes grew accustomed to the diminished light, I made out shapes, the contours and corners of the room. I could see a chair pulled up close to the bed on the opposite side. I sensed it was where Nick had held his vigil. Machines and monitors were positioned on either side of the bed where John lay.

As I neared him, my breath caught in my throat. He looked like something in a horror movie, a being like Frankenstein's monster, assembled in a lab and connected to half a dozen tubes that monitored him, fed him, sustained him. The tubes led to IV bags suspended from a stand next to the head of the bed; another bag filled with blood and urine hung against the side of the bed; an array of machines and monitors beeped and hummed, displaying his vitals. An orchestra of sounds.

It hurt me to look at him, at the pallor of his face, his utter stillness. I moved right up to the edge of the bed and stared down at him and was nearly overwhelmed by such powerful emotions that I gripped the railing to steady myself.

"John." I leaned over him.

His hair looked wild against the white pillowcase. His

beard had been shaved off, and it took me a moment to get accustomed to the sight of him. He looked like the Bob I'd known thirty years ago. I ran my fingers lightly over his chin, my thumb traced the shape of his mouth. He didn't move. I leaned closer and listened to him breathing. Was it my imagination, or did his breath sound like it was rattling in his chest?

I pressed my mouth to his forehead. He was hot.

"John, can you hear me?"

No reaction. My heart felt as though it were seizing up, then breaking apart, then restructuring itself in some new way. *Please come back to me.*

I folded back the top edge of the sheet that covered him and nearly keeled over. He had a drain in his left shoulder, and the bandage around it was large. I didn't fold the sheet down any farther. I didn't want to see the bandage on his stomach.

I pulled the sheet back over him, walked around to the other side of the bed, sat in the chair where Nick had undoubtedly sat, and took John's hand. I was careful not to disturb the IV needle in the back of it. "John," I whispered, "come back. Come back to me, to Nick and Nina, to all of us. Can you hear me?"

No reaction.

I squeezed my eyes shut and prayed silently. Then I slipped my hand under the sheets and beneath his hospital gown to gaze at his tattoo of the Archangel Michael. I believed he had always protected me and was protecting John now. When I opened my eyes, I leaned toward him again and whispered, "If you can hear me, squeeze my fingers, John. Can you do that?"

Nothing. No sign at all that he'd heard me.

My phone vibrated, and I slipped it out of my pocket. A missed call from Luke, Paul's son. I listened to his message: "Sweet Christ, Mrs. DeMarco, I'm . . . so sorry." His voice was soft, choked. "Am headed for . . . New York. I . . . I got a call a while ago . . . from the hospital administrator. Dad . . . isn't expected to live. Call when you can."

I disconnected from voice mail, pressed the phone to my forehead, and murmured a prayer for Paul, for his son, for John, for Prince, for all of us. How had it come to this?

You know how. Just make sure it never happens again. I sat down in the chair right next to him.

That voice seemed to come from some other, wiser part of my being. Maybe we all had that wiser being within us, but we had to arrive at a certain level of consciousness to hear it. Was this wiser being my connection to the divine? And if so, could it bring me some sort of sign that John was going to live? That my pattern with men had been broken by this tragedy? That things would now turn around?

"Excuse me . . ."

My eyes snapped open, and I gazed across John's bed at an Asian man coming through the doorway. He wore jeans and a wrinkled cotton shirt with a wild print that made him look as if he'd just flown in from Honolulu.

"Yes?"

"I'm Dr. Cho." He strolled over to the bed with his iPad in one hand, his other hand extended. "And you are . . . ?"

"Samantha DeMarco." I got to my feet and we shook hands. His grip was firm but not overbearing. He had kind, gray eyes set in a nest of tiny wrinkles, a quick smile, and gray hair threaded with black. I liked him immediately. "I'm just checking in on him, talking to him, encouraging a response."

"Good, that's always good. There's considerable evidence that patients in comas can hear, that it's the last sense to go."

To *go*? What did that mean? Was John on his way *out*? "Is he that bad off?"

He scrolled through his iPad. "When the physical body has been badly traumatized, a coma is like a respite, a place of restoration. He's also heavily medicated, with morphine, for pain. Didn't you read his chart, Nurse. DeMarco?"

"I was in a hurry and left my iPad in my locker downstairs."

"The shoulder injury was serious, and the gunshot wound to the stomach was even worse. His fever right now is a cause for concern; so is his dropping blood pressure. Have you checked his vitals since you got in here?"

"I, uh, haven't had a chance to check yet. I just walked in here a minute before you did."

"What was your name again?" He eyed the spot on my uniform where I should have been wearing a name tag. "Your name tag is missing."

"It's in the locker with my iPad. DeMarco, Samantha DeMarco."

"Are you new? I've never seen you around the hospital."

"I just got transferred to the graveyard shift two days ago."

Frowning, he scrolled some more through his iPad, then suddenly glanced up, pinning me with his small eyes. "Wait a minute. Samantha DeMarco. You're a patient here. Why're you dressed like a nurse?"

Busted.

"Because they wouldn't let me see him," I burst out. "Because I'm not family. But . . . but he was shot because of me, because the lunatic who did this was out for revenge, for . . . Never mind."

I shut up. I sounded hysterical. And, bottom line, the story was too damn complicated to explain in fifteen seconds, which was probably all that I had before he called security.

He didn't say anything. He just kept looking at me in an unsettling way, until I could feel his eyes moving around inside of me, as though he were reading me from the inside out.

"I . . . *had* to see him," I rushed on. "And I was sitting here, talking to him, asking him to . . . to come back to me, to his son, to the people who love him. That's all. If that's a crime, then arrest me, just arrest me."

With that, I sank into the chair next to John's bed and took his hand in my own. Dr. Cho stood there for a long moment, proceeded to check the monitors and machines, and entered data onto his iPad. And while he did this, he talked.

"Your name. Now I know why it struck me as familiar. It's your screenplay they were filming. I'm sorry I didn't realize that initially. I didn't mean to be . . . insensitive. Mr. Steeling is a partner in Gallery Studios, right?"

"Yes." *And my lover.*

"And Mr. Jannis . . . was the producer."

"Until he was fired."

His head bobbed. I could see he was connecting the dots on his own and that he wasn't going to turn me in to the hospital police or to the psychiatric Big Brothers. "The odd thing is that no one has to be a victim because of his or her past. And I think that's what this is all about." He motioned toward John. "His injuries. Our shoulders carry our burdens. His left shoulder took the brunt. The left side of the body is ruled by the right brain. Intuitively, he understood that and chose this injury to make a point."

Huh? "I don't understand."

"We create our realities from the inside out. Through our thoughts, intentions, beliefs. Nothing is random. There are no accidents. The dramas we experience are those we create."

He was beginning to sound like Tolle. "But how's he doing? Is he . . . going to live?"

"All things considered, he's doing remarkably well." He

smoothed his hand over John's forehead, then checked the drain in his shoulder. "He's sweating, so his fever is breaking. I'm going to cut way back on the morphine. If we're fortunate, Ms. DeMarco, and I think we will be, he'll be out of here in a week or less. He's physically fit; that's a big help." He lowered his iPad and gave me his full attention. "I, uh, appreciate why you sneaked in here. But it's probably a good idea if you sneak out in the next ten minutes or so."

"I-I'm in a room downstairs," I stammered.

"The head nurse on duty tonight is a bitch on wheels, and she keeps a close eye on her ICU patients. I'm going to have Mr. Steeling moved out of ICU tomorrow morning and into the general population." He turned off the drips on two of John's IVs, emptied the catheter bag. "And after he gets out, maybe you should surprise him with a trip— some romantic spot where the weather is warm and perfect and the two of you can thrive."

Was this Dr. Cho for real? "Got any suggestions?"

"I do, actually. Savannah is particularly beautiful this time of year."

My eyes suddenly awoke to the feel of John's fingers. As I looked up I realized that I must have been dreaming. John's fingers twitched against my palm, and I glanced down at our hands, wondering if I'd imagined it. "John?" I whispered, leaning close to him. "Can you hear me? Move your fingers if you can hear me."

His fingers twitched again. "Oh, my God, Dr. Cho, his fingers . . ."

I looked up—and Cho was gone.

Just *gone. Was this a dream?*

"What the hell." I slipped my hand away from John's, stood, hurried over to the door, and looked up and down the hall. No Cho. I turned and saw that John's head had moved, that it was facing the door. Facing me. And his eyes were open, cognizant, aware, fully present.

"Sam," he whispered, and I rushed over to him, slipped my arms under his head, lifted it gently, and kissed him.

"John. You came back. You came back."

"Someone . . . was here . . ."

"This doctor who . . ." I pulled back, away from him, but his eyes were shut again, his body felt limp. I pressed my ear to his chest, heard the steady beat of his heart. As I raised my head, I felt his breath against my cheek, like a caress.

Okay, he was alive, definitely alive.

It was nearly midnight; I didn't want to get caught in here by the bitch on wheels, as Cho had called her. "John, I'll be back in the morning."

I disengaged myself from him, slipped out of the room, and stole back down the stairs to the third floor. I saw only two other employees, and neither of them paid any attention to me. I thought of how quickly Dr. Cho had disappeared and wondered if I had hallucinated him. That had to be it. No other explanation made sense, but why?

In my room, I quickly shed my nurse's uniform and shoes, put on my hospital gown, and crawled into bed. A nurse, Lita Hernandez, appeared ten minutes later, saw that I was awake, and asked if she could get me something to help me sleep.

"No, thanks. I'm fine."

She went through her checklist on her iPad. "You're being released in the morning."

"Thank God."

"Frankly, I'm not even sure why you were kept overnight, Ms. DeMarco."

"Me neither. Can you tell me how John Steeling is doing?"

"Are you related?"

"We're lovers."

Lita started scrolling through her iPad. "Wow, this is remarkable. As of the ten p.m. check, Mr. Steeling was listed as still being in a coma, with a fever of one-oh-three; his blood pressure was very low, and internal bleeding was suspected from the wound to his stomach.

But as of the most recent check, his temperature is normal, his blood pressure has stabilized, and he's conscious and hungry. The drain will probably be removed from his shoulder tomorrow morning. He has definitely turned the corner. In just two hours."

I knew right then that I hadn't hallucinated Cho. Ghost, spirit, angel? He was my divine sign that a significant shift had occurred. And as crazy as this may sound, someone was looking out for us, and I surely wasn't going to question this . . . at all.

chapter

NINETEEN

Eight weeks after Paul's rampage—at the end of July—
Brooklyn Story was scheduled to resume shooting. John had
been released from the hospital less than a week after the
shooting, just as Dr. Cho had predicted. We had attended
memorial services for Barbara, who had died on the scene
in the park, and for George Prince, who, despite the doctors' best attempts, had died within forty-eight hours of
being shot.

Paul had survived his injuries and was recovering, according to Luke, in a psychiatric hospital on Long Island.
Once he was released, he would be face multiple homicide
charges. Isabella had flown back to L.A. with Liza, King,
Marvin, and Flannigan, and she would be staying with Liza
until I returned to the West Coast. Since Brooklyn now
seemed off limits for filming, King had decided the rest of
the filming would take place in L.A.

John and I decided to fly into Savannah Airport, rented
a car, and drove toward the historic district. Instead of taking the interstate, we followed an alternative route that
showed up on my GPS. After all, we weren't in any hurry.
These roads followed the Savannah River south to the city. I
felt as though time had slowed or stopped altogether. Maybe
it was the tremendous trees that lined the road; live oaks

and cypress trees loomed like giants, their massive branches forming braided canopies overhead, webs of Spanish moss hanging from them. Or perhaps it was that the past was steeped in the very air we breathed.

Established in 1733, Savannah was the first colonial and state capital of Georgia. I could almost see the Southern gentry sipping mint julep tea on the wide front porches of their plantations, women decked out in their finest clothes and fanning themselves in the heat.

We lowered the windows, and the rich, warm scent of the river, the sea, and the salt marshes blew through the car, an aroma that was somehow liberating, uplifting, and blissfully distant from the tragedies of New York. The salt marsh seemed to extend all the way to the curve of the blue dome of the sky in the distance. The tide looked as if it was coming in, and pools of glistening water broke up the continent of brown reeds. Birds swooped over the marsh—gulls, cranes, blue herrings, and others I couldn't identify.

I slipped off my sandals and pressed my bare feet against the glove compartment. My blue toenails looked odd against the black of the glove compartment, like a line of chorus girls on Broadway. The breeze blew up under my sundress, puffing it out like a balloon.

"Mary Poppins," John said with a laugh, and brought his hand down gently against the skirt and then slipped his hand under it and caressed my thigh.

I leaned toward him and slid my hand between the buttons on his shirt and nibbled at his earlobe. "Three days just for us."

"Paradise."

"So tell me why you chose Savannah," John said. "An S city!"

"Do you remember anything about the time you were in a coma?" I asked.

He thought about it for a moment, his eyes darting

from the road, out to the salt marsh, then back to the road. "The little I remember is weird. After I got shot . . . and was on the ground, I remember seeing you scrambling toward me on your hands and knees. Then I blacked out and came to briefly while I was on a gurney, being rushed, I think, into surgery. And then suddenly I was above my body, watching all the activity. I . . . I saw this team of doctors and nurses trying to shock my heart into starting, and I knew I had died."

"*Died?* No one told me that."

"I talked about it with this grief counselor who came around shortly before I was released. She checked with the main surgeon, and he said I was dead for maybe thirty seconds. Except that I wasn't dead. I was aware of everything, Sam."

I had read my share of books on near-death experiences, everything from Raymond Moody's classic from the 1970s to Kenneth Ring's works later on. Consciousness survives death: that was what their research proved. But until now, until this very second, I'd never known anyone personally who had died and returned.

"Did you . . . see a tunnel of light or anything like that?"

"Not a tunnel, but a doorway filled with this incredibly beautiful light that emanated such warmth and peace that I was drawn to it. But before I reached the doorway, this guy hurried toward me. And this is the strange thing, Sam. He says, 'It's not your time yet, John. You can go if you want to, but you'll be selling yourself short.' I asked him what he meant, and scenes started flashing through my head, then all around me, these . . . I don't know, they were like holographic images, except that they pulsated with life."

"What kind of images?"

"Of the future. At least, I think that's what they were. I don't remember the details now."

I felt strangely unnerved by his story and squeezed his

hand, reassuring myself that he was here with me, in the car, and that he was real, tangible. "Did you know this man?"

"Nope. But afterward, when I was conscious, I thought of that scene in *What Dreams May Come* when Cuba Gooding Jr. first appears to Robin Williams after he has died. Remember that?"

I nodded. I'd seen the movie several times, and every time I watched it, I discovered something that I'd missed in earlier viewings, some detail about the afterworld that the Williams character now inhabited. "So you think he was, what, like a guide?"

"That was my impression."

"Did you see anyone else?"

"If I did, I don't remember."

If I had a near-death experience, would Grandma Ruth appear? Or my mother? Or Alec?

"You still haven't told me yet why you chose Savannah."

"Dr. Cho suggested it."

"Who?"

So I told him the story, start to finish. Frowning, he asked, "What'd he look like?"

I described him. "He tended to you and assured me you were on the road to recovery. I thought I had hallucinated him because he vanished so fast."

"My God, Sam, that's who I saw, a little Asian man in a Hawaiian shirt. *He's* the one who advised me to go back. This is incredible."

I reached for his hand and squeezed it. Whatever it was that had happened in the hospital—a miracle, a visitation by an angelic being—I knew it had been a spiritual turning point for me. And it had definitely been a turning point for John. Within a few hours of that visitation by Cho, John's fever had dropped.

We crossed a bridge—another bridge, my life seemed to be filled with bridges that I needed to cross—and saw a construction site under way along the river. Live oaks and cypress trees shaded the site, and I was immediately struck by one of the model homes we passed, a gracious Southern place with tremendous windows, a long front porch, a curving driveway lined with flowers.

John glanced over at me, his expression as inscrutable as the words written in a fortune cookie. "You and I are coming at life from our gender perspectives, but have arrived at the same place, Sam."

"So what's that mean?"

"That we should buy one of those homes under construction. How would a river view inspire your muse?"

"My muse has been out to lunch lately. I'll have to ask her. But she would probably love it." Was he saying what I thought he was? That we had a future together? Or was I reading something into it? "And when we were in this house, it would hum along on automatic like your other places."

He laughed. "Yeah. I could arrange shoots down here. I mean, honestly, look at this place, Sam. It's *Gone with the Wind* for the twenty-first century. I can see Scarlett O'Hara sitting under those trees." He gestured at a thicket of live oaks on our right, the Spanish moss on their branches swaying gently in the breeze.

"And Rhett races in—"

"And the entire places goes up in flames."

"Truth time," I said. "Since I moved to Malibu, I've written two paragraphs on my next novel. That's it. When I have the free time to write, I don't feel like doing it. I don't know what the story is, who the characters are, what the plot is. I don't know what I want to write next. I don't know whether I want to write another novel or do a screenplay first."

"Doesn't matter. You've got all the time in the world."

Yeah, it was nice to hear but wasn't exactly true. If I'd learned nothing else during the past months, it was that at any moment your life could turn on the proverbial dime. Rags to riches, bliss to despair, love lost and found, life and death. "I guess that right now, there's not room for a whole new story with new characters. I just want to see *Brooklyn Story* finished. It's my healing."

"Makes sense. I thought my healing was prison, but it was really my almost dying. I think it helped me let go of the past."

He said it so matter-of-factly that I glanced over at him, drank in the sight of him—his beautiful profile, his jaw stubbled with a new growth of beard, his hair still sort of wild. I loved him already, but I was afraid of loving him too much, too deeply, because it would leave me way too vulnerable. At the moment, though, I was just happy to see him alive and healing and happy.

"Let's stop and look at the model, Sam."

"Really?"

"Sure. We don't have to be anywhere at a particular time."

"Okay, let's do it."

He made a U-turn and drove back to the site. We parked in a lot next to the office and got out. The scent of the river was powerful, intoxicating, and drifted like a promise through the hot air. Gulls careened above the river, diving now and then to scoop up fish. The trees on the property rose like majestic beings. Birds sang in the shadows, from the branches. I imagined myself and John here, the place where we would come to dive into our various creative projects. A new novel, a new script, a whole new life.

He slipped his arm around my shoulders, kissed me, and we went into the office. We looked at an artist's rendition of what the neighborhood would look like when it was completed—not a gated community, but a place where every home sat on at least an acre of riverfront property. Bikes paths would meander through the trees, jogging trails would follow the river.

"We'd like to see the model," he told the Realtor.

"Y'all are just going to love it," she replied in her rolling Southern accent. She was a short, petite woman with carefully coiffed auburn hair, probably in her mid-thirties. "Where y'all from?"

"Brooklyn," John said.

"Are y'all vacationing here?"

"For a long weekend."

"Well, let's see if we can get y'all to extend that long weekend, shall we?"

She unlocked the door, and John and I, holding hands, walked inside.

It was five thousand square feet, with four bedrooms and three and a half baths, and a family room that was all windows and overlooked the river. There was a long swimming pool out back, an outside shower, a room for Isabella, and a guesthouse for other visitors. It sat on more than two acres, so our closest neighbors wouldn't be able to hear our dog bark. Never mind that we didn't have a dog right now. We would. A dog, a cat, maybe even a bird—a conure, a cockatoo, an African gray.

The floors were tile, the kitchen was divine, there was enough space to accommodate anything we could imagine. But . . . where did marriage fit into that equation? Did it figure in at all? And why did that word, *marriage,* suddenly pop into my inner dialogue?

I was forty-five years old. Next year, my daughter would graduate from high school and then would head off to college. And that October, I would be forty-six, closer to fifty than forty. And year after year, that number would increase. John was the man I loved, no question about that anymore. But for me, that kind of love meant full commitment, a life partner with whom to share it all.

I wasn't interested in some cohabitation deal where we were *sort of married,* enjoying the perks but not bound by the legalities. I wasn't the least bit interested in a roommate with benefits. I could have that anywhere in Malibu, at any time. I wanted a romantic partner who was also my creative partner. I wanted what might very well be impossible.

But John, like me, had been married before. We both carried baggage from our marriages—a son and a daughter, respectively, and a host of psychological issues with which a shrink would have a field day. I realized that none of our issues were easy fixes. My father had been a deadbeat; John had never known his real father, and his adopted father had been a mafia don who had used him for his own agenda, his own gain. In this sense, we were both orphans who had made our way—somehow—through the world to where we were now. And how strange that we had come to this odd slice of paradise to find ourselves—and each other.

That hadn't been my intent when I had booked this trip. I had only wanted time away for the two of us, a place for us to heal. Now I understood that nearly everything in our relationship until now had involved other people and their issues. But Vito and Paul were out of the picture—if not forever, then at least during our time here.

Here, it was just John and me and *our* issues. That was what travel did. It took you outside your normal routines, away from what was familiar, and forced you to confront who you were. *Here you are together, people, free to be whoever you want.* And right then, I understood this trip would be either our nemesis—or our salvation.

"What do you think about this place, Sam?"

"It's fantastic." *But . . .*

He touched my arm and led me through an arched doorway, into a cozy room with a riverfront view, sliding-glass doors, a fireplace, a mahogany computer table, floor-to-ceiling bookshelves. "Here's where you're going to write your next novel. Or screenplay. Isn't it fantastic?"

"It's . . . perfect."

The Realtor strode across the room and opened the sliding-glass doors. "Y'all just have to see this deck."

John and I walked out onto the deck with her. In addition to the swimming pool, there was a Jacuzzi, an outdoor shower, and a shaded area for a table and chairs. The deck extended the width of the house and was lined with plants in large, ceramic pots. It had a pass-through window to the kitchen.

"Let's walk down to the river, Sam." He looked at the Realtor. "We'll be back in a few minutes."

"Y'all take your time."

"This place, Sam. It's awesome. It's a *location*. This place, Savannah, Tybee Island is ten miles away . . ."

"But what's the *story*?" He and I had talked about stories before, during the weeks since his discharge from the hospital. But it was always in vague terms. Love story or time-travel story? Or a combination of both?

"My favorite time-travel/love story is *Romancing the Raven*," John said. "It involves Edgar Allan Poe."

I put the book on my mental list of must-reads. John had been such a reader. I didn't understand how he read so many books.

"Sam, I felt like I saw the afterlife. It wasn't as colorful as what Williams saw in the movie, but it was that same sort of magical feeling. When I thought about it later, I figured my unconscious had been coughing up images from the movie. Now I'm not so sure."

"Describe what you saw."

As he continued to talk, we walked along the river, and my muse, dormant for so long, came shrieking out of hiding and dropped what amounted to an information download in my head. I stopped and sat down on the riverbank and kicked off my sandals. My toes ran through the grass.

"John. I . . . I've got pieces of the story."

"Tell me. Fast. Before it gets away from you."

As we sat there, two people completely out of their elements, out of time, I described what I was seeing. *A woman, heartbroken and despairing over the death of her husband from some awful disease. A man, recently released from prison for a crime he didn't commit. Both of them are struggling to come terms with their lives. They meet at the resort, spend an idyllic two days together . . . and then discover they are separated by fifty years in time.*

John thought about it, but not for long. "It's too similar to *Somewhere in Time.*"

No, it wasn't. He was wrong. "Only in the sense of love and moving through time. In Matheson's story, a *penny* is the portal between the past and the present, *a stupid penny.* But in this story, *love* is the portal."

"Maybe that's it, Sam," he finally said. "Maybe you're right, and it doesn't matter whether the portal is something physical, like a penny, or whether it's an emotion. Either one can create a particular state of consciousness . . ."

Yes, yes. I was in the flow, in the groove, and I already knew my protagonist was a blonde. I've often wondered what it would be like to be blond and tall and skinny, like some California surfer girl blessed with good looks, smarts, and money. Now I would know. Now I would crawl into that surfer girl's skin. I would feel what she felt, experience her travails, live as she lived.

Overcome with emotions I hadn't felt since I'd written *Brooklyn Story*, I lay back against the grass and peered up at the gorgeous blue sky, letting the scenes unfold in my head. John stretched out alongside me, his head supported in one hand. "I'll produce it with you. This could be the new production for your company, Sam."

I laughed. "I just have to write it."

He plucked a piece of grass and drew it along the side of my cheek. "I love you, Sam. I'm completely in love with you. I have been for a long time. I need for nothing, I have my Stunner."

I drew his face toward mine. "When I thought I'd lost you"—I felt tears burning the backs of my eyes—"I didn't know how I could survive it. That's how much . . . I love you."

He kissed me. Words between kisses never felt so good. Then he sat up. "Do you still have my iPad in your purse?"

"Uh, yeah." I sat up and dug out his iPad, puzzled by this rapid transition from *I love you* to *Do you still have my iPad?* I handed it to him.

"I have to show you something." He pressed the home button to bring it to life. "When I was in prison, there were a lot of days when I thought I was going to explode if one more guard told me what to do or not do. When you're incarcerated, the only control you have is over your own thoughts. So I got to the point where I created this private little space in my head. I trained myself to go into that space whenever I felt I was going to explode. I decorated it. I gave myself a TV, bookcases filled with good books, comfortable furniture. Then the one room expanded to include a kitchen, a bedroom, a balcony that overlooked the Mediterranean. And in that space, I started writing stories and scripts, and shooting movies."

As he spoke, I slowly began to appreciate the scope and breadth of his imagination. I could almost see this fictional John Steeling in his imaginary rooms. It reminded me of scenes from some Stephen King movie, maybe it was *Dreamcatcher,* where an alien controlled the body of a young man, and his consciousness, his soul, had sealed itself off in an imaginary room that the alien couldn't penetrate.

"I met my muse in that room, Sam. A guy. He loves music. He reads graphic novels. He's a movie fiend. He enjoys good stories. And, quite a few times, he's shown me the future."

"What do you mean?" I was so taken in by his story that

I just wanted him to keep talking. "How can an imaginary guy in an imaginary room show you the future?"

"I don't know. After the first few times it happened," John went on, "I started keeping meticulous notes. Over the years after I was released, I converted all those notes I made in prison into electronic files. Here's an example."

He turned the iPad so I could see the screen. The entry was dated September 12, 1992, at 2:11 p.m.:

> So Mr. Muse who lives in the basement of my head supposedly decided to show me scenes from my future. I figure he's a great bullshit artist. But if he's for real and not just some part of me, then he does it to keep me sane until I get the fuck outta this hole.
>
> As we're sitting in the imaginary room, he picks up the remote control and turns on the TV. "I'm gonna show you your creative partner, amigo. You're gonna have to go through some shit before you two connect, but trust me on this."
>
> The screen flickers, clears. I see this dark-haired beauty and recognize her immediately. Samantha Bonti. I knew her years ago in Brooklyn, kissed her under a mistletoe one night. I have no idea where she is, what she's doing.
>
> I suddenly realize Mr. Muse has been digging around in my subconscious like some dog digging for bones he buried long ago. I laugh at him, at my muse. "Yeah, right."
>
> "Dude. Seriously. She's the one. You run into each other in L.A. You've both got baggage. Don't mess it up."

I read the entry twice, looked up at him, then read the entry a third time. Here we were, two people sitting on the banks of the Savannah River, while a Realtor waited inside the house for us, but none of that mattered. Something special was happening here. I knew it the moment a huge chunk of my next book or screenplay fell into place. "I want to call it *Baggage*."

"How about *Love Baggage*?" he suggested.

Spoken aloud, it sounded absurd, and we exploded with laughter. "Gag," he said. "Maybe *Hollywood Baggage*?"

"Worse. We need an alliteration."

"Alliteration." John ran his hand over his head. His hair had grown back, but not fully, and I rather liked this version of John. "Okay, I think I've got it. I think I've got the title."

"What?"

"Hello, Hollywood."

I rolled it around in my head for a moment. The best movies I'd seen, the best scripts I'd read, usually had strong, powerful titles. *E.T., The Hunger Games, Minority Report, The World According to Garp, Indiana Jones, Star Wars, Thelma & Louise* . . . How did *Hello, Hollywood* stand up against them?

Pretty well, I decided, and threw my arms around John's neck. We fell back against the grass, laughing like fools, hugging and kissing, then laughing some more. "It's a good working title," I said.

"Ha. It's solid all the way. . . . You think we can write this script, Sam?"

"Sure. We've already started it."

"Do you want to write it here, in this house, on the banks of this river? At least part of the time?"

"It'd probably get written faster here than in Malibu, that's for sure. Why?"

How about, what if, do you think . . . I knew I didn't want to buy a house with a man who simply wanted to live with me. But I couldn't think of a diplomatic way of saying that, so for at least a full minute, I didn't say anything at all. I stared at my fingers, picked at my nails, watched a school of fish leaping in the water. I felt that curious exhilaration that comes from the high of creative adrenaline, a kind of bliss you experienced when you sensed your life had taken a ninety-degree turn for the better.

When I looked up, John was just sitting there, holding something in his cupped hands. "Sam, will you marry me?"

In the light, I could see a small gray ring box, and then he opened it and my heart caught in my throat. The blue diamond, a light blue, the color of the sky, the sort of sky where magic flourished and dreams came true. I realized he had bought this ring before we'd left New York, and that, for him, this trip had been about what he'd just said.

A simple question. *Will you marry me?*

The talk about the house, whether my muse could write here, hadn't been some casual off-the-cuff thing about the two of us living together. It had been about the two of us being married, being creative partners, and doing our creative work here, away from places that held pieces of our darker personal history: New York, Malibu. I suddenly understood that, for John, the road to this moment probably had been clear from that second we'd laid eyes on each other at Blu Jam. *I* was the one who had thrown up issues, blocks, drama. I was the one who had created a labyrinth of challenges. *Me, shit, me.* Right up until this moment, this instant, I had been my own worst enemy.

"Yes," I whispered, and wrapped my arms around him; he hugged me as though these moments were our last on the planet. "I love you . . . so . . . Sam."

"I love you, John."

"My Rapunzel, you are liquid love through and through."

When we finally peeled ourselves away from each other, he took my hand and slipped the ring on my finger. It fit perfectly. "I knew it would fit."

For a moment, I sat there admiring the ring, turning it this way and that on my finger, then I looked at him again. The light revealed his elation, as though he had reached the end point in a journey begun long ago, perhaps when he was in prison and his muse had shown him the future. But the end point was also the beginning—I saw that, too—a new chapter, a new journey, and it was one we would make together. Then it hit me. I thought of Priti and how she said to me how her country is the perfect place to be married. The ceremony, the colors, the taste of it all.

"Can we get married in India?" I asked.

"Wherever you want. Pluto. The Space Station. India. It doesn't matter to me." He cupped my face in his hands and kissed me. The he leaped to his feet, grabbed my hands, and pulled me up. "Let's go put a down payment on this place."

We ran back along the river, both of us barefoot and laughing like fools.

That evening, from our B and B in downtown Savannah, we started making calls—to Isabella and Nick, then to everyone else.

A few weeks later, we wrapped the shooting in L.A., and I got serious about the wedding. Priti had made my dress, chosen the location, and I bought plane tickets for the people who would be in the wedding. On Labor Day, John and I boarded an Air India flight with the people we loved, our family and closest friends, and two days later, we were married.

The wedding was magical. In honor of our union of love, John surprised me with a beautiful Buddha tattoo with wild white daisies surrounding it. It was one of the most captivating pieces of artwork I'd ever seen. As for me, I wasn't quite ready to be inked up so fast, only time would tell.

The music at the wedding fit everything we had lived through together and separately: "You've Made Me So Very Happy" by Blood, Sweat & Tears.

> *But you said, "Try, just once more"*
> *You made me so very happy. I'm so glad you came into my*
> *   life . . .*

I am here to tell you that dreams come true. That love does come. They may not unfold in the ways you think they will, the details may not be exactly the way you imagined. But if your desire is powerful and clear, if you can get out of the way so that you aren't your own worst enemy, then you're in for the wildest and most beautiful ride of your life. And I promise you that none of it is predictable.

epilogue

It was one of those moments to savor, a moment burned into my brain forever. John, Isabella, and I walked onto the Oscars' red carpet together, our arms linked as though it was the three of us against the rest of the world.

We were interviewed, photographed, and I knew that, somewhere, Paul was watching, and that maybe Vito and Tony Kroon were watching, too. But I didn't give a damn what they thought. This was *our* moment—John's, Isabella's, mine. *Brooklyn Story* had four Oscar nominations—Best Picture, Best Actress, Best Supporting Actress, and Best Art Direction.

For months—while the filming wrapped up, while John and Isabella and I adjusted to our new reality, while Marvin and Flannigan got married, while Liza and Brian bought a home together—I had envisioned this moment, imagined it, *willed* it into being. I had felt it in my blood, my bones, and savored its reality to the point where I had awakened one morning a month ago and thought the Oscars had already happened. I thought it was a done deal.

We sat close to the stage, the three of us with King and Liza, Marvin and Flannigan, Renée, and all the others. So many others. My Gallery Studios family.

I knew that the deaths of Prince and Barbara gave us a pity card, but I also knew that *Brooklyn Story,* on its own, without that pity card, was a solid, stellar story.

And when we won Supporting Actress and Best Picture, a cheer went up from our section of the theater, and the entire cast and crew, and King and John and I, went onstage to receive the award. As we were all onstage, all I could hear was Grandma's voice in my ear. *Mazel tov, Samelah, mazel tov.*

acknowledgments

This being the final book in my trilogy, I now think back on all the memories that are on paper and I must say, my words, my sentences, my books, they cured me. Through the written word I was able to really forgive and understand why the things that happened to me really happened and to find out once and for all where and what my true destiny was to be. I am honored that God gave all this to me. He gave me the strength to go on and heal my past and to bring in wonderful people to guide me along the way. I needed to wrap up all my loose ends and really give credit to people who had done things for me that no one could ever even begin to understand. Sometimes in life people come in and do what they must, then leave, while others stay on your train until the end. Doesn't matter how long, what matters most is what they do, what they leave you with, whether a smile was needed or a hundred bucks to get food. Whatever it was or is, they were there to make a difference and to add to one's life at that given point. To those people who have done just that for me, I have true gratitude for all of you. And you know who you are.

Faith is something bigger than you and me and has nothing to do with what religion you are or whether or not you believe in God. It has to do with not believing in your own ego and stepping away from the mental aspect of living. Taking a moment to step into the unknown and knowing that it (or whoever) has your back and is leading you toward the answers to your prayers. When we lose faith, we lose ourselves, and that is when bad things happen to good people. In the long run, I don't mind any wrinkles on my face as long as they are from me smiling.

I'd like to thank my publishers, Louise Burke and Jen Bergstrom (still the hot blondes) at Gallery Books/Simon & Schuster. My editors, Lauren McKenna and Natasha Simons, for giving me a fabulous ending to yet another new beginning in my life. And all my true supporters at S&S who never gave up on me or my words. My beautiful agent, Susan Ginsberg, who always has my back, and that's a nice feeling to have. And my girl, Trish McGregor. Your Moon will always float with mine!

Samantha, my daughter, my girl. I always remind myself of how blessed I am to have you in my life. Thank you for always sharing the comforter and pillows, I will never forget, and, oh yeah, the music of Harry Styles, too! I am just a Brooklyn girl with a story to tell, since stories are all I have and telling them is my gift. And finally—to true love that lives and yearns within all of us. There is no other force that's greater. And remember, a life without love is no life at all.

Printed in the United States
By Bookmasters